GRAVY

by Faith A. Colburn

Prairie Wind Press

Dedication

I dedicate this novel to my mother for all her bull-headed, inflexible, dogged stubbornness. Neither of us would have survived without it.

Acknowledgements

I'd like to thank my two-and-a-half-year-old grandson, Bruce, and his parents, Ben and Misty, who let him hang out with me a couple of days a week. He kept me grounded enough to work through all the isolation of this pandemic. I especially appreciate the few minutes of conversation at drop-off and pick-up times.

Thanks to my four beta readers, Jim Arrowood, Mari Beck, Dorothy Ramsey, and Katherine Wielechowski. I know this is a long book and that a critical read takes precious time away from your own writing.

Thanks to the Nebraska Library Commission for the Nebraska Book Award for Fiction given to my second novel. It was so well timed that it got me writing again when I was slipping too deep into a purple funk to work.

And at this time, it seems appropriate to thank all the people who kept my city and county running so I could keep on keeping on. I appreciate all the medical care providers who took care of those who needed help, all the utilities workers who kept the lights on, all the people who stocked the groceries, ran the cash registers, and pulled product for pick-up and delivery, and all the quick-stop attendants. I applaud your courage for showing up every day and working among all the plague rats who refused to wear masks and/or keep their distance so that you could be safe. I hope this will be over soon so we can get out and see each other in person. I can't forget the road crews who kept our highways and byways open so, when I couldn't stand another minute in my house, I could go on a photo excursion to, as my mother used to tell me, "blow the stink off," and maybe come home with something worth sharing.

Introduction

My series, of which this is the third novel, seeks to explore family and resiliency in the face of trauma.

In the first book, *The Reluctant Canary Sings,* you meet Bobbi Bowen. It's 1937 in the second dip of a double dip depression. The only way Bobbi, then 15, can save her family is to sing, and she faces a workplace where everyone, by definition, is drinking, and with no law or policy regarding sexual harassment or assault. She has very little support from her family, but then they had little or no support themselves. Her grandmother (her mother's mother) has been institutionalized for paranoid schizophrenia. Her father is an orphan. As her mom says, "How would I know how to be a wife and mother?" Does that lack of function have to pass down through the generations?

In the second book, *See Willy See,* you meet Connor William Conroy and his close-knit family. It's 1940 and Connor has just returned from wandering the Western United States, riding the rails, subsisting in the national parks, and depending on the generosity of strangers. Throughout the war and the Depression preceding it, he has kept in touch with his family by letters— particularly his sister, Nora, who's serving with the U.S. Foreign Service, starting in Paris just before the Nazi invasion. Can such remote support sustain these two adult children through a generation of horrors?

In this third novel, I throw Connor and Bobbi together to see how they'll respond to the aftermath of the two traumatic decades of the 1930s and 1940s. Just to stir in a bit more adversity, I've added a medical assault on Bobbi in an era with little, but not zero, recourse to malpractice law. In this book, I wanted to explore ways in which a supportive family can rescue, not only its own, but also others who have floundered alone. Can a loving family help overcome generations of fear, distrust, and illness?

Forward

Part of the impetus for this book was the medical assault that appears in the center. Like the two previous novels, it's a hybrid that incorporates a few facts I actually know and a great deal of make believe. Although this is a work of fiction, a doctor actually performed the so-called procedure on my mother. Mom was unable, more likely unwilling, to describe the implement involved, but she made clear that it existed. She did not describe the effect of each procedure on her body. She focused instead on the fact that it had no effect on the need for surgery. She spoke often about the days her doctor waited to do the necessary caesarian and his prognosis for the baby—a short life, mine, with little or no intellectual capacity. I have not used the doctor's correct name. I suspect he has died by now. (He would be at least 100.) I have no desire to punish any descendants he may have left behind.

Table of Contents

Part I

May 27, 1945

"Incoming!" He yanked the man next to him to the ground, yelling. In seconds, he was back on his feet, crouched and running. "Behind the rock!" He heard garbled screaming. "Behind the rock, dammit. They're shelling us again. Get down."

He felt someone crowd in beside him. Another rumble and crash sent him cowering at the base of the rock under a sharp pounding of shrapnel and rain. "Where's Jakes? What happened to the guys in the kunai grass?"

"What guys, Connor? We have to get out of this before we get beat up."

The simultaneous bellow of ordinance and the deluge that drenched him had ripped him from a quiet break. A flash blinded him just as he heard the voice again, like a distant whisper. *Tokyo Rose?* He peered around the rock, but the downpour masked the enemy, like usual. He heard the voice again.

"Connor. It's okay. It's just rain and hail."

He leaned into the rock, his forehead against its cold surface. *Am I losing my mind too?* Another roar deafened him, and a flash bled red through his eyelids.

"Connor!"

GRAVY

Was the ordinance coming from the ships offshore? He didn't recognize the artillery. What caliber was it? *Where's my rifle?* He looked around himself, trying to focus on the man next to him.

"Connor, you're safe, but we gotta get outa here."

He frowned. What the hell was going on? He trembled, raising his head, trying to make sense of the drenched woman crouched beside him.

"Connor, you're not in New Guinea anymore. This is Colorado."

What's she doing here? How'd she get here?

"Connor, it's me. Bobbi. You're in Colorado."

"Colorado?" He hesitated, scrunching up his face, thinking. He shook his head. "Nurses aren't supposed to be at the front."

"Connor, you're in Colorado. This isn't New Guinea."

He rolled his eyes, taking in the rain and hail, the red rocks, the continuing roar and flash of the storm, and the barefoot woman beside him.

"It's Bobbi, Connor. You're not in the war anymore. You're safe."

He frowned. He couldn't understand who was talking to him. As he started returning to reality, he said his cadence. "Mendez, Green, Moore, Wilson, Hidalgo, Hayes, Gordon, Reese, Trigg, Menardo, Martinez, Eisler." He whispered, "Mendez, Green, Moore, Wilson, Hidalgo . . .

There was that voice again. At least he could understand it this time.

"Let's go back, Connor. Maybe you can tell me about it."

GRAVY

As he became fully conscious, she pulled him by the hand. In the downpour, he stood, ducked, and ran to the car with her. Settled into the driver's seat, he gave her an embarrassed look. "I really went nuts back there, didn't I?"

"Yeah."

"I wish I could tell you it would never happen again." He shook his head. "It's loud noises mostly now. I only hope it gets better in time. I've heard it does." He stared out the windshield. "I suppose we'd better start back so you can get dry."

"I'd drive us back, but I don't know how to drive."

"I'll teach you . . . if you ever agree to go out with me again. I'll understand if you don't."

Bobbi glanced across at him. "Let's worry about that later. Are you okay to drive?"

"Yeah. I'm okay now."

"At least the hail stopped."

"Yeah. You're gonna be pretty bruised up."

"Could I go back and get my shoes? I dropped them when you grabbed me."

"I'll get them. I'll try to pick up the food too. I suppose the boxes will have melted by now."

"I'll go with you. We're both already drenched."

Connor turned the heater on full blast, and they jumped out to gather their picnic. Minutes later, they slammed back in, soaked and shivering. They barely spoke as Connor drove Bobbi back to her barracks.

GRAVY

April 5, 1945 — Colorado Springs, Colorado

Bobbi Bowen had given up a few short weeks too soon or she'd never have been in Colorado—clear out in the boonies—where anything might happen. She'd been singing with the Jimmy Jones orchestra when the Japanese attacked Pearl Harbor. Then, one by one, the men in the orchestra had received their draft notices and, next thing she knew, she was sitting on a bench in the bed of a cattle truck, jostling over her first gravel road. She wondered what she'd got herself into as she bounced against a bunch of other new recruits, on the way to basic training at Fort Des Moines, Iowa. After a cattle truck, how much worse could it get?

She found that out during the first couple of days in the Women's Auxiliary Army Corps, waking up in the dark to a screaming whistle and marching, and marching, and marching. She only had time late at night to regret the radio show she'd missed because she'd already signed up with Uncle Sam. That would have meant a steady income and no more touring. On the other hand, she couldn't regret the three squares a day and the warm roof over her head after four years of scrapping to keep her family alive. That's why she'd signed up in the first place. The Army hadn't let her down, and it did get better once she had her specialty training and a duty post building and installing radios for B-24 bombers, called Liberators. In Colorado Springs, right at the east face of the mountains, she got a part time gig singing at a nightclub when she was off duty. She guessed it could have been worse and maybe she'd still be able to take that radio job after the war. Or maybe . . . she might marry Tony. They'd dated for a while before they both joined up and got sent all over the place. She didn't love him, but he'd take care of her. They'd made no promises. Neither was a letter writer. She didn't even know if he was still alive.

She'd met a lot of flyboys at the club and also when she worked on their radios at the airfield. At the club, she also met soldiers from Camp Carson. Many of the men had been arrogant with their contempt for WACs showing on their faces while they

4

spoke with her—if they deigned to speak with her at all. She found them more friendly at the club when she was out of uniform. Many of them had been skirt-chasers. She knew the type from her nightclub gigs before the war. She'd met a few she liked, some she liked a lot, but most of the airmen got posted overseas once they'd finished training.

One night, a soldier had turned up at the club with an MP band on his arm. He'd had her attention right away, even though he'd only stood at the back of the club scanning the crowd. She'd watched him turn to leave as she started into her next number, *Blues in the Night,* and smiled when he turned back and leaned in the door frame to listen. He'd left during the song, but something about the way he'd watched said that he'd be back.

While Bobbi had begun her career as a singer, Connor William Conroy had left his parents' Nebraska farm to see if he could find work in California. For several years he'd been a hobo, hopping freight cars and subsisting in the national parks where he and a man he'd met in a boxcar had caught fish, trapped little mammals, dug tubers, and picked berries. Connor had returned home in 1939 and begun to build up his own farming operation as the war in Europe spread. At his urging, his sister, Nora, had taken classes so she could find "interesting" employment. She had joined the U.S. Foreign Service and, over his strenuous objections, took a post in Paris just months before the Nazi invasion.

Reasoning that he'd be sent to Europe where he could look out for Nora, Connor then enlisted in the Army, leaving behind a girlfriend who'd promised she wouldn't wait. She hadn't. In fact, he hadn't received a single letter—only her engagement announcement in a letter from his parents. To top off his frustration, after basic training, the Army sent him to Panama, instead of Europe. After Pearl Harbor he had trained for jungle warfare with the 158th Army Infantry Regiment, made up of the Arizona National Guard including Whites, Hispanics and members of twenty-two tribes. Almost a year after the Japanese attack, he boarded a ship for Australia. From there he went to New Guinea where he joined soldiers already island hopping from one battle to the next.

Connor, through field promotions, had become a platoon sergeant during a battle that left only one Navajo soldier who'd lost a leg, and himself, from a squad of fourteen. But the jungle, in the end, had defeated Connor. He'd recently returned from the Southwest Pacific with a virulent case of malaria called Blackwater Fever, sailing under the Golden Gate Bridge on a hospital ship. After treatment in San Francisco, the Army had sent him to Camp Carson near Colorado Springs, to serve out his enlistment as a military policeman.

With his partner, Connor walked into the Peterson Club, blue with cigarette smoke, looking for drunk and disorderly soldiers. He and Sam had spotted no trouble there, and they'd turned to leave for the next bar, when the drummer started a steady tom-tom. *Blues in the Night*. A 1941 tune the band leader said. New to Connor. A woman stepped up to the mic. He leaned in the door frame, wishing he were off duty, then in minutes, took off with Sam to break up a brawl across the street. Offenders loaded into a paddy wagon, he and Sam tramped down the strip.

"Hey, d'you see that canary they got in the Peterson Club?"

"Yeah. She's a looker, ain't she?"

"Pretty nice voice, too." He stopped walking. "Hey, Sam, you got a date this weekend?"

"Nah. Why?"

"Because you're the only man I know with a car, and I want to borrow it."

"She'll be workin'."

"Yeah. I know."

GRAVY

April 7, 1945

Connor had leave that weekend so he headed straight for the Peterson Club. When he stepped in the door, he saw the singer behind the bar, mixing drinks. She and the barkeep, Ed he thought, were not rushed and he noticed that she'd stopped, chatting with a sharp-looking guy in Air Force blues. He stepped up to the bar, hoping to divert her attention, but Ed waited on him. *Damn it!* Connor glared at the airman while Bobbi laughed with him.

Ed grinned. "She's about to start another set anyway."

"I'm not the only poor bastard trying to get her attention, am I?"

"Nope." Ed took a swipe with the bar towel and moved away.

When Connor glanced down the length of the bar again, the girl, still laughing, turned and headed toward him. Connor started to say something, but she gave him a quick grin as she rounded the end of the bar and took her place on stage. He turned around and leaned his elbows on the bar behind him so he could watch her. She glanced his way for a moment, then grabbed the mic off the stand and turned to the band leader.

At the end of the set, as she bustled back to mix drinks, he grabbed her, bent her over his arm, and kissed her. When he released her, she stood glaring at him.

"What'd you do that for?"

He grinned. "Seemed like the thing to do." He decided, while he had some momentum, he should go ahead. "How 'bout I buy you a drink?"

"No thanks."

Uh oh. I've pissed her off.

She started to walk away, but the jukebox began playing, *Bewitched, Bothered and Bewildered.* Connor didn't ask. He curled an arm around her waist and led her to the dance floor. He felt her resistance relax when they stepped onto the polished surface.

"You look like you're just back from the war."

A shock of guilt ran up his back, like an electrical charge— Mendez, Green, Moore, Wilson. *Control yourself man.* The slow dance rhythm helped him calm himself.

"Yeah. New Guinea. Came down with malaria. Otherwise, I'd still be there. My name's Connor Conroy, by the way. My friends call me C. Willy C."

"Willy for William?"

"Yeah." *Now what do I say?* He hid in silence for a moment. "Did you grow up around here?"

"Gosh no. Cleveland."

"How'd you get here?"

"I got tired of starving to death. I saw a poster and joined the WACs. I'm stationed at Peterson Field."

"So, you're a WAC?"

"I am. Do you mind?"

"Mind? Why would I?

"Most GIs don't like the WACs."

He frowned. "You know, I punched a guy on the way back from New Guinea for saying I'd marry a WAC. Don't know why. I don't care." *Better change the subject.* "How'd you end up singin' here?"

"I'd been singing with a regional orchestra before the war. Did pretty well for a while. Then everybody started getting drafted."

The music stopped and she stepped away. "I've gotta help Ed."

"Hold on a minute."

She turned to him.

"Can I take you home after your last set?"

She closed her eyes. When she opened them, she frowned. "I really don't like being manhandled."

He hung his head. "I'm sorry. It's just been so long and I'm so nervous. I don't know how to act anymore." She stared at him for a long moment, then nodded as she moved off.

Connor ordered another drink and settled down on a bar stool to wait for the last song. He figured he'd already pushed his luck to the outer limit, so he left her alone between her last sets. While the band packed up their instruments, he waited for her to change clothes and walked her to Sam's old Ford. By the time he'd dropped her at her barracks, he'd worked up a sweat trying to keep up a conversation. He wondered how long it would take to become comfortable with regular people, especially women.

Camp Carson

Back in his barracks, he thought about how long it had been since he'd taken a woman out to dinner or dancing—anything. Years. The whole idea terrified him, but he'd at least taken a first step, no matter how awkward. He decided he needed some expert advice, so he started a letter to his sister, back in the Paris Embassy after De Gaulle's triumphant return.

> Dear Sis,
>
> Well, here I am, still alive. The fevers have pretty much subsided. I still get a teeth-chattering chill sometimes, but I'm at altitude and it gets cold.

GRAVY

They've made me an MP while I wait for my discharge. It's easy duty tramping up and down the main drag here, breaking up brawls. I'm still worried about being with normal people.

Do you hear anything from Daniel? You said he was still somewhere in the thick of it. From what I'm seeing in the papers, it's almost over on that side of the world. The Japs won't give up until the last one dies, though.

You know what? I've met a woman. I don't know what to do about it. She's a WAC. She's a singer too. Sings with a local orchestra when she's off duty. Her voice calms me. Feels like a lullaby. I've only just met her, but I like her a lot.

The trouble is, Sis, I don't remember how to be with civilized people, especially women. I didn't do too well with Pauline, after all. The only women I saw for years were nurses in the evac hospitals and the ship—too sick to appreciate them. What the hell do I talk about? I've only been stateside for four or five months and half of it in the damn hospital at Leatherman. I don't know anything about music anymore. Haven't seen a movie in years. I sure can't talk about what I've been doing these last couple of years.

Anyway, my nerves got the better of me and I did something really stupid. She'd come down off the stage and when she walked by me, I grabbed her and kissed her. She didn't hit me or anything, but that glare was enough to scare me to death. Then instead of apologizing like I should have, I grabbed her again and hauled her out onto the dance floor. When she started to run off to help tend bar, I did apologize. I asked if I could take her home and make up for my boorishness. And she let me.

Enough about my troubles. I hope you're doing
well, and that Paris will settle down to some kind
of normal now that the Allies have taken the war
to the Germans on the Continent.

Connor

He poked the letter into an envelope, licked the flap, pasted on a
stamp, and headed for his bunk.

April 12, 1945 —Peterson Field

Inside the tube of a B-24 cockpit, working on a radio array,
Bobbi heard something blaring from the post loudspeakers. She
squirmed out of the tight fuselage, hustled down the stairs, and
stepped out the bomb bay door.

Gloria, who'd been working on the engine, stood beside the props
looking in the direction of HQ.

Bobbi glanced at her friend. "What's up?"

"Don't know. Everybody's supposed to report to the parade
grounds. Immediately."

Bobbi checked her watch. "Four-thirty. Late for a drill."

The two women walked to the parade grounds along with
hundreds of other personnel. In a few moments the loudspeaker
squawked.

"This is Lt. Col. Hutchinson. We've just been informed . . ." he
hesitated and cleared his throat, "we've just been informed that
President Franklin Delano Roosevelt has died . . ." he cleared his
throat again, "of an apparent cerebral hemorrhage . . ." he
faltered, "at 5:47 Eastern Time." Bobbi could barely hear him
murmuring with someone else. "Vice-President Harry S. Truman

has been sworn in and will now take over the Presidency." Bobbi heard some paper shuffling. Hutchinson went on. "We will continue to carry out our normal activities unless otherwise advised." He paused. "That is all."

No one stirred for several minutes. Bobbi heard a light wind stirring the grasses at the edge of the field. She stood motionless, trying to understand what it meant. "But," she whispered, "the war's not over yet." She turned to Gloria. Her friend's eyes were wet. People started moving back to their duty stations, the crunch of their feet on gravel the only sound.

Camp Carson

A few miles away, Connor couldn't believe he had a letter from his sister already. He was going on duty, though, so he didn't have time to read it. He had just slipped his MP band over his left arm when the loudspeaker crackled. "All personnel to the parade grounds. On the double."

"What the hell?"

Sam shrugged. "Ours not to reason why."

The two men jogged to the parade grounds where they heard the news that had been broadcast at Peterson Field. In the silence Connor tried to picture Harry Truman as he'd appeared in the newspapers back when he'd been inaugurated with Rooseveldt. He and Sam turned back to the motor pool.

"It'll probably be quiet tonight."

"I guess it's normal activities for us." Sam shook his head. "I don't know what's normal anymore."

Connor grabbed a set of keys. "Me neither." He pointed with his head. "That's our jeep."

They found Main Street deserted. *Bobbi ought to be on her way to the club.* Connor scanned the street. *This is like Judgment Day. Everybody's gone wherever they're going. Just me and Sam to carry on.* Silence on the usually-busy main drag spooked him. Hardly any cars sat along the curbs and none moved. He breathed a heavy sigh when the Peterson Bus sailed around the corner at about seven thirty. *At least someone's alive.* He passed the parked bus at the Peterson Club. Bobbi got off by herself. He saw no other faces in the windows. *Jesus!* He drove to the far end of town and turned back.

"This is spooky."

Sam nodded. "You can say that again."

Connor stopped at the club. "I want to check on Bobbi."

"Bobbi? You don't even know her."

"She let me take her home the other night."

"God, Connor, you're really smitten."

He shrugged.

He left Sam in the jeep while he stepped inside, where the band was tuning up. A few patrons sat scattered around the place. *I wonder if they've heard.*

Bobbi stepped onto the stage and whispered something to Kramer. They'd started into the first bars of Bobbi's theme, *Blue Moon,* when Ed stepped up.

"I need the mic, Bobbi."

Connor heard a murmur from the crowd as Ed stood breathing into the microphone. "There's been an announcement." His voice broke and he hesitated for a long moment. People shuffled their feet. "At 5:47 this evening, President Roosevelt died." He took a deep breath and sighed it out. "I'm closing the Peterson Club until further notice." He looked around the room. "Good luck." He handed the mic back to Bobbi and stepped off the stage.

GRAVY

No one made a sound. Connor walked up and took Bobbi's hand, helping her off the stage while customers stood and filed out, making a little ripple of noise. Connor and Bobbi sat on the nearest vacant chairs.

She reached for his hand, tears spilling. "What're we gonna do?"

"Truman's already been sworn in. He'll be all right."

"You really think so?"

"Sure. I don't think much'll change."

"He was a really good President."

"Yeah. Hey, we're on duty. I just wanted to make sure you're all right."

"I'm okay. Just stunned."

"We all are. Gotta go. Don't worry." He started to leave, then turned back. "Sam and I will take you back to the base," he offered.

He waited for Bobbi to change into street clothes, and they left. Connor tucked her into the passenger seat, and he perched behind her for the short hop.

When Connor returned to the barracks after his patrol of mostly deserted streets, he was finally able to read his letter.

> Dear C. Willy,
>
> I'm glad your fevers are better. I've been worried about you. In answer to your question, I have heard nothing from Daniel, but since the Germans surrendered on the Ruhr, I'm hopeful that he's okay—unless of course, he was hurt before that.
>
> Congratulations on finding a woman you like. You should just ask her out. I hope it works for you,

14

but I don't think anything's going to be
particularly easy or predictable, even once this
war's over. Don't give up on yourself. I think
Pauline loved you, or at least liked you a lot, but
just couldn't deal with worrying about her
brothers and you, too.

On a brighter note, dear brother, Cousin Keith
stopped by to say hello. You knew he's in the Sixth
Armored Division? He was in Paris getting some
R&R and he looked me up. He looked weary, but
at least he's all in one piece—for now anyway. We
had dinner and he had to go back.

Oh, I hope this will be over soon, but even when it
is, it will be years, many years, before Europe's
rebuilt. When I look out at Paris, I want to cry.

Just be well, brother, and have faith that you can
make a life for yourself.

Nora

Connor folded the letter and put it back in the envelope,
wondering if anything would ever get back to normal. But then,
what was normal?

April 16, 1945

Connor took his sister's advice right away. As he and Sam paced
the streets, he detoured into the Peterson Club to ask for a date.
When they both had a free evening, he arrived at the airfield
early. He stood smoking while he waited for Bobbi. He spotted
the red dress with its swishing full skirt as she stepped out of
the barracks. He dropped his cigarette and stomped it out.

GRAVY

"I don't know about those ruby slippers. Do you really want to dance in those?"

Bobbi shrugged. "I'm used to them."

"My sister, Nora, was too but she was a glutton for punishment. I marvel at what you women put yourselves through." He took his place at the wheel. "Where would you like to eat?"

They decided on a steakhouse along the strip.

"Back home, we ate seafood a whole lot more than steaks, Bobbi said, "Cheaper, you know? Because of Lake Erie."

"I'm a meat and potatoes man, but I've eaten a lot of stuff. Charlie and I killed a rattlesnake and roasted it. It was actually pretty good. We trapped marmots, squirrels, and rabbits. We ate service berries, raspberries, and blueberries. Dug wild parsnips. Ate dandelion greens and morels. We roasted acorns. Charlie always had some fishhooks in his hat and some string in his pocket. We caught mountain trout." *Good Lord,* he thought, *what does she care about that?*

"That must have been awful not having enough to eat."

"It did get a little thin sometimes, but we didn't go hungry very often. We always had a can of beans or something. My grandmothers were midwives and knew a lot about what you can eat. At home, we always ate stuff like lambs quarters and dandelion greens."

"But wouldn't you have been safer in town? What if you ran out of beans?"

Connor pulled into the steakhouse parking lot and jumped out to open Bobbi's door. They continued their conversation inside. "What about you? How'd your family weather the Depression?"

"Not very well, Connor. My parents couldn't get work." She studied the tablecloth, tracing a pattern with her fingernail. "I guess you might as well know. I'm not as smart as you. I didn't even finish high school."

He reached across the table and lifted her chin. "A lot of people didn't get to finish high school, Bobbi. So tell me what happened. I know it's not because you're not as smart as me."

"Mom was scrubbing floors in a bank and then they cut her hours. Dad had a job with the WPA and then he broke his leg— bad—so the summer before eleventh grade, I auditioned and got a job singing in this nightclub a few blocks from home."

"Bobbi, I'm sorry. You couldn't have been very old if you were still in high school."

"Fifteen."

"I can't believe they hired you. You weren't much more than a child."

"I told them I was eighteen."

"And they believed you?"

"I doubt it. But I'd won this singing contest at Euclid Beach and I'd been singing with the house band there all summer, so I already had my name out there. The club, LakeView it was, tried me for a while and I was bringing in new customers, so they kept me, and I could support my family. But about all I can do is sing."

"But Bobbi, you can sing. Most of us can't. At least not like you."

"Most people think I must be a slut because of the way I make a living."

"I don't. I admire the sheer guts it took to do what you did when you were just a kid."

"Really?" Bobbi's smile lit up her face. "I *was* really scared at first, and it looked like the customers were going to have their

17

hands all over me." She sighed. "First time one of them touched me, just reflex, I slapped him."

Connor grinned. "See what I mean?"

"But he grabbed me, and I don't know what he would have done if Tony hadn't got there in time. Took the guy right out the door into the alley."

"Tony?"

"The bouncer."

"Did they stop molesting you then?"

"The manager came huffing and puffing to my dressing room and told me I can't just slap his customers around and I said I wasn't going to put up with guys feeling me up. He thought about it a minute and said he'd have Tony escort me from the stage to the dressing room and go around with me when I chatted up the customers. Everybody figured he was my boyfriend, so they left me alone."

"*Was* he your boyfriend?"

"He was really sweet, but more like a big brother."

"I'm glad you had him."

"Me too." Bobbi hesitated. "Nell and Ed have been great friends too."

"Nell and Ed?"

"The owners at the club. But that's enough about me. Tell me about your farm."

Connor wanted to know more but respected her subject change. "We've got 640 acres, four quarters."

"How big is that?"

GRAVY

"A quarter is a fourth of a section and a section is a mile on a side."

"Is that big?"

"We might be able to work another quarter or two, I guess, but we made a good living on half that—at least when the dust didn't blow, and the prices were decent. Even during bad times, we survived. Mom had her garden and her chickens, and we milked cows, so we sold eggs and cream. We had cattle and hogs and we grew the feed for them, so there wasn't much expense. Pop never borrowed money, so we were never vulnerable to foreclosure."

"Sounds like an awful lot of work."

"We work really hard from planting time to harvest. Not much in the winter. Give the cattle some hay, milk the cows, feed the chickens and pigs, gather the eggs. That just takes a couple of hours out of the day. With Mom and Pop and me, that doesn't amount to much."

"Seems secure."

"We never went hungry. I could have stayed home through the worst of it, but I wanted to do something on my own. I don't regret a minute of it. I saw some beautiful country and met a lot of nice people. I have a better idea now how this country works—at least the western half of it."

"I did get hungry once, really hungry, and I never want to do it again."

Connor reached across the table for her hands. "I'm sorry you had to go through that, Bobbi."

"It's over now." The waiter delivered their steaks. "I'm certainly not going to starve tonight."

Connor tucked into his steak. *She gives me a glimpse then slams shut. Musta had a really rough time.*

19

When they finished eating, Connor would have liked to talk more but Bobbi was on to the next thing.

"Where we going?"

"How about that new club on the edge of town?"

"The Springs? Great idea! I've heard they have a pretty good canary. I'd like to hear her."

"Okay, The Springs it is."

When they walked in the door, the band was playing the final notes of *Stardust*. "She *is* good," Bobbi said as Connor paid the cover. Then the band swung into *One O'Clock Jump*.

"You ready?" Connor held out his hand. *I hope I can still do this.*

"You bet." Bobbi strode with him to the dance floor. As they hit the boards, he swung around to face her. They fast-walked into the rhythm. Connor pulled her against him and see-sawed a few steps before he pushed her out, off-arm reaching for the ceiling. He pulled her in again.

"You ready?"

She looked into his grin. "For what?"

"For this." He lifted her off her feet, swung her between his legs, stepped over and stood her on the other side. "I guess you were ready." He noticed that most of the other dancers had cleared a space and circled them, clapping along.

"Hey," someone in the crowd yelled as they left the floor panting. "How long you guys been dancing together?"

"First time," Bobbi shouted.

"Can't be!"

They found a table and ordered drinks. Almost as soon as they sat a fight broke out a few tables away and spread to several others. Connor stood. "Hold on."

Shielding the table with his body, Connor took a moment to assess the situation. He stepped in and grabbed one of the fighters. He whispered something in the man's ear. The guy peered at him over his shoulder and headed for the door. Connor grabbed a pair by their collars and again spoke some quiet words. They left, ending the struggle.

"What did you say to them?"

"I told them I'd call the MPs. I think some of them recognized me."

"Why didn't you?"

"What?"

"Call the MPs?"

"Those guys have been through hell and back. They're mad and they can't figure out what to do about it. They need a chance to adjust before we start throwing them in the guardhouse or giving them dishonorable discharges."

The band played the opening bars of *Perfidia* and Connor held out his hand.

"I don't know how to dance to this one."

"Sounds like a rhumba. You know how to waltz?"

"Yes."

"How about a Cuban Walk?"

"No."

"Okay. I'll show you. I learned a lot of Latin steps in Panama."

21

"Panama?"

"They sent us there to guard the canal. In Panama City, I looked for the Panamanians' dance clubs."

"Aren't they all Panamanian in Panama?"

"They had clubs for the soldiers and tourists, but when you found the natives' clubs, you got a real treat. A couple of times, I was the only white guy in a roomful of Negroes. Those colored senoritas can really dance. Come on."

In a quiet corner Connor demonstrated the Cuban walk. "The step is slow-two, quick-quick. You hesitate a count on the first step. The hard part is the hip swing. You keep your weight on your right foot—left for you—and move forward—uh, backward— with a slightly bent knee. When you transfer your weight your hip swings. Try it."

Bobbi did.

"Now you combine that with the waltz box step." He stepped forward and took her in his arms. After a few stumbles, they moved together smoothly.

"See, it's easy."

Bobbi leaned into his arm. He loved holding her, the warmth of her body through her dress, and the light, fresh scent of her perfume.

"You ready?"

She nodded and he began a turn to the left. Soon they moved together, hips swaying, through an intricate pattern of turns, pauses and open breaks.

She leads like a feather. What a great dance partner.

"That was fun," Bobbi said as they left the club.

He grinned. "I haven't had this much fun in a coon's age."

"You're foolin' with me."

"What?"

"A coon's age? You don't talk like that."

"Thought you might like to hear my farmer voice."

"Connor, I'm sorry. I never met a farmer before."

"I know. Just don't jump to any conclusions about us. It's not a bad life."

Connor closed her door and walked around to climb behind the wheel. *I wonder how she'd adapt to a farm—big city girl like her. She's used to a lot of glamour I couldn't give her. Myself, I wouldn't want to live like that.*

When he dropped her off, he watched her walking to her barracks in the moonlight before he started the car and headed back to Camp Carson.

Camp Carson

Back at his barracks, Connor couldn't sleep. Instead, he squatted against the wall outside with a cigarette, smoke curling straight up in a breezeless night. The vision of Bobbi standing in the moonlight in that red dress wouldn't go away.

Maybe I shouldn't even try to date a woman in my condition. Do I even deserve to have a life after leading all those good men to death? He started the cadence: Mendez, Green, Moore, Wilson, Hidalgo. . .

God! I've gotta stop it! I can't do anything about those men. We didn't have a chance. None of us. I don't know why I'm alive at all. Nora says I've got to pack many lives in mine for all the guys who didn't make it. But I can't possibly live long enough, and I've lost too much already. I'm thirty. Haven't done anything with my

23

GRAVY

life. Just killed a bunch of Japs. What kind life achievement is that?

He started pacing. *I can't wait to get on with it, though. I've already given up eleven years. May not have much time. Who knows about that blackwater fever? Who knows? I could drop dead tomorrow. A virgin. I wonder how Gracie and Marvin are doin.' Maybe I should have taken the opportunity when I had it. But shit. The boss's wife? What was she thinking? Or that girl in Australia. I think she'd have had me. It's just . . . I want something like Mom and Pop and Grandma and Granddad. Even the old folks—you might come in any time, unexpectedly, and Grandma'd be sittin' on his lap, and they'd be kissin.'*

Do I even have it in me anymore? So much hate . . . hard not to just be a cog in somebody's wheel. We all were. We didn't ask for it. That bastard MacArthur, always sending troops on ahead before the job's done. He killed more men than the Japs did.

He closed his eyes and there was Bobbi again, walking away in the moonlight. *No knowin' what she's been through. Poor kid. Workin' in nightclubs instead of goin' to school. Maybe she won't be able to have a normal life, either.*

He heard someone in the barracks, yelling.

"Shut your trap," someone growled, and the barracks went quiet again.

What about kids? What if I have a family and one of the kids toddles in and touches me when I'm sleeping? Will the nightmares be gone by then? Will I be able to wake up suddenly without killing something? Maybe I should just build me a cabin somewhere and live like Uncle Harry, so I don't damage anyone.

But Bobbi stood before him again, this time in the nightclub, singing, songs like *Serenade in Blue, Stardust, Tenderly.* He leaned against the building and reached into his breast pocket for another cigarette. *God! Her voice just brings me down, makes me feel as calm as if I were cutting hay with Star and Rusty. And*

24

the way her body moves in my arms, dancing. We hardly know each other. But there's something there.

"Whachoo doin' out here in the dark, Conroy?"

"Johnson. Just thinkin'."

"Best not do too mucha that. It'll scare ya to death."

"I'm finding that out. What're you doin' out here?"

"Aw, Parker woke me up with his squallin' an' now I can't get to sleep."

"Have a coffin nail." Connor shook out a fag and held out his pack.

"Thanks."

They smoked in silence for a while.

"Whacha thinkin' *about*?"

"A woman."

"Not that broad from the Peterson Club?"

"Yup."

"She pretty uptown for a country boy like you."

"She seems to like me."

"Yeah, I like ya, too, but ya ain't wastin' any time out here thinkin' about me."

"Aw. I didn't know."

"Keep it to yoreself."

They smoked for a while.

"Maybe I should cut and run right now, before it's too late."

"I would. Who wants a dame messin' things up? Next thing ya know, yore married and ya got a buncha brats runnin' around."

"Sounds kinda good to me."

"Ain't yore life complicated enough already?"

"Huh."

"Well, suit yoreself. I'm goin' to try and get some shut-eye," Johnson ground his butt out under his heel.

"Sweet dreams."

"Aw."

I wonder if we'll have to think, every time we go out, whether we ought to do it again. I wouldn't be surprised if she's out next to her barracks with a cigarette, trying to decide if she can risk going out again with an aggressive soldier who might manhandle her. Wish I hadn't grabbed her like I did. At least she went out with me once. Bet she looks real sexy standing there smoking and thinking. Guess I'll see if I can get her to go up to the Pike Forest with me some time. He turned, ducked into the barracks, and tried to get some sleep.

Peterson Field

Bobbi lay on her bed, hands behind her head, thinking about Connor and his farm. She wondered if she could adjust to a farm. She hadn't even seen a farm until boot camp at Fort Des Moines in Iowa, and she certainly hadn't spent any time on one. Her only clues about how they worked had been her friend Bonnie, whom she met that first confusing, chaotic night in the barracks. A South Dakota farm girl, Bonnie obviously loved the farm. "I think the greatest thing," she'd said, "when I was a kid, I could get up in the morning and wander outside by myself and walk around. You know, look at stuff."

"Just walk around?"

"Yeah. There was so much to see. We had a plum thicket at the edge of the farm. In spring it would be wild with bloom and bees. It smelled so sweet. And sometimes I'd crawl in there and listen to the bees."

"Didn't they sting you?"

Bobbi remembered the other woman glancing over at her.

"No. I didn't *mess* with them." She sat up on her bunk. "The air would be so soft, you'd feel snuggly all over."

Bobbi couldn't even imagine soft air. "What else?"

"Hmm. The babies. They're so shiny and new. You know. They come out and they're all bloody and dirty. And then the mother licks them . . ."

"Ugh."

". . . and just like that, they're clean and bright. They're gangly little things, lying there in the straw. They start floundering and then they stand, splayed out all over the place. They totter over to their mothers and suckle."

"Sounds . . ."

"Boring," Bonnie finished for her. "I know."

"That's not what I was gonna say."

"What?"

"I don't know . . . safe? That sounds silly, doesn't it?"

"Not so silly." She stared at the ceiling. "I guess I hadn't thought about it that way, but yes. It did feel safe. I had two brothers."

"Gosh, it must have been nice to have brothers."

"You only have sisters?"

"Neither. Just me."

"Must have been lonely."

Bobbi studied her fingernails, pushing back the cuticle with her thumb. "Well, I had a few friends. We were close. Then, these last four years—working nights—we lost touch."

"My brothers teased me and pulled my hair and snitched my stuff, but if anybody said a bad word—or even looked at me the wrong way—they were glowering and puffing up—you know how a man rolls up his shoulders and makes himself look bigger— they looked pretty silly, but nobody was allowed to mess with me."

A shrill whistle blew, somebody screamed *"Lights out!"* and, in that instant, the barracks plunged into darkness.

As Bobbi drifted off to sleep—again—she realized that, although it all sounded foreign, none of what Bonnie had told her seemed so bad. In fact, some parts of it sounded pretty good, especially the safety part.

May 9, 1945 — Camp Carson

The day after Germany surrendered, Connor received a letter from Nora. Before he headed to the Springs for what he assumed would be a long shift, he lay on his bunk to read it.

> Dear C. Willy,
>
> It's almost over here. Hitler is dead. We hear he killed himself. I had dinner with our favorite cousin again, Apparently, he's about to get out on points, but what a horrible thing he had to witness

before he left the front. He helped liberate a concentration camp called Buchenwald. He wouldn't tell me everything, but he said they had airtight rooms. They herded people inside and then pumped in cyanide gas. He said they had ovens where they burned up all the people they murdered. He said the smell hung over the entire camp and the neighboring town like a fog. But, he said, the living people were almost too much to bear—starved and sick and filthy and just shuffling around, when they could walk at all. He apologized for telling me, but I think he just had to talk to someone. We'd already got the first prisoners liberated from Germany about a month ago, so it was no shock. The prisoners' arrival was, though.

It's what Daniel and I feared, but even worse than we could have imagined. On a Saturday, they flew in thousands of men in American transports, but we didn't see them. It was the first women the next day that nearly broke my heart. They came in by rail. The Parisians stood ready to welcome them with bouquets of lilacs. We all stood on the platform with the scent of the lilacs surrounding us and the women started stumbling out of the cars. Their sunken eyes looked dead in greenish faces.

They wore whatever discards they'd received at the camp, probably taken off the dead. The flowers fell from hands too weak to hold them, making a carpet of trampled blossoms, their perfume mixed with the smell of disease and dirt. Years will pass, maybe decades, before we understand the full horror of what happened. God knows if we humans will ever recover.

We've seen the worst of it, haven't we, you and I? What will we ever tell our children?

GRAVY

Nora

Connor slipped on his armband and headed out with Sam. They worked a long shift, policing celebratory brawls all over Colorado Springs. As he patrolled the bars and nightclubs, he noticed a few soldiers sitting in morose silence in the midst of the chaos.

Must have fought in the Pacific. The Japs will never give up until the last man dies.

Time had begun to blunt the shock of retrieving one of his men from a mound of flies feeding on his tortured body, the men dismembered by bombs, and the throats slit in the night while the man in the neighboring hammock slept. He still hadn't sorted his thoughts about the sick, starving Japs they'd found on Arawe and Noemfoor.

They should have given up when we cut their supply lines. Any sane human beings would have surrendered rather than starve, rather than carve roasts from their friends. He shivered. *What would make a man do that when he could just wave a white handkerchief and get fed?*

Interrupted by a fight bursting out of a bar, he ran with Sam to break it up. Once back on the street walking, he returned to New Guinea.

We probably would have fed them and sent them back to a prison camp on Finschafen. They would have had intelligence value.

Connor couldn't forget the Japanese officer bounding from the back of that cave, yelling an unintelligible curse, and plunging a jeweled ceremonial dagger through his own gut. *Who would do that? I've spent a lot of time with people who have very different ideas. Hell, my own squad—Navajos and Pimas and Apaches and Mexicans. But damn, they were at least sane.*

"What's goin' on, Connor?"

Connor started. "Sorry. Got a letter from my sister about the concentrations camps we've been reading about. One of our cousins was among the first into Buchenwald. It kind of threw me back into New Guinea."

"Well, at least it's over in Europe."

"Yeah, but from what my sister says, it'll be years, maybe decades, to recover."

They kept walking.

May 27, 1945 — Peterson Field

Bobbi had spent the day after Germany's surrender in the fuselage of a B-24, installing a radio. That night the nightclub surged with celebrants, many of them drunk and disorderly. The chaos continued for most of the week, then settled down to a normal that allowed her off-duty time with Connor. She hardly noticed that Connor had monopolized her time. When she worked the club, Connor met her there and took her home, if he were off duty himself. Often, they simply sat in Sam's old Ford and talked. It had seemed like a dream until the stormy picnic.

Once Connor dropped her off that afternoon, Bobbi scuttled into the barracks, dribbling water all the way. She took a hot shower, changed into dry clothes, and mopped up her drips. Then, she lay on her bed, snuggling under the Army-issue blankets.

Will he ever get over it. Maybe if he didn't need to be outside in the storms . . . But what if something sets him off and he thinks I'm a Jap? What then? What are you thinking about Bobbi? Are you crazy? There's not going to be a next time. You just met this man. End it here, before you fall in love. She put her hands behind her head, staring at the ceiling. *But he's so good-looking and he dances divinely and he's gentle.*

Her roommate interrupted her thoughts.

"Bobbi, what the heck are you doing in here all by yourself?"

Bobbi glanced up. "Oh, it's you, Gloria. I'm thinking."

"What about?"

"A man."

"Aren't we all? The one you told me about who's tall, dark, and handsome, but probably not rich because his shoes aren't shined?"

"You make it sound so weird."

"Don't you think it is a little weird to choose your husband by how he shines his shoes?"

"When you put it that way." She sat up. "But you know, if a man can afford to have his shoes shined, maybe he can afford other things."

"What were you thinking about your man with no spit-shine?"

Bobbi watched Gloria change from her work jumpsuit. "We went to Garden of the Gods this afternoon. We found this lovely spot among the red rocks. The peaks in the distance were a jagged sawblade of blues and purples. The foothills, dotted with shrubs and trees, undulated like a green blanket. Clouds billowed tall over the hills. Perfect, you know?

"We talked. He told me about being a hobo during the thirties. Said he'd carried a camera all over the West, taking pictures in the national parks. Said he and his buddy had lived pretty well on what they could scrounge. Said they both had packs with food and stuff and when they started to run out, they'd leave the park and get whatever job they could find—you know, to replenish their supplies."

"Sounds a whole lot different than my experience of the thirties."

"Mine too. Anyway, when we finished eating, we packed up our stuff, then we sat there on this blanket he'd brought. He pulled my feet into his lap and I thought, 'What're you doing?' But he talked about the clouds and the way they were climbing up the sky. He said it would rain sometime that afternoon. He took off my shoes, tucked my socks inside, and lined them up together. Then he began stroking my feet."

"Wow. You may want to keep this one."

"Oh yeah. It felt heavenly. He talked about going dancing with his sister when they were in high school. We talked about how we'd both wanted to go to college and then the stock market crash and the bottom fell out. He's a farmer, you know."

"A farmer? You're dating a farmer?"

"I told him he's too smart to be a farmer and he gave me this lopsided grin. He has a beautiful smile." She played with a string that had come loose from her blanket. "Then he told me that farmers aren't hayseeds. He told me about all the things farmers have to know and how they have to figure out how to survive when a hailstorm wipes out the crop just before harvest." She sat up and hugged her knees. "And then he kissed me. He just brushed my mouth with his lower lip and then waited until I kissed him back." She smiled. "It was wonderful. He wasn't all over me."

"Here. Look at my face. Do you see it turning green?"

"Here's the problem. We were kissing and it was wonderful. I noticed it got darker. The air suddenly chilled and a stiff wind came up. We looked up and he said the clouds looked like hail, so I grabbed my shoes and we each grabbed a box, and we were running to the car when it cut loose—and that's when he went crazy."

"How so?"

"He thought he was in New Guinea."

"What did he do?"

"That first clap of thunder was really loud. And then the lightning flashed. He dragged me to the ground and lay there looking for Japs." She leaned her chin on her knees. "But that wasn't the worst of it."

"What's worse?"

"When he finally calmed down, he started saying these names, over and over, like a cadence, without any expression at all."

"I'd take the names, but I'd worry about whether it's safe to go out with him again."

"Yeah. I'm pretty strong, but not like him and he's a lot bigger. With those long legs, I don't think I could outrun him."

"Seems to me that any time you have to worry about outrunning your date, it's time to stop dating him."

"I suppose, but how many dates have you had when you *didn't* think about it? Besides, I think he might be the one."

"What one?"

"You know The One. Mr. Right."

"Don't tell me you believe in that stuff."

"Sort of."

"That kind of thinking can get you beat up or killed, Bobbi."

"It's not his fault. When he's not scared out of his mind, he's the gentlest man I've ever met."

"If you could get just the times he's not scared, that would be wonderful. But you get the whole package."

"I know, but he'll probably get over it in time."

34

"In the meantime, he could really hurt you."

"But he's sweet . . . and a good kisser."

"God, Bobbi. What about that Air Force major who's been flirting with you. Or Lieutenant Adams. You remember him, don't you?"

"I don't know, Gloria. I've got a bad feeling about the major. He flirts with everyone. I don't think he'd ever settle down, even married. You know, in my business, I've seen plenty of other women's husbands."

"I can imagine."

"Not in that way!"

"Bobbi! Don't be so sensitive. I didn't mean it in that way. You've worked in bars and nightclubs where that kind of guys congregate. That's what I meant."

"Boy, that's the truth."

"Well Bobbi, my advice to you, if you're looking for it, which you're not, is to ditch the combat veteran. He's too dangerous. What if you like him enough to marry him? What if you had babies?" She buttoned her last button. "Hey, it's time for chow and I'm ready. Let's go get some chow and you think about it."

Camp Carson

Back at the base, Connor took a hot shower and flopped on his bunk. For hours, he stared at the wall. After mess, he decided a "talk" with his sister might help. Connor figured she could understand him if anybody could. He got out the air mail stationary he'd switched to from the trusty Big Chief tablet that he'd carried all over the West.

> Dear Sis,
>
> Got your last letter a couple of weeks ago. You must have written before the surrender. I'm sure

you would have mentioned it if not. So how is the peace going so far? I imagine now that it's official, you'll be seeing even more refugees every day. How are the authorities able to accommodate them?

I told you about Bobbi in my last letter. I took your advice and asked her out. We'd been going out for several weeks when she wasn't fixing radios or singing, and I wasn't MPing. Things had been going okay despite my awkwardness. But this afternoon, I found out I haven't got over being bombed and shot at yet. I took her on a picnic this afternoon. We were talking and laughing (I managed although I was a nervous wreck). We even did a little necking, you know? Well, a hailstorm blew up when I wasn't looking, and I went off. Thought I was back in New Guinea. I think I scared her half to death, although she stuck with me like a trooper. She'll be bruised up pretty bad. I kept her out there, yelling and screaming about taking cover and looking for Japs while the hail beat us to a pulp. I thought it was shrapnel, of course.

I suppose she'll think I'm too dangerous to go out with again. I don't blame her. How do you suppose I can convince her to try again? How can I convince her I won't always be like this?

Maybe I *will* always be like this. I'm haunted by my memory of Pauline's Uncle Harry, sitting all alone in that tiny house, hour after hour, day after day, in that bent-backed chair, staring at that pot-bellied stove. I don't want that for myself, but I don't suppose Harry did either.

On that uplifting note, I'll close, wondering if you have these daytime nightmares, too, and hoping you don't. And what about Daniel? Have you seen him lately? Is he okay?

C. Willy

Connor smiled as he folded the letter and stuffed it into an envelope. Amazing, he thought, he and Nora could live on far sides of the world, but he always felt better when he wrote to her. At least now he had an address so she could answer him— unlike the years when he hoboed all over the West and sent letters home, but could never receive them.

May 28, 1945 — Peterson Club

The next night when Bobbi spotted Connor at the back of the club, she tripped on the mic cord and took a running leap across the stage. Once she'd righted herself, she stepped off, stage right, while the band played *Moonlight Serenade.* She tried to calm herself as she decided what to do. *I ought to tell him I'm busy. I ought to tell him I'm dating that flyboy. I ought to tell him I'm engaged.*

At the end of the set, he stood waiting to hand her down. "We have to talk."

She flashed him a smile, "What about?"

"My weirdness."

"You're not . . ."

"Please, Bobbi. Just listen."

She sighed. "All Right, but I'm not making any promises."

"I'm pretty short on promises myself."

"I'll see you at closing."

37

GRAVY

After her final set, Bobbi took a corner table with Connor. He took both her hands. "I want to apologize for the other day. I must have scared you half to death."

Bobbi stared for a moment. "There's nothing to apologize for," she said finally.

"Of course, there is. I went completely nuts. I'm afraid that may happen to me sometimes—for a while. I'm determined that I *will* get over it. I don't want to be a danger to you or anybody else. I want to have a real life."

"I understand, Connor, but you're so big and strong, I can't protect myself."

"I know, Bobbi. It's all on me. I know that. The thunderstorm the other day took me by surprise. When I got back to the states, I spent several months in the hospital at Leatherman. No storms since I got here. I grew up with the prairie's furies. It never occurred to me they could set me off. I know that now, so I'll make sure I'm never in a thunderstorm with you until I'm over this."

"And how long will that be, Connor?"

"I don't know. To be honest, my girlfriend had an uncle who never got over it."

"Girlfriend? You never mentioned a girlfriend."

"Ex-girlfriend. She grew up next door and we were dating when I signed up. She said she wouldn't wait—and she didn't."

"Dear John?"

"Nope. Never wrote."

"That stinks."

"I get it now. She had brothers to worry about." He shook his head. "I suppose she married some 4F that she wouldn't have to

38

worry about." He closed his eyes. When he opened them, she saw a glint of determination. "Uncle Harry never got over it, but *I'm* going to."

"But what if something else sets you off? What if I startle you and you think I'm a Jap?"

"I don't know, Bobbi. I've been talking to guys whose wives have joined them here. They say the women make noise before they enter a room—kind of like coming up on a wild creature. Bobbi, I know I can beat this, especially if I have someone like you to get over it for."

"But we just met."

"Oh, I know. And I don't know if you're the woman I want to spend the rest of my life with, but I sure like you a lot. I think there's something there to grow on."

"Me too, Connor, but right now, you frighten me. And I don't know if I can tippy-toe around my man for the rest of my life."

"I know and if you never want to see me again, I'll understand. But I just heard you thinking out loud about spending a lifetime with someone like me. I'm looking for a chance to rebuild my life. It used to be a good one. Maybe we could go dinner and dancing, or a movie. That way, I probably won't have any surprises."

"We could try it."

"I haven't seen a movie in years—except old ones they used to show up to keep up morale. How about dinner and a movie next Sunday. I'll see what's playing." He hesitated. "We should probably try to arrive after the newsreels."

Bobbi hesitated a long moment. "All right Connor. I like you a lot, too. But I'm scared."

"Fair enough." He ran his thumbs over the back of her hands. "I'll pick you up at the base tomorrow. How's seven for dinner?"

"Seven's fine. I'll see you then."

Peterson Field

Back in her bunk, Bobbi stared at the ceiling, dimly lit by the lights on the airfield. She hoped she hadn't made a mistake. In the old days, she'd have smacked someone who grabbed her like Connor had, but she'd seen a lot of shell-shocked vets since then and those guys might hit back.

She let her mind wander over her year at Peterson. Like Gloria had reminded her, she'd met a lot of flyboys including Andrew. She'd met Andrew before the Army sent him to the front in Europe. His trainer had come in on its belly one morning when the landing gear refused to deploy, taking a couple of bounces along the way. When they got it into the hangar for repair, Bobbi climbed into the fuselage to check the radio system. She found several of the largest vacuum tubes shattered, leaving glass shards inside the radio. She'd picked them out and dumped them into a sack, noting what replacements she'd need. She'd started to descend the steps when a flight officer stepped through the bomb bay door. She moved back and stood at attention, transferring her sack of broken tubes to her left hand.

"What the hell. D'you murder somebody in there?"

Bobbi stood, staring. "No, sir."

"At ease, Private." He frowned. "What happened to you?"

"What do you mean, Sir?"

"You've got blood all over your face."

She brushed a hand across her cheek, smearing blood into her hair. "I thought it was sweat. It's hot in there."

"It's blood. I assure you."

"I must have cut my hand when I took out the broken tubes."

She pulled a handkerchief out of her pocket and wiped her face and hands.

"I'm taking you to the Infirmary."

"I'm sure it's not bad, sir. It doesn't hurt."

"Let me see." He took her hand. "That's pretty deep. Sometimes a clean cut like that takes a while to hurt. C'mon." He led her to a jeep just outside the hangar and tucked her in. "Name's Calvin Andrews. "I won't ask you to shake hands."

At the Infirmary, Bobbi asked for a bandage.

"Bandage hell," said the corpsman. "I can't get a stitch in there, so I'm going to wrap it. You'll have a straight finger for a while." He handed her a Form 81.

"Look," said Andrews. "You'll just be off duty for a while."

"It's a finger. You really think the Army's gonna give me a week off to nurse a finger? It's still on there."

He walked her back to the jeep. "Stubborn, aren't you?"

She climbed aboard. "I call it persistent."

He sighed. "Where can I take you?"

"Supply so I can replace those tubes."

Adams walked around and climbed into the driver's seat. "Won't it be awkward working with that finger?"

"Probably, but you want your plane back, don't you?"

He started the jeep. "Listen, how about you meet me at the PX tonight and I'll buy you a soda?"

"Can't."

"Why not?"

She snickered. "You're an officer and I'm a grunt. We're not allowed to fraternize."

"Technically," he says, "I'm really a non-com. By the way, what's your name?"

She told him.

"So, let me pay you back for getting hurt fixing my radio." He stopped in front of Supply. "I'll wait and take you back to the hangar."

"Okay."

"Okay what? You'll let me take you back or you'll let me buy you a soda."

She climbed out of the jeep. *It's just a soda. It might be nice.*

"Both," she said.

As she crawled back into the plane with her bag of new parts, he wandered around to check on engine repairs. She heard him talking to Gloria.

"What's goin' on with Bobbi?

"She cut her finger."

"Stitches?"

"Nope. She's all taped up."

"I don't think you've done much damage here. Just the skin under the belly."

"I'll be back to check on her tomorrow."

"Her who?"

42

"What do you mean?"

"The plane or the radio repairman?"

That's Gloria, Bobbi thought, *she probably winked, too.*

"Both," he'd said.

She'd seen him several times during the following few weeks. She'd liked Andrew. She didn't get to see him much, but he seemed to see her—not a WAC or a canary, but as herself. Anyway, Andrew had finished his training and shipped out to England. She'd received a couple of letters. She felt guilty about not answering, but it didn't take him long to stop writing. She didn't even know if he were still alive.

She liked Connor, too, even more than she'd liked Andrew. She had to decide how dangerously she wanted to live. She'd risked another date, so she'd soon find out.

June 11, 1945 – Peterson Club

After a few more—uneventful—dates, always checking the weather forecast if they'd be outside, Bobbi sat at a table in the Peterson Club waiting for Connor. She'd finished her last set and he'd planned to take her home. While she waited, she wondered what life would be like if she married him like Gloria had suggested. She tried to imagine living on a farm. *How about slopping hogs, I've sometimes heard about that—what's that like? Would I have to milk cows? Do they kick you? How do you get eggs away from the chickens? Do you have to go find them?* She'd seen big fields of corn and wheat in Iowa during basic training at Fort Des Moines. *Would I have to plant stuff? How would I do that?* Her friend Bonnie from South Dakota had told her they had machines to do it, but she wondered if she'd have to operate those big machines. *Would I have to dig around in the dirt and plant a garden, so we'd have something to eat?*

43

She decided not to worry about that yet, because she had an idea. Maybe they didn't have to live on a farm. She ordered a drink while she waited. She lit a cigarette and set it in the ashtray. "Connor," she whispered to herself. "I need an agent to take care of my business." She grimaced. "No. That sounds wrong. Connor, I need a business manager and . . . No . . . Connor . . ." She took a drag from her cigarette and put it out. "Connor you're so smart. You could really help me out . . ." She lit another cigarette, took a drag and laid it on the edge of the ashtray. "Connor, what would you say if I asked you to be my business manager?" *Oh rats! Does he even think what I do is business?* She took a drag on her cigarette and ground it out in the ashtray just as Nell delivered her drink. She took a sip and lit another cigarette. "Connor, wouldn't it be fun to travel all over the country together? I could sing in nightclubs and you could be my business manager . . . Damn," She lit a cigarette. When she reached for the ashtray, she realized she already had one and put them both out.

She started again just as Connor strode across the nearly empty club and sat. "Bobbi, I got a letter from Pop today. He says there's another quarter available just a mile from home. He knows I want to graze more cattle and it's mostly grass. He's talking about travelling with Mom and starting to turn the operation over to me. Isn't that great? How would you like to be a farmer's wife?"

Bobbi stared, her mind churning. *What about my career? What would it be like? How could I live out in the country with the cows?*

"Bobbi, say something."

"Um." She finally focused on his eyes.

"What?"

"I don't know."

"You don't want to marry me, do you?"

44

"I do. You just surprised me. Shocked me."

"Surely you knew . . ."

"I knew we were getting closer."

 "You're ashamed of me."

"God no. Why? Because you're a farmer? No. Just give me a minute to think."

He pulled a pack of cigarettes out of his pocket and offered one to her, which she declined. He lit up and waited. That was one of the things she liked about him. He didn't rush her. He ordered a drink. She took a sip from hers, staring at the table.

"Okay. Here goes. I was about to make you a proposition—that's why it was such a shock. I wasn't ready for you to make a proposition."

"It's not a proposition."

"Oh, I know. But mine is."

"What kind of proposition?" He flipped ashes into the tray.

"A business proposition." She hesitated, watching the smoke rise, choosing her words. "I really want to be with you. Forever. But I've worked really hard to be a singer. I've taken voice lessons and put up with the bar scene."

"Yes, I know. I thought you were tired of bars."

"Well, but I'm not tired of singing and that's where I have to do a lot of it. I was going to ask you to be my agent."

"Your agent? What does that mean?"

"You would book my singing engagements and promote me and handle the money."

Connor's face turned red. "I would be your pimp."

"No," she cried. Heads turned all around them. She dabbed at a few tears that threatened her makeup. "You said you didn't think of me like that. You don't understand."

"You're right. I don't. I'm sorry, I really don't. You can't expect a self-respecting man to live off a woman."

"You wouldn't be living *off* me, Connor. You'd be my business manager. You would keep me from getting stranded without any money for food, like I did that time I almost starved. You would check the venues where I'd sing and the bands I'd sing with and make sure they're legit. You would contact people and write contracts for me. We could travel all over the country together, Connor. We could stay in nice hotels and meet all kinds of new people."

"Geez, Bobbi, I don't know anything about the music scene. I don't know how to write a contract. I don't know how to see if a club is legitimate. I wouldn't have any idea about how to manage your career. I'd just get us both into trouble. It doesn't sound very secure to me, anyway. Always on the move, never in one place long enough to even know who pays his bills and who doesn't. See, where I come from, I have history. I know old John Stokes pays his bills on time, so if I do some work for him, I know I'll get paid. And I know that people talk about the cars Ansel Barton sells and I wouldn't buy a car from him. As a matter of fact, we'll probably have to go to Hastings to buy a car. Anyway, how would I know anything about any of the people you do business with?"

"That's why it's so hard, Connor. That's why *any* performer needs a manager. You're really smart and you could learn."

"God Bobbi, you've knocked me for a loop."

"Just think about it, would you, Connor? And yes, I do want to marry you. I just want other things, too."

"I see that, Bobbi." He remained silent, smoking and finishing his drink. "What've you been doin' here? Looks like you lit half a pack of cigarettes and put them out."

"Yeah. I was trying to think of how to ask you."

"I wouldn't hurt you."

"You think calling me a prostitute didn't hurt?"

"Aw, I didn't mean *that.*"

"It sure sounded like it."

He ordered another round, then turned back to Bobbi. "Do you want a family?"

"You mean kids? I guess I hadn't thought much about it."

"I do. I know I've got to get over the blow-ups, but I want to be a dad. What kind of life would it be for a child to get dragged all over the country?"

"Lots of performers do it. Just think about it, would you Connor? Maybe we could do it for a few years and then settle down somewhere."

"What is it you want to do that you haven't done already. What would happen in a few years?"

"I want to sing with the Dorsey band or the Glen Miller band. I know he died, but his band's still touring. Or Bennie Goodman or Duke Ellington."

"God, Bobbi, you don't want much."

"I think I can do it. And then I could get a radio show where I would stay in one place and sing for radio. Then we could have a family. I had an offer, but I'd already enlisted."

"Okay, Bobbi, I will give it some serious thought, but I'm not promising anything."

June 13, 1945 — Camp Carson

A couple of days after Bobbi's proposal, Connor continued to consider like he'd promised, but he couldn't imagine the kind of life she'd suggested. He recognized how the glamour might appeal to Bobbi, and he'd always sought new adventures himself. Her kind of night life might be fun for a while, but not for life.

He remembered city boys he'd worked with in the Civilian Conservation Corps. They'd been terrified of the forest. At first, every night sound had them trembling in their tents. Maybe Bobbi was scared too.

Growing up on a Nebraska farm, Connor had heard coyotes yipping before he could speak. He loved to walk in star shadows, spotting raccoon and occasional bobcat tracks in the mud by the creek. Sometimes he spotted a coyote slinking along a fencerow or a jackrabbit zigzagging across an open field. He'd heard cows breathing in the pasture and sometimes they had come to the fence to greet him. He'd heard the clank of the neighbor's windmill and seen its silhouette against the starry sky. Maybe he could help Bobbi get comfortable with his world. After all, she'd adjusted to the Army, even in Iowa. He could start in the mountains and the trees. Pike National Forest was not a farm, but it wasn't a city either. Maybe she'd learn to love it like he did.

As usual, when he felt frustrated and confused, he turned to Nora.

Dear Sis,

GRAVY

You won't believe what Bobbi wants me to do now.
She wants me to be her manager. She says I would
book her appearances and check out the venues. I
would travel with her and hang around the clubs
when she sings. I promised her I'd think about it,
but what the hell do I know about nightclubs and
bands and singers? Hell, I don't even know the
words. Venue, what's that? Can you see me sitting
around nightclubs every night and *living off a
woman?* I'd feel like a pimp. She says it's not like
that and she was pretty upset with me for saying
so. She says it would be a partnership with me
doing the business end.

What do you think? Could I do it? Should I even
consider it? Damn she's a complicated woman.
Wants to sing with the name bands like the
Dorseys or Duke Ellington. Thing is, I think she
could do it. But what kind of life would that be?

While I think about it, I'm going to try to give her
a different perspective. Maybe if I get her
comfortable with my world, she might like it. Can't
take her to a farm, but we can go to the
mountains. Wish me luck and let me know what
you think.

Connor

He'd no more than sent his letter than he received one from
Nora. He ripped into it on the spot. He hoped his sister's life was
less complicated than his.

Dear C. Willy,

It's really hectic here. With the German surrender,
we're faced with rebuilding Europe and millions of
refugees. What is the world going to do with all
the people being rescued from concentration
camps? How will they ever find their mothers and

fathers, children, sisters and brothers, husbands and wives? How will they ever recover their ability to make a living? Where will they go? The war demolished more than a million buildings in France alone. Back home, that's probably an impressive number. I know what it looks like.

You asked about daytime nightmares. I do understand something of your problem. Those couple of trips with Daniel smuggling American and British pilots out of France, I saw things I wish I hadn't. There was plenty I'd rather not have seen during the bombing of Paris. I hope I'll never be that scared again. The difference is, everyone here is in the same boat so I don't stand out. That said, Connor, I have every confidence in you. You will adjust and you will find a way to vanquish your demons.

Now about that city girl. I think it's a good sign she stuck with you during your blow-up. She sounds level-headed. My concern would be the fact that she's probably used to a lot of glamour, and we don't even have electricity on the farm. How would she adjust to that? From what you wrote, she's been on her own for a while. How will she adjust to a partnership?

You'll have to feel your way, big brother. Daniel and I have some big gaps to fill, too. He's at the vinyard now figuring out if there's anything salvageable of his family's properties. His parents both died during the war. His sisters were among the first refugees he smuggled out. We don't know yet where they ended up. Between us right now, mine is the only reliable income we have.

We don't know where we will live. France? The U.S.? We don't know what we'll do. We're just

taking it a day at a time. It's hard to plan
anything because the whole world is in shambles.

Nora

Partnership. He guessed Bobbi would adjust just fine to a
partnership, but not necessarily the kind that he, or Nora, had
in mind. All he could do was keep thinking as he began his
campaign.

June 17, 1945 —Peterson Field

Gloria watched Bobbi slip into shorts and a sleeveless blouse
over her swimsuit. "So. You're still dating that soldier."

"It's been going okay so far—except that one blow up. We
checked the weather forecast. It's supposed to be sunny."

Gloria sighed. "You're taking an awful chance."

"His blow ups don't worry me as much as the fact that he's a
farmer. That worries me. Where would I sing? Some little
honkytonk bar?"

"You're going to have to figure out what you want if you keep
going with him—the man or the career."

"I have another idea, though. I asked him to be my manager."

"How'd that go over?"

"Like a lead balloon. But he promised to think about it. So I
hope." Bobbi grabbed a towel and sat on her bed. "I'm scared to
give up singing. What if I get married, to him or anybody for
that matter? What if he starts gambling like my dad? What if he
doesn't get better and he starts drinking away all our money? I
see that all the time at the club. I don't know if there are any

51

guys left who haven't been in the service. What if he dies from that Blackwater Fever? How would I support myself? I can't jump back into the business when I'm 40."

"We all take risks when we love someone."

"I know. I know. But I nearly starved once. How can I give up knowing I can feed myself?" She checked out the window. "He's here." She glanced back at her roommate and grabbed her bag and the picnic basket. "Maybe he'll take me up on being my manager."

"Don't hold your breath," Gloria hollered as Bobbi shut the door.

Pike National Forest

Heading west into the foothills on U.S. 24, they entered the forest almost immediately. Connor glanced over at Bobbi. "I'm looking forward to showing you some of the country I saw when I was wandering around the West. Maybe someday we'll have a couple of days and I can take you up into the real mountains."

 "You said there was a lake up there, so I wore my swimsuit. I've missed swimming."

"It'll be cold."

They proceeded in comfortable silence for a few moments. "Connor," Bobbi said, "tell me about farming. What's it like? All I know is what I saw in Iowa during boot camp and what my friend Bonnie told me."

"Who's Bonnie?"

"She grew up on a farm in South Dakota. She said her favorite thing was crawling into a plum thicket and listening to the bees. Do you have any plum thickets on your farm?"

"Oh yeah! That's great! Nora and I used to have a little hands-and-knees trail into the big bushes. We'd lie in the middle of the underbrush and smell the plum blossoms and listen to the bees.

We'd have the shade of the bushes, but the sun would warm the air. The sweetness and the warmth and the drone would make us drowsy. I think we napped in there at least once every spring—even the spring before Nora left for Paris."

"Did you have many baby animals?"

"Of course. The cattle pretty much look care of themselves, but we had a runt pig or two in the house for a while every year."

"In the house?"

"Yeah." He grinned. "We'd wrap them up in rags and put them in front of the oven door in a box."

"Didn't they smell?"

He frowned. "Not really. We didn't just leave them there in their own mess. "Once they get warmed up, they're just so bright-eyed and alert." He went silent for a few moments. "They have such solid little bodies." He laughed. "If they get out on the road, you don't run into them, you go over them. I upset mom's Model A the spring I graduated. Came up over a hill and there it was."

"Did you kill the pig?"

He chuckled. "Nah. He just ran off. Probably bruised up for a day or two. Had to get a couple of neighbors to set the car up on its wheels and get it back on the road."

By the time they found the lake, they were both ready to eat. Connor brought out the familiar blanket and Bobbi unpacked the food. "I brought some Sangria, just because I like it. We should have white with chicken, but what the heck."

"No point in getting all fancy, schmanzie. It's a picnic, let's just enjoy it."

She glanced up at the rock face across the lake as she removed food from the basket.

"Connor." She grabbed his arm. "Isn't that a mountain lion?" She began snatching food and shoving it back in the basket.

"What are you doing?"

"Let's get out of here."

"She won't bother us. She's just watching."

"But look at how big she is."

"Isn't she a gorgeous creature?" Connor put an arm around her shoulder and pulled her close. "Now that we've spotted her, she'll probably wander off." On cue, the cat stood and yawned. "Look how her smooth muscles ripple when she moves." She disappeared over the back of the rock. "See. There she goes."

"Won't she come after us?'"

"No. Wild animals don't like people. I don't think we taste very good." He gave her a little squeeze. "Just relax, Bobbi. It'll be fine."

She hesitated, glancing around at the trees and, one by one, took the lunch items back out of the basket. "Here, have some tomatoes. They're fresh. I got them from that little stand at the edge of town."

He released her, forked one of the tomato slices, and popped it into his mouth. "I'm in heaven. I haven't had a home-grown tomato since I went into the Army." He forked another and held it on his tongue.

"Aren't they wonderful?"

"They are. Where'd you get the pastries?"

"The croissants? I borrowed Nell's kitchen. My dad used to run a pretty high-class restaurant before the banks folded."

He grinned. "He taught you well. What's for dessert?"

She took two small oven dishes out of the basket.

"What is this?"

"It's a baked apple, silly."

"Mom's baked apples never looked like this,"

"Instead of sugar and cinnamon, I fill them with red hots."

"They look great." He dug in. "Mmmmm, what a great dessert. That's probably what attracted the cougar."

Bobbi looked over her shoulder.

He grinned. "You might want to snuggle up closer to me, in case she comes back."

"You cad." She leaned against him and popped a bite of apple into her mouth.

"Got me the girl, didn't it?" He put his arm around her and forked another mouthful of apple from his oven dish one handed.

When they'd finished eating and packed up the basket, Bobbi stripped off her shoes, shorts, and shirt, and headed for the water. "Holy cow! This is cold."

"It's mountain water, Bobbi."

"Ha," she said as she turned around to find him hip deep. "You thought you were going to sneak in so I wouldn't see your Army-issue underwear. You think I can't see through this clear mountain water?"

He blushed and reached for her. "I'm freezing."

They embraced as they adjusted to the temperature, then they inched out farther, hand in hand.

"Watch out, Bobbi, these lakes suddenly drop off and there's no bottom at all."

She gasped as she crouched to submerge herself, then swam farther, treading water about fifty yards out. "Oh, my gosh, Connor, this is wonderful, like Lake Erie early in the spring. Come on."

She watched him submerge himself and swim out to meet her. They played together, for a while, ducking and splashing, then headed back to the blanket. Side by side, they lay in the sun to dry and warm themselves.

She sat up, hugging her knees. "When I was a kid, my friends and I spent almost every afternoon at the beach." She looked down at him. "I looked at a map of Nebraska the other day. I didn't see any lakes around Willow Grove."

"If you came to Nebraska with me, we could go to Crystal Lake sometimes. It's not the Great Lakes of course, but there's a swimming beach and a dance pavilion. In winter it's a skating pond." He turned over with an arm over his eyes. "Pop said they're planning a big flood control dam on the Republican River. That'll be a lot of water when it's finished." He sat up and took her in his arms, brushing his lips across her mouth.

"Mmmm," she said without opening her eyes. "You've got a month to cut that out."

He deepened the kiss, and she felt his tongue exploring just inside her lips. She ran the tip of her tongue across his. He pulled her over on top of him and she lay her head on his shoulder as he stroked her back. "Hmmm," he murmured. He began slipping her straps over her shoulders.

"Connor, no."

"I won't do anything."

"Connor, I've been fighting men off since I was fifteen. They all thought I was easy because I sang in those places. But I'm not. I barely know you."

"You're right, Bobbi. I'm just so glad to be alive and I feel so good with you."

"I like being with you, too. But not . . . I'm just not that easy."

She watched as he got up and paced the lake shore. He stopped and nudged a pebble with his toe, picked it up and skipped it across the lake. "You want me to take you back?"

She joined him on the shoreline, picked up a rock, and tried to skip it. It plunked and sank.

"No. I just can't let us get carried away." She stood beside him and scooted under his arm.

"Do you mind if I critique your rock skipping?" Connor asked.

She chuckled. "Critique away."

"You need a flat rock, Bobbi." He let her go and picked up a likely candidate. He skipped it three times. "The object is to get the rock to skip as many times as possible."

She found a smooth, flat rock. "Like this?" It sank.

"You got the right kind of rock. It just needs a little English."

"English?"

"Here. Try this rock. You kind of settle it in the curve of your index finger and then flick your wrist." He stood in front of her and motioned a side-arm throw, then handed her the rock.

She took it and threw, skipping the rock twice, turning to him with a smile. "I think I've got it."

"See." He picked up another rock. "This one's perfect." He wound up and threw. "Five skips. Not bad."

She found a thin, flat rock with a lot of surface area. "How about this one?"

"Perfect."

She threw and the rock kept skipping.

He counted. "One. Two. Three. Four. Five. Six. Seven. Now that you've humiliated me at rock skipping, maybe I ought to take you home."

"Does that really bother you? The rock skipping?"

"Of course not. I'm just worried I've offended you and I don't want to press my luck."

"I'm not offended exactly. Just cautious."

"You're right. though. We barely know each other."

She smiled with a coy look. "Guess we'll have to spend more time together."

"You're willing to risk it?" He took her in his arms. "I guess we both have scars. I'm sorry I sparked yours."

"How about we get dressed and just snuggle up on the blanket for a little while?"

"Is that okay with you?"

"As long as we keep our clothes on."

They spooned and fell asleep.

Bobbi awoke to a strange sound that echoed in the silence. Hoo-oo-oo-oo hoo hoo. She sat up, scanning the dark meadow. "What's that?"

Connor sat up beside her and she cowered against him as a silent shadow skimmed across the clearing. He put an arm around her shoulders. "It's just an owl. Great horned, I think. One of the big ones."

"It's so dark."

"Let your eyes adjust. You'll see star shadows. All the trees and grass will look silvery." He pulled her close. "Look over there," he whispered, gesturing with his head, "see the doe tiptoeing out of the trees? Look at those long shadows. See," he said as her babies followed, "she's got twins."

They watched the deer grazing the edge of the meadow.

"What if the mountain lion comes back?"

"She won't come anywhere near us. I've camped in these woods all the way from Canada to Arizona, and they've never bothered me. You're safe with me."

She shivered. "I'm cold."

"Let's get out of here. We don't want to be late getting you back to the barracks. It's full dark now, and the sun sets late in the summer."

Camp Carson

Connor ended the night back at the base with a letter to his sister.

> Dear Sis,
>
> Well, she's still going out with me. I thought maybe if I get her comfortable with the out-of-doors, the quiet, she might adjust to the farm. She seemed comfortable with stepping into the trees to do her business anyway. She was afraid of the mountain lion we saw. I managed to calm her down, so maybe the coyotes won't scare her.

GRAVY

It's a campaign, you know, to get her used to the country. She saw farms and farmers in Iowa when she took basic training in Des Moines, so she has at least some idea what it's about.

I don't know, Sis, I really want this to work, but I see all the pitfalls you've mentioned. I'm gonna keep taking her away from the bright lights, because I've decided I just can't take her offer. If I had any desire to manage a singer, she'd be the one, but I don't want that life.

Now to your problem. If Daniel can resurrect his family's concern, you said they had a vineyard, then I assume you will go there. But what if he can't go back to that? I think you could start a vineyard in the Republican Valley. You could settle near Riverton, Inavale, or Guide Rock. You wouldn't want to run power and water lines too far because you'd have to pay for them yourselves. But a good well and a windmill might work.

That's assuming you're ready to settle down. If you haven't had enough adventures with the Foreign Service yet, you could keep that job and maybe go back to Paris and be with Daniel. How far is the vineyard anyway?

I have to admit, I've had enough adventures and it would be great if I could go back to Willow Grove and you would be close enough that our kids could play together.

Luck to both of us.

Connor

Connor switched off the light and fell asleep smiling.

GRAVY

June 19, 1945

Connor glanced at the silhouettes of the peaks west of town as he and Sam wandered the strip, looking for trouble. The snow had receded from all but the tallest peaks. *Looks cold up there.* He sighed. *I'm avoiding the issue. What the hell does she want from me?* He remembered the sleazy character who hung around outside Camp Carson, trying to get business for "his" girls.

Bobbi's not a hooker. She's offering a legitimate business deal. He scuffed along, studying the cracks in the sidewalk. *But I'd feel like a pimp—or what's that word—a gigolo. Even sounds sleazy. It's a whole different way to live; hanging around nightclubs, sleeping till sometime in the afternoon, never seeing the sun rise or laying in the shade of a tree, or smelling new-mown hay. What kind of life is that for a man?*

"Connor, what are you thinking about, man? New Guinea getting to you again?"

"Nah. It's Bobbi." He glanced at Sam. He'd almost forgotten his partner, walking right beside him.

"What's she up to?"

"She made me a proposition and I promised to think about it, but it's rubbing me raw."

"God, Connor! What kind of proposition?"

"She wants me to be her business manager."

"Well, that's not so bad, is it? What would you have to do?"

"She says I'd have to book her appearances and keep track of the money and make sure everybody pays up."

"Sounds like a good deal for you. She'd do all the work. You'd get to listen to her sing every night."

GRAVY

"I'd feel like her pimp. Imagine sitting at a table in some nightclub while every man in the place ogles your girl. How's that different from a pimp?"

"Well, for one thing, Bobbi's not a hooker. For another, you'd be protecting her from the people who wouldn't pay or dead-end jobs that wouldn't advance her career."

"You'd make a better manager than me. You've lived in cities all your life and you know how to talk business and write contracts. I don't know a thing about the music business and my experience with business in general is a handshake with the local merchants. What could I do for her?"

"If you're worried about the business end, I can help you with that. I can probably find you somebody who knows the music scene, too. But I don't think that's the problem, is it?"

Connor kicked a piece of rock down the street ahead of him, intent on his feet. He glanced up at Sam, then back down at his feet. "No. It's not. I just don't see how any self-respecting man can live off a woman. Oh, she says I'd work just as hard as she would, but that's not the point. There's just no dignity in this. And what kind of a way to live would that be—spending all our time in nightclubs, up until four or five in the morning? Never seeing the sun, except to watch it come up as you go to sleep. Never doing any real work. We couldn't even have a dog."

Their feet crunched on loose gravel at the edge of the street.

"Well," Sam said finally, "What kind of life would you give Bobbi if she married you and moved to the farm? Do you have electricity, flush toilets? How often do you hear a car go by or somebody laugh or footsteps on the street?"

Connor groaned and they crossed the street to check the other side.

"From what you've told me, Bobbi's been on her own for, what, seven years? How do you think she'll take to having you make all the decisions?"

62

GRAVY

"But that's what she asked me to do."

"Well, maybe, but she's still the star. How do you think she'd feel about giving that up? What does she want to do?"

"Says she wants to sing with the Dorsey Brothers or Duke Ellington or the Glen Miller band."

"Holy shit!"

"Yeah."

They stopped in the middle of the street. "You think she could do it?"

"Maybe. Then she wants a radio show of her own where we could stay in one place and raise a family."

"What would *you* do then?"

"That's a damn good question. I just don't see how I can do this for her."

"It *would* be tough for a man like you and I'm not sure nightclubs are the place for men who've been through what we've been through. Be easy to drown in a bottle. Look at all the guys we're hauling out of bars every night, just trying to forget. But you gotta admit that Bobbi'd have to give up a hell of a lot to marry you."

"You think I don't know it? She says she wants to get married, but that might change if she has to give up her singing career."

"You guys have talked about marriage?"

"Yeah. I asked her the other night. Got a letter from home. Pop's located some more land. He's ready to retire and let me start taking over. So I asked her and here she has her own ideas."

"How long have you known her, Connor. It can't have been very long."

63

He thought back. "A couple of months, I guess."

"That's not very long."

"Yeah, but look, I'm almost thirty. I lost all those years—five years hoboing around during the thirties. Then I no more than got home and started back to farming, and I ended up in the Army. So that's another five years. I just want to settle down and have a damn life." He glanced at Sam. "But what do I do about Bobbi? My girl back home has already married somebody else."

"Can't tell ya, pal, but I feel for ya."

"Right. With a ten-foot pole."

"It's your problem, my friend, and I wouldn't want any part of it. I wish you luck."

They kept walking, sticking their heads in a bar now and then. Fortunately, the night remained quiet, and Connor had plenty of time to think. Sam patrolled with him in silence. By the end of the shift, Connor hadn't changed his mind. Sam's comment about drowning in a bottle just added fuel to his reluctance. By the time he got back to his barracks, he'd decided. *Nope. I just can't do it.* He crawled in his bunk. *Now, I have to find a way to tell Bobbi.*

June 25, 1945 — Peterson Field

A week after their trip, Connor still hadn't given Bobbi an answer, even though they'd spent at least a few moments together every day. She hoped that meant he was really thinking about it, but her step dragged as she returned from the intricate work of building radios for the Air Force. She felt like she'd climbed Everest when she finally got into bed after her night at the club. The whole night had felt like swimming in pudding.

GRAVY

He's going to turn me down. I know it. Can't think of any way to change his mind.

He's not how I imagined farm boys. He could fit beautifully into any sophisticated crowd. He looks wonderful in slacks and a sport coat and I know he'd look great in a tux. But he doesn't seem interested. I had to work my butt off to figure how to act, but it's easy for him. He dances divinely and has a quick wit. It just doesn't matter to him. He wants to go home. That's great for him. He has a home to go to. She sat up, looking around in the dark. *I don't suppose a farm family would accept me. Then what?* She turned over and fluffed her pillow. *But maybe they would. What would that be like?*

She dropped off to sleep, smiling, imagining a home—how it would feel, how it would look. She imagined Connor's warm arms around her, protecting her.

In her dream, she sang with the Miller band—Glen Miller leading. A nightclub with polished marble columns, granite floors, and crystal chandeliers. Connor sat at a table covered by white linen, with a bud vase and a red rose. She smiled at him.

Then she was in a dressing room with a sweet little girl who watched closely as she touched up her makeup. "Can we go home now, Mommy?"

"Not yet, sweetie. Mommy's got to sing some more."

"Sing to *me*, Mommy."

"Not right now, Darling."

Bobbi left the dressing room and the child. As she walked away, she saw thick, hairy fingers reaching. She tried to go back, but she was frozen in place, forced to watch the man with the fingers grab her little girl, rip her dress, and fondle her thighs under her little skirt. Bobbi tried to scream, to shout at the man, to call for help, but what came out was a song—*Don't Sit Under the Apple Tree with Anyone Else But Me.*

"No!" She woke panting, wrestling with the blankets. She forced herself to take a deep breath and exhale slowly. *That seemed real.* She recognized Carl Short, the man who had tried to rape her years before. She rearranged the covers and snuggled back down to sleep, but her mind kept going back into the dream, trying to save the little girl. *You need to stop this, Bobbi. It was just a dream.* Eventually, she slept.

In her next dream, she walked down a dark street. She recognized the entrance to Lake View Cemetery in Cleveland where she'd nearly been abducted. In her dream she was with the little girl again—a silent child this time, looking around with big eyes, peering into the darkness inside the gate. Bobbi felt the hair stand up on the back of her neck. She, too, peered into darkness she couldn't penetrate.

"C'mon, Sweetie, let's run." Before she could take the first step, a dark figure, swept out of the cemetery and disappeared back into the gloom with the child. The last thing she saw as the child was torn from her grasp was the tiny hands reaching for her and huge, terrified eyes. She pursued a figure she could barely see. Once, she spotted a flicker of black crossing before a white tombstone. Something tripped her and as she fell, she heard a childish voice, moving away, singing *I'll Be Home for Christmas*.

She started awake shivering.

Gloria's disembodied voice startled her. "What's goin' on?"

"Bad dream."

"Musta been pretty bad, you were yelling."

"I'm going out for some fresh air." Bobbi slipped into her shoes and headed for the door. Outside, she leaned against the wall and lit a cigarette. *I don't know where that little girl came from. Connor talking about kids maybe.* She stood smoking, calming down. *We would have beautiful children together.* She paced until she finished the cigarette, then threw it down, ground it out, and went back to bed.

She kept dreaming. She walked into a frigid world where a bitter wind blew down deserted city streets. Again, she walked with the child clinging to her hand. The little girl's eyes appeared sunken. Her fingers, hanging onto Bobbi's, seemed skeletal, hardly the fingers of a soft little girl. The child had hollow cheeks and thin hair, reminding Bobbi of survivors from the Nazi concentration camps, pictures she'd seen in news photos. The child plodded along beside her in silence. Bobbi noticed a man, walking just ahead of them.

"Connor," her dream-self called. "Connor, are you all right?"

The man stopped and stared at her, hollow-eyed.

"I'm sorry, Bobbi. I don't know what to do here. I don't know how to find a job. I just don't know."

His voice trailed off as he turned and continued walking, hobbling really. As he moved away, she lost the monotone of his voice in the wind, singing *Brother Can You Spare A Dime*.

Bobbi opened her eyes and peered through the dark in silence, tears running from the corners of her eyes, down her temples, and into her hair. *God, I don't want to go to sleep again. It just keeps getting worse. It's like living the very worst of my life all over, and taking everyone I love down with me. Is that what it would be like if Connor agreed to represent me? Could it really be that bad?*

She tried to visualize herself singing with the Glen Miller orchestra, as she'd imagined a thousand times before, but the dream had snuffed that out. Every time she closed her eyes, she saw that emaciated child.

"I don't know what to do. I just don't know what to do."

GRAVY

June 24, 1945 — Rocky Mountain National Park

Almost from the moment they'd met, Connor had talked about taking Bobbi to Rocky Mountain National Park. When they finally had a couple of days' leave together. Bobbi had her doubts about spending an overnight alone with him. She knew he wouldn't force himself on her, but she didn't trust herself either.

When she met him in the parking lot next to the much-borrowed car, he was grinning like a Cheshire cat. "You seem chipper," she observed as he held the door for her.

"Sun's shining. Sky's blue. I've got a couple of days to spend with you."

She chuckled. "Where will we stay, Connor?"

He walked around and slid into the driver's side. "You'll see. I'm pretty sure you'll like it."

"Rustic?"

"Very."

"Log cabin?"

"You'll see. It's going to take about half a day to get there, so make yourself comfortable. It's a beautiful drive."

As they followed the Front Range on U.S. 85, chatting about their lives before the Army, she kept seeing glimpses of the tortured baby's face and hearing a weak voice singing. They stopped for lunch in Denver before heading west into the foothills on U.S. 36. As they left the high plains and headed into the trees, they lapsed into silence that left spaces for Bobbi's nightmare. She remembered that some expert thought our dreams tell us something. She tried to imagine what hers meant. *I guess the obvious message is, don't try to have a family and a singing career.*

68

"You're awfully quiet," Connor observed.

"Just looking."

"Anything wrong?"

"I had a dream so real that I'm having trouble getting it out of my head."

"Wanna talk about it?"

"Nope."

They waited for a herd of elk at the Big Thompson Creek crossing. "I didn't have a rifle when I was wandering around here during the thirties, so I never had a chance to shoot one of them. It's probably just as well because most of the meat would have spoiled before we could eat it, anyway."

"Didn't they have seasons on them?"

"I'm sure there were, but people ignored the seasons at lot, just to get food in their bellies."

"I'd have been happy to have some elk when I was in Buffalo."

"There were a couple of times I'd have given a lot for an elk steak, myself."

As the animals ambled away, Connor edged through the herd, nosing the car on into the park.

He could survive out here. He's comfortable and he knows what to do. I wonder if he ever would adapt to the cities.

When the road turned into a series of tight switchbacks, Bobbi glanced out the side window a couple of times, then focused straight ahead, gripping the armrest with white knuckles.

Connor grinned. "Scary, isn't it?"

"I'll say."

When they got to Bear Lake, Connor pulled into a little parking area. Bobbi stepped out, glad to get her feet on solid ground.

Connor pulled in a big breath and started to unload the trunk. "Smell those pines, Bobbi."

"What have you got there?"

"Let's see. I brought a couple of steaks and a rack to broil them. I packed them on ice to keep them fresh, some potatoes we can roast in the coals." He handed her a roll of aluminum foil. "We can wrap them in this." He continued unpacking the trunk. "We can swim here. Pick a convenient tree for a changing room."

"What about you?"

"I'll get the fire started first, then I'll pick my own tree. There will probably be people driving up through here, so we should keep out of sight to change."

He spread a blanket on the ground and busied himself while Bobbi watched. "Okay, you get comfortable, and I'll make our fire pit." He returned to the car for a trenching tool and dug a pit, surrounding it with rocks. He placed four inside the perimeter.

"What're those for?"

"For the grate, so we can grill our steaks. We probably won't want to eat yet, although I'll want plenty of time for the fire to burn down and make coals. Do you want to swim for a while first?"

"Yes! Last one in's a rotten egg." She hurried to the car and fumbled through her overnight bag, dragging out her swimsuit and half her other clothes. She shoved them back in and slammed the car door, leaving them draped over the edge of the case—too late. Connor had already rushed off to a clump of trees. He'd changed and stood at the edge of the lake before

Bobbi got out from behind her tree. He stepped onto a rock at lake's edge and dove.

Bobbi watched for him to come up as she strode toward the water. When she stepped onto the rock, she could see him through the clear water, but he kept sinking, not coming up.

"Oh, my God." She watched for movement, but he kept sinking. "No!" She gulped air and dove, cutting the water and going deep.

By the time she reached him, he'd started to struggle, but she didn't hesitate. She maneuvered behind him, reached over his shoulder, cupped his chin in her left hand, and started dragging him upwards with strong scissors kicks and a grasping right arm that pulled water down toward her. As she kicked and pulled upward, she felt like her lungs would burst. *What if he drowns before I can get him out?*

In just a moment, they broke the surface, both gasping. She felt him breathing and relaxed a bit but, with a lungful of air, he started struggling.

"Stop it, Connor." She towed him toward shore, laying on her right side and scissor-kicking as she stroked with her right arm. "You're gonna drown us both."

He lay still in her grasp.

"You alright?" she demanded when she dragged him onto the sand.

"I think so." He coughed.

"You weren't moving. I thought. I didn't have time to think. I thought you were dead. I was diving and swimming for you and I thought you'd hit your head and . . . You weren't moving. You just sank and sank, and I thought you were dead."

"Well." He grinned. "I'm not dead. I jumped in there and liked to froze the instant I hit the water. I thought I was having a heart attack. Just couldn't make my arms and legs work for a minute. Seemed like a very long minute."

"It *was* a very long minute." She sat on the sand panting.

"And then you were there, just when my body started working again."

"It wasn't working very much. You barely moved until I got you to the surface. And then I didn't know if I should just let you go. You were struggling, but I didn't know if you had the strength to swim."

He turned to face her. "How did you . . . Bobbi, you're crying. Are you okay? Did I hurt you?"

She broke into sobs. "I thought I'd lost you. It all happened so fast, and I thought I'd lost you."

He moved onto the beach and wrapped her in his arms. "I'm right here, Bobbi. I'm all right. I'm probably not going to jump into any mountain lakes without testing them first, though."

"Is your heart okay?"

"Of course, I may not be fully recovered from the fevers, but I'm all right."

"Connor, you scared me half to death." She pushed away. She cupped her hands in the water and splashed her face. "Connor," she looked into the depths of the lake and saw no bottom. "I don't ever want to be scared like that. If you'd gone down much farther, I don't know if I could have got you back."

He gazed into the depths as if hypnotized. Eventually, he shook his head and looked over his shoulder at Bobbi. "I wonder how deep it is. As clear as this water is, you'd think you could see the bottom." He shivered lightly, then stood and got a couple of Army-issue towels from the open trunk. "Not as plush as the Hilton, but we can dry off a little. How about some steaks?"

GRAVY

"I not hungry yet, but the fire would feel good."

"Right. It'll cool off fast at this altitude. Tell me something." He started building the fire. "How did you know how to get me out of there without drowning yourself?"

"Oh, like I said before, we all used to swim in Lake Erie—every day." She frowned. "I knew a guy who taught me lifesaving."

"What's the matter?"

She stared at him for a moment. "Jack's dead now."

"War?"

"No." She gazed out across the lake. "Murdered."

He stepped around the fire pit and took her in his arms. "I don't even know what to say. Was he a close friend?"

"We'd been going together for a couple of years." She hesitated. "I read it in the paper."

Connor said nothing for a moment, then as though her story had taken time to sink in, he said, "Oh, Bobbi," tightened his hold, and rocked their bodies back and forth.

Eventually, she stepped out of his embrace. "That was a long time ago. I don't want to think about it." She stood on the other side of the fire wrapped in her towel and they were both silent while he blew the little rags of flame into life.

"Connor," she looked into the spreading tongues of flame, "I'd have been devastated if I'd lost you in there."

Connor looked into her eyes without a word.

"I don't want to lose you, too," she said.

He stood and moved to her side of the fire in an instant, holding her in his arms and kissing her. "I love you too, Bobbi."

They stood together for a few moments until Connor remembered the fire. "I'd better get some fuel on this or I'll have to start it again. Why don't you get dressed while I cook."

By sundown, they'd eaten, and they sat on a blanket, watching the last of the fire burn down.

"Bobbi," Connor took her hands. "I've thought about your proposition. I've thought about it a lot. But it's the man's place to make a living. I'd feel like a complete waste with you putting yourself out there every night while I just sat around and drank booze. Pretty soon, I'd be taking a poke at every man who ogled you or tried to talk to you or put his hands on you. You know I've seen and done some awful stuff and now I need to feel like my life's worth something. And I'm afraid. I don't know if I can be around bars that much without turning into a drunk."

She started to speak, but he hurried on, "Besides that, I do want a family and I can't imagine raising kids without a real home. I know you grew up without one and you turned out all right, but I don't think it made your life better or happier."

He stopped. "Okay, I'm done. If you don't want to marry me now, I understand, but I still want you to come with me to Nebraska."

"Do you remember that nightmare I told you I'd had that I couldn't shake?"

"I suppose it was about living on a farm in Nebraska."

She laughed ironically. "No. It was about the city. It was about every awful thing that's happened to me since I started singing in nightclubs—only all those things were happening to the people I love. There was a little girl, and she must have been my daughter and you were in it and we were in a city and we were all starving."

"Sounds ugly. What do you make of it?"

"Well, maybe a warning? Like I could ruin everyone I love."

74

"What do you want to do?"

"I *want* to live happily ever after with you in our kingdom *and* I want to sing with the Glen Miller band." She smiled. "But I'd give my life for you. I didn't realize that until we nearly drowned this afternoon. I didn't even have to think about it. I just jumped in and I guess the only solution for me now is to jump right in. I want to marry you and live with you, wherever that may be."

"I was hoping you'd say that." Connor kissed her, wrapping her tightly in his arms. "Bobbi, I can't promise you a lot," he murmured between kisses, "but I *can* promise that you will never, ever be hungry again. We can eat meat three times a day and we'll have all the eggs and milk we want. We have a sweet well that never went dry, so we can at least irrigate a garden, even if I have to do it in buckets."

They packed the car and headed higher into the mountains as Connor tried to describe what a farm is like. Even though he did his best, Bobbi really couldn't visualize how a room lit by kerosene lantern looked. Although he explained that not having electricity meant using an outhouse, Bobbi hadn't thought of having to traipse out there in the dark or in the middle of winter—or of using a chamber pot. And she couldn't possibly imagine the quiet.

When they topped the tree line, Connor pulled onto the shoulder. She stood next to him, with his arm around her waist, while he pointed out a large cluster of twinkling lights in the distance. "That's Denver."

"It's so quiet here."

He turned to her for a kiss, their breath a frosty cloud rising along the flank of the snow-covered mountain. "Now," he said when they separated, "Let's go find our accommodations."

He turned around and headed back down the mountain. "We *do* have to go back into Estes Park."

GRAVY

"Nope."

"Then what?"

"You'll see."

Soon he pulled into an access road barely wide enough for the
car. When they came into a clearing, he announced, "This is
Kaley's-in-the-Pines."

"What cute little cabins."

"A guy from back home owns them. I've rented one for us."

"But . . ."

"It's all right, Bobbi. You can have the bedroom, and I'll sleep on
the Murphy bed in the other room. Unless you change your
mind—since you just told me you'd marry me."

"We'll see." She gave him a sideways glance.

Once they'd checked in, they sat on the couch, Bobbi straddling
his lap. Connor unzipped her jacket and began unbuttoning her
blouse. She remained silent, nuzzling his neck and shoulder as
he held her against his chest, his hands warm on her bare back.
He slid the blouse off her shoulders and smoothed his palms
along her sides as though molding her shape. He reached for the
back of her bra and fumbled with the hook until he released it,
then slipped the straps off her shoulders and dropped it on the
floor. Then he looked for a moment.

"Ah," he whispered, "They're gorgeous."

Her nipples hardened as a slight draft brushed them. She
watched his face as he cradled them in his hands, the hollow of
each palm over a nipple as he stroked and squeezed. The draft
persisted, leaving her feeling completely exposed but at ease.
She'd have never guessed she could sit bare-chested in front of a
man and feel so free.

76

She kissed his forehead, and he scanned her face. They kissed, then remained, lips touching, open mouthed, sharing ragged breath. As he rolled her nipples between his fingers, she felt a response between her legs, like a low jolt of electricity. She drew a deep breath and arched her back as he tugged at her waistband. He unbuttoned it with trembling fingers, and she stood to step out of her slacks and kick them away. He stood before her, stroking her skin, running his hands down her sides. Looking. And she looked back, studying his face, running her hands over the swell of his muscular chest and shoulders.

He started to slip her panties off, then withdrew suddenly. "Damn it!" he growled, grinding his teeth in frustration.

She gasped, stunned. "Connor!" She came out of her trance. "What are we doing?" She tried to cover herself with her hands, looking for her blouse. "We can't!" she collapsed on the couch, hands over her face. "We can't!" she moaned. "I can't believe I've been such a slut!"

"You're not a slut, darling. You're a beautiful, desirable woman and I'm going to make love to you sometime soon." He knelt in front of her, cradling her chin and raising her face. "Just not tonight."

"You must think I'm easy," she whispered.

"If you are, then I'm doubly so."

"You're the one who stopped."

"I wouldn't have . . . I just realized I have to protect you. I don't have a condom, Bobbi. I didn't realize we'd make such a commitment today and now the last thing I want to do to you is get you pregnant. I know we're going to get married, but we've got a lot to work out and it'll be tough enough. Let's not start with a baby."

They spent the night spooned on the bed. Neither of them slept much.

GRAVY

June 25, 1945 – Camp Carson

Driving back down out of the mountains, they'd made wedding plans. "I imagine you'll want to get married in Cleveland."

"Connor, my parents can't afford a big wedding, or at all. I'm signed up for another year, so unless you want to wait for me, we'll have to get married here. Then I can get out."

"We'll have to get married in uniform. Regulations."

Bobbi remembered her dreamed-of wedding with its formal gown and her groom in his tux and the crystal chandeliers. She hesitated. "Do you suppose they'd throw us in the brig if we didn't?"

Connor grinned. "Probably not. Is that what you want to do?"

She frowned. "No. I guess not. I'm proud that I'm serving my country."

"Then we'll get married in Colorado Springs."

"When?"

"I get out in a week."

"A week! You didn't tell me."

"I just got my orders. It seems like things kept happening and we had other things to talk about. I forgot."

"We need a place."

"We could do it in the chapel."

"We could. How about Ed and Nell's back yard? They have a nice lawn, and we wouldn't have many guests. We could get some folding chairs."

GRAVY

By the time they reached Colorado Springs, they had a plan. Connor dropped Bobbi off at Peterson Field to apply for leave and make whatever arrangements she had to make with the Women's Army Air Force, and he went to Camp Carson to return his friend's car and make similar arrangements.

When he got back to the barracks, he found a letter from Nora. He ripped it open, knowing he had to respond right away.

> Dear brother,
>
> I think you're on the right track with Bobbi. If you can make her comfortable with a quieter life, she might adjust. Like you said, she already has a start with her military experience. But this is her whole life you're trying to change. Even if you win the damsel, you will have to help her adjust and it's likely to take years. As to Daniel and me, we have to make some big adjustments too. We'll see. They've just signed the peace after all. He hasn't even been back from checking the vineyard and he's still scouring the registries for his sisters.
>
> I have to tell you about VE day here. Remember how Grandpa used to talk about the whole earth's crust moving with living things at night? It was like that here in Paris when General de Gaulle announced the surrender over the government loudspeakers. People started moving in the sunshine and on into the dark. They filled the Champs-Elesées and poured around the Arc de Triomphe. The sound of shuffling feet and murmuring voices almost drowned out the church bells. We heard the canon only as a background rumble. We stood on the balcony and watched and wept with the crowd.
>
> Oh, how sweet is the peace, but how excruciating the rebuilding. We've years ahead of us. People will subsist in tents and bombed out buildings for

the foreseeable future—without sanitation or running water, and very scant rations. I don't know how the people returning from the concentration camps can begin to regain their health in current conditions.

Anyway, just keep doing what you're doing, brother, and I hope it works for you.

Nora

Connor folded the letter and stuffed it back in its envelope, thinking about how his sister had seemed to get the worst of the war. He immediately grabbed pen and paper to tell her so and to let her know about his impending discharge and upcoming marriage—in just six days.

June 30, 1945

In less than a week, they'd pulled it all together. The weather cooperated, with clear mountain air and high-flying clouds. By one p.m., the chaplain and their few guests had arrived. Connor walked in with his campaign badges pinned on upside down and his combat infantry badge out of place.

"Hey, Connor," said Sam. "Let me straighten you up." He righted the misplaced insignia.

In Nell's bedroom, Bobbi fussed with a uniform that didn't quite fit. "Bobbi, this will have to do."

"But I look fat."

"Can't be helped, dear, unless you want to postpone the wedding. I talked to the cleaner myself and he said he definitely would not have your uniform ready until tomorrow."

"I took it to him a week ago," Bobbi wailed.

"I know. Apparently, it got lost somewhere in the back of the shop."

Bobbi tugged at the jacket. "Maybe this is a sign."

"A sign? Of what?"

"Maybe I'm not supposed to get married."

"Bobbi, something always goes wrong with a wedding. Nobody, and I mean nobody, ever gets through it without a hitch."

"Oh, I don't know, Nell."

"Well, now's the time to back out if you're going to."

"No." Bobbi squared her shoulders. "He's the one."

"You'd better be sure."

"I am."

The Peterson Club House Band was playing Mendelssohn's *Wedding March* as she started to walk out, when a stray dog wandered into the yard. Black and scruffy, he slunk around sniffing. Several of the guests tried to shoo him out, but he snarled at them and kept out of reach. Bobbi didn't spot him until he met her in the center of the aisle, snarling and growling. He snapped at her, but she stood her ground and he leapt to the side, upsetting a vase of flowers onto Gloria's dress. Gloria gasped and jumped up, brushing the water off her skirt.

Bobbi stood, staring at Connor and the chaplain. *Maybe I should turn around and run as hard as I can.* She saw all the faces turned toward her. *God, what am I doing here?* She took another step. *I should follow that scruffy dog and get out of here.* She stepped forward again. *I don't know how to be with a husband. I don't know how to be a wife.* She kept walking until she stood beside Connor, facing the Army chaplain. She heard almost nothing of the ceremony as her mind ran like the dog, still trying to find an outlet to safety.

"Bobbi," Nell whispered, touching her elbow.

"Do you take this man?" the chaplain repeated.

Connor stared into her eyes. She looked back for a long moment. "I do," she whispered.

Turning to Connor, the chaplain continued the ceremony.

"You can back out now," Connor said, too low for anybody but Bobbi to hear.

She shook her head.

Connor glanced back at the chaplain as he finished the recitation. "I do," he responded firmly.

Before the chaplain could tell him to kiss the bride, Connor bent Bobbi over his arm, as he had once before, and kissed her. When he set her back up, they were both breathless, but he swept an arm around her waist and strode down the aisle, into the house and out onto the street before she could protest.

He bustled her into the car and took off. Neither of them spoke until they'd travelled a few miles out of town.

"Bobbi, you didn't seem very sure about saying I do. Are you still afraid of me?"

Bobbi thought about that for the first time since she'd dragged him out of Bear Lake. "Well yes," she said finally. "I've only seen you blow up once. That was frightening. There's an edginess about you all the time. But that's not it."

"What is it, sweetheart?"

"There was that scruffy dog, and it was like I went into a trance watching him try to get away. I saw all the places where I used to sing and heard all the noises a city makes and all the lights and the people talking and shouting and cars and car horns; footsteps on pavement; smells from the back doors of restaurants; just everything I've been used to all my life. Even on the base there are a lot of people and noise and confusion. And I wondered what my life will be like from now on."

Connor pulled over to the shoulder and turned to face her. "It will be different. Very different. It will be quiet. I can barely hear myself think in the city, but I know it's different for you."

"Connor, sometimes I don't want to know what I'm thinking. I don't know how to be a wife. My parents fought all the time. My mom threw dishes at him and yelled at him and he yelled and slammed doors. I guess I just got carried away by the wonder of having a man respect me. I've never had that."

Connor stared out the windshield. He sighed and turned back to Bobbi. "We can turn around and get the marriage annulled."

"No! I love you, Connor. I know I don't sound like it. I'm just scared. This is all so new and different. I don't really even know what I've got myself into."

"Would you like to go back and think about it?"

"No. No. I want to go on a honeymoon with my husband. We've only got two days. I want to make love and just be together and think about this later."

"Bobbi, I think we can feel our way through this and make a good life together. But I know you're giving up a lot. I'll try to respect that."

"I know you will. Let's just go, though. I want to get you back in that cabin and finish what we started."

Connor grinned. "You got it." He pulled back onto the highway and hit the gas.

Part Two

July 2, 1945 – Union Pacific, Central Plains

Connor sat by the window, watching the high plains rumble by with its sagebrush and dust, his Army duffle on the floor under the seat. As he counted cadence under his breath, he wondered if he could remember how to be part of a family and if he could calm his nerves. Bobbi would never know the effort he had expended keeping himself under control, trying to be reasonable, when all he wanted to do was go out on the sagebrush desert screaming and ripping out hair. He was glad for the cross-country train ride alone to compose himself while Bobbi went back to Ohio to tell her folks about their marriage and to muster out of the Army.

He looked forward to seeing his folks. When he'd got home on his first furlough in December, he'd just curled up behind the cook stove and shivered. Remembering the teeth-chattering chills and fever gave him a shudder running down his back. *I hope I'm done with that.* The rhythm of the rails lulled him, and he dozed for a couple of hours. He woke when the train pulled into the station at North Platte. He stepped out to stretch his legs and get a sandwich at the Canteen.

He got back on the train with a paper plate full of chicken, green beans with bacon, and some sliced cucumbers soaked in vinegar. *Hasn't changed a bit.* He found his seat and dug in. A little awkward with his Army knife, but he didn't have time to eat at the Canteen where he could use real silverware.

He changed trains in Grand Island for the short hop to Willow Grove. Looking out the windows, he began to see old friends' houses, places he'd visited often when he went to school in town, fields he'd helped work. Would any of them recognize him now? He guessed he looked the same, but he didn't feel the same. He felt like he'd been dropped from another time into vaguely familiar country. He didn't feel like he fit anymore.

When the train pulled into the station, he spotted his parents, Henry and Claire, standing on the platform. He was pleasantly surprised to see Nora standing with them. He dragged out his duffle, slung it over his shoulder, and stepped into the sun.

His dad's face looked solemn as he reached a hand to shake. "I'm glad to see you, Son, and we can't wait to meet your new wife."

His mother threw her arms around him and sobbed into his shirt. He set his duffle on the platform so he could put both arms around her.

"I'm okay, Mom."

He held her and looked over her head at Nora. He smiled. "How ya doin,' Sis?"

"It's great to see you, Connor. I moved heaven and earth and a couple of Congressmen so I could be here when you got home."

"It's great to see you, too. How long have you got?"

"I've got a month. Considering travel time, about two weeks and a couple of days. I hope Bobbi will be here before I go back."

"What about Daniel?"

"He found his sisters in London. They're doing okay. They want to stay where they are. The oldest is married. Daniel is still in France sorting things out."

Connor chuckled. "You gonna try to make a plainsman out of him?"

"His family had a vineyard. I think he could start over here."
Nora grinned. "I may be contented to come home after all."

"Damn. Be nice to meet the man who could make my sister say
that."

His mom finally released him and stepped away. "We've got a lot
to do to get ready for Bobbi."

"I know. Mom. Nora, she's really nervous about living on a farm.
I'm counting on you to help to her find her way around a little
bit. She didn't really have a family growing up, so she needs to
feel like she's a part of this one."

"How long before her discharge?"

"It's in the works. She's on furlough right now, home telling her
folks. She'll probably muster out in Illinois, then jump on a train
for Willow Grove."

They all climbed in the car. "What's she like?" Nora asked.

"Like I said in my letters, she's been singing with the big bands
since she was a kid, so she's tough."

"It's hardened her, then."

"No. Not like that, although she had to learn how to look out for
herself. She just had to have a lot of guts to go into that first
nightclub when she was fifteen."

"Fifteen! That's just a child."

"I know, Nora." He started to loosen up with his sister. "Oh, and
she can dance."

"Maybe they'll start having dances again, now that the war's
almost over."

"It could last a long time yet, Nora. I think Japan will fight until
the last man's dead or disabled." He looked out the window,

trying to ignore the chill running up his spine as he remembered the Jap soldier running his own dagger through his gut in that cave in New Guinea. Connor still couldn't fathom what would induce a man to do that.

"Connor? you okay?"

He looked at his sister. "Yeah. Just remembering something."

"By the look in your eyes, it must have been grim."

"It was."

"I'm sorry."

"It just is. Nothing you can do about it. I imagine you saw some things, too."

"Worse than you can imagine," she whispered, glancing at their parents in the front seat. She leaned back, crossing her arms over her chest. "I suppose you *can* imagine."

"I think I can." He struggled to stop the images until he got a strong whiff of new-mown hay through the open window and his body relaxed.

"Mom made you a lemon meringue pie." His grin spread across his lean face.

July 3, 1945 — Willow Grove, Nebraska

The next morning, while Claire and Nora cooked, the men drove off to the east. A mile from home, Henry pulled into an overgrown driveway and followed it to a worn-looking house.

"The Robinson's place." Connor stared at the house and barn, the outbuildings and a fence line that needed repair. "I had a lot of good times in that house. What happened?"

87

GRAVY

They both stepped out of the car and leaned on the hood, looking at an orchard and a shredded windbreak.

"Your mom wrote you that Luke died at Pearl Harbor on the Arizona?"

"Yes, and Fred died somewhere in Europe. What happened to Cecil?"

"That's what broke their hearts. He was working in that munitions plant southeast of Hastings. I told you about that plant, didn't I?"

"Yeah. Three brothers in our unit got kicked off their farm to build that plant. They were pretty bitter. Joined the Army so they could send some money back to their folks."

"That was a dirty deal for all those families."

Connor nodded.

"Anyway, about six months ago, Cecil was working in that plant and something lit a spark. The whole building went up. They couldn't even find pieces of those people to bury."

"That might have been merciful in a way."

"What do you mean?"

"I think it would be awful for a parent to see what an explosion does to a body."

"Oh." Henry dropped his eyes to his toes, blinking back a stubborn tear. He took a deep breath. "It just took the gas out of Howard and Rosemary. He couldn't get a crop in. The neighbors helped. Planted the fields for him, but we all got busy and couldn't keep up with his crop too. And then he couldn't pay his taxes."

"He lost it for taxes?"

GRAVY

"Well, I offered to pay the taxes for him so he could keep on, but he just wanted to quit. So, I bought it from him for the taxes owed and some extra to get set up somewhere."

"Like you did with the Green's before the war?"

"Yeah. They've already paid me back, by the way."

"So, we own this quarter now?"

"Yup. Not next door like the Green quarter, but it's only a mile."

"What'd you have to pay?"

"$1800."

"That's a bargain."

"Taxes was $600. So I gave him $1200 and the boys had sent him their Army pay—until they died. So he and Rosemary have a start. The girls are all married."

"Just looks sad."

"Well, let's go take a look."

They walked through the house, already familiar to Connor from years of visits.

"It's still sound."

Connor kicked some debris on the floor and a mouse scurried away."

"You'll have to set some traps or get a bunch of cats. It's kind of a gamble, but I thought you and I could take out all the plaster and lath. It's in pretty bad shape anyway. And we could run electrical wire and put in some plug-ins—and light fixtures. Harm Obermeier's an electrician. He's been taking care of everybody in town."

GRAVY

"So you think REA will get here pretty soon?"

"I think it will be several years yet, but as long as we're gonna have the walls open anyway, we ought to be ready. It'll be cheaper to do it now than to do it after the walls are all closed up again. We can put in some of that fiberglass insulation."

"Makes sense."

"You and I can fix that porch. We'll probably have to take the whole thing off and start over."

"Looks that way. What happened here anyway? This looks like more than neglect, especially the windbreak."

"Howard had really let things go, but we had a tornado last spring. That just took the cake. As if the poor guy didn't have enough to deal with. It touched down in that field over north and zigzagged to the windbreak. Howard said it kind of popped up then and jumped over the house or swung around it somehow. He wasn't clear. Anyhow, it chewed up the orchard and outbuildings before it was done with him."

"Pop, it'll take weeks just to get those stumps and snags out of here."

"I know, Son. You can plant your new windbreak in among them while you work on getting the dead stuff out."

"Good idea, Pop. Those old snags will give the new trees at least a little protection from the wind."

"You'll have plenty to do for the first year or two. I hope Bobbi's a patient woman."

"Me too."

"Let's go look at the barn."

"Still looks nice and square. Should be sound. We spent a lot of hours in that loft, swinging from a rope Luke snagged from somewhere—playing Tarzan."

As they walked around looking at the feed bunks and stanchions, the wind blew a loose door shut with a bang.

"We'll have to fix that door." Henry turned to Connor. "Connor?"

Connor pushed himself off the floor into a crouch, his eyes swept the barn over the edge of a feed bunk.

Henry stood without moving. "It's all right, Son." He used the same quiet voice he'd used decades before when he carried Connor on his shoulder through the first nights after his mother had weaned him from her breast. "You're home."

Connor looked back over his shoulder at his father's familiar face. Gradually he stood, still scanning the barn. Satisfied that he and Henry were alone, he relaxed. "Sorry, Pop."

"It's all right. You're liable to do that for a while. I can't say I understand 'cause I've never been shot at, but I know a lot of men come back from war a little jumpy."

"Pop, you've got a gift for understatement."

Henry smiled.

"What have we gotta do here?"

They climbed into the loft.

"We need to replace the rope on the drop door. See how frayed it is? The augur door into the feed room needs a new board. It's been left unlatched a time or two. I wired it shut until we can get to it."

"Before we leave, I'll do the same on that door that's flapping in the breeze downstairs. What else, Pop?"

GRAVY

"You wanna walk the fences?"

They walked six miles of fence, noting needed repairs. Henry had been making a materials list on a little pad he kept with a stub pencil in his bib pocket. When they got back to the farmyard, he walked around the barn and noted the materials they'd need to repair the doors.

"I think I've got most of what we'll need at home. So what do you think? Can you make this place work?"

"Sure, Pop. It looks good. Looks like the pastures have had a rest. Too bad Howard couldn't keep up with that little bit of cropground."

"Connor, I think there were a lot of days he couldn't get out of bed. Said without his sons, there just wasn't much reason to keep workin'."

"That's a cryin' shame."

"How about my thinkin' on the house?"

"I agree with everything you said."

"Allright, I'll call the workmen tomorrow and get 'em started. You think we can get that plaster and lath out in a couple of days?"

"Oh sure. If I learned one thing in the Army, it's that demolition is quick and easy. It's the building that takes time."

"Okay. I'll see if I can get Obermeier started—this is Wednesday. I'll see if I can get 'em out here by Monday. You and Bobbi'll probably have to stay with us for a while. I think it will take a few months to get everything done. We'll start by ripping out the plaster and lath, then while all the ruckus is going on in the house, you and I can take care of the fences and the barn—and plant some trees. It's late in the year for that, so you'll have to water them by hand."

GRAVY

"How about the well? I seem to remember it kept pumping all through the thirties. Do I remember right? I was gone several years."

"It's a good well and it never ran dry. You'll be fine. May have to pull it and replace the leathers, though. It's running a little slow." Henry hesitated a moment. "You may want to wait until spring to buy cattle. That way you can grow some winter feed while they're grazing the pastures."

"I'd like to build a lane along the north fence like you did on the home place, so I can just open a gate and let them meander to the new grass when they're done with one pasture."

"That's a good idea, Connor, but it may be next spring before we have time to do it—unless we get an open winter. Seems like we don't get as much snow since the drought."

Over supper, Connor drifted in and out of the conversation, trying to concentrate but always pulled back to his cadence. It was torture trying to concentrate on trivia—which neighbor had married, which had bought more land, which was off somewhere fighting the war. That last, particularly, set him off. He should be over there with them, finishing this thing off, not eating lemon meringue pie with his folks, not married to a beautiful woman who'd given up her dream for him.

When the meal finally ended, he wandered onto the south porch to watch the drab little hummingbird moths sucking syrup out of his mom's four-o'clocks. He leaned back into the leather of the chair that his mother used to shell peas and snap beans before she took them into the house and stretched his legs. He wished he could just sit there until the jitters stopped, until every loud noise stopped propelling him onto his belly or behind a rock, until he could stop saying the names of all the good men he'd left in New Guinea without even a "so long." He smelled the alfalfa again. It must be ready to cut. They ought to do that rather than working on his house.

GRAVY

His dad joined him, sitting in a twin chair. "I noticed the alfalfa across the road's beginning to bloom. You're gonna have to demolish by yourself until I can get it down."

"I was just thinking that. I smelled it. You want me to cut it? You can take the morning off for a change."

"Naw, you go ahead and get started on that house." Henry leaned back. "You know a lot of us bought tractors these past few years. Just to keep up with feeding you boys off fighting."

"I know, Pop. That will save a lot of work."

"It will. It has. But I'm not sure it's an altogether good thing."

"Why?"

"What'll all those boys do when they get home? Farms will get bigger, and they won't need as much help." Henry held his gaze. "I study about things like that sometimes."

July 4, 1945

Next morning, Connor dug out a couple of bandanas, took the truck, and started on the house, a bandana around his neck and another over his nose and mouth. By noon, he had the upper floor stripped, plaster and lath heaped in every room. He dusted himself off as best he could and climbed into the truck. When he got to the home place, he stopped in the tool room for a couple of shovels and a big tarp. After a stop by the stock tank to dunk his head joined the rest of the family for dinner. He couldn't be sure if he rinsed out the dust or just made it into mud. He thought by the end of the day, he and his dad would have to compete for the wash tub and the hot water in the reservoir.

His dad was already at the table when he got inside. As they all sat down to eat, Henry grabbed the platter and served himself a

94

chicken thigh. "Hay's down," he said, "so I'll come with you while it dries."

"I'm coming too," Nora said.

"This is filthy work, Nora."

"So is Paris. I won't be home for long, so I want to be with you. I spent the morning with Mom." Nora supplied herself with a bandana and tied a scarf over her hair."

Connor grinned. "That's not gonna help much, Nora. Dust filters through everything."

"Better than nothing."

They piled in the truck and headed for the house.

Nora started downstairs with a hammer and a pry bar, knocking out plaster and ripping off lath. Henry sorted out most of the lath for other uses and stacked them in a corner while Connor went upstairs with the tarp and scoop shovel. He began by helping Henry sort, then scooped all the plaster, and broken bits of lath, onto the tarp, and hauled it, load by load, down the stairs and into the bed of the truck. Each time he dumped a tarp, another room was clear. By suppertime, they'd cleared the house.

"While you eat, I'm gonna get out the washtub," Nora announced. "I'll need some of that water in the reservoir for my hair, too."

Connor grinned. It wouldn't be the first time he'd bathed in the stock tank while his sister monopolized the hot water and the kitchen. Fortunately, it was mid-summer.

That evening, Connor and Nora wandered out onto the section line road as the day mellowed into sunset.

"I'm back into some semblance of civilization now," Connor began, "but you didn't say much in your letters about Paris. How bad is it in Europe?"

"The anger and hate frighten me. They take it out on themselves—women especially. It's always the women, isn't it?"

"What do you mean?"

"It's the collaborators. The women who slept with German soldiers, or who they suspect. They drag them out into the street—whole screaming gesturing mobs. They rip their clothes off and shave their heads. You can smell the tar boiling." She gave her brother a long look. "They didn't have enough fuel to keep themselves warm, but they can heat tar." She paused, walking along the roadside in silence. "Then they smear tar on them." She kept walking. "Even in the Embassy some days, I can hear them screaming and crying; I can smell the tar and burning flesh. I try not to imagine how they get it off or how badly they scar."

"Jesus."

"The men don't fare a lot better. They've turned on the resistance fighters and some of them have turned up dead. They think they're communists. Many of them are, and the Russian Revolution has people scared. I'm afraid for Daniel."

"It must be anarchy there. Are you sure you're safe?"

"Yeah, but I rarely leave the embassy. I just don't get that patriotism or nationalism, or whatever they call it. Everyone was trying to get along as best they could. They survived bombing, and rationing, and their neighbors were getting dragged off to God knows where—well we know now. They are the survivors, and they can't even forgive each other?"

Connor continued walking without a word. At the section corner, they turned south. "In New Guinea, we hopped onto this neighboring island. Noemfoor, they call it. We'd broken their

96

supply lines and the Japs were starving and sick. We found corpses that had been cannibalized."

Nora shuddered but said nothing.

"That last day in the jungle, I found a man who had been carved and eaten, and then I came on another one who was all in one piece. Maybe he'd eaten part of his buddy—I don't know. Anyway, I was so mad at the way the little bastards had tortured Beacon, Chet Eiseler, I kicked him. I thought he was dead. He wasn't, but he was dying. His eyes popped open, and he looked at me. He didn't say anything, probably too weak, but he just kept looking. And I was thinking this guy didn't want this any more than I did, couldn't stop it any more than I could. I sat down on the jungle floor and pulled his head into my lap. Just held him that way until he died.

"I left him there for the jungle to eat him up and walked on. I'd lost my squad, so I wandered around until I collapsed. Figured I'd die there too."

"But you didn't."

"Nah. The guys came back and found me. Hauled me to the field hospital."

Connor scuffed up some dirt along the roadside, pointing out a track with his toe. "Will you look at that? Deer. Maybe a doe and a couple of fawns."

"Maybe the Game Commission will manage to bring them back."

Connor walked on ahead. "Do you think Europe will ever recover?"

Nora kept walking for a moment. "I think I told you about all the demolished buildings." She glanced at him and continued. "Reconstruction is already behind schedule—as if you can schedule such a gargantuan job amid all the misery." She paused and he listened to their footsteps on gravel. "Even if they could get supplies—the rail lines are ripped, bridges bombed, cars and engines destroyed, seaports simply inadequate—where would they get workers? Think of all the missing people—architects and engineers as well as plain old workers. I don't know how many were killed in the war. Then we have people who can barely hold their heads up coming out of the concentration camps. They live in tent cities that probably don't seem a whole lot better than the camps. We still have people in prisoner of war camps in Germany and there are hundreds of thousands of wounded who can't work.

"They can't grow any food because of the land mines. That's what Daniel's working on now. Clearing mines. Last winter was awful. I felt guilty because we had adequate food and heat at the embassy, but there were thousands of people sleeping in doorways and bombed-out buildings. They were starving, Connor."

He stopped and pulled her into his arms. "I'm sorry Nora, but you can't allow yourself to feel guilty about it."

"Huh," she said, looking at him with tear-stained eyes, "like you never feel guilty about all the men who died. At least you can call out their names."

He released her and continued walking. "Logic doesn't work, does it?"

"You mean, the logic that says that we didn't cause this so there's no reason to feel guilty?"

"Right. But damn! I should be back there helping the guys who are left."

"No Connor, you shouldn't. You've already done your part and who knows how it's going to affect you for the rest of your life?"

"You mean the malaria?"

"Yeah. Do they think you're cured?"

"I don't know. I haven't had the fevers for a while, so maybe."

"But how much damage did it do when you had it? Remember Grandma and what scarlet fever did to her."

"I can still hear."

"I know, Connor. My point is that fevers do all kinds of random damage we don't even know about until later. Grandma didn't lose her hearing right away."

They didn't mention the nightmares and flashbacks, or the grief. They just walked the remaining three-and-a-half miles around the section in silence, watching the sun set in a prairie display of orange, scarlet, and gold. Turning east, they faced the moon, floating upward like a silver bubble lighting the raccoon tracks in the bottom next to the creek.

July 11, 1945

Day by day, Connor helped his father with the farm. They worked on the new place together when they had time. While the electrician worked in the house, they forked hay onto the hay wagon and into the loft, cranking up the door when they finished. As he threw hay into the barn, Connor began noticing the calm he sometimes felt.

With the loft full, they joined harvest crews, moving from farm to farm around the neighborhood, cutting wheat. As they worked, scooping wagon load after wagon load of golden grain into the bins, local workmen put up walls and ceilings in Connor's house. His cousin Keith had returned from Germany. The two men didn't say much. Just a few words during noon break or when they finished up for the day. Maybe as they headed for vehicles and home to crawl into bed, "You still got nightmares, wake you up?"

"Yup."

GRAVY

Maybe sitting on the ground, leaning against a truck tire waiting for the combine. "Loud noises bother you?"

"Next thing I know I'm on the ground, lookin' for the next shell."

Or maybe lying in the shade under a truck after a big dinner, "You been huntin'?"

"*Hell* no. Probably shoot somebody."

Or washing up at the stock tank, "Gettin' any better?"

"Think so."

Those few words provided affirmation. They weren't alone. They weren't crazy. They might get better.

That evening, Bobbi called with her arrival time on Saturday at six a.m. Instead of Willow Grove, she would debark in Hastings. "Because, I'd have to wait half a day for a connection," she said. "You said it was close."

July 14, 1945 – Hastings, Nebraska

Not wanting to spend the money for a sleeper, Bobbi had sat up in her compartment for forty-eight hours. She felt sweaty and bedraggled. The moment she saw Connor standing on the platform, though, she forgot her fatigue. She snatched her bags and shoved her way off the train. She almost bowled her husband off his feet when she leapt into his arms.

"I thought I'd never get here. It seemed like that train stopped in every Podunk town between here and Cleveland."

Connor smiled. "We Podunk residents like to go places, too, Bobbi."

"Sorry. I didn't mean to insult little towns. I'm not off to a good start, am I?"

"Let's go see what one looks like. Is this all your luggage?"

She turned back to the train car. "No. I have two more."

In minutes, they had her luggage loaded into Henry's car, a Chrysler New Yorker. "Wow!" Bobbi said. "Posh car."

"Yeah, gettin' old, though. We've had it since before I went in the service. I've ordered a new one for us, but they're not making any until the war's over. I don't know when we'll get it."

Wow, a new Chrysler New Yorker. That would even impress Mom. "How will we get around until it comes?"

"We'll have to borrow this or use the truck."

Bobbi'd gotten used to riding in a truck during boot camp and at least she wouldn't have to ride in the back. "How long will it take to get to the farm?"

"About forty-five minutes."

As they left town, Bobbi stared out the window at harvest crews working in the wheat. "What are those men doing?"

"That's wheat and you'll get to see it up close in just a little while. We're harvesting grain at the farm right now."

"So that's what wheat harvest looks like?"

"Sure is."

When they pulled into the farmyard, Nora and Claire came running from the house to welcome their new family member.

"We're so glad you're here." Claire gathered Bobbi into her arms. Overwhelmed, Bobbi just managed to hug her mother-in-law back when Nora stepped up with a sisterly peck on the cheek. "How was your trip out? Not too tiring, I hope."

"It was okay."

"Connor, why don't you take Bobbi's luggage up to your bedroom. Maybe she'd like a nap."

"No. I'm too excited to sleep."

Connor hauled the luggage upstairs as Nora took Bobbi's hand and led her into the house. "We're feeding a harvest crew today, so we're in kind of a mess. I don't guess you're gonna have much time to get acquainted first. We're dropping you right into the heart of things."

Claire pulled a chair in from the dining room. "Why don't you sit here. We can chat while we get the meal ready?"

"I know how to cook. What do you want me to do?"

"If you really want to help, here's an apron." Nora pulled one out of the linen drawer and handed her a knife. "How about peeling and slicing these cucumbers. Just put the peelings in that bucket." She looked at Bobbi for a moment. "That'll go out to the hogs."

A few minutes later, Connor reappeared, dressed in tan work pants and shirt with a bandana around his neck. "Looks like you're pretty well occupied." He gave Bobbi a peck on the cheek. "I'm sorry I don't have much time to spend with you today. We've got weather predicted and we need to get the rest of the wheat in before it storms."

"Okay. I guess I'll see you later."

"I'll be in for dinner."

In about two hours, the three women had put the finishing touches on a substantial meal as the crew of men, smelling of wheat dust and sweat, hair wet, faces and hands scrubbed in the tank, came trooping in, giving Bobbi a quick look-over before they found their places at the table. As the women set platters and bowls on the creaking table, the men kept their eyes on their hands as they began filling their plates and passing food to their right. They spoke barely a word. In the kitchen, pulling pies from the oven, Bobbi heard the clink of forks on plates and an occasional request to pass something. Claire or Nora often stepped into the dining room and collected a dish to refill.

"What about the pies?"

"Let's take them in right now. I think they're about ready for dessert."

As quickly and quietly as they came, the men left, scraping their chairs away from the table and giving the women a nod as they stepped back outside.

Connor stopped in the kitchen for a moment to check on Bobbi. "You got everything you need till suppertime?"

"I guess so. I'll just help Claire and Nora."

"We'll keep her busy, Connor."

"Bobbi, maybe we can go look at our house tonight."

"Oh, I'd love that."

Connor winked. "It's a date." He stepped outside.

"Where'd they all go?" Bobbi looked out the door. "I don't see anybody moving and the trucks and tractors and wagons are all still here."

"Look in the shade under the trucks and under those trees over there." Claire pointed.

"My gosh. What're they doing?"

"They're taking a nap. In almost exactly one hour, they'll get up and go back to work."

"I thought they had to hurry to get the wheat harvested."

"They do, but they're doing dangerous work. They worked hard all morning and they have to give their bodies a rest, so they don't make mistakes and hurt themselves . . . We'd better eat now. They will work until late tonight, so we need to get more food ready."

Bobbi followed her mother-in-law back into the kitchen. "I've never seen anybody eat so much."

"They work hard, Bobbi, and they burn up a lot of fuel."

"What're we making for supper?"

"Do you know how to pluck a chicken?"

"No, but I'm sure I can learn."

"I'm sure you can, too. Nora, is that water boiling yet?"

"Just about."

"Let's go get some chickens."

Bobbi followed the two women who turned left around the house toward a cluster of chickens chasing grasshoppers next to a fenced garden. With her right hand, Claire grabbed one by the legs. Before the flock scattered, she had another in her left hand, as did Nora.

Nora handed one to Bobbi. "Could you hang onto this?"

Stunned, Bobbi automatically took the bird. She lifted it and looked into its face. It blinked.

"Here," Claire said. "Hold this." She handed Bobbi another chicken and grabbed the one in her left hand by its head and spun it until the head popped off. She dropped the head and, as the chicken danced around the yard, she took one of the chickens Bobbi held and wrung its neck. Soon all four were either dancing or lying on their sides, jerking. Bobbi could only stare.

"I suppose it seems pretty barbaric," Nora said, "but the first twist breaks their necks, so they're already dead."

"Oh."

"Let's get the water to scald them."

"Aren't they already dead?"

Bobbi followed Nora to the house. "We scald them to loosen up the feathers."

The two women carried a bucket of boiling water to where the chickens lay lifeless. "Here," Nora said, "take one and dunk it into the water a couple of times. Like this." She took a chicken by its feet and dipped it, swishing it around in the bucket. She took it out and pulled on the thigh feathers. They came out readily, so she continued plucking. Bobbi followed suit and Claire dipped another bird. In minutes they had four birds lined up on a tray. Nora emptied the water on the ground and Claire took the tray back into the kitchen.

"You know how to butcher a chicken?"

"We always got them already opened up and then used a cleaver."

"Here, I'll show you." Claire opened the bird and sorted through the entrails. "See this green thing? That's the spleen. If you puncture it, any meat it touches will be ruined." She saved the heart, liver, and gizzard and taught Bobbi how to dismember an animal at the joints. "Your turn." She handed Bobbi another chicken.

"I'll put these to soak while you girls pick apples."

105

GRAVY

"Don't we need a pan or a bucket?"

"We've got our aprons." Nora stepped outside. Bobbi followed.

When they returned with aprons full of apples, Bobbi offered to make the pies. Nora and Claire agreed, and they worked in silence for a while.

"Connor says you like to dance," Nora said as she sliced some tomatoes and cucumbers.

"I do, and your brother dances divinely."

"I taught him everything he knows."

"Did you really?"

Nora chuckled. "No. More like he taught me. He said he learned some new things in Panama. I'm eager to learn from him."

"Oh yes. He taught me the rumba and the Cuban walk. It'll be fun to go to a dance together."

"They stopped having dances until the war's over and I have to go back in a couple of weeks. But we have a record player. Maybe we'll have some time when harvest is over. I think we're the last place this year."

They chattered through the afternoon, getting to know each other. Occasionally, Bobbi glanced at Claire who worked silently but seemed to listen to everything.

At six o'clock, Henry came in. "We got heavy clouds comin' up in the southwest. We need to eat fast and get back out there."

"Everything's ready, Henry. We'll set it out while everybody gets washed up."

The women bustled food onto the table and stood back while the men consumed it and left. No naps this time. Again, Connor stopped a moment to check on Bobbi and then rushed out the door.

Claire watched them leave. "I really hate to see them go back to work without any rest. I'm always afraid for them." She turned back to the kitchen. "Oh well, we'd better grab something to eat ourselves."

When they'd finished eating and cleaning up, Claire began pacing, watching the sky as a heavy cover of clouds built up. "Claire," Bobbi asked, "have you had any noisy storms since Connor got back?"

"No. Why?"

"If there's thunder and lightning, he may go a little crazy. The noise makes him think he's in New Guinea. He's really frightening. I don't know what to do for him."

"Nothin' you can do, Bobbi. He has to work it out himself."

"That's what he said."

"Maybe the men can help him some. Keith was in Europe. He saw some awful stuff there. I don't know, Bobbi. He suffers so. He's not the same as when he went. He broods a lot. And he seems to be saying something under his breath all the time."

"I've heard it too," Nora said.

"He's counting cadence. It's the names of all the men in his unit that didn't come back."

Claire blanched. "Like Harry." She reached for a chair and sat, head bowed, wringing her hands in her lap.

"Who's Harry?"

"He served in World War I. He never recovered. Just sits in his little house and calls out the names of the men who died."

GRAVY

"Pauline's uncle. Connor mentioned him. That must be how it got into Connor's mind to do that. It's eerie, but it seems like he's already doing better than Harry."

"What do you mean?"

"Well, he's out harvesting with the other men and he's been getting our house ready and helping his dad. From what you said, Harry doesn't do any of those things."

Claire gave Bobbi a weary smile. "You're right, Bobbi. I just hope he can keep getting better because he's not my Connor anymore. No pranks, no handsful of wildflowers. I just don't know. Well," she stood, "it will be what it is. Let's go check all the doors and make sure they're latched."

"What doors?"

"We need to make sure all the doors on the barn and the outbuildings are closed so the wind doesn't blow them around and break them up. The augur doors will probably be open, since the men have been putting grain in all day. Come with me and I'll show you."

Out in the field, Connor had watched lightning for an hour. Occasionally, he noticed Keith doing the same. In the yard, they scooped off a load as distant thunder rumbled. They exchanged a glance. Connor stood, still, wild-eyed, feet buried in grain.

"We're gonna get through this, Connor," Keith said. "Take a deep breath and smell that wheat, and the dust, and the rain. I been noticin' that smell. That's not war. Concentrate on that."

Connor gave him a tentative grin and started scooping again.

The sky let loose with a downpour just as they ran the last of the grain through the combine augur into the truck. Henry drove into the shed with that last truckload and crawled out of the cab, grinning. "We got'er all," he announced, slapping Connor on the back. The crew members scattered to their own vehicles and headed for their respective homes.

GRAVY

August 1, 1945

"Come on Connor, I need to learn how a farm works if I'm going to be your partner."

"This is man's work, Bobbi."

He knew that look. He'd seen it a lot lately.

"Your mom told me all about Great-great-grandma Flaherty and homesteading on her own when her husband died."

He sighed. *Sometimes Mom talks way too much.* "I've been teaching you to drive the tractor, but not this time. If you should slip off, I'd have you sliced into stew meat before I could stop. I won't take that chance."

She argued briefly, but Connor wouldn't budge. He climbed on the tractor and engaged the power take-off to test the sickle. He shut it off, lifted the blades, and pulled out of the yard.

A couple of hours later, Connor and his dad unhitched the sickle and prepared to disc down the wheat stubble. "I don't know what to do with her, Pop. She does her share of the cooking and canning, but she wants to follow me all over the place." He handed his father a box end wrench. "I'm surprised she isn't out here now."

"Think, son. All the girls you knew before grew up on farms. They knew how things work." He tightened a bolt on a disc blade. "Hand me that three-quarter inch." He tightened another bur. "She has a lot to learn."

"That's just it, Pop. I'm afraid she'll get hurt."

Henry squatted on his heels. "Then you'll just have to be extra careful and explain everything. You've always said you want a partnership like your mom and me." He stood. "She can't be your

GRAVY

partner if she doesn't know how the operation works. She has
been patient with you." He looked over at his son. "It's almost
noon, let's check on that heifer."

Earlier that morning, Henry had found a heifer trying to give
birth. "Musta been that time last winter when the bull got out on
me," he said at breakfast. "It's way too early for that little
heifer."

When they'd finished eating, Henry and Connor had got her up
and walked her to the barn where they'd been checking her
throughout the morning. When they saw that she hadn't
delivered, Henry called his father-in-law.

"Bobbi, when Granddad gets here, you might get in the way."
Connor said at dinner. "If you slow things down, you make it
harder for the heifer."

"I want to see how you pull her calf. What's that like?"

"It's pretty hard on the heifer sometimes, but if we don't get that
calf out of her soon, she'll die."

"Do you actually pull the little calf right out of her?"

"That's exactly what we do. It's pretty messy. There'll be a lot of
blood and they always shit on us. Why don't you just hang
around in the house this time?"

Bobbi said nothing more, but soon after his grandfather arrived,
Connor spotted her perched on the feed bunk where she had a
good view of the stall. He hoped Grandpa Frank wouldn't see
her.

The older man rolled up his sleeves, knelt, and reached into the
animal, probing with a loop of rope for front feet and nose. When
he looked up over her flank, he spotted Bobbi. "Get her out of
here. This is no place for a woman."

"Bobbi," Connor said, "just go on back to the house."

"If you want me to be your partner, I have to know what's going on."

"There are plenty of men to do this, Bobbi, you don't need to know."

"If you're out harvesting a crop, you won't have time to take care of a cow."

"We breed them so that they won't have their calves at harvest time."

"And yet here we are."

Connor caught Henry's chuckle as he turned away. "Just let her be. She's not in the way. Remember what we said."

"No place for a woman," Frank growled as he trapped the calf's front hooves and tried to turn its nose.

Connor saw his wife open her mouth and he tensed, but she closed it and kept watching as the calf slid onto the straw. He heard her gasp when the little animal lay without moving. He started to pick it up by its hind legs to clear its breathing passages, but it began kicking and struggling. He grinned when it wobbled to its feet. "How's the mama?"

"Pretty weak. Might have to put that little guy on one of the milk cows." Kneeling by the heifer's head, Henry talked to her. "C'mon, little girl, you've got yourself a baby. Let's get you up."

She lifted her head and struggled onto her front feet, then rested before lunging onto all fours. She started licking the calf as it nuzzled for its first afternoon snack.

"I swear you can sweet talk an animal into doing anything," Frank remarked as they stood watching. "Looks like she'll be all right."

GRAVY

Connor was right behind his grandpa and his wife when they left the barn. Frank leaned into Bobbi. "Pretty level-headed for a city girl."

Connor grinned, pleased and surprised at the old man's acceptance. But then, Grandpa Frank knew about old Grandma Flaherty, too.

August 2, 1945 — Willow Grove

The next day, Nora and Bobbi took the car shopping for records in Hastings.

"What was Connor like as a kid?" Bobbi asked as they pulled out of the farmyard.

"Curious."

Bobbi glanced at her sister-in-law. "What do you mean?"

"Well, he always wanted to know what the wild critters were doing. There was a little prairie dog town in the middle pasture, and he'd spend hours sitting on the hill watching them. One day he came in jumping with excitement. Said he'd seen a black-footed ferret."

Bobbi smiled. "He said he tamed a parrot when he was stationed at Camp Paraiso."

"He mentioned it in a letter. He used to catch bugs and put them in jars so he could watch them grow. We climbed a lot of trees and looked into birds' nests."

"Sometimes he talks about plant breeding."

"He wanted to go to college and study horticulture so he could develop new crops. He had a whole wildflower garden in the yard

112

behind the house. He was always studying how to grow those plants because some of them didn't transplant very well and he searched for just the perfect environment for each one of them."

"Did he have a lot of friends? We haven't talked to any of his old friends yet."

"Yeah. His best friend Ralph died in France. D-Day invasion. Most of the other guys are gone now too."

"Gone? They got killed?"

"Oh, I don't know. Mom told me we had almost as many men in the service from Willow Grove as had graduated from the high school in more than a decade."

"Wow. Did she know them all?"

"Yes—or their parents. The paper ran all their names."

"Haven't they come back?"

"Some probably have, but probably only if they're wounded our sick and unfit for service." Nora chuckled. "When they were seniors, Connor and Ralph and a couple of their friends got together and carried the superintendent's car up the steps and through the freight entrance behind the gym. They set it sideways in the hall with only about a foot between the wall and the car on each end."

"I'll bet that got them in trouble."

"Oh, Superintendent Nash just laughed and made them carry it back out where it belonged."

"I haven't seen him laugh much, Nora. Do you think he'll get that back?"

"I don't know Bobbi. It seems like we don't have as much fun as we get older. And it'll take time to get over the war."

"He still has the blow ups."

"I worry about you a little bit when he gets confused."

"You know, so far he seems to mistake me for one of his men and he tries to protect me. I just hope he never takes me for a Jap."

Nora agreed.

"What amazes me. I've only been here for a couple of weeks, but you and your folks treat me like I'm part of your family." She stared out the window so Nora couldn't see the tears in her eyes, but she could feel the other woman looking at her.

"You are, Bobbi."

"I am what?"

"You're family. You're my brother's wife. Your children will be Mom and Pop's grandchildren."

"They've accepted me. I never could have expected that. Not so soon. They don't even know me, but they're done everything to make me comfortable." She smiled. "Pop took me into town with him to do some tradin'." She glanced at Nora. "He took me into every store on Main Street and introduced me to everybody we saw. Felt like he was showing me off—but not like a celebrity or an entertainer or anything. Just like me."

"Of course."

"Everybody smiled and greeted me like a friend, like I had some kind of aura."

"You do. We all do, you, and me, and Connor. Our parents' aura. Mom and Pop are not only well respected in Willow Grove, they're also well loved. Over the decades, they've helped a lot of people, especially during the thirties. They didn't have much, but they shared what they had. You haven't been around them long enough to know it yet, but they *rarely* say anything bad about anybody, no matter how richly deserved." She turned right

114

onto East Second Street. "I'm convinced they've managed to help people be better than even they thought possible, just by expecting it."

When Nora parked in from of the little record store, they sat in silence for a while.

"For the first time I can remember, I feel safe. Connor and you and your parents. I feel safe. I know it sounds strange coming from someone who just met you all, but I feel like I've come home."

"You have." Nora pushed her car door open. "But now, let's get some of those Latin records and see if we can liven things up a bit before I go back to Paris. I want to see Mom and Pop dancing the rhumba."

August 6, 1945

Unlike his son, Henry tinkered. When he'd bought machines to keep up with the farm work during the war, he'd spent winters in his chair by the cookstove, reading and studying the manuals that came with them. Connor knew his dad had worked hard all his life and he was happy to do the farm work when he could persuade Henry to go tinker with the equipment. It always needed something. That's why Henry was in the house, after supper checking on the specs for the corn harvester, while Connor knocked down a second cutting of alfalfa. Bobbi and Claire had canned summer apples that day. The women cleaned up to the accompaniment of radio music following the evening news. As Bobbi dried the last dish, a special announcement blared from the box, introducing U.S. President Harry Truman. The President didn't bother with niceties of time zones when he described the bomb an American airman had just dropped on the Japanese city of Hiroshima. An atomic bomb, it had the firepower of 2,000 times the munitions used elsewhere, he said. It was, he said, harnessing the power of the universe.

The house went silent. Bobbi spoke first. "What does that mean?"

"Well," Henry considered for a moment, "maybe it means the war's about over."

"Do you really think so?"

"I don't know, but something will surely stop them."

"I'm gonna go tell Connor." She jumped into the car and drove to the field where Connor was cutting. She'd learned never to approach the tractor from the side with the cutting blade, so she floundered through the standing alfalfa to reach her husband.

He shut off the mower, but when he heard the news, he just shook his head. "That'll never stop them. If you won't quit when you have to eat your buddies to keep from starving, no bomb's gonna stop you."

"But 2,000 times the firepower."

"A bomb's a bomb. It'll kill more people, but they seem to have plenty to go around."

Bobbi deflated as he engaged the cutting bar and finished the field.

Three days later, when Connor heard the second announcement, he remembered the emaciated men on Noemfoor, shaking with fever and shitting their guts out. They would not quit. He shrugged and went on with the farm work.

GRAVY

August 14, 1945

Startled from his roast and mashed potatoes, Connor waited for the two longs and one short ring before he stood, grabbed the receiver, and listened. "Yeah?"

He motioned and Bobbi turned on the radio. They listened for a couple of minutes.

"We hear it." He grinned. "Yeah. Bobbi's dancing around here singing." He paused, watching his wife's gyrations. "What?" He chuckled. "Hold on." He held the phone away from his ear for a moment, then talked into the mouthpiece. "Oh, it's *Happy Days Are Here Again*." He laughed. "Yeah. Goodbye, Sis." He started to hang up. "Hey wait!" He made a quick decision. "Hey, we're going to town tonight. How about you?"

Bobbi laughed. And laughed. And laughed. Connor watched her, holding the receiver to his ear. "Bobbi's hysterical," he said.

"No, I'm not," she gasped.

"Then what's so funny?"

"I don't know."

"What, Sis?"

"Yes, I know. I'm pretty happy, too. What? I . . . yeah. There's getting to be a few back from Europe, Sis, and even one or two like me with malaria. They're back too. Hey! You want to go to the Legion Club with us?"

Nora agreed and when he hung up, Bobbi grinned. "Let's hurry up and eat so we can get dressed and go to town. Connor, we can initiate that new Legion Club."

Connor hadn't realized how shallowly he'd been breathing until he took a long gasp, like a man returning from the dead. "Well, all righty then."

GRAVY

The town had built their Legion Club in the old telephone central building—big enough for all the boys who had gone, as well as the wives they would bring back, and the hometown girls they would choose. Most weekends, the hall still echoed with just a few voices, but that Monday night the whole town came to celebrate. They couldn't scare up a band on such short notice, but they had a record player and several people brought records. They laid the PA system's mic next to the speaker and soon Bobbi and Connor were showing off their dance moves.

By eight o'clock, they'd danced a polka, which Bobbi swore to him she didn't know how to dance, a few rhumbas, some jitterbug, and some two-step. Nora had found a single farmer or two to dance with, as well as Cousin Keith. When the floor got so crowded that they couldn't maneuver, they stepped out of the hall with Nora and Keith. Just as they stepped outside, someone lit a string of firecrackers at the bottom of the steps. Connor reacted before anybody could even grab his arm. In an instant he had the man on the ground. Keith and Nora tried in vain to pry his hands off the man's throat while Bobbi went inside screaming for help.

In just a few minutes, six healthy farm boys had lifted Connor and set him down, still fighting and struggling, on the grass at the edge of the street. "I'm all right guys," he said as he regained his composure. "Thanks for taking care of me."

"Wasn't you we was taking care of."

"I know. How is he?"

"Still chokin' but he'll be all right."

Connor crawled over to where the other man lay gasping. "You okay?"

"No thanks to you."

"The firecrackers. I thought I was back in the fight."

"Never been shot at. I wouldn't know."

118

"Nothin' I would choose."

"Nah, I don't 'spose so. Name's Munroe, George Munroe."

"Connor Conroy. Don't remember you. What you doin' in Willow Grove?"

"Came over here to trade for some breedin' stock and heard the news."

"Welcome to Willow Grove. Sorry about my welcome."

"Yeah. I'd pass on that next visit."

The men shook hands. Connor stepped up and put an arm around Bobbi. "Do you mind if we go home. These blow ups just wear me out." He glanced at his sister.

"I'll take her home," Keith said, and Connor headed for the car with Bobbi practically running to keep up.

September 24, 1945 — Willow Grove

With Nora gone back in Paris and Connor out making hay, Bobbi felt even more eager than ever to have her own home. She borrowed her in-law's car and drove over to the house in progress. As she wandered through the rooms, she imagined the furniture they would buy and where she would put it. When she stepped onto the wrap-around porch, she found that Henry and Connor had ripped out the floor but hadn't made much progress putting it back. She studied the tongue-and-groove lumber and how they'd installed what they already laid.

She picked up a board and fit the tongue onto the last board the two men had laid. *This can't be any harder than building radios in those tiny B-24 cockpits.* She stopped to study what Connor and Henry had already done. She picked through the toolbox,

119

fitting tools to the task. Her first effort went well so she tried another. She had to cut it, so she picked up the saw, then put it down. She'd seen Henry measure, so she got the tape and square, measured, marked, and took the board to the sawhorse. Tongue between her teeth, she cut it, one careful stroke at a time. She checked, found it straight, and nailed it in place. Soon, she worked much faster, singing as she tapped grooves onto their corresponding tongues. She forgot she had Henry's and Claire's car, and that she and Claire had planned to can peaches. Late in the afternoon, she heard the truck pulling into the driveway.

"Bobbi," Connor called. "Bobbi, are you alright? Where are you?"

"I'm here, Connor," Bobbi shouted. "Come look what I've been doing!"

Connor stepped up on the porch. "What the hell?"

"See, I got all this done."

"Mom's canning peaches by herself and you're over here fooling around with the flooring. You've got Mom and Pop's car. What the hell are you doing?"

"You can see what I'm doing. I got a lot done, too."

"You don't know what the hell you're doing here."

"I copied what you and Pop did."

"You'll get it crooked and we'll have to rip it all out. We'll lose time and materials."

"I am not getting it crooked. You can't even tell where you and Pop left off and I started."

"I'll get to it. I just have to get that second cutting of hay in the barn. Then I'll get to it, I promise."

"I'm not worried about that, but I can help here. What was all that about being your partner? I can do this, and our house will be ready that much quicker."

"You *are* my partner."

"Partner, not housewife. You knew I wasn't ever going to be a housewife."

"Of course not, no farm wife is, but this is man's work."

"That again. Like carrying water to hogs and feeding cows."

"That's different."

"Different how? It's a whole lot harder carrying five-gallon buckets across the farmyard, water sloshing into my shoes, than cutting and nailing a few boards."

"Well, Mom never hammered a nail."

"I am *not* your mom. I love your mom, but I can't be her. I learned growing up that, if you want something, you'd better figure out how to make it yourself and that's what I'm doing. If you don't like it, that's just tough!" She threw the hammer onto the subflooring and stomped to the car, roaring off in a cloud of dust.

By the time she reached her in-laws' house, she'd slowed down. "I'm sorry about the peaches, Mom. I forgot."

"Are you all right? I started with the canning and didn't notice how much time had passed. Then I worried about you. I sent Connor to see if you were all right."

"I'm fine, Mom. It looks like the sheetrock crew finished with it so we can paint and get out of your hair. I noticed where Connor and Henry had started working on the porch. And I thought I could help, so I started nailing on boards and lost track of the time. I'm really sorry I wasn't here to help you."

"It's fine, Bobbi, there are plenty of peaches for tomorrow. Let's get supper on the table. Where's Connor?" She started carrying food into the dining room.

Bobbi grabbed a couple of bowls and followed her. "I thought he was right behind me. I'm sorry you got stuck making supper by yourself."

Claire nodded without a word.

Oh-oh, the whole family's mad at me. She heard the truck pulling into the yard.

Connor glared at her as he walked in and took his place at the table. She glared back.

Henry came in, drying his ears with the towel he'd snatched as he passed through the kitchen, and sat looking over the bowls and platters of food.

"I got two dozen quarts of peaches canned today," Claire said. "Bobbi and I will finish them tomorrow."

Connor shot a grim look at his wife.

Henry frowned. "I thought maybe we could work on that porch floor while the hay dries."

Claire looked at her lap and Bobbi stared at Connor. "Maybe we should leave that to Bobbi," Connor snarled.

Henry looked at Connor glowering at Bobbi, then at Bobbi, staring back, a flush rising on her face. "What's this about?"

"I . . ."

"She . . ."

"Bobbi, what's going on?"

GRAVY

"I borrowed your car and drove over to the house to plan how to
arrange it and what color to paint the rooms. Then I noticed the
porch floor. I thought I could do that, so I worked on it all
afternoon. I'm sorry I left Mom without a car and I didn't help
her with the canning." She looked at her hands in her lap. "I lost
track of time."

"What's all the glaring about?"

"Connor said that's man's work and I should let you do it."

"Do you have any carpentry experience?"

"No, but I did it just like you did."

"Didn't she do a good job, Connor?"

Connor stared at his wife. "She did an excellent job."

"So what's this man's work and woman's work stuff?"

"I'll get to it, Pop."

Bobbi kept her head down. Apparently, Connor wasn't ready to
give up being mad. They all ate in silence, leaving Connor to his
sulk. After supper, he stepped outside. Bobbi watched him walk
to the west pasture and climb through the fence.

"Just let him be," Claire said.

"He'll get over it," Henry said. "I think he just feels like he's not
doing enough for you."

January 15, 1946 — Willow Grove

Before corn harvest, the family had set aside a couple of days to
paint Bobbi and Connor's new house. Henry had helped with the
painting and Claire had made sure they had plenty to eat. In

early October, the new owners picked out their furnishings and rugs, taking a couple of days to haul everything home in the stock truck. Bobbi made drapes on her new Singer® sewing machine. When she'd had a little time between cooking, cleaning, laundry, and preserving food for the winter, Bobbi continued working on the porch floor. Sometimes Connor and Henry worked on it too, and they had it done in time for Connor and Bobbi to move in before corn picking.

By the first snow in January, Bobbi had experienced almost everything the farm had to offer. Corn picking had progressed much like the wheat harvest. They'd had a bumper crop on the cob, filling the corn crib and setting up a wire ring to hold the surplus outside.

Late in the fall, they'd butchered hogs, shooting them in the morning to hang by doubletrees in the middle of the corn crib, where Henry and Connor gutted, scraped, and aged them. Bobbi learned where all the lard her parents had used so liberally in their restaurants came from —fat trimmed from the hogs and simmered on the stove, then strained of "cracklings," the crispy remains that tasted so heavenly with salt. Henry had smoked the salted hams in a little building that looked much like an outhouse and buried them in the wheat when they were done. Bobbi and Claire had canned beef from a steer the men butchered later. While it was fresh, they had roasts and steaks, then switched to cubed, canned meat later. And there were always chickens, canned during the summer—one three-pound chicken intricately stuffed into each quart jar.

She'd arrived too late for the cherries and the wild chokecherries, but she helped pick the wild plums from the road ditch west of the house and make them into plum jelly. She hoped she'd get to laze in the plum thicket with the bees when it bloomed in the spring. Canning winter apples with her mother-in-law, Bobbi remembered what Connor had told her before their marriage. A farm is hard work from spring through fall, but it gets easier in winter. She couldn't wait for winter, although she loved lining up all the jars of food in the basement. Like Connor had promised, they would certainly eat well.

GRAVY

She had hesitated a long moment when Claire explained that the cobs she burned in the cookstove came out of the hog lots. "We feed the corn on the cob directly to the pigs," Claire explained. "So, when we have a few minutes, we pick up a bucket or basket full of cobs and store them in the cob house. That's the little shed out by the back gate."

Bobbi couldn't feel any fondness for laundry in the well house next to the windmill. By switching a valve, she could run water into the tubs which she heated on an old cookstove salvaged from some old house. She'd washed plenty of clothes on a washboard in her parents' apartment, so that wasn't new, but the layers of stubborn dirt that accompanied farming was daunting and wet overalls posed their own challenge, just picking them up, let alone wringing them. When the temperatures dropped below freezing her hands suffered as she hung the wet clothes outside on the line. At least, she thought when she remembered the damp air and ducking drying clothes in the apartment, she could be grateful that the mess was all outside. Bringing in freeze dried clothes did pose its own challenges, especially the overalls and jeans that she stood in a corner until they thawed.

Bobbi especially despised the outhouse. The actual structure didn't bother her so much, she just didn't like the trek out the back door, through the back gate, and across that windy bit between the fence and the outhouse. Her fondness for catalogue pages waned with their use as toilet paper—especially the rough color pages. She had no enthusiasm for carrying out the chamber pot either, especially after the first snow.

Some of the leisure Connor had promised came with the snow. For one thing, the days got shorter, so they had fewer hours to work. With the crops harvested, the animals sold or butchered except the breeding stock, the workload dropped to almost nothing but feeding and watering the remaining animals. They wouldn't build a new chicken house until spring, so Bobbi got all her eggs from Claire. They had a cow to milk, and Bobbi learned how, but she thought the cow must hate having her teats yanked on every day. She wondered if she shouldn't apologize to the long-suffering animal.

Between Henry's and Claire's house and the Connor and Bobbi's house stood a tall hill. Accustomed to short vistas between buildings. Bobbi hadn't noticed the view from the top of that hill until she drove home from her in-law's one day after a few inches of show. Suddenly, there was her house near the bottom with the barn a few steps away and nothing but endless white all around. Connor's trees, 300 of them she remembered, looked like little sticks. It gave her a creepy feeling of isolation like she'd never experienced. The emptiness that first winter gave her only a moment's pause, though. The short days gave her a lot more time alone with Connor for snuggling, and petting, and exploring each other's bodies. Those times didn't seem so lonely.

May 13, 1946

As Connor planted corn, he watched clouds billow up in the southwest. He smelled rain and hurried his planting so he could get the equipment into the yard and under cover. Thunder rumbled in the distance like naval bombardment.

Pulling into the farmyard, he cleaned out the planter box as the storm swept over the hills and the rumbling came closer. A flash made his hair stand up and he dropped the lid of the planter box. He continued scooping, hands shaking. He spilled handsful of seed but kept working.

This is gonna be a bad one. Moving slow. Won't be over for a while. Maybe if I get inside. turn on the record player. Maybe I'll be all right."

He cleared the planter and parked the tractor as light dimmed. He hurried to the house where he paced from window to window peering at the storm and waiting for Bobbi. *I wish she'd stay in town. At least she'd be safe from me.* He flinched at a particularly bright flash, saying his names between clenched teeth. He stalked to the back of the house where he peered out the west window. *I wish she'd get home with the groceries. She could run off the road in the mud or get lost again.* He considered his wife and the storm, listening to a scratchy recording of her voice. He still felt like ducking under something. *Guess I don't know what I want.*

He continued to stare out the window, his back to the front door. The noise had become so loud he could no longer hear household noises—the refrigerator motor, the clock ticking, the fan on the table, the record player spinning in the blank at the end. His jaw clenched so tight it hurt, he moved to another window, whispering names.

When he felt a touch on his shoulder, his reality shattered. Spinning around, he grabbed the enemy soldier, knocking him flat and pinning him with a forearm across his throat, knee jammed into his chest. He grabbed the throat and began bashing the head. He heard the voice. It sounded wrong. He focused.

Oh God, no!

He let go, stood, and walked away, his voice frantic. "Mendez, Green, Moore, Wilson, Hidalgo . . ." He couldn't stop trembling. When he turned back to his wife, she remained on the floor, gasping for breath.

"Bobbi."

She struggled, levering herself with her elbows.

"Bobbi, are you alright?" He reached out to help her, but she flinched, staring into his face. He couldn't meet her eyes. "I just. The thunder and lightning. Like landing on those islands. Bobbi I . . ."

"It hurts, Conner. I can't breathe."

He crouched and tried to scoop her into his arms.

She groaned. "No, stop."

He remained squatting on the floor, waiting for her to catch her breath, the sounds of the storm crowded out of his mind. "How can I help?"

"I think it would hurt less if you helped me stand."

"Bobbi, I'm sorry."

"Just help me up." He stood and she reached for his hands. She moaned but kept pulling. On her feet, she held her left hand against her chest, taking quick, shallow gasps.

Connor couldn't look her in the eye. His shoulders drooped. "Listen, can you walk to the car?"

"I think so."

"I'm taking you to the doctor."

She hesitated. "In this storm? It seems to be hanging there instead of moving on. And what will we say happened?"

"I'll tell him I hurt you. What else would we say?" He felt a tear spill down his cheek. "Bobbi, I don't ever *want* to hurt you, but I'll always take responsibility."

In town, old Doc O'Neill listened to Bobbi's chest and lifted her left arm. She moaned. "I'll bet it hurts to breathe," he said.

She nodded.

"I'm pretty sure you've cracked her sternum," he told Connor. "About the only way to treat it is plenty of rest. He turned to Bobbi. "Twice a day is a little more than I'd like to see you."

"Twice? What twice? I thought you were getting groceries."

"That too."

"Are you alright? No, of course you're not. Is something else wrong?"

"You're gonna have to get those blow-ups under control," Doc interrupted, frowning at Connor. "Your wife's pregnant."

Connor looked at Bobbi who smiled and nodded. "Oh, my Jesus Lord!" Connor exclaimed, sitting abruptly in the nearest chair. "What am I gonna do?"

"I thought you'd be happy," Bobbi cried.

"Bobbi I am. I've never wanted anything so much in my life. But look what I just did to you. I'm terrified, Sweetheart. I'm scared of myself, and I don't know what to do."

"Are you able to sleep, Connor?" Doc demanded.

"Sometimes."

"How often sometimes?"

"I get a few hours almost every night."

"I thought you were sleeping okay," Bobbi said. "You don't get up and roam around."

"No. When my nightmares wake me up, I just lie there and listen to you breathing. Sometimes that puts me back to sleep."

"And the rest of the time?" asked O'Neill.

"I'm afraid to go to sleep."

"You need to sleep. That'll help. I'm gonna give you something," He frowned at Connor again, bushy white eyebrows nearly hiding his eyes, "and you take it. You can't take it for long. I'll prescribe thirty of them. Take them at bedtime. I think things'll look better if you get some real rest. Who do you have to talk to?"

"Bobbi and my folks."

"No, I mean who do you talk to about the things in your nightmares?"

"I couldn't talk about those things. No one wants to know what I know."

"I do," Bobbi said.

"No. You don't, and I don't want you to know. If you think you're scared of me now . . ."

Just then thunder roared and lightning flashed. Connor ducked.

O'Neill interrupted again. "Look, Connor, you did what you had to do. Don't ever forget that." He stopped a moment still staring at Connor. "There's a new guy in town. I don't know how he came to be here, but he's got a welding shop over by the tracks. He was with the first Marines at Guadalcanal. He's a Bosque. I want you to look him up."

"Aw, I've got so much to do."

"That wasn't a choice. You need to get better before that baby comes. Your family's gonna need you. And you need to talk about it. Gene needs somebody too."

"The Army debriefed us."

"Debriefed my ass. Pardon me, ma'am. You need to talk to somebody who's done what you've done and seen what you've seen. Oh and, if Bobbi hasn't had a chance to tell you she's pregnant, I'm sure you don't know yet that she'll have to have a Cesarean birth. That means she'll need extra help. So get yourself together. Figure out what calms you down and do it." He scribbled a prescription, ripped it off and handed it to Connor. "Get this filled and get yourself home. I don't like the looks of that sky. I think that front coming in is gonna be a bad one. It's already stalled for a good while."

Connor did as he'd been told, helping Bobbi to the car and letting her wait while he filled the prescription. Coming out of the drugstore, he got a good look at the sky. He jumped in the car and hit the accelerator.

"Slow down, Connor. You're scaring me."

"I know, Sweetheart, but Doc's right. This looks bad. I'm gonna drive us to Mom and Pop's. They've got a storm cellar and we don't yet. Looks like we might need it."

About a half-mile from Henry's and Claire's house, the wind suddenly died. Connor leaned forward and peered through the windshield. "Mendez, Green, Moore, Wilson . . ."

Bobbi laid a tentative hand on his arm. "Connor, this is Nebraska."

"It's okay, Bobbi. I'm here. But we need to be in that storm cellar—now."

When they pulled into the yard, Henry and Claire had just stepped out of the house. Henry carried a lantern. Claire bent and peered into Bobbi's car door. "I'm so glad you got here. I've been trying to call. We're heading for the storm cellar."

Connor took another look at the sky, nudging his mother out of the way. "Bobbi, I know it hurts, but you've got to hurry." He didn't point out the funnel he saw forming in the clouds.

Claire backed away, glanced at the sky and ran. Connor helped Bobbi out of the car, wrapped an arm around her waist, and practically carried her down the cellar steps.

Henry had already taken the lantern into the darkness underground. Connor saw a match flare as he let the door down with a bang, blowing it out and pitching the cellar into complete darkness. He heard Henry scrabbling in the dark for another match. "Bobbi, just stand still. I'm going to open the door a little so Pop can see." By the time he'd spoken Henry had lit it.

Connor pulled out a chair with trembling hands and held it for Bobbi. Gradually the lantern's dim glow brightened the little table as Henry adjusted the wick. Once the women were seated, Henry and Connor squatted, leaning their backs against the cool underground wall. Then they waited.

"How will we know when it's time to get out?" Bobbi asked.

"Well," Henry said with a tiny smile, "we'll wait a while and if we don't hear anything crashing around, I'll lift the door and check."

They'd only waited for a few seconds when they heard the wind pick up as suddenly as it had stopped, screaming over the cellar door and rattling it on its hinges. "You don't think it'll suck up the door, do you?"

"We've heard it rattle like that before, I think it'll be okay." The scream built up to a roar. Connor saw Bobbi pull her head even further down into her shoulders. They all waited in silence. They couldn't have heard each other if they'd tried to talk.

When the roar suddenly died, they heard rain pelting the cellar door. "It's safe to go out now," Henry said, "but we're all gonna get soaked." He led the way, Claire right behind him. Connor waited for Bobbi, supporting her with an arm around her waist and taking a moment to shut the cellar door. He moved slowly enough with Bobbi that he noticed what he *couldn't* see. The hulk of the little grain bin seemed to be missing. Bobbi stumbled on a piece of broken branch, gasping for breath as he steadied her. He looked up into the maple and saw only a skeleton.

Once inside the house, Henry set the lantern on the dining room table and paced from window to window. "Can't see a thing through this rain."

"I think the little granary's gone, Pop. I could see the outlines of all the other buildings, but that one doesn't seem to be there."

Henry checked through one of the north windows, looking where the building was supposed to be. "I don't see it either, Connor. I'm sure glad the wheat's all in the big bin—what we haven't hauled to town already.

Claire had disappeared with the second lantern almost as soon as Connor and Bobbi slammed in from the porch. She returned in minutes with dry towels.

"I think some of Nora's clothes will fit you, Bobbi, so we'll just go shopping upstairs."

"Mom, could you go up and pick something out and help Bobbi in your bedroom?"

Claire gave him a sharp look.

"I hurt her. Thought I was in New Guinea." He hung his head. "Doc says she's got a cracked sternum." It might have been the hardest thing he'd ever said.

"Oh, Connor."

"He feels bad enough already," Henry said. "But somehow we've got to protect Bobbi until he gets better."

"It's my own fault," Bobbi said. "I was trying not to startle him, so I walked up behind him, quietly, and when I touched him, he exploded. That was dumb of me."

"Bobbi," Claire said, "It's not your fault."

"But he can't help it and it isn't his fault, either."

"Let's not waste time figuring out who's to blame. Connor just has to figure out how to get over this and we have to figure out how to help him."

"Doc said . . ."

"Oh, you've been to the doctor, Connor. That's wonderful," Claire interrupted.

"Well yeah, I took Bobbi. Anyway, Doc gave me a prescription for something to help me sleep. He thinks that will help."

"And he told you to go see that new guy," Bobbi reminded him.

Connor grimaced. "Yes. He did."

"And you're going to go see him. Right?"

"Yeah, I guess so."

"Who's the new guy?" Henry asked.

"Oh, he's just some guy who was at Guadalcanal. Went through some of the stuff I went through," Connor said. "Doc thinks it will help to talk about it."

"And he says you'll be helping the other guy, too," Bobbi reminded him.

"You don't forget a thing, do you?"

Bobbi grinned at him.

"We can talk about that later," Claire interrupted. "We need to get Bobbi into some dry clothes before she catches her death." She looked at Connor. "Some of your old clothes are still hanging in the wardrobe upstairs." She looked him up and down. "See if you can find something you can still get into."

"I'll hang around here and keep Bobbi company," Henry said.

In a few moments, Connor and Claire were back downstairs. "Let's go back to our bedroom and get you dried off," Claire said.

When they'd all changed to dry clothes, Bobbi crooked a finger at Connor. He bent to hear her whisper. "Should we tell them?"

He couldn't help smiling. "You go ahead."

He saw the twinkle in her eye.

"We have more news," Bobbi said, smiling at her mother-in-law. "I'm going to have a baby."

"I knew it," Claire exclaimed, smiling and dancing a little jig around the dining room.

Henry stared.

"Doesn't it make you want to dance, too?"

He laughed. "I guess so, but I've never seen you do—whatever it is you're doing."

"I've never been gonna be a grandma before."

"It's not even born yet," Bobbi protested. "In fact," she said sobering up. "I'm going to have to see a specialist because I need a Cesarean section."

"Oh, that's not so bad anymore," Claire said. "They do 'em all the time. Kate Robinson had one." Connor saw her frown and make the pushing gesture she always made when something came up that she didn't want to think about. She picked up one of the lanterns and started for the kitchen. "I'll just make us some popcorn."

That was strange. Connor shook his head and looked at his dad who also stared after Claire. Henry shrugged.

When the rain stopped, Connor and Bobbi went home. "Connor," Bobbi asked as her husband plowed mud, throwing clumps onto the side windows. "Did you notice how Mom suddenly clouded up when I said I had to have a C-section?"

"No. It seems like she just went to get popcorn to celebrate."

"Yes, but all the laughter and chatter just died. I wonder what that was all about."

"Probably just your imagination."

"Hmmm. Maybe so."

Connor thought for a moment. "But then, Mom lost a baby. She had us all at home. They did that back then. The doctor brought an infection. Killed the baby and almost killed her. She couldn't have any more kids after that." Connor glanced across at his wife. "She was probably remembering."

He recalled Claire's expression. She remembered.

Part Three

May 24, 1945 - Hastings

Bobbi arrived at the clinic early and sat in the lobby when Malcolm Powers entered, whistling, door catching the wind and slamming shut. She could barely hear him murmuring to himself. "How I love my work. Not long now. Technique perfect. Name in every newspaper." When he entered the reception area, she looked through the window to see him staring over his receptionist's shoulder smiling. *Anybody that happy in their work should be really good at it.*

Bobbi had fought the wind, white knuckled, all the way to Hastings. On an east-west stretch, a dust cloud from newly disked summer fallow had blown across the road, blinding her. She feared being rear-ended.

When they called her name, she entered an examining room and submitted to the usual examination. "I believe we can help you have a normal birth," Powers told her, smiling. "You know you can only have one or two babies by Cesarean section," he said, "but if we can stretch those ligaments that hold your pelvis together, you can have as many babies as you want."

She nodded. *How can he do that? Doesn't seem possible.*

"It will reduce the chance of infection, as well." He frowned at her. "Through the centuries, we've lost hundreds, thousands of mothers and babies to infections. C-sections just make it worse."

137

GRAVY

"But don't we have antibiotics now?"

"Yes, but an ounce of prevention is worth a pound of cure."

"Can I get up now?"

"No. We'll do the first treatment this afternoon and then another at each pre-natal visit until you go into labor."

"What are you going to do?"

"First, we're going to loosen up those ligaments with a little heat." He took a big, fluffy towel from a warmer in the corner. He tucked it around her pelvis, then sat back down on the stool. She heard a click and felt cold metal begin to enter her vagina.

"Oh," she said, surprised. "I think that one's too big."

"It's just right. This *will* hurt a little bit and you will bleed." He expanded the instrument, increasing the already painful pressure. "Just remember the benefits of avoiding major surgery."

Bobbi gasped as soft tissues tore. "We reduce the risk of infection," he repeated, "plus you will be able to have more children."

"Dr. Powers. That really hurts."

"I'm afraid it will. We must stretch those ligaments before that baby comes. I won't do a C-section until we've exhausted all other possibilities. You'll see. It's better this way."

He put more pressure on the speculum and she heard him lock it into place. She felt like her entire pelvis was ripping apart.

"Stop this. This is wrong!"

"Who's the specialist here, Mrs. Conroy. I know what I'm doing. Where did you get your degree?"

"But it hurts. I don't think it's supposed to hurt like this."

"Stupid woman! Childbirth hurts. In sorrow thou shalt bring forth children," he quoted.

"I'm not giving birth *now*."

He chuckled. "Often, for women like you, it's agony. Mostly women like you died, but just relax. We won't expand this anymore today We need those ligaments to release a bit at a time, so next time we can make more progress. I'll be back in a half-hour to remove the apparatus." He left the room, whistling.

Confused, she looked around, realizing that she was completely exposed from the waist down, spread out in the stirrups without even a sheet over her. For half an hour, she remained trapped by an apparatus she couldn't remove herself, unable to move or do anything but hurt.

As she lay motionless, her mind spun. She fought off images of Carl Short with his pudgy hands reaching down her blouse. She told herself that had nothing to do with what was happening in the doctor's office. She struggled to understand how the treatment could work. *Could he really stretch me to deliver normally? Where else could I go to get the Cesarean if I don't stay with Powers? He's the only qualified doctor anywhere near. He is a qualified doctor. I saw his license in his office when I talked to him before going to the exam room. Why didn't he mention his treatment before the exam? Is it so routine, he didn't even think to tell me. He probably thinks I know all about it. It still seems weird to think he can stretch bone. No, he's going to stretch the ligaments. Why didn't he put a sheet over me? I feel so exposed.* Listening to the wind buffeting the walls, she felt blown before the gusts.

After what seemed like hours, Powers returned, and removed the apparatus. As she struggled to sit, he worked at the counter, whistling. "Okay," he said when she sat on the end of the examining table, blood oozing onto the drape, "that went well.

We expanded you a half centimeter." He handed her a sanitary pad. "I'm afraid you've got some bleeding, so you'll want this."

"But I don't have a belt."

"I'm sure your underwear will hold it in place. Don't worry, we'll repair the stretching when you give birth so you will be nice and tight for your husband."

He looked her in the eye. "You need to do this or I won't even think about delivering that baby. You don't need that C-section. Just take it slow for an hour or two until your body gets used to its expansion. You can get dressed now. Make an appointment for a month from now." He left, closing the door behind him.

She stumbled as she climbed off the table and stood on quivering legs. She got dressed, waddling around the room picking up garments and stepping into them. Then she stood inside the door, pulling herself up as tall as she could. She took a few steps around the room until she could walk normally. She made a new appointment, then walked to the car with brisk steps, pushing against the wind. She yanked on the car door, struggling against the wind, and crawled in. The door blew shut on her ankle.

A couple of miles out of town, she pulled onto a side road and stopped in a field entrance. She stared out the windshield at a stream of dust, dry leaves, corn husks, and tumbleweeds passing in front of her. *What am I going to do? Can he really do what he says he can do? What can I do about it anyway? He says he won't deliver unless I take his treatments and he's the only qualified surgeon within a hundred miles.* She remembered the route to Lincoln. Connor had taken her to the State Fair. Fifteen miles of dirt roads, about fifty of gravel before reaching pavement. It had taken half a day.

If I tell Connor, there's no telling what he'd do. It hurts like hell. How many babies do I have to have? Wouldn't two be enough? I'm not worried about infection. I'm strong and healthy and we have antibiotics now. But what can I do? If I weren't so tiny, not like

140

normal women, I wouldn't have this problem. He's just trying to fix me. Oh God!

A wave of nausea struggled up her throat. She opened the door and leaned out. The vomit blew back onto her skirt and down the length of the car. She slammed the door and beat her fists on the steering wheel.

She screamed, and screamed, and screamed until her voice cracked, then sat, staring out the windshield. She wiped the tears she hadn't known she'd been shedding and turned the car toward home. *I can't think about this anymore, I just can't.*

That afternoon

When Connor reached the house after checking on the livestock, he found the screen door shattered—with pieces lying on the step and the spine hanging with torn screen material still attached to the hinges. *Must have gotten away from Bobbi in the wind. That'll take a new door.*

"Bobbi," he called stepping onto the porch. He heard a muffled sound from the storeroom on the right. "Bobbi?" He found her on the floor, curled around a washbasin she'd pulled off the shelf. "Bobbi, what're you doin' in here?"

"I couldn't stop throwing up."

"Oh." He reached for the reeking basin. "What's happened? Why are you on the floor? Why are you crying?"

"Couldn't make it to the kitchen. Kept throwin' up." He took the basin, set it aside, and lifted her off the floor.

She reached for the basin.

"I'll get a pan so I can empty that."

He carried her into the living room and laid her on the couch, scrambled to the kitchen for a pan, and rushed back to Bobbi's side just as she unloaded again. She dry-heaved while he held her head. "You done?"

"For now," she whispered.

He emptied the pan into the basin and took it back to her. "I'll take this other thing out and empty it."

She lay back, tears still streaming. When he returned from the outhouse Connor sat on the edge of the couch and took her hand. "What happened with that doctor?"

"My eyes are just watering from throwing up."

"Is there something else? There must be something else. What happened with the doctor?"

"Oh nothing. He thinks I may not need the Cesarean after all."

"What's making you so sick? Did you eat something?"

"Must be morning sickness. I got sick the other day when Mom and I were canning beef."

"That's pretty awful for morning sickness."

She groaned.

"So was Doc O'Neill wrong about the C-section?"

"Maybe. I don't know. Powers thinks so."

"I suppose he knows his stuff. He *is* a specialist."

"That's right," She turned her face away. "We'll have to trust him."

"Bobbi, you're sure nothing else is wrong?"

"Yeah. But I'm hungry."

"What do you want to eat?"

"I don't know."

"Maybe some of that beef you and Mom canned the other day."

"Too heavy."

"Chicken soup. Mom swears by chicken soup."

She gagged.

"I thought you liked chicken soup."

"Not now."

"Milk?"

"No." She let her head fall back onto the arm of the couch.

"Beef broth?"

She opened her eyes a slit. "Uh uh."

"How about if I make you some mashed potatoes."

She said nothing. Connor thought she'd fallen asleep and began to get up.

"I think I could hold that down."

He got her a blanket and went to boil the potatoes. When he brought them back, the smell started her gagging again.

"I'm calling Mom."

She moved her head. "Okay."

Claire came immediately. "How are you?" She felt Bobbi's forehead as Connor stood by waiting for orders. "No fever. What's been goin' on?"

GRAVY

"I can't keep anything down."

"How about some soda crackers? I never had morning sickness, but Mom used to say if you nibble on soda crackers . . ."

Bobbi tried nibbling, but even bits of crackers set her gagging. Claire and Connor conferred in the kitchen.

"We've got to get some sugar and fluids into her. You'd better go to town and get Seven-Up." She paused while Connor grabbed the car keys. "I'll try some of Mom's old recipes."

When they returned to the living room, Bobbi had fallen asleep, so both headed off to do their errands.

Bobbi woke up when Connor and Claire returned. Connor handed his little grocery box to his mother and sat next to Bobbi while Claire bustled into the kitchen. "I've got something else for you to try," she hollered a few moments later.

She offered Bobbi a cup of dusty, mint-smelling liquid.

"It's beebalm. Grandma says it works when all else fails."

Bobbi sniffed and took a sip. When nothing happened for a few minutes, she tried another. In a few more moments, she downed the whole cup and gave Claire a weak smile. "So far, so good."

"We'll let it settle before we try the Seven-Up."

"Seven Up?"

"If you can hold it down, it will get some sugar in your system and the fizz bubbles up some of that sour in your stomach." She took the cup and saucer. "And then, maybe. We can try for something more solid.

The next day started the same. Bobbi threw up and cried. Claire had left some beebalm leaves and Connor brewed tea. Bobbi sipped it and stopped gagging, but she didn't stop crying.

"Bobbi, what's wrong?

"I don't know," she wailed. She pulled the blankets up to her chin and shivered. "I don't know. I just feel like crying. I'm hungry, and I can't eat anything, and I feel like crying."

"But why? This has to be more than morning sickness."

"I. Don't. Know. I just don't know."

Later, Claire arrived asking the same questions with the same results. "Bobbi, this isn't just morning sickness, is it? There's something very wrong. Did Connor hurt you?"

"No, no of course not. He hasn't had a blow up since that one when it stormed."

"So what is it? Are you worried about having that baby?"

"A little, I suppose, but I just can't stop crying."

"Bobbi," she asked again. "Did something happen that you're not telling us about?"

God! I wish they'd quit asking! I can't tell anybody about that doctor. Connor would kill him. Anyway, he's a specialist. He knows what he's doing. Besides, that wouldn't make me throwin' up sick.

"I just went to the doctor and then I came home and got sick. That's all that happened. Remember I got sick that day we canned beef, too."

Bobbi got better in a few days. Although her stomach remained queasy, she could eat a little bit, at least.

May 31, 1946

One glorious spring day a week later, Connor worked alone
hoping to have his landscaping all done before the baby. He
knew he wouldn't have much spare time after that. Although he
couldn't carry a tune when he sang, he whistled a jaunty
rendition of *In the Mood*. It echoed full, rich, and right on key.
Transplanting a truckload of trees, bushes and flowers, he
realized that years had passed since he'd felt so peaceful and
confident.

The smell of yellow sweet clover from across the road filled the
air as he turned rich, black soil out of the hole he dug for his
weeping willow tree. Reluctant to sell him the tree, Emil at the
nursery had told him they don't do well with the winds in
Nebraska, but Connor knew he could make one grow just fine.
The tree would be the centerpiece of his landscaping, with the
driveway circling around it. With the tree set in place, he dug a
moat around it to hold water on its roots and carried four
buckets of water to fill it. He would have to bucket water to it
every night when he came in from his fieldwork. That effort
seemed miniscule compared to all the hundreds, maybe
thousands of crates of weapons and equipment he'd dragged up
beaches in heat and humidity that would kill a rattlesnake.

Next, he lined out his box hedge, leaving a gap on either side of
the sidewalk, another big gap between the house and the barn
and a last one leading to the orchard and the outhouse. He
planted seven dozen fast-growing Chinese elms that he could
keep clipped about waist high. He'd just about finished with the
hedge when Bobbi called him for dinner.

"You looked like you were actually having a good time out there
working yourself to death," Bobbi said as she stirred the gravy.

"I am, Bobbi. I don't know as I've ever told you this, but if I'd had
a chance to go to college, I'd have been a horticulturist." He took
the basin out by the front step and pumped some water from the
pitcher pump, to wash up before sitting down at the table.

Bobbi set the gravy on the table and joined him. "You could use the G.I. Bill."

"I'm too old. The government decided they didn't want to send us old folks to college with the kids. I'll just take some ag classes and play around in the yard here in my spare time."

"That's not fair! You had to do everything the younger guys did."

Connor shrugged. Nothing he could do about it. As soon as he'd got back on furlough, his dad had offered to send him, but he'd decided when he got married that college was probably a pipe dream. He'd given it up twice before. The third time seemed anti-climactic.

After they ate, he helped her clear the table and then took her hand. "The dishes will wait. Let me show you what I'm gonna do out here. I hope you'll like it."

He led her first to the willow tree. "See, when people come; they'll drive around the tree and park over here." He grinned. "It'll have to be watered every day." He walked her to the opening he'd left in the hedge. "People will come in through here. It will be up to about here," he gestured. "I'll keep it trimmed square. They call it a box hedge."

She nodded. "Sounds like a lot of work."

"Great work for Sundays," he beamed at her, his teeth glinting in the sun. "Then up against the house, I'll plant the spirea under the windows, so we'll have a cascade of little, white flowers drooping down to the ground. They'll bloom in the spring. In summer, we'll have some yellow roses, like Mom's, to smell up the yard."

"Connor, I'm used to concrete and asphalt. I'm trying, but I'll get it when I see it." She turned around looking at all his plants. "So you're telling me all those little sticks will be tree and flowers?"

He chuckled. "They sure will."

GRAVY

"I can see they're making you happy, so I love them too."

When he'd finished walking her through his landscaping plans, she reminded him that he needed to get cleaned up soon because they planned to go out. He followed her glance to the new car. "It'll be fun to drive our own, won't it?"

She nodded and went inside.

Whistling *Moonlight Serenade,* he set an American elm on the south side of the house for summer shade. He dropped the shovel and stamped dirt tight around the tree, then shoveled more dirt into the depressions made by his feet. After repeating the process a couple of times he took his buckets to the stock tank and brought them back full of water, pouring it on the roots and watching the water disappear.

Then, he stuck his head in the front door and yelled, "Bobbi, I'm going up to Mom's to get some of her yellow roses. I'll be right back."

He'd already asked Claire about taking the roses, so he jumped out of the car and started digging. Claire came out on the front step, wiping her hands on her apron. "You seem happy today."

"Yeah, I almost feel like a normal human being doing normal stuff." He dug up a few likely-looking canes, stuck them in a bucket, and put them in the car.

"What's Bobbi doing?"

"You mean, is she crying?"

Claire nodded.

"No, Mom. She seems to be having a good day, too. We're going to go over to Jake and Mary's tonight."

"Nice night for it."

"I think so. I gotta go get these in the ground. See ya tomorrow."

Back in the car, he whistled a few bars of *Ain't Nothin' Like a Dame* on the way home. He was still whistling when he climbed out of the car with the bucket and set the roses at each end of the clothesline, making a mental note that he would have to be sure to keep them pruned so the thorns wouldn't snag the clothes—or his wife.

Finally, he made beds for the tea roses on either side of the front step. He planted the Crimson Glories on the left and the Peace roses on the right. Then he hauled buckets of water to everything he'd planted and put his tools away in time to get ready for their night out.

He'd only been in the house a few minutes, though, when he started feeling jittery. At first, he just ignored the feeling, dipped some warm water from the stove reservoir into the big washbasin and bathed. When he climbed out of the tub and dried off, though, the feeling intensified. He slipped into his underwear and started pacing, pushing his arms into the sleeves of a dress shirt.

Bobbi looked up from polishing her nails. "Connor, what's going on? You're pacing around here like a tiger in a cage." She dipped the brush back into the polish bottle. "We've got plenty of time."

"I don't know. I'm just keyed up for some reason."

"What about?"

"I don't know. Something just feels weird."

"Like what?"

"I don't know. Something. There's not a cloud in the sky, so it's not that."

"Are you worried about the cows?"

"Not any more than usual. We've got some great calves."

"We haven't gone out in a while, is that getting to you?"

"I sure don't think so. I've been looking forward to it."

"Me too." She turned her attention back to her fingers.

Connor sat and picked up the newspaper. He read for a few moments, then crumpled it and threw it on the end table. He pulled on his pants, slid on some socks and tied his shoes. "I'm going outside."

He stood on the front step and took a deep breath, scanning the farmyard for the source of his anxiety. He didn't see anything out of the ordinary. He walked to the corral to check the tank and found plenty of water. The hogs seemed perfectly content, mud-caked and sleepy. Walking back to the house, Connor realized he felt much better.

When he stepped back inside though, he hit a wall. "What's that smell?" he demanded.

"I don't know. What smell?"

"I'm not sure." He walked around sniffing. As he approached her chair, she slipped and got polish on her knuckle.

"Now look what you made me do!" She reached for the polish remover and a cotton ball.

When she opened the remover, he frowned. "There's something about that smell."

"What?"

"I said I don't know." He sat down and grabbed the novel he'd been reading. That didn't last long. He jumped up and got a drink of water.

He watched Bobbi jerking on the polish brush with white knuckles. He paced. "Just sit down," she said. "You're making me nervous.

"I'm going outside."

"Go."

"I think I will." He stomped out, slamming the door, but slammed back in seconds. Bobbi was wiping polish off the back of her hand with remover.

"Darn it!"

"What's the matter?"

"You startled me when you slammed the door."

"I didn't slam the door."

"Yes, you did. What is the matter with you?"

"What's wrong with me? What's wrong with you? You've been snapping at me all afternoon."

"I have not. You've been stomping around here, scaring me and making me mess up my nail polish."

"You can't use that against me all the time, Bobbi. I know I have my fits, but . . ."

"And you're having one now."

"No, I'm not. I'm just a little keyed up."

"And you've been pacing and stomping around and slamming doors."

"I didn't slam that door," he shouted. "I'm going outside!"

"Fine."

He checked all his new plantings, spotting a yellow rose that had wilted. He grabbed a bucket and gave it some water. *Seems like that smell is setting me off. It reminds me of something.* He opened the car door and sat on the seat. *What is that smell? It's in the nail polish. It smells like.* He frowned, absently rubbing his ear. *It smells like that place, I can't even remember where we were now, where they shelled the hell out of us. Arawe maybe. There were bananas rotting all over the place. We were on the beach unloading. That's it. That's what's driving me nuts. Banana oil.*

He stood and shut the car door, walking around the willow tree and looking toward the road. *I wonder what the hell else will set me off. At least I didn't attack anybody or break anything.*

In the house, Bobbi hurriedly finished her nail polish, so it could dry before Connor startled her again. She put the polish away and got dressed, thinking about their quarrel. *I don't know why I can't be more patient with him. I'm not much of a wife if I can't realize what he's been through and how hard he's trying to get better. I'm not even woman enough to have his babies the normal way. I have to have these treatments.*

The thought of Powers's treatments brought her up sharp, clenching her fists until her newly polished fingernails cut into her palms. She began pacing from window to window, wondering where Connor had disappeared to. She wished she could tell him about the treatments, but she still feared he wouldn't understand. Hell, she didn't really get it. And Connor? No telling what he might do. *There's no other doctor anyway. It just hurts so much and five more treatments. Can I take five more treatments?*

She stopped walking, staring out the front window. *I can't do it.* She stood rigid in the middle of the living room trying to stop the tears that threatened to spill over and ruin her makeup. *I just can't do it.* She sobbed. *But what else can I do? I can't have the baby without Powers, and I can't tell Connor.*

She brightened a little. *I could tell Claire. Maybe she can help me think of a way out of this. There must be a better way.* She sagged on her feet. *But no, Claire would probably tell Connor, or she'd tell Henry. I couldn't stand it if Henry knew.*

She resumed her pacing, wringing her hands, furiously wiping tears that she couldn't stop. "Oh, I don't know *what* to do," she moaned, sitting and burying her face in her hands.

She barely heard Connor return to the house a few minutes later. "Bobbi, we ought to go pretty soon, I think. Our reservations are for seven o'clock . . . Bobbi, what's wrong?" he demanded, striding over to the chair and kneeling to pull her hands away from her face.

"Nothing, Connor, just nothing."

"It's not nothing, Bobbi, you're crying. What is it?"

He tried to put his arms around her, but she pushed him away. "Leave me alone!" She jumped up and stalked across the room where she stood with her arms crossed.

"I'm just trying to comfort you."

"I don't want comfort." She turned away. *He can't understand why I don't want to make love anymore. He keeps asking what's wrong—if he's done something wrong. I don't know what to tell him.*

"What do you want, Bobbi? What can I do for you?"

"Just leave me alone."

The look on his face when he turned and left the house made her want to call him back. *But what would I tell him? After those treatments, it hurts too much, but that's not what I tell him. I say I just don't feel like it. I can see the hurt in his eyes, but I just can't, and I don't know what to tell him. I don't imagine that's helping him get better either and I don't know how I can ever—at least until after this baby is born.*

If I weren't so inadequate. That's what Dr. Powers said. I have an inadequate pelvis. I'm not fully developed like most adult women. I need these treatments to have this baby, he says. He's a

153

specialist, but I can't believe him. I have to believe. He's the doctor. O'Neill trusts him, so I should.

I'm just like that little heifer—too small to get this baby out. It's my own fault. I'm just too narrow down there.

Connor stepped back inside the door. "Do you want to cancel tonight?"

"No, I'm almost ready. Let me check my makeup."

She stepped into the bedroom and applied some foundation under her eyes. She sighed, grabbed her purse, squared her shoulders, and walked out to join him. He was still standing on the front step when she got there.

July 19, 1946

About a month later, Bobbi spent another couple of days doubled over the basin, crying, and a month after that, the day before her next doctor visit, Connor came in from checking on the new pigs. "Did you see my fencing pliers anywhere?"

"No, they're probably where you left them."

"I'm sure they are, but I thought maybe you'd seen them."

"I'm busy. I can't imagine why you'd bring them in the house, and I can't be expected to keep track of where you leave your tools."

Connor hesitated, staring at Bobbi's back. "I don't expect you to keep track . . ."

She turned, holding a glass she'd been washing, and pitched it at his head. He ducked. The glass shattered against the wall. Soapy water ran onto the floor. He grabbed her hand and slapped her across the cheek. She stared back at him. *He's going to beat me to a pulp.* She began crying.

"Don't you ever do that again."

She covered her face with soapy hands. "You hit me!"

"What's the matter with you? You can't go throwing shit at people. I thought I was the shellshocked lunatic around here."

She ran into the living room and threw herself on the couch sobbing. Connor followed and knelt next to her. "What's wrong Bobbi? You haven't been yourself lately."

"Stop asking me that. Just stop it. I can't help it."

Connor stalked out of the house, slamming the door behind him.

After Bobbi went to bed that night, Connor curled up by the stove with his writing tablet.

> Dear Nora,
>
> How are you and Daniel doing? Has the chaos of refugees and rebuilding let up even a little bit? Has Daniel made any headway with the Gaullists getting a new government set up?
>
> I'm still trying to get control of my blowups. How are you doing with that? Doc O'Neill prescribed something to help me sleep, so for a month I slept like a baby and grogged around all day. I guess it did help some, so I'd recommend it. Getting some real rest makes me less jumpy and seem to have less nightmares now. Doc also prescribed conversation, if you can believe it. He sent me to talk to this new guy in town. His name is Gaetan Bergara and he's a Bosque. Don't I remember the Bosques guided Daniel and his refugees across the Pyrenees? Gaetan joined the British Army and landed with the Brits on D-Day. So, we can talk

about just about any brutal thing we've seen. I guess it helps some too.

The trouble is, Nora, I'm not the only one going crazy now. Bobbi seems to be having some kind of breakdown. I wrote you a couple of months ago that she's pregnant, but she can't eat anything without throwing it back up. She gets better for a while and then she'll have a few days when she can't keep anything down. Along with all the upchucking, she cries and cries and cries. Mom says that it happens sometimes when a woman's pregnant, but I can't help thinking something's really wrong. Everybody tells me it'll pass and she'll have a nice, strong, healthy baby, but I'm scared. Grandma Flaherty doesn't say much, but I think she's worried, too. I don't know what to do.

Connor

The stove ticked and the house creaked as it cooled for the night. Connor blew out the lamp and crept upstairs, undressing in the dark and sliding in next to his wife's warm body, a body he was no longer allowed to touch.

August 12, 1946

"Mom? You got a minute?" Connor had stopped in at his parents' house between jobs.

"Is everything okay?"

"No, Mom. Bobbi's crying and throwing up again."

"You want me to go see to her?"

"No, that'll just make her mad. But I've been noticing a pattern."

Claire frowned. "What kind of pattern?"

"Every time she has an appointment with that doctor, she gets sick a few days before and a little after. Have you noticed that?"

"No. Can't say as I have."

"Maybe I'm making it up. I want to understand so bad—so I can help her."

"I know you do, son, but I think it's just that women sometimes get real emotional when they're pregnant." She sighed. "Grandma says she's never seen anyone get it that bad, though."

"Do you think there's something else going on?"

She shook her head. "I don't know what it would be, I truly don't."

"I don't either. I just wonder if that doctor's scaring her to death."

"Why on earth would he do that?"

"I just don't know. She won't talk about it, but there's something." They stood silent in the kitchen listening to the wind rustling around the corner. "Aw hell, Mom, I gotta get back to work.

Connor got the mail that evening and picked out a letter from Nora. He sat next to the mailbox at the end of the lane to read it—in case Nora'd answered his concern about Bobbi.

> Dear Connor,
>
> I hope you sold a lot of wheat this summer because we're desperate for it here. As if the war hadn't done enough damage, we've had drought here. Ambassador Caffery is begging for supplies of wheat. We still have refugees living in camps all over Europe and we must feed them somehow.

GRAVY

Imagine surviving a concentration camp and then starving in a refugee camp. I'm ashamed of my country because we have so much but we allowed so few to immigrate back when we could save lives—and now we only let a trickle of survivors in. I feel so helpless!

As to Daniel, I think he's about to give up on politics. It's such a struggle. He's also been working himself to death trying to save the grapes. Like all the other food crops, they're stressed by drought. I worry all the time that they haven't cleared all the mines and Daniel will step on one. Wish him luck. He'll need it.

I don't know what to say about Bobbi. Just keep taking care of yourself and doing whatever you can for her. Her misery does seem extreme, but remember when we were in high school and I helped Aunt Eva that summer? It seems like she cried all the time too. I'd ask her what was wrong, and she'd say, "I don't know." She got better when Luke was born, so I'll bet Mom's right. Bobbi will be fine in the end. But you'll have to be extra gentle now.

I'll never forget the Bosques. You asked if they guided Daniel and his refugees across the mountains and the answer is yes. There was an old fellow who took us across that trip I made with Daniel. He was a gentle soul but could be ruthless when he needed to be. I'm glad you found your Bosque to talk to. I think it does help. Like I said before, we're all pretty much in the same boat here, so we don't have to say much. We just nod and maybe add a word or two about a specific horror.

Gotta go. The workload never lets up.

GRAVY

Nora

Because of the drought in Nebraska, Connor stuffed the letter in his pocket instead of burning it. He'd put it in the stove when he had a chance. Usually he shared, but he didn't want Bobbi to know he and his sister discussed her.

He took the rest of the mail and walked on home.

August 16, 1946

Connor saw the dust when Bobbi pulled into the lane and stopped at the mailbox after her appointment with the obstetrician. He headed for the house as soon as he saw her drive into the circle, jump out of the car, and run inside. *Sick again. That doctor's doing something. I don't know what.* He helped her get comfortable on the couch with her inevitable pan and, once she was done, he grabbed the mail. Surprised to get another letter from Nora so soon, he ripped it open immediately.

> Dear Bobbi and Connor,
>
> I don't rant very often so please bear with me. I am just furious with Harry S. Truman. You see, there are about a quarter of a million Jewish refugees stranded in displaced persons camps all over Europe. Nobody can figure out what to do with them. Heaven forfend that we invite them to come into our country. Instead, we have formed a Committee of Inquiry with the British to figure it out. It reminds me that the Nazis had committees to figure out what to do about the Jewish Question as well.
>
> The Jews themselves want to have their own country in Palestine. There's been a Zionist movement for decades and a few people have been

159

going there over the years. Who can blame them for wanting their own homeland? The Axis powers tried to exterminate them. The Allies didn't want them. The Arabs don't want them either, but at least they're going back to territory they had once inhabited.

The Committee has decided it can send about 100,000 Jewish refugees to Palestine. When I think about that, I remember what you wrote me about the Indians who served with you. I remember how we European whites settled on their lands and used up their resources, or destroyed them, as if nobody at all lived there. The Committee seems to have that same attitude. What will happen if we (the Brits and the Americans) resettle 100,000 new people on that little strip of Palestinian desert—as if nobody lives there? Where do the people who do live there go?

The Committee wants to specify that there will be no Arab and no Jewish state. The Committee also recommends a statement that neither Jew nor Arab will dominate in Palestine. That's better than nothing, I guess, but the Brits are furious with Truman because he approved the resettlement without even those provisions. Ambassador Caffery isn't very happy either.

I can't imagine this will have a peaceful solution.

Okay. I'm done now. Of course, I don't know everything about the negotiations, but I can't help thinking the world will pay for this. I think our next war will start in the Middle East.

I guess I'm getting a little depressed. The recovery is so slow here and so punishing. Daniel says the vineyard looks a total loss. It's a real shame, too. Some of the vines are at least a hundred years old.

Daniel says that if he wants to stay here, he will
have to dig up and transplant as much stock as he
can and start over. If he has to dig everything up
anyway, why not ship it all to some place where he
doesn't have to worry about stepping on a land
mine, or more political upheaval, or shortages of
the very things he needs to start over.

Thanks for "listening."

Nora

By the time he'd finished reading, Bobbi had dozed. Connor
tossed a blanket over her and went out to do chores, wondering if
his sister had guessed right. *Are we doomed to endless wars?* He
shuddered as he walked toward the barn, thinking of
increasingly efficient killing machines.

He shook his head as if shaking the thought out of it. *How about
Daniel and Nora? Maybe they will bring those ancient grapes to
Nebraska.* He tried to imagine a bunch of kids playing together,
rolling down hills of prairie grasses and running back to the top
to do it again.

Part Four

February 28, 1947 — Willow Grove

Thick flakes of snow fell when Connor and Bobbi awoke. A furry blanket already lay on the ground. Connor dressed and hustled outside before breakfast to check on the new calves.

"If the wind picks up, this could be trouble."

Inside getting breakfast, Bobbi felt a twinge in her lower back. She stopped with the plates in her hand and frowned, but it went away so she went on to the stove with them. She checked out the window to see if Conner was on his way in, but the snow was thick enough all she saw was shadows. She set the plates with eggs, bacon and toast on the back of the stove to stay warm. She decided to sweep up while she waited and was struggling with the dustpan when Connor stepped in with a cold packet of air.

"Here, let me help you."

He held the dustpan so she could stand and wield the broom.

"Calves okay?"

"Yeah. The mamas have them in the corral, up next to the barn. I'll have to go back and feed after breakfast."

Later, back inside after feeding the stock, Connor paced from window to window.

"What're you looking for, Connor?"

"Just hoping this doesn't turn into a storm with you almost ready to have the baby. And all the new calves out there." He

162

turned to his wife. "I think we should go into Hastings now, in case it starts blowing."

She felt another twinge in her back and across her lower torso. She frowned and held the dish she was putting in the cupboard for a bit before she grabbed another handful and stored them. "No. It's not time, Connor. I've got stuff to get ready here."

"Maybe not, but it's close and I want to be safe."

"Where would we stay? In a hotel? I'm not ready yet. I have lots to do. I'd go nuts."

"Bobbi . . ."

"I'm not going now. Who's having this baby anyway?"

Connor shook his head and went back to pacing.

Several times during the day, a cramp got Bobbi's attention momentarily and she wondered if she might be beginning labor. It didn't seem as intense as she expected so she ignored it. She'd made up her mind, months before, that she would *not* call Dr. Powers until the very last minute. She couldn't be sure of much, but she knew she didn't want to spend more time with that man than she must. Throughout the day, the cramping got a little more intense, but still scattered. She went on with her work, although Connor's pacing had begun to get on her nerves.

When he came in from evening chores, stamping snow on the porch, they barely spoke. With supper finished and dishes done, they went into the living room where Connor spent a few hours reading and Bobbi crocheted some things for the baby. When they went to bed, Bobbi felt a particularly intense cramp, but she blew out the lantern and pulled the covers up to her chin.

By morning, the cramps had become more intense and more frequent, but Bobbi got up and prepared breakfast without a word.

"You okay?" Connor asked as he bundled up to take care of the stock. "You've been awful quiet the last couple of days."

"Yes. I'm okay." She endured another of his long, questioning looks, and then he was gone.

With Connor out of the way, Bobbi started timing the cramps, thinking that they'd become regular. Every half-hour, she discovered. *We have to go. It's coming whether I'm ready or not.*

She remembered the last time she saw Dr. Powers and she felt nauseous. She started gagging.

"Bobbi, we're going now. Snow's up to my mid-calf and pretty soon we won't be able to get out of . . . Bobbi?"

She looked over her shoulder.

"Are you all right?"

"Yes. I'm all right."

"No, you're not all right." He picked up the knocked-over cookware and stacked it back in the cupboard. Just as he turned to his wife, a contraction ripped through her and she couldn't help groaning.

"What's going on?"

"Nothing. I just had a little cramp."

"That didn't look like a little cramp to me. I think you're in labor."

"No, I'm not. It was just a cramp."

"How often are you having those little cramps?"

"I don't know," she lied. "Every once in a while."

He stood watching her a moment. "How are you doing?"

"Fine Connor. I'm just fine."

"We're going to Hastings."

Another contraction snatched her, and she grabbed the back of a chair with trembling hands. She saw herself in the stirrups again, waiting for Powers to return and remove his obscene instrument of torture. Again, her stomach heaved, and she retched into the dishpan on the countertop.

"Where's your suitcase?"

"Not now! You hear me? Not now!"

"Yes now. We're going now if I have to pick you up and carry you to the car."

They stood staring at each other. "Where's your suitcase?"

"In the bedroom."

Connor got the bag and hustled it out to the car, then looked around for Bobbi. He strode back and slammed through the door. "Can I help you?"

"No, I'm fine. I'm putting on my boots."

She walked out the door and across the porch while Connor closed the house and rushed ahead of her to open the car door. She saw him holding the door and stepping from foot to foot. When she finally got into the car, he slammed the door and rushed around to the driver's side, started the car and pulled around the willow tree and out the lane.

"There's no hurry, Connor, we've got plenty of time."

They rode in silence as Bobbi again visualized herself and Dr. Powers with his treatments. "Stop the car, Connor," she said about halfway to the hospital.

"Why?"

"For Heaven's sake stop the car!" Before he came to a full stop, she'd opened her door and stepped out.

"Bobbi!" he yelled as she doubled over, retching. "My God," he said when she got back in, "wait until the car stops at least."

"Didn't have time."

When they reached the hospital, Bobbi was retching again. Connor grabbed the suitcase out of the back seat, then opened Bobbi's door.

"Bobbi, you're trembling!"

"I know. Just help me get in this place before I throw up on your shoes."

Connor put an arm around her waist, and she leaned on him for support in the slick, snowy entrance. At the front desk, he turned her over to a nurse with a wheelchair while he filled out paperwork. Someone showed him to the maternity waiting room where he waited—and waited.

March 2, 1947 — Hastings

Connor stalked the waiting room. He'd already stormed the labor room the second day and Bobbi looked like she couldn't take any more then. *What has another day—two days—what is it? How exhausted is she now? Can she even survive surgery?* He couldn't stop pacing and repeating his names, Mendez, Green, Moore, Wilson . . .

Henry and Claire had arrived the previous day, but Henry had returned home to take care of the stock.

Suddenly, a nurse burst through the door of the operating room and Connor got a glimpse inside, a glimpse of blood and his wife's exposed internal organs. His shocked brain flashed images of soldiers ripped apart by shells. He gagged. He remembered Beacon, captured by the Japs, hanging from a tree. His stomach rebelled, sending bile up his throat. He rushed for the nearest bathroom, gagging.

"What happened?" Claire asked when he came back wiping his mouth with a paper towel.

"Blood."

"What?"

"Got a glimpse of Bobbi. She's gonna bleed to death and I can't do anything."

"Connor, the doctor's a specialist. He must know what he's doing."

Half an hour later, Powers finally came out to talk to them. He wouldn't make eye contact. *Christ! He's killed her. What about my baby?*

"They're both alive," Powers said. "Bobbi's very tired and we'll have to be vigilant about infection . . ."

"And the baby's alive?" Connor demanded.

"Yes, but I don't expect her to live very long. She's likely to be seriously impaired by the long labor . . ."

Connor didn't wait for another word. He grabbed the doctor by the throat and propeled him flat against the wall. "Impaired by the long labor, you son-of-a-bitch. Impaired how?"

The doctor gargled.

"Connor!" Claire shouted, pulling at Connor's arm. "Let him go!"

"What have you done to my baby!?" he screamed in the doctor's face as it turned a deep shade of red and his eyes bulged.

"Connor! Stop it!" Claire kept trying to pull him away. "You'll kill him."

"I'm *gonna* kill him. He let her suffer and he's hurt my baby."

They heard someone running toward them. "Connor, let him go!"

A security guard rounded the corner, glanced at Connor and Powers, lowered his shoulder, and took a tackling run at Connor. Connor went down, losing his grip on Powers and burying Claire under his body with the guard on top of all of them. They all lay tangled together for a moment before the guard struggled to his feet and pulled Connor off the others.

"What the hell you think you're doin' here?"

Connor looked at Powers, still struggling on the floor. "He nearly killed my wife and he's crippled my daughter."

Powers, who had managed to sit himself up against the wall, tried to speak, but only managed a croak. The guard knelt beside him. "I want this man charged with murder," he whispered.

"Who's dead?"

The guard looked around as Connor gave Claire a hand up. "I'm sorry, Mom, are you okay?"

"I guess so." She stood smoothing her dress. "What about the doctor?"

"I don't give a damn about the doctor."

"Who's been murdered?" the guard repeated.

"Attempted murder then," the doctor croaked.

"The police are on their way. It'll be up to them."

Connor stood and studied the guard's face for a moment. "I know you from somewhere." He frowned. "Where'd you learn to tackle like that?"

"Name's Robertson." He helped Powers to his feet. He frowned, studying Connor's face. "And I learned it tackling *you* back in 1933, last game of the season."

"No shit? You played for Cowles?" He looked harder. "I remember you. You broke my arm."

"Whadaya mean? You played the whole game."

"With my arm taped to my side."

"No shit!"

"Hey," the doctor rasped. "That man tried to kill me."

"Well, he's not going anywhere, is he? I'll turn him over to the police when they get here. Streets are pretty bad out there." He turned to Connor. "How about that touchdown in the third quarter?"

"You mean that leaping, one-handed catch in the end zone?"

"Yeah."

"Wish I'da caught it."

"That guy graduated and walked on at UNL."

"No shit!"

The two men chatted about football for a few moments, until Connor asked if he'd be allowed to go to the nursery and see his little girl. Powers protested, as loudly as he could, but Robertson gripped Connor's elbow and took him along the hall. "You didn't hear it from me, but a lot of Powers's patients are here for a very long time and more than one of the babies has died."

"Christ! What am I gonna do? Wish I'da known that."

Connor gazed at his daughter, her skin still very red. "She looks all right, doesn't she?"

Robertson studied the baby for a moment. "Looks good to me."

They waited back in the waiting room until the police arrived. "Mom, I think she's going to be all right," Connor said to Claire as she sat wringing her hands. "I don't know how she even survived . . ."

"Maybe she'll be okay."

"If she's not," rasped Powers, "it's not my fault."

Connor and Claire both stared at him until he started gagging and choking again. The other three ignored him. When the cops arrived, stamping snow from heavy boots, they took statements from all four. Powers insisted that Connor must be hauled off in handcuffs, but Robertson walked them to the front entrance where he encouraged the cops to remove the cuffs.

Back in the Waiting Room

Once Powers, coughing and glaring at her, got to his feet, Claire demanded an explanation. "What do you mean the baby may be impaired. Impaired how?"

"In these long labors, the baby is often oxygen starved and there's sometimes brain damage."

"You knew that, and you let her labor for *three days*? Why?"

"If she could have a normal delivery, there would be less chance of infection."

"At cost of the baby? What's the matter with you?"

He shrugged and scurried off. Claire hurried to the nursery to see for herself how the baby looked. The infant lay quiet, barely moving arms and legs, but her eyes tracked the nurses. Claire headed to recovery. She knew right where to go—in the same place as 50 years before—to watch over Bobbi as the new mother regained consciousness. Claire figured she'd been helpless and vulnerable in this hospital long enough.

She stood gazing at her exhausted daughter-in-law. Bobbi's eyelids appeared translucent. Her deep tan had faded, In just three days. Only a shade darker than the sheets. Bobbi's chest barely rose and fell. She tucked the girl's cold hand under the blanket and pulled the covers up to her chin. Bobbi's eyelids fluttered.

"It'll be all right," Claire whispered. Her own memories of that same hospital flitted through her memory. "You're strong. You've gotta believe in yourself. You'll make it through this. If we have to cry, we'll cry with you. Then we'll go on."

Swift, quiet footsteps, the tinkle of medical instruments, soft, urgent voices in the hallway reminded her of when she'd lost her own baby. She took a deep breath and focused on the emptiness that comes with the smell of crisp, fresh sheets and antiseptic, accompanied by an undercurrent of stale urine, pus and infection that breaks through in just a whiff and disappears. She let it go, exhaled until she emptied her lungs. She gazed at Bobbi's hair flattened with sweat and tousled by thrashing on the pillow. Dull, dark circles underscored the eyes—the mouth drawn tight and straight. *The girl's shrunk in just three days. Somebody should have made that doctor do that surgery sooner.*

Bobbi stirred. She seemed to be saying something. Claire leaned down to hear. "Oh my gosh," she whispered when she finally made out a pattern in Bobbi's weak voice. "She's singing. She really can't help herself. Even unconscious, she has to sing."

I sure didn't sing after my surgery. She calculated in her head. *Almost thirty years ago. They thought I couldn't hear. The doctor told Henry I'd die.* She took Bobbi's hand. *I tried to tell 'em, but I couldn't speak. Couldn't move. Burned up with fever. Couldn't*

GRAVY

even feel where they cut out my insides. The grieving came later when I realized what they'd taken from me.

She tried to send her own strength to her daughter-in-law, remembering her struggle to survive and how much she'd wanted to live. The doctor who delivered her baby at home had been treating blood poisoning before he came to her. A couple of days later, she began feeling really bad. By the end of a week, as she slipped in and out of delirium, her family panicked. Her mother, always calm and capable, told Henry to take her to the hospital. Henry needed no prompting.

While he hitched up the horses, her mother wrapped her tightly in a sheet and a couple of blankets. Back in the house, he smelled a little like tack leather and horses. Henry was a small man, a little shorter than she, but he hoisted her in his arms and carried her to the buggy. She could feel the air moving across her face as he strode swiftly outside and set her carefully on the seat. She felt the buggy jerk and she almost fell over when Henry climbed up on the seat beside her and leaned her hot body against his, holding it tight to his side with the arm that held the reins. She felt the swing of his other arm as he whipped the horses, something he never did, and the terrifying jolt of the buggy as it raced toward Cowles, where they could board a train for Hastings. She heard Henry muttering, "You'll be all right Claire, I swear. You'll be all right."

"Of course, I will," she murmured, but he couldn't hear her for the thud of the horses' hooves and the wind blowing into the buggy.

That ride seemed to go on forever, the bruising jolt of the seat pounding her nearly inert body and the hot wind and sun burning her face. Once or twice, she felt the buggy come off the ground, sailing for a few feet and landing with a teeth-jarring bounce. She could only lean into Henry and endure, listening to the unaccustomed snap of the whip and hoping it would be over soon.

Dr. Powers interrupted her thoughts as he stepped, whistling, into the room.

"What are you doing here?"

"Watching over my daughter-in-law."

"You get out of here. We don't allow anyone in recovery. Go see the baby until we get her into the ward."

"No. I'll stay here. That's what families do. We watch over each other."

"That's what nurses are for. Now go on." He made a shooing gesture at her.

"I'll stay right here."

Powers' eyes narrowed. "What's she been telling you?"

"Nothing. That's what worries me."

"Well, you get out. You're not sterile. You'll give her an infection. We'll let you know when she's in her room."

She smiled. "That's all right. I'll stand here until she wakes. We'll have more to say to you later."

Bobbi stirred. "No. No. Keep away from me."

"See, you woke her up."

Without a word, Claire looked back at Bobbi, ignoring the doctor until he left. "You have to tell us, Bobbi," Claire pleaded. "I don't know what happened, but it's tearing you up. Did that doctor do something to you?" She glanced at the sleeping woman. *Seems more like a daughter than an in-law.*

She smiled. She'd taken to Bobbi the moment they met. For all her glamorous career, to Claire she seemed down-to-earth, although a little starry-eyed. *But something has happened. That doctor won't admit how dangerous his delaying the caesarian was, but I know.* Suddenly the sky darkened as scudding clouds blocked the sun. Claire stepped over to the window. *Looks like another storm.* The sky opened and closed again with the fast-moving clouds. *The air must be electrical.*

Bobbi shifted on the bed. "Where am I?"

"You're in the hospital, Bobbi. Do you remember anything about the last three days?"

"Umm. Oh, it hurts! What happened to me?"

"You've had surgery. You're just waking up."

"What kind . . ." she drifted off again. Claire watched Bobbi sleeping, stirring, beginning to feel the pain, shifting her body to ease it. She didn't look forward to Bobbi's waking. The poor child would feel like she'd been beaten by a sledgehammer. They'd have to tell her about the baby.

Bobbi moaned. Claire watched, making sure she didn't bump against the rails. When the thrashing left her uncovered, Claire pulled the blankets back into place. Finally, Bobbi's eyes popped open and she looked at least semi-conscious. Claire took the girl's hand in hers. "How're you feeling?"

"Am I still alive?"

Claire smiled. "Yes, Bobbi, I think you're gonna make it."

"I thought I was gonna die."

"We were all worried about you, but you're strong and you hung on—by the skin of your teeth, I think."

Bobbi'd already drifted off again. Claire stepped back to the window. She wondered if Henry had managed to get Connor out of jail yet. She'd called him as soon as the police left.

GRAVY

Bobbi's and Connor's lives won't be easy. If that baby's brain's damaged like the doctor said, it will be awful.

When Bobbi finally woke up, the nurses settled her in a room. Claire followed along. She took Bobbi's hand and held it for a while before she began. "You've had a little girl. She's beautiful, of course." She spent a moment looking at the floor.

"What's wrong?"

Claire sighed. "The doctor says she may have brain damage because of the long labor."

"Because of the long labor . . ."

Claire interrupted. "We'll deal with him later—after we know more about the baby. She looks perfectly normal, so let's not despair yet."

Tears dripped along Bobbi's temples into her already-damp hair. "It's all my fault," she said. "I'm not woman enough to have a baby. I'm not normal."

"Why, that's nonsense, Bobbi. Where did you get such nonsense?"

"Well, it's true. If I'd been built like a normal woman, she wouldn't have had to go through all that."

"Bobbi, you're not the only woman who's needed a Cesarean. That doesn't mean there's something wrong with the baby."

"And it's like the doctor said, it's the babies that get hurt. If there's something wrong, it's my fault."

"No, Bobbi. That's not true. The doctor should have done that operation days ago."

"He was just trying to help."

"Help! Whatever do you mean?"

GRAVY

"He gave me these treatments to stretch me out so I could have a big family."

Claire narrowed her eyes. "What kind of treatments, Bobbi?"

"Where's Connor?" Bobbi struggled to raise herself on her elbows.

"He's in jail, Bobbi."

She dropped back on the pillow. "What for?"

"He tried to choke the doctor."

"No!"

Claire hesitated a long moment. "Bobbi, the doctor wants him charged with attempted murder."

"Murder?!"

Claire sat silent, hands resting in her lap.

"What're we gonna do? It's all my fault."

Claire rose and smoothed Bobbi's hair back from her forehead. "It is *not* your fault. You just get that out of your head right now."

"I can't. I'm ruining everybody I love. I've got to *do* something."

"*You* are going to concentrate on recovering and taking care of your daughter."

"But what about Connor?"

"Henry's on his way. But the roads aren't all plowed so I don't know how long it'll be."

"Plowed?"

"All the time you've been in here, it's been snowing, Bobbi."

"Snowing! Still? How long have I been here?"

"Since—four days now. Don't you remember? You came in the snow. There are at least four feet out there."

"What can Henry do?"

"He'll try to get him out on bail and find him a lawyer."

Bobbi groaned. "I'm gonna be raising a baby all by myself."

"No! You're not!"

"He'll never get out of this."

"He didn't kill anybody, Bobbi."

"They'll just put him away forever. They will."

"No, they won't."

They lapsed into silence. "All those months of taking those treatments—for nothing."

Claire took her hand. "Tell me about those treatments, Bobbi. I can't imagine what kind of treatments he could have done."

Bobbi's wan complexion turned scarlet. "I can't . . ."

"Bobbi, tell me."

"He . . . he said he could make me bigger so I wouldn't have to have a caesarian. He said I could only have a couple of babies if I had the surgery. He said . . ."

"Wait a minute. How on earth did he expect to make you bigger?"

She covered her face with her hands. "He had this instrument that he put inside me and kept expanding it. He said it would stretch the ligaments that hold my pelvis together."

Claire could barely make out her words through her hands, but she got the gist. Her own hands shook, and she took several deep breaths to steady herself. "I can't imagine how much that must have hurt."

"Like fire."

"Why didn't you tell us?" She wanted to run but she kept talking, keeping her voice calm. "We could have found another doctor."

"I didn't know what he was going to do and then I was afraid Connor would kill him." She took her hands away and looked into Claire's eyes. "Don't tell anybody. He's a specialist. Isn't he supposed to know what he's doing?"

Claire shook her head. "I don't know what kind of specialist puts his patients through what you've been through." She sighed. "Let's think about that later. I want to talk about you and the baby. First off, no matter what happens with Connor, you're not on your own."

"I can't earn a living here!"

"Nobody's talking about that. We'll take care of you. You're my daughter now."

Bobbi's tears welled up again. "I don't deserve you."

"Of course, you do, Bobbi. I don't know what's going to happen, but we'll take care of you and that baby. You can count on it. She's our first grandchild, you know."

Bobbi lay looking at the ceiling. "It just seems like everything I touch goes bad."

"Don't be thinkin' like that. Take hope."

"Hope," Bobbi murmured, drifting off to sleep. "Maybe we could call her Hope."

Later That Afternoon

Bobbi awoke to the sound of rapid footfalls in the hallway as the nurses hurried from patient to patient. When she opened her eyes, she saw Powers, humming and glancing through her chart.

"Well," he said cheerfully, "Our little experiment didn't work, did it?"

Bobbi, still groggy from the anesthetic, just stared at him. "What experiment?"

He smiled down at her, "Why, our attempt to stretch out your pelvis so you could give birth normally."

Annoyed by the doctor's manner in the face of all her pain and fear, she caught on the one word. "Experiment?"

"Why yes." Dr. Powers beamed. "It didn't work this time, but maybe next time it will."

"Wait a minute," Bobbi said, struggling to sit, her voice rising. "You used me as an experiment?"

"Calm down, Bobbi, you're getting hysterical. I did have to do the Caesarian, but it went well and next time . . ."

"Went well? You're telling me my baby may be badly damaged and you think it went well? And what the hell do you mean 'next time?' I want to know about this experiment."

"You're still recovering, Bobbi. You're likely to be a little confused."

"I am not confused. "You just said *your* experiment didn't work. The one about stretching me out. I want to know. You put me through all that torture for all those months for an *experiment!*"

GRAVY

"Now, Bobbi, you've just had major surgery . . ."

"I thought your so-called treatments were common practice. Now you're telling me they were an *experiment*?"

"I told you it didn't always work."

All the pain and humiliation of her prenatal visits and the agony of the past three days, trying and failing to deliver a child that was too big to bear combined in a rage with the confirmation that her suspicion had been correct. Dr. Powers was up to something besides delivering a healthy baby.

"Has it ever worked? Has it?"

"Now, Bobbi . . ."

"Don't Bobbi me. Has it ever worked? Has anyone else ever done this to his patients? Who else have you tortured?"

"I'm not torturing anyone. You're overwrought. You've just had surgery. You'll rupture your stitches."

"How many women have you tortured like this? How many babies have died while you let their mothers push themselves inside out? You miserable excuse for a human being."

He bristled, red creeping up his neck. "Now see here . . ."

"Get out of my sight. Don't you ever come back. Ever!"

"You've gone completely insane. I'm going to call the authorities and have you institutionalized." He turned and fled. She could hear his shoes slapping on the tiled floor as he hurried down the hall and she wondered if he could really put her in an institution like her grandmother.

Left alone with only the echo of her own voice, she realized the hospital had turned stone quiet. Leaning back on the pillow, she covered her face and wept, remembering the months of treatments and the humiliation. She remembered herself on the examining table, uncovered, feet in the stirrups, the hard, mechanical device ripping everything inside her just as an aide came into the room carrying food. She smelled peas or pea soup—something green and chalky. She gagged once and then, before the aide could get a basin for her, she leaned over the side of the bed, tears streaming, and splattered the bile from her empty stomach on the floor. Leaning there with her head hanging, she couldn't stop gagging and every one of her stitches seemed to rip with each heave.

March 3, 1947

Bobbi'd been dozing when she heard Henry's voice in the corridor.

"I know it's not visiting hours, but we waited three days for that baby to come and I've been busy all day seeing about her father."

"I just can't let you in."

"See, I need to see my daughter-in-law for myself, so's I can tell my wife. If I can't report to her, I'll be sleeping in the barn."

Bobbi heard the smile in Nurse Jolene's voice, "I doubt that, Mr. Conroy."

"You don't know Claire. She can be real mean."

"Well, if you'll be very quiet, I'll let you take a peek."

Bobbi heard Jolene's soft footsteps hurrying away.

Henry poked his head in.

"Hello, Pop."

He took her hand. "How are you, Bobbi? You don't look real good, if you don't mind me saying so."

"What is it you say? 'I feel like I been rode hard and put up wet?'"

"You do have that look."

 Did Mom tell you about the baby?"

"Yeah, but I wouldn't get too worked up about that. I'm not big on false hope and don't know much about what that doctor thinks is wrong, but I went over to see her. She looks all bright and smart—just like Connor and Nora when they were born."

"You think she'll be all right?"

"I think there's reason to hope. Only time will tell. I'm more worried about you."

"I'm all right, but I'm sure not gonna work any cattle with you this week."

Henry smiled. "That's the ticket."

"What're we gonna do about Connor?"

"Them lawyers have got the judge to let me bail him out, so I'm goin' to the jail after here."

"I didn't think they'd ever let him loose. If Powers had his way, they'd hang him."

"Nobody's gonna hang anybody, Bobbi. I reminded them lawyers that my boy's been over there fighting them Japs so they could sit here and make money."

"Did that make any difference?"

"The war ain't been over long, Bobbi. They'll still do just about anything for the soldiers. Anyway, I wanted to be able to tell 'im how you're doin' before they let 'im go. So he'll be prepared. He can't afford to blow up again."

"Tell him I'll be all right, Pop. I'm just plain exhausted and I feel like I'm torn up every which way but loose . . . Don't tell him the torn-up part."

"I'll tell 'im. You rest now; I'll go get 'im."

"Hurry, Pop. I want him to see the baby."

She smiled as Henry left. *It's sure nice to have someone to take care of things. I wish I deserved it.*

Henry left Bobbi to go to the Adams County Jail and pay Connor's bail. "Well. How is she?" Connor demanded once they'd climbed into Henry's car.

Henry glanced at his son, then back at the street. "She looks like something the cat dragged in . . . but she'll be all right."

Connor looked at his father, then back at the street. "What about the baby?"

"No telling yet, but she sure looks bright and alert. What did *you* think?"

"Aw, I barely saw her, they hadn't even cleaned her up yet. But she seemed all right."

"Cute as a button; all eyes watching everything that moves. I think that's a good sign."

Henry slowed for traffic, skidding a bit on the icy street.

"So you think she'll be all right?"

Henry responded as he gently accelerated. "I don't know, son. We'll just have to wait and see."

"What if she really *is* damaged?"

GRAVY

"If it comes, we'll deal with it, whatever it is." He slowed, rolled down the window, signaled his turn and made it, rolling the window back up. "For now, we'll just enjoy her."

In the hospital parking lot, Connor started to open his door.

"Just a minute," Henry grabbed his son's arm. "Before we go in there, I want you to know something."

"What's that?"

"That wife you brought home? She's as strong as they come. You want to keep her if you can."

"Boy Pop, I know it and I intend to."

"Just keep workin' on them blow ups."

Connor ducked his head. "I know, Pop. I'm tryin.'"

"I know you are, son, and I can see some difference, but what you did yesterday tells me you're not done. Just keep workin' on it."

They walked into the hospital together, their blue silhouettes preceding them on the snow: a tall, broad-shouldered son with his short, skinny, bandy-legged father.

They met Jolene again as they approached Bobbi's room.

"You again!"

"Yup, and this here's Connor, the baby's father."

"You're the one . . ." she began.

Connor gave her to a sheepish grin. "Uh huh."

"You're kind of a hero around here"

"I am?"

184

She looked over her shoulder. "Nobody much likes Powers."

Connor digested that for a moment. "I don't suppose that justifies choking him."

"Probably not." She gave him a long look. "Go on in. Just remember, she's been through the wringer. She's putting on a brave face. Try not to upset her."

"We promise," Henry said.

"I'll get the baby. I was on my way." She bustled off.

Connor walked in first, hanging his head. "I'm sorry, Bobbi. I shoulda been here."

"Look at me, Connor, I'm all right. It's my fault you went to jail."

"It was not. How can you say that?"

"Well, it is. If I'd just been able to have a normal birth . . ."

"You stop that right now. You can't blame yourself. It was the doctor. Bobbi, I don't want that doctor anywhere near you again. He's messin' with your mind."

Jolene popped in, carrying the baby. "Oh, you probably don't need to worry about that."

"Why not?" Bobbi and Connor asked together.

"I heard him asking one of the other surgeons to follow up with you, Bobbi."

"Really?!" Connor said. "I don't suppose he wants to see *me* again."

"Actually, I think it was Bobbi."

Connor turned to his wife. She blushed. "You heard that, Jolene?"

"I think everybody in the hospital heard it."

"What?"

"Oh, Connor, he just came in when I was still groggy and, instead of thanking him for trying to help, I yelled at him."

"What did you say?".

"Well, she . . ." Jolene began, but Bobbi gave her a little shake of the head.

"She told the doc to back off," Jolene mumbled, handing the baby to Connor. "Here you are. Just support her . . . Oh. You already know."

"I was the first grandchild, so I always had a lot of little cousins to babysit." He turned to Henry. "I guess Edna's were the last ones."

"They were the last when you were in high school."

"If you don't need me for anything . . ." Jolene took off to answer the buzzer they could hear in the corridor.

"I've been thinking, Connor."

"Me too. I'm really sorry I blew up like that. It's just that Powers told us that our little girl . . . he left you so long . . . and then he said she'd been injured."

"I know, Connor. That's what I've been thinking about."

"What about it?"

"Well, since Powers doesn't give her much of a chance, I think we should call her Hope."

Henry grinned. "Now you're gettin' it!"

186

"I was thinking Faith, as in 'have faith and it'll turn out all right," Connor said. He thought a minute. "But I like Hope better."

"Then we'll name her Hope. Everybody's tired of calling her 'the Conroy baby.'"

Part Five

March 18, 1947 — Willow Grove

Two weeks later, Bobbi left the hospital. The snow had melted and dried up, but a cold wind blew steady from the northwest. As she stepped out of the car with Hope in her arms, she surveyed her home, a stark little white house that was open to the sky. She glanced at Connor's little trees and wondered how long before they could protect the house. She'd never thought about shelter from the wind before she left Ohio. She wished she could turn off the storm in her head.

Claire arrived early every afternoon and helped, but Bobbi couldn't seem to regain her strength. She moped around listlessly, afraid to make eye contact. She feared that Connor might see something in her eyes. After his attack on the doctor, she realized he could never know what the doctor had done.

On Easter Sunday, they all had dinner at Henry and Claire's. Bobbi stood in the kitchen, helping, when Henry came in bleeding from a barbed wire cut to his palm. "Where's the iodine?"

"I don't think there is any." Claire said. "There's alcohol in the cabinet. Bandages, too."

Henry got out the alcohol and poured it into the cut. Bobbi got a whiff of it, and Dr. Powers's examining room flashed into her mind. She dropped the pie she was carrying. She stood crying and shaking.

Claire gathered her in her arms, "What's the matter?"

"I don't know. I just dropped the pie."

"That's not important. We'll clean it up."

"But it's Connor's favorite."

"It doesn't matter, Bobbi."

"I ruin everything."

"No, you don't, Bobbi. What are you talking about?"

"I . . . oh I don't know."

Henry finished with the alcohol and replaced the lid, wrapping his hand in gauze, as Bobbi calmed. He frowned at his wife who shrugged, then turned back to her daughter-in-law as he left the room.

Claire released her. "Look, I'll just clean this up and then we'll go in the parlor and talk."

"I'm all right."

"I think you need to talk about it."

"I've already talked too much." She took a step closer, lowering her voice in a fierce whisper. "You can never tell Connor." She blinked back tears. "Or Henry either, or anyone." She squeezed her eyes shut, then looked deep into Claire's. "Promise me!"

"Or course not, but is there anything I can do?"

"I don't think so. I just have to forget it. It's just little things I don't expect. Smells. A sound. I'm being silly."

Claire grabbed her shoulders, giving her a gentle shake. "You're not silly. You've been through torment and you need time to get over it."

With Bobbi calmer and the mess cleaned up, they all sat down to dinner. Connor joined them a little late.

GRAVY

"I got that fence spliced," he said. "How's your hand, Pop?"

"Gonna be sore, but I got it wrapped up."

Bobbi heard the men's discussion of farm prices, work that needed doing, and the weather as a comforting buzz. "Bobbi," Claire said as they finished the meal, "I've been thinking. We'll have the corn in the ground before long."

Bobbi nodded.

"Your mom and dad haven't seen Hope yet. Maybe you and Connor should go to Cleveland for a week or so to show her off."

Bobbi looked at Connor. He smiled, "That's a great idea. What do you think? Let's go show off our baby!"

"I don't know. They're pretty busy with that new restaurant."

"We could call them and see. Maybe there's a time . . ."

"A restaurant's a lot like milking cows, Connor. You have to be there every day."

"Maybe your mom could take a little time while your dad covers for her. Let's just call."

"Okay," Bobbi said. "It would be nice to see some of my friends, and I guess we could see my folks at the restaurant if nothing else."

When they finished dinner, Bobbi and Claire cleaned up while Henry rocked Hope in the cradle he'd made for her while the two men talked about their timetable for spring planting.

"What do you think?" Connor asked when they got home that evening. "Would a little time with your mother help get over the baby blues?"

"Probably not." Bobbi swaddled Hope for the night. "But it would feel really good to see some of my friends."

GRAVY

May 3, 1947— Cleveland, Ohio

Bobbi and Connor arrived in Cleveland late on a Friday evening. They thought the restaurant would be closed on Sunday so Bobbi could catch up with her friends on Saturday and spend time with her parents on Sunday. After two days of travel, they checked in to their hotel, put Hope down for the night and fell into bed, exhausted.

Connor slept poorly. Bobbi knew because he couldn't be still.

"What's wrong?"

He sighed. "It's the constant din. Doesn't it ever stop?"

Eventually, they both slept and next morning they were parked across from the café. "Bobbi darted through the first opening in traffic, but the bleat of a car horn made her turn to see Connor juggling the bassinette, hurrying to catch up.

Once inside the building. Connor caught his breath for a moment and chuckled. "Here I am juggling the baby with people bouncing off me on both sides and you're practically dancing on the street, ducking between clumps of people. How do you do it?"

She shrugged. "I don't know, Connor. Been doing it since I could walk."

They stepped inside her parents' restaurant and found a table, then they took Hope into the kitchen. Her dad cooked while Mom waited tables—just like the old days. Bobbi wondered if they had quit screaming at each other after the divorce.

"Hi, Dad." Bobbi grinned, holding up the gurgling infant. "I brought your granddaughter."

"Hi yourself." He glanced up from the eggs he was frying. "When'd you get in?"

"Last night."

191

"Baby looks okay to me."

"We think she's gonna be all right."

"Hope so." He turned the eggs.

"Mom's out front?"

He nodded without interrupting his rhythm.

"Well . . . I guess I'll see you later."

Back at their table, Bobbi waved when she spotted her mother, but Ella nodded and kept running meals out to her customers.

"They knew we were coming?"

"Yes. Remember what I said. A restaurant's a lot like milking cows. You have to be there every day. Every single day."

"Looks like."

"Maybe Mom'll have a minute to talk when she waits our table. It looks like it's slowing down."

"Maybe so." Connor looked at the menu. "What would you like to eat?"

She slipped Hope back in the bassinette. The baby lay kicking and reaching for a rattle Connor had tied to the handle, cooing to herself.

"I was afraid she'd be scared or fussy, but she seems contented." Bobbi checked the menu. "This sure isn't Mowry's, but it's good they got back into business."

She chose an omelet and Connor decided on steak and eggs with hashed brown potatoes.

Ella came up to the table from behind Bobbi to take their order.

GRAVY

"Mom! How are you?"

"I'm very busy."

"I thought it looked like you were slowing down a little."

Ella scanned the restaurant. "Not much. What'll ya have?"

Bobbi looked back down at her menu, while Connor ordered for them. "I knew they wouldn't have time." Ella hustled away. "I guess I just hoped." She trailed off.

"Maybe they'll have a little more time later."

They ate their breakfast and waited for the Bowens to have a little time, but even when the breakfast crowd cleared out, Ella remained in the kitchen, prepping napkins and silverware for the next shift. Paul made up his grocery list and checked the accounts. Bobbi took her daughter and Connor back to see them once more.

"Mom, Dad, this is my husband, Connor."

"Pleased to meet you." Her dad shook Connor's hand and went back to his books.

"Likewise." Ella looked him up and down without stopping her napkin folding.

"Wouldn't you like to see the baby?" Bobbi took Hope from the bassinette.

"Saw 'er." Paul entered a figure in his account book.

Ella laid the napkins down and took the baby from Bobbi. She held her up and looked her over. "Don't see nothin' wrong with her." Ella handed her back and started filling mustard and catsup bottles.

"Well, I guess we'll go back to the hotel."

"Okay," Paul said.

"I'll see you tomorrow?"

"We'll be here."

"I thought you were closed Sundays."

"Got to catch up. You know how it works."

Bobbi sighed and returned Hope to the bassinette. "Let's go, Connor." She saw him frown. "We knew they'd be busy on a Saturday." They walked out on the street. "Let's go find a phone. I want to call Mary. I wrote her I was coming, and she wants to meet you."

"There's phone in our room. We can go there and get comfortable. Maybe Mary can meet us."

As soon as she had Hope changed, fed and settled down for a nap, Bobbi called her childhood best friend. They arranged for Mary to join them. "I can't wait," she said.

"Me either."

When Bobbi opened the door about a half-hour later, Mary burst through, grabbing her in a bear hug. The two women held each other for a long minute, then Mary pushed away and took a good long look. "You look great! Just great! That fresh farm air must be good for you." She turned to Connor. "And you must be that big handsome husband I've been hearing about!"

Connor grinned. "I'm the husband anyway. It's good to meet you."

Mary turned back to Bobbi. "We had some really good times, didn't we Bobbi?"

"Sure did. Is Euclid Beach Park still the same?"

"Pretty much. Hey, Kate was wondering yesterday when you'd get here. We gotta call her."

"How about Helen?"

"You haven't heard? She joined the WASPs, those service pilots. You know about them, don't you?"

"Yeah. I'm surprised she didn't bring any planes into Peterson Field. Where is she now?"

"I don't know. We kept in touch for a while, but I lost track after the war. But where's that baby? I want to see her for myself."

When Mary peered at her, she saw Hope's wide blue eyes looking back.

"My gosh, look at those blue eyes—and that blonde hair! Can I pick her up, since she's awake?"

Mary lifted Hope from the bassinette and cradled her on her shoulder, bouncing her slightly. "Is she always this quiet?"

"She's been a really quiet baby." Bobbi glanced at Connor. "We're worried . . ."

"She's been an angel coming over here.," Connor interrupted. "Seems like she's just taking in all the changes, looking around at everything."

"She slept a lot in the car and just laid in the back seat playing with her toes when she was awake."

Hope snuggled into Mary's shoulder.

"You've always been kind of a natural mother, haven't you? You always took care of the rest of us."

"Except you. You, by golly, took care of yourself!"

"I was a little hard-headed, wasn't I?"

"Still are," Connor smiled.

Bobbi gave him a squinty-eyed look.

"It's one of the things I love about you."

"Speaking of taking care of yourself—you seen Ella and Paul yet?"

"We just came from the restaurant."

"They doin' all right?"

"I guess so. They didn't really have any time."

"They never did."

"Well, it's Saturday. Their busiest day."

She walked around joggling Hope on her shoulder, her eyes flashing. "They didn't!"

"Not a whole lot, I guess. They were struggling."

"Who wasn't? I'm sorry, Bobbi, but they were too busy slashing and jabbing at each other to take care of you. Sending you out . . ."

"Let's not talk about it anymore," Bobbi pleaded, but Mary hadn't finished.

She turned to Connor. "You should know this girl was the only parent in her family an' a damn good one she was, too."

"Mary!"

"All right, I'll shut up."

Connor glanced at Bobbi and changed the subject. "What about your friend, Kate? Weren't you gonna call her?"

Kate joined them in minutes and after her introductions, the two Clevelanders explained that their husbands and kids were waiting to meet them at Euclid Beach Park. "The dining room on the lake's still open," Mary said, "and we can all afford it now."

Ralph and Ed, Mary and Kate's husbands, had organized the beach umbrellas, bathing suits, and kids while their wives met with the Conroys.

"You brought bathing suits?" Kate demanded.

Bobbi giggled. "Of course."

A few minutes later, as they passed under the arches at Euclid Beach, Bobbi felt a twinge of unease—like a lost life. The sudden memory of Jack gave her a sharp, unexpected ache. Their last night at the beach and the *Plaindealer* headline reporting his murder a few months later swam into her mind.

"You alright?"

She glanced up at her frowning husband. "Just a memory."

"Doesn't look like a very happy one."

"They weren't all good times." She tried to perk up. She smiled. "But this will be."

After romping on the beach and a cold swim—only Bobbi and the kids braved the early temperatures—they packed up and dropped the kids with Mary's mom. Then they had a slow dinner at Mia Bella's in Little Italy and moved on to Danceland where Freddie Caloni's musicians—back from the Army, performed as house band. They took tables near the bandstand. Carloni immediately recognized Bobbi and asked her to take the mic for a few numbers. Then the friends danced and chatted until closing.

Bobbi and Connor returned to their hotel with Hope and sore feet. "You looked like you really enjoyed singing," Connor remarked as he undressed for bed.

197

"I did, kind of," she said, smiling.

Sunday, May 5, 1947 — Cleveland

The following day, Connor paced the dining room while Bobbi tried to chat with her mother. They'd found her parents at the café at eight in the morning.

"Well," Ella said, "this is our only chance to clean up and take care of things we always put off when we're busy—which is all the time."

"But Mom, couldn't you take a little time just to chat? You don't have any customers on Sunday."

"Time's money, honey. We're makin' some money here and your dad's too busy to spend it on the ponies and booze. And, since you're not sendin' us anything anymore, we gotta keep working."

Connor stopped his circuit around the café. *So that's her beef? Bobbi's not sending them money anymore?*

"Mom, I have a husband and baby now. It's not mine to send."

"Well, it's different for us. We don't have anyone to pay our bills for us."

"But Mom, you seem to be doing very well here."

"We're doin' all right. But we're not kids. We gotta make it now while we can. Remember all those years we didn't make anything."

"Because you were too busy collecting Bobbi's checks," Connor muttered under his breath. He continued walking, wondering why Bobbi didn't tell her mother to buzz off.

"Bobbi, I've got to get back to work." Ella walked away.

Connor watched Bobbi wilt, staring at her mother's retreating back.

"C'mon, Bobbi." He took her elbow. "Let's go back to the hotel. Mary said she was gonna call you and we don't want to miss her."

Bobbi snuggled Hope and stood, walking along beside her husband without a word. Back im the car. Conner saw tears in her eyes. "Why isn't anything ever enough for her?"

"I don't know, Bobbi. You've certainly given them more than any parent should ever expect. I know you're hurt, but it's not you. It's them." He pulled out in traffic.

"I don't think they ever wanted me."

"Oh Bobbi, that's not true." He rolled down the window and signaled a left.

"I think I was a nasty surprise and there's nothing I can do to make up for it."

"Bobbi, your parents wouldn't appreciate a solid gold Cadillac." He signaled a right and rolled the window back up.

"Well, I *did* kind of leave them in the lurch when I got out of the Army. I'd been sending money home."

"I sent money home, too, but my dad saved it for *me*."

"I know, but Mom and Dad have never had anything—no land, or home, or money to start in business." She glanced at him. "Remember, Dad was an orphan and Mom's parents disowned her for marrying him."

"Now don't you go hanging your head." Connor pulled up beside the hotel and turned his keys over to the valet. He took the bassinette, slung the diaper bag over his shoulder, and handed Bobbi out of the car. "Let's go call Mary. She'll perk you up."

"She's busy, Connor. She said she'd call me."

"So, no reason you can't call her instead, is there?"

They headed for the elevator, but the concierge stopped them in the lobby with a note. Mary had already called.

"How'd it go with your parents this morning?" Mary demanded as soon as she answered.

"Oh, they're pretty busy."

"So, they won't even have time for dinner with you?"

"They're ordering next week's groceries, catching up the books, cleaning up—you know, prep stuff."

"You and Connor and your baby are all alone?"

"I guess that's right."

"Nope. Not right. You're having lunch with us and dinner, too. I want you to get right back in your car and get yourselves over here right now."

"Mary, I couldn't impose on your family."

"The heck you can't. You get right over here, or I'll come and get you."

"Mary, you've grown into a regular drill sergeant." She hesitated a minute. "Let me ask Connor."

Bobbi's smiled at her husband. "Mary wants to know if we'll come over now for lunch and dinner at her house. Is that all right?"

Connor grinned. "Sounds like we don't have any choice. Let's get right back in our car and get ourselves right over there right now."

GRAVY

"You heard."

"Couldn't miss a drill sergeant voice like that."

On the way over, Bobbi told Connor about how Ralph and the rest of her friends had helped build up crowd enthusiasm for her when she entered the contest that started her singing career. "And Ralph brought all his brothers and sisters," she concluded, "and that's a big crowd. I think there are ten of them. Some of them were married and they brought their families."

They arrived to an enthusiastic welcome, especially from Mary's little boys, Chet and Jim, who had decided the previous day that Connor would be their buddy. While the women set the table, Connor thanked his new friend for all the help he and his family had given Bobbi.

"Aw, we all loved Bobbi. We thought she deserved a break . . . although I'm not sure we did her a favor."

"How's that?"

"Seems like we gave her folks the idea she could support them forever."

"I don't know about that, but they didn't have to take all her Army pay to buy that restaurant. They could have got a loan like everybody else."

"I don't know what to think. Doesn't seem like they've treated her very well."

"Don't seem very grateful for everything she's done for 'em."

Mary interrupted with orders for Ralph. "Come carve the roast." He shrugged and left Connor with the boys who piled on him the moment their dad left the room. "Whoa guys," said Connor, but before long, he had one under each arm spinning them around.

201

"Hey!" Ralph returned from the kitchen. "What do you guys think you're doing? Connor isn't here to rough house with you." He turned to Connor. "Sorry."

"It's fine. It was kinda my idea."

"I can imagine."

"It was, Dad," the boys chorused.

"All right, all right. If it's okay with Connor."

Connor grinned. "It is." He watched them run off to wash up. "Good kids."

Wish we could have a couple of boys like that, but after the fiasco having Hope, that doesn't seem likely. Maybe one. That would be okay. He sighed. *But maybe not.*

June 2, 1947 — Willow Grove

Bobbi sat alone on the couch, staring at a little bit of cloth in her hands. At last, Hope had fallen asleep, and Connor had taken a load of corn to town. She'd had to argue with him to go.

She'd smiled and told him to "get going," but, only a half-hour later, she wished she hadn't sent him away. Hope's cough was worse and her low, rattling struggle for breath frightened her. The way every one of her little ribs stuck out when she sucked in a breath made Bobbi want to jump in the car, and take her to Doc O'Neill, but Connor had taken the car to his dad's place to get the truck. She had to wait for him. She fiddled with the sleeper she'd been sewing, hearing the baby's breathing in the next room.

Oh my God, I've got to do something. She paced, throwing the sleeper on the couch. *What can I do? She's gonna die while I sit here thinking what to do.* She ran into the kitchen and cranked the telephone.

"Mom, I don't know what to do," she cried the instant Claire picked up the receiver.

"What's wrong, Bobbi? Are you all right?"

"Hope's sick!"

"Connor said she had a little croup."

"Mom, she can't breathe. I can hear her breathing, even in the next room."

"I'll come." Claire hung up the phone.

By the time Claire arrived, Bobbi sat on the couch, beating her fists on her thighs. She'd bitten her lip until it bled. Claire walked directly into the nursery with Bobbi right behind.

"Bring me a sheet."

Bobbi ran to the linen closet and grabbed one.

"Here's what we're gonna do." Claire began draping the sheet over the crib. "Give me a hand." Once they had the crib draped, she went into the kitchen and dipped hot water from the stove reservoir with Bobbi following close behind. "Bring one of the kitchen chairs," she ordered over her shoulder.

Bobbi fetched the chair. "Now put it next to the crib—just so she can't reach it."

Bobbi set the chair in place.

"Facing the crib."

She turned it around.

"Now, we'll put the steaming water on the chair." She demonstrated. Take that sheet up and over the back of the chair."

She stepped back. "Good. We've made her a little tent. She gets more of the steam that way."

She put an arm around Bobbi's shoulders. "The water will cool pretty fast, so we'll have to change it. In fact, let's heat some more on the stovetop."

She found a suitable pan, filled it from the little pitcher pump just outside the door, quickly pumping the handle, and set it on the stove.

"Now." Claire sat on the couch, pulling Bobbi down beside her. "We're not going to wake her, because sleep is the best thing for her, but I brought some Vicks and when she wakes up, we're gonna rub it on her chest."

"Will she be all right?"

"I'm sure she will, but I'm more worried about you."

"Me?!"

Claire caught Bobbi's gaze and held it. "Bobbi, most people don't beat up on themselves when they have a sick child."

"I'm not."

"When I walked through that door, you were pounding on your thighs with your *fists*. Your lip's still bleeding. How can I help you get past what that doctor did to you??"

"There's nothing you can do."

"You've been saying that for months now. You've got to let me help you."

Bobbi exploded into tears. "I can't even have a baby right!"

Claire gathered her daughter-in-law into her arms. "There's no right way to have a baby, Bobbi. You just have it the best you can."

"She's damaged and it's all my fault. She's gonna die because of me."

"She is *not* going die. She has croup. Babies get croup. It doesn't have anything to do with you."

"But the doctor said . . ."

Claire leaned back, holding Bobbi by the shoulders and looking into her eyes. "Doctors don't know everything."

"But he says I can only have one or two more babies."

"So? How many do you need?"

"Connor wants a big family." Bobbi sniffled and grabbed a tissue.

"I did too, Bobbi, but I didn't get it and life went on."

"But . . ."

"Let's not worry about big families. One or two's plenty, don't you think?"

"For me . . . but how do I keep from getting pregnant? Connor wants . . . well you know what he wants."

Claire chuckled. "I guess I do, but mothers don't usually think of their sons that way. Didn't that doctor help you with that?"

"With what?"

"With not getting pregnant."

"He explained about 'safe days' but by the time he was done, it seemed like there weren't any."

GRAVY

"How about rubbers? How about a diaphragm?

"He said rubbers break about seventy percent of the time and, since I'm too narrow to give birth normally, I couldn't use a diaphragm."

"What?"

"He said . . ."

Claire raised her hand. "I heard. I just don't believe."

"I'm not making this up."

"Of course not." Claire sat silent for a few minutes. Bobbi watched her face for any sign of disgust or rejection.

"Bobbi, Doc O'Neill can help you with this. I don't know too much about it because we always wanted more children, but Doc does, I'm sure. That doctor in Hastings—I don't know what he's up to."

"Oh Claire, I can't anymore."

"Can't what?"

"I can't . . . you know."

"Does it *still* hurt?"

Bobbi hung her head. She whispered, "I don't know. We haven't done it. Every time we try. It's like I'm in that doctor's office again."

"You have to tell Connor."

"I can't."

"But Bobbi, he needs to know so he'll understand. He'll give you time."

"Mom, he already tried to kill that doctor once. They're gonna try him for attempted murder. He can't know."

Claire got up and peeked into the nursery. "No. you're right. But you've been bearing this all by yourself for all these months. I'm so sorry."

Bobbi twiddled the tissue in her lap. "It's all right."

"Bobbi, look at me," Claire commanded. Bobbi raised her eyes from her lap. "It is *not* all right. None of it's all right. But I'm here and I hope you know you can talk to me."

Bobbi nodded, tears seeping from the corners of her eyes.

"Connor doesn't try to pressure you, does he?"

"No. Never. But he's just so disappointed."

"Look, Bobbi, we're gonna solve this somehow." She remained silent for several moments as Bobbi wept quietly. "Connor's been asking Pop and me what to do. Now I know what I'm gonna tell him."

Bobbi looked up, fear in her eyes.

"No, I won't tell him your secret. I'll just say that women sometimes go through a real bad emotional time after they give birth, and you need time to recover."

Bobbi nodded.

"Now I hear that water boiling, so we need to put it in the nursery."

The two women sat and chatted about the farm and the crops, recipes and the new linoleum they would lay in Claire's kitchen in the spring—until Hope woke. The baby still panted, but Bobbi saw an improvement. They rubbed her chest with Vicks and wrapped her up in an undershirt and fresh sleeper.   Then Bobbi watched her mother-in-law walk out to the car. She wondered if Claire was right. Would she ever recover enough to enjoy her husband again?

June 15, 1947

Connor and Bobbi limped along, each suffering outbursts when they least expected them. They watched Hope for signs of trouble, but at less than four months, they had no idea how she would develop. Between watching and waiting, they even managed to have a few good moments.

Connor crawled out of bed before dawn, soaked in sweat, exhausted and stiff from trying to get some sleep without thrashing around and waking Bobbi.

"Bad night?" she mumbled.

"Mmmhmm. Go back to sleep."

"Let me get you some breakfast."

"Not hungry. Go ahead and sleep some more."

She rolled over, still half asleep, and drifted off while he slipped into his clothes and stepped into the dimly lit cavern of the kitchen where he sat at the table with his head in his hands. He glanced at the table under his elbows and noticed a tablet and a pen. Bobbi had written letters the previous evening. He picked up the pen and started doodling, but soon realized he'd written names. Mendez. Green. Moore. Wilson . . . *I'm turning into Uncle Harry.* He dropped the pen and scrambled for the door. In rising daylight, he practically ran to the barn. *I wonder what I'm doing here.* He glanced around trying to get his bearings.

Leaning against the wall in the feed room, he noticed a scythe still standing in the corner. He picked it up, raising a puff of dust. *Old Robinson must have left it. I wonder why I haven't noticed it before.* He remembered the grass growing in his new shelterbelt, the rows too close to mow with the tractor. He took the scythe outside and made a tentative swing. He tested the blade—still sharp.

Connor carried his prize to the trees and started swinging— swish, swish, swish—slicing big bluestem with its turkey-track awns, needle-and-thread, crested wheatgrass, bunches of little bluestem, and a scattering of wildflowers—purple coneflower, blanket flower, brown-eyed Susans. Soon he whistled, *Oh Susanna*, in rhythm with the stroke of the implement.

When Henry arrived at the neighboring hayfield, he found Connor swinging the scythe. He stopped the tractor and walked over, smiling." "We have machinery to do that now. It's faster."

"I know." Connor continued the swinging slice of the two-handed implement. "But I wasn't thinking tractors when I planted these. The rows are too close for the sickle and this actually feels pretty good."

His dad watched for a while. "You sure haven't forgotten how to use that thing."

"Used to be my favorite job and the swing, the swish of the slice, the smell of the new-mown hay. It's kind of soothing."

"Well, you just keep cutting. I'll pick up the sickle-mower in the yard. I'll have this one done by noon."

"Dry as it is, we can probably rake this afternoon."

"Maybe stack in a couple of days."

Connor moved on with the scythe. He noticed white and yellow sweet clover as they fell before the knife, along with little bluestem, love grass, and brome.

He inhaled the sweet clover and sighed. Underfoot, he noted some purple poppy mallow and buffalo grass. Silver-leaf scurf-pea stood out with its grayish foliage. *This grass looks healthy—*

a few legumes to add nitrates, some good, nutritious grass, even some wildflowers for the bees. He smiled to himself. For a few hours, the rhythm of his work, the sun's warmth, the blade's swish, and the smell of cut grass had erased, at least for a moment, the guilt of survival. Connor stood right inside himself, in his trees, in his present moment. He felt, for that moment, as though he'd nudged a stuck phonograph needle, endlessly repeating a fragment of sound, and released it to play the music.

He grinned. He felt like dancing.

July 20, 1947

Somehow, Bobbi felt keyed up—like her life had gone out of kilter again. She wanted to sit on the front step and cry. *About what?* Nothing unusual had happened since her bored cocker spaniel had crawled into the hog lots and got his fur all clotted with mud wallowing with his favorite runt pig. Connor had said a spaniel wasn't a good farm dog, but he'd been so cute in the pet store.

Maybe I'm bored. She shook her head as if to shake cobwebs out of it. *Doesn't feel like boredom. Feels like jumping out of my skin.* It had come on her—like a tub full of dirty laundry poured over her head—when she was making the noon meal. She hadn't cooked anything complicated, just a beef roast with potatoes and carrots. She'd heated a can of peas to go with the roast. She'd felt a little queasy as she set the table.

Connor stepped in and washed up, then swept Hope out of her bassinette. He swung her over his head, careful not to bump her head on the low ceiling. He paced around the kitchen, chucking her under the chin.

"Take her in the living room. You're in my way."

Bobbi noticed her husband's sharp look as he complied.

210

GRAVY

When Connor and Bobbi sat down to eat, Bobbi propped Hope in her highchair and grabbed some peas she'd mashed. She aimed a spoonful at Hope's mouth, but her daughter didn't open. She put the spoon back into the bowl and took a few bites from her own plate. Her throat closed a little bit when she sampled the peas, but she swallowed and returned to feeding Hope.

"What do you think about going to the Legion Club Saturday night?" Connor asked.

Hope spit the peas back. "Stop it!"

Hope shrank back into the chair.

"What did you say?"

Connor was frowning when Bobbi looked up. "I asked what you think about going to the Legion Club."

"Fine. Do whatever you want." She turned back to shoveling peas into Hope's mouth.

Connor frowned and said nothing. Hope kept spitting the peas. Bobbi became increasingly agitated.

"Would you like me to feed her this time?"

"No. I wouldn't like you to feed her. You let her spit out more than she eats."

"I'll clean it up then."

"No." She kept shoveling peas.

Connor sighed. "How about I get something else for her."

"She's got to learn to eat her vegetables." *Why can't I let this go? Why am I so angry?* She didn't remember that she'd been eating peas in the hospital when Powers had revealed his experiment. She tried another spoonful, but Hope had clenched her jaw.

GRAVY

Bobbi scraped the peas off her daughter's face with the spoon and offered it again. Hope didn't budge.

"Eat your peas!"

"There are other vegetables, Bobbi."

"Just leave us alone!"

"Bobbi, it isn't worth . . ."

"I know what I'm doing!"

"You're scaring her."

"I'll scare her all right. Just let me be."

"Bobbi . . ."

"Enough."

Connor stalked off while Bobbi tried again. When Hope refused to cooperate, she released the highchair tray, grabbed the little girl and smacked her bottom.

Connor strode back into the room. "Bobbi. No."

Bobbi returned her daughter to her highchair, crying, and started again. "She has to learn!"

"Not like this."

Bobbi got a spoonful into Hope's mouth. The baby gagged and threw up on the tray. Bobbi's eyes watered and she swallowed a heave. "You little brat!" She grabbed the child out of the highchair and spanked again. Hope screamed.

"Give that baby to me. Now!"

Bobbi glared at him but handed over the child. "She wants to cry? I'll give her something to cry about." She remembered hearing the same words in her mother's voice. *What am I doing? I swore I'd never say those things if I ever had kids.*

Connor frowned. "You already have." He cuddled the sobbing child against his chest, then he crouched next to Bobbi, who was crying herself. When he put an arm around her, she relaxed a little against his warmth. "Bobbi. Calm down. We'll figure this out."

Tendrils of scent—warm peas—continued to circulate in the room. Bobbi couldn't quite put them together with what she felt, but she broke out of Connor's grasp, grabbed the jar of peas, stepped out onto the porch and pitched them as far across the yard as she could.

"There. No more peas. Ever."

Connor stared at her. She saw the question in his eyes but had no idea how to answer.

Later Outside

Once Connor had assured himself that she'd regained control, he went to check on the sows in the Wahoo building. The pigs were ready to separate and fatten. He'd decided he could move them and stay close to the house, where he could check on Hope and Bobbi throughout the afternoon.

When he had the feeder pigs moved to the empty west lot and the sows kicked out of the farrowing shed, Connor returned to the house. He found Bobbi, red-eyed, hands in dishwater. He didn't ask why it had taken two hours to wash the dishes.

"Where's Hope?"

Bobbi pointed at the bassinette in the corner with her chin.

"You all right?"

She shrugged. He handed her a dishtowel, turned her away from the sink, and slipped an arm around her. He looked into her eyes. "Tell me."

She shrugged him off and sat on a kitchen chair, hands covering her face. "I can't help myself." She glanced up at him. "I'm so mean, and I don't know why." She looked at the bassinette. "I've turned my daughter against me."

"You haven't turned her against you."

"But I have. Every time I try to cuddle her, she pushes me away."

Connor picked up his daughter, he held her at eye level, and looked into her eyes. Then he set her on Bobbi's lap. Careful not to frighten the infant, Bobbi petted her, smoothing her sleeper and combing her hair with her fingers.

"She'll get over it, but I don't think peas will ever be her favorite food."

Bobbi groaned.

"I don't like 'em much either, but it hasn't ruined my life."

"I'm sorry Connor. I'm not much of a mother."

"You're a good mother most of the time, Bobbi, but something has happened to you. I don't know what it is."

"I'll do better, Connor, I know I can."

"Bobbi, I know you're trying, but something's happened to you. Is it what Mom says? Did having the baby make you depressed?"

"I don't think so."

"Mom said sometimes the hormones get all out of whack. She said it gets better."

She handed Hope to him and left the room. He followed her.

"Let's not talk about this anymore right now."

He dropped his head. "I have to get back outside," he said finally. "I've got a cow out."

"Just go take care of the cow."

"You're more important than the cow."

"Just go."

He handed Hope to his wife and left the house.

After chasing the cow around the wheat stubble a few times, Connor almost blew up himself. The wind had picked up and that didn't help his attitude or the cow's. He finally got lucky when he had her lined up with the break in the fence for the fourth time. As she turned her head and bolted past him again, a piece of an old feed sack came loose from the wagon and spooked her right into the pasture. "Well halleluiah," he muttered as the cow trotted off, tail raised.

He grabbed the fence stretcher, cut a piece of wire, and repaired the hole. He thought about Bobbi and Hope as he ratcheted up the barbed wire. The blow up he'd just witnessed had him worried. *What happens when I'm not there?* He caught his thumb on a barb, jerked his hand back, and sucked his thumb. "Damn." He wiped it on his trousers.

She's almost as shellshocked as I am. I don't know what she would have done if I hadn't been there. He gathered his fencing tools. *Maybe it's me. Maybe my craziness just gets on her nerves so much it's making her crazy too.* He placed the fence stretcher on the wagon and reached for the coffee can of staples just as a gust of wind upset it, scattering staples into the stubble.

"*Damn it!*" Squatting on his heels, he picked up staples, shoving wheat stubble aside to find the hidden ones. *She can't stand to have me touch her anymore.* He poked around in the dirt. *I try to*

215

be gentle and wait for her, but I've been waiting a long time. He picked up a final staple and stood. *Something happened to her when she was pregnant. She's not the same. She's all bowed down, and then she blows up.*

As he put the tools in the shed, he considered what he could possibly do to protect Hope without frightening Bobbi. It seemed obvious she feared something. Connor knew what fear looked like.

He walked to the house, to check one more time, and found Hope asleep and Bobbi working in the kitchen, singing. "Mmmm," he said. "I love to hear you sing. Are you feeling better?"

She flung her arms around his neck. "Much. You don't have to check on me anymore. Go ahead and get your work done. Supper will be ready in about an hour."

August 1, 1947

Bobbi stepped outside to pull a few carrots from the garden for a roast. As she dug a handful of vegetables, the wind suddenly gusted, blowing dirt in her eyes. Blinking and crying, she gathered them up and hurried to the house. Back outside she filled a bucket from the pitcher pump. The wind picked up to a steady roar while she splashed her weeping eyes, blinking out water and dirt.

She checked on Hope, still blinking away tears and wondering how long the baby would nap. She wiped her eyes on a dishtowel and peeled the carrots, adding them to the roast and sliding it into the oven. She stood, hands on her hips, listening to the wind howling around the corner of the house. She couldn't get used to that sound. She heard a door outside, banging in the wind. She ran out to latch it.

GRAVY

Out in the field planting winter wheat, Connor got a face full of dirt from the first gusts. He ducked his head and narrowed his eyes when he turned into the rising gale. Finishing the last pass, he raised the planter and headed for home.

His tears made streaks in the dirt on his face, but he kept working to park and unhook the planter also emptying the planter boxes. He'd just finished when he heard a door banging. Following the sound, he watched black clouds climb the sky as he ran. He spotted Bobbi just before he reached the tool shed. He shot the latch shut as she came up beside him.

Click.

The sound of the wet latch closing became Dr. Powers' "spreader" locking. Bobbi screamed, pounding with her fists on Connor's chest. She felt him trying to restrain her, but she bit and kicked, struggling to escape. She barely heard the thunder tearing across the prairie like a runaway team, wild-eyed and snorting. She kept fighting as Connor pulled her to the ground screaming, "Incoming."

She felt herself dragged, helpless, feet off the ground. Unlike her kidnapper years before, this man held her face-to-face. She didn't know how to escape. On the ground, he dragged her through the mud, rain coming in sheets.

"Let me go," she screamed, gagging. She sobbed and gagged as he dragged her underneath a thrashing cedar. "Let me go."

When she finally gave up, trembling with cold and exhaustion, they lay in each other's arms, burrowed under the tree.

"Keep your head down, Eiseler," she heard him murmur. "We'll get out of this. Goddamned rain. Goddamned the fuckin' mud and Goddamn the stinking, starving, skinny little Japs."

The storm seemed to hesitate directly overhead as they cowered beneath the tree.

217

"Get that thing away from me," Bobbi yelled.

Connor covered her mouth with a muddy hand. "Shut up," he whispered, "they're out there. You're gonna get us killed."

Exhausted, Bobbi lay still, and Connor removed his hand. "See, they're over there," he whispered, gesturing toward a line of trees thrashing in the wind.

An hour later

Bobbi returned to reality first, shivering in the cold rain and wondering where she was. Connor's mud-soaked shirt and cedar bark were all she saw.

"Connor."

His grip tightened. "Be still. They're all around us."

"Connor, it's me. Bobbi."

"Shshshsh."

"Connor, we're not in New Guinea. Look around."

"Don't move."

"Connor, I'm cold. We need to get out of this rain."

He subsided into his cadence. "Mendez. Green. Moore. Wilson . . ."

Bobbi tried to get onto her hands and knees, but the lower limbs pinned her. She took Connor's hand and started scooting backwards. "C'mon. Let's go in the house."

Her husband didn't move. "Hidalgo. Deer. Gordon. Reese . . ."

"C'mon." She began singing, low and quiet so he would have to strain to hear her. "Blue Moon."

"Trigg, Menardo, Martinez, Eisler . . ." He stopped, listening.

"You saw me standing alone."

"Mendez . . ." He stopped again to listen.

"Without a dream in my heart."

"Mendez . . ." He stopped.

"Without a love of my own."

"Green . . ." He roused himself, looking around, water dripping onto his confused face. "How'd I get in here?"

"I'm not sure, Connor."

"What're you doin' here?"

"I think you dragged me. Something about Japs movin' in the rain."

Connor fell silent for a moment. "Why were you screamin' at me . . . and punchin' me?"

"I don't know. I was scared."

"Of me?"

"I don't know."

"Let's get out of here." He began moving.

"I've been trying."

He glanced at the cedar limbs, inches from his face. "We'll have to belly crawl." He began scooting backward as Bobbi, too, began to get the hang of it.

Suddenly, she stopped moving. "Oh my God, Connor, Hope's all alone in the house."

GRAVY

They inched their way out from under the tree and ran to the house through the downpour, both mud-soaked, with twigs and cedar foliage in their hair. They stopped on the porch, panting, and listening for any sound from their daughter. They heard nothing.

"Was she in the crib?" Connor demanded as he stripped out of his wet clothes.

"Yes. Napping." Bobbi hugged herself, shivering.

"Get out of those clothes. I'll check on Hope and bring you some dry stuff."

Bobbi began to strip. "Hurry."

He left his mud-drenched clothing in a puddle on the floor and tiptoed into the house, dripping water all the way, and found Hope asleep with pools of tears in the corners of her eyes. He looked at her for a long moment, then looked at his mud-caked hands., He grabbed a blanket off the couch, between thumb and index finger and tossed it to Bobbi. "Here, wrap up in that while I wash up."

He tiptoed back into the kitchen, dipped water from the reservoir, and poured it into a basin. He washed his hands and face and splashed water into his muddy hair, combing it out. He carried the dirty water outside, emptied it, and dipped some more for Bobbi.

"You can wash up a little bit while I get some dry clothes and towels." He tiptoed into the bedroom and gathered some clothes, taking them out to Bobbi.

"Bobbi, I've seen you naked before. Get out of those clothes and put these on."

"Well, I've got all but my underwear off." She washed her hands and face and ducked her head into the basin, rinsing out the mud and wrapping the towel around her wet hair.

He turned his back and pulled on dry clothes to give her the privacy she seemed to need lately.

"Hope's all right?"

"Sleeping . . . but it looks like she's been crying."

"What're we gonna do?"

He pulled her into his arms. "I don't know, Bobbi. I know what happened to me out there, but what happened to you?"

"I don't know. I went a little crazy."

"You were acting like you were shellshocked, too. Won't you tell me what's going on?"

"Nothing, Connor. Just nothing." She scrubbed at her eyes.

"It's got to be something, Bobbi. You're not yourself." Connor paced, absently picking cedar twigs out of his hair.

Bobbi dropped the towel and picked at her hair, too. "Maybe this *is* my self. I'm not much of a wife."

"That's not true, Sweetheart, but something's eating at you. Please tell me . . . or tell Mom. Tell somebody. Please."

"It's nothing, Connor. I'm just a bad wife."

"Stop that, Bobbi. You are not. But you're not happy. I haven't heard you sing in months. Well, until under that tree."

"I'm sorry, Connor. I'll try to be happier."

"That's not the point, Bobbi. Something's eatin' at you and I wanta help."

"There's nothing to help," She stepped into the kitchen to check the roast. "Supper'll be ready in a few minutes."

GRAVY

The baby started crying. "I'll go change Hope's diaper. Then I'll get supper on."

Connor shook his head. "I'll change her. You go ahead in here."

Part Six

August 2, 1947

Next morning, Bobbi and Connor ate breakfast without a word, both buried in their own thoughts. They'd talked late into the night, trying to figure it all out, but Bobbi hadn't connected the door latch sound to Dr. Powers's abuse so she couldn't explain her break-down, even if she dared. Bobbi turned her cheek when Connor bent to kiss her as he went outside. When he stepped through the door, he turned back to his wife. "I'm going to see how much damage that storm did to my trees." He turned to go then stopped. "I know last night was terrifying, but we'll work it out, Bobbi." Then he closed the door and she watched him through the window.

Alone in the house, she washed the dishes and got Hope out of bed, bathing and dressing her without the usual song. The baby fussed a little, but mostly watched Bobbi's face until her mother set her on a blanket on the floor. *I'm going crazy like Grandma.*

She hadn't told Connor that her grandmother died in an insane asylum, and she didn't intend to. Connor had suggested counseling a couple of times, but she shied away, terrified that a counselor would see it—that she's as crazy as her grandma.

For a moment, she remembered her one visit to the institution with her mother, door after locked door, people yelling and screaming and reaching out to grab her as she passed. And her grandmother, skinny old crone of a woman with glassy eyes and garbled speech. Bobbi knew she didn't want to go to a place like that.

What'll I do? What can I do? I can't stay here. I can't take care of Hope—what if I blow up and hurt her? She scrubbed harder on

223

the stained countertop. *But I can't leave her with Connor. He's getting better, but what if he blows up?*

She realized she'd dropped the cleaning rag and begun pacing the kitchen, wringing her hands. She looked at Hope. "What're you doin' down there?" Bobbi squatted on her heels and held out her arms. "Here, come to Mommy."

Hope reached up for Bobbi then leaned back in her mother's arms to touch the tears Bobbi didn't know were flowing. She brushed her face with the back of her hand. glanced out the window. "At least the storm didn't hurt the willow tree." She remembered the day Connor planted it and how he had whistled around the yard. Amazing how he transformed the barren little plot in just a couple of years. A breeze wafted in a teasing scent of yellow sweet clover. She remembered how hard he'd worked that day, and many others, planting, watering, and trimming. Almost the secure, ivy-covered cottage she'd once dream of.

And now I'm going crazy. She turned away and plopped down on a chair. In seconds she jumped up and carried Hope into the bedroom, where she deposited her on the bed. *I have to get out of here before I do any more damage.* She looked at her daughter. *I'll hurt you and I couldn't stand that. I've already hurt you by not giving birth the normal way.*

She dragged her battered suitcase from the back of the closet, glancing at the worn edges and remembering all the times she'd dragged it from one show to the next. *I guess I was never cut out to be a wife and mother.* She threw her clothes into the bag. *I sure have loved the security—knowing I would always have food on the table.*

She sat on the bed. *How can I leave Connor?* She watched Hope drift off to sleep. *I can't. But I'm an awful wife, denying him every night. Lying. Telling him it still hurts. It was so wonderful with him before the baby. He was so gentle and sweet. I don't know why I can't . . .*

She jumped up and stuffed a handful of underwear on top of the skirts and blouses, shorts, shirts, and slacks she'd already packed. *I'm a terrible, terrible mother.* She looked at Hope. *Leaving you alone last night. Alone in that storm with no one to hold you and comfort you.* She sighed. *You must have been scared.* She turned to the closet, reaching into the back for the gowns she'd worn when she sang. She laid them out on the bed. *I'll just put these on the hook in the back seat.*

She bent over the bed, smoothing one of the gowns, then leaned on her knuckles, eyes closed, fighting back images of men's hands reaching for her as she walked by them wearing those gowns. She balled her hands into fists as a grinning image of Carl Short flitted across her memory followed by Dr. Powers whistling to himself as he looked at her chart. *I can't think about that.* She straightened up and turned back to the closet. *I'll have to support myself. Maybe I can still get that radio show.*

She sat. *I've never had it so good, have I? A handsome husband who loves me and a beautiful child. I have to write him a note, so he knows I'm not lost again.* She grabbed a writing tablet and a pen from her night table. *I'll leave a note for Mom. Connor can give it to her. I hope she'll take my baby in until Connor gets better. Then he can take care of her himself.* She moaned. *What if he gets married again?* She stared at the wall, barely noticing the wallpaper she'd hung. *I can't think about that. I can't take a chance I'll hurt you.* `

She scribbled a note to Connor and one to Claire. She took the notes into the kitchen and propped them on the table, then she grabbed her cosmetic bag, biting her lip as she swept things off her dressing table and into the bag. She grabbed Hope's diaper bag. *You'll need diapers and rubber pants, a change of clothes in case you spit up or your diaper leaks.* She picked up the sleeping baby, laid her in the bassinette, and grabbed the bag. She hauled them out to the car and stowed them in the back seat. *Mom can get whatever else she needs after I'm gone.* She dragged her suitcases to the car and stowed them in the trunk. She rushed back to the house, grabbed her gowns and hung them on the hook inside the back door.

GRAVY

August 2, 1945 — U.S. Highway Six

"Okay, let's go," she whispered as she started the car and headed to her mother-in-law's house. She told Claire she was about to run out of formula and needed to run into town. Claire agreed to take care of the baby until she returned. Then she climbed in the car and drove away leaving Claire standing on the step, Hope straddling her hip.

When she reached the four-mile corner, she pulled over and stopped. "I can't see," she murmured, as she gripped the steering wheel, white-knuckled, letting tears run off her chin. When she heard a truck motor behind her, she glanced in the rear-view mirror. "Oh no, there's Oren." She grabbed a handkerchief scrubbed at her face, rolling down the window while the neighbor walked up beside the car.

"Oh." His face pinched into a weathered look of concern. "It's all right, Missus Conroy. You're not lost. See, ya just turn right here and ya turn left at the stop sign and before ya know it, you'll be in town."

"Thanks, Oren," she managed. "I don't know what I'd do without good neighbors."

"It's all right, Ma'am. You'll get it. This country must be hard for a city girl."

"I guess I'll just sit here a while and compose myself."

"Yeah just do that. I've got this here load of pigs to take to the sale barn."

"It *is* sale day, isn't it?"

"Yup, sure is." He turned, trudging back to his truck and pulling around her with a wave.

She waved and sat, silent, watching his trail of dust blow over the hill. She thought she remembered that she could get to the highway by turning left. She blew her nose, slipped the car into gear, and made the turn, remembering Connor's frown of concentration during those hot afternoons when he taught her to drive. He'd never said a word, but she could almost hear his teeth grinding when she slipped the clutch or ground the gears.

A few more tears slipped down her cheeks, but she caught herself. *There's no time for this, Bobbi. No time at all.*

When she reached the highway, she took a deep breath and turned onto pavement. She pushed the car north. *I'll go to Mom or Dad's place until I can find an apartment. They probably won't be thrilled, but they won't throw me out—I don't think. I took care of them for years. I won't call them. I'll just show up."*

As Bobbi sped toward Cleveland, she tried to keep her mind on the future, rather than what she'd left behind. She crowded her thoughts with what she had to do when she arrived in the city. First thing, she'd call Mary and Kate. She should do that immediately, so they'd know she was coming. Maybe one of them would have room for her so she wouldn't have to stay with her parents. She smiled at that thought, at least until an image of her baby's smile crowded into the picture. She gritted her teeth and steered her thoughts back to Cleveland. The next time she stopped to fill up, she called Mary, telling her friend nothing except that she would arrive late the next day. Then she hung up before Mary could ask questions.

Back behind the wheel, she tried to plan her next steps. She'd call Freddy Carloni. Maybe he'd have some work for her—more than a guest appearance. She'd check the newspapers for auditions. She'd visit nightclubs. She wondered if Perry Como would host any more Chesterfield Supper Club shows on NBC. Maybe she could get him to introduce her on the program. That would get her back in front of an audience. She would definitely call station KFAU. Maybe they'd still consider giving her that radio show. Probably not right away, but as they planned their next season.

Bobbi had listened to the radio, even on the farm. She knew the new Latin rhythms had become popular. She could sing them. Connor loved "Begin the Beguine." She groaned. *I can't think about him.*

She picked up U.S. 6 in Hastings and followed along to Omaha, barely noticing the farms and fields along the way. Enclosed in the capsule of the car, Bobbi felt isolated and a little frightened by the open expanse of sky. At least at the farm, she knew the neighbors. They always helped her find her way when she got lost—like Oren that morning.

She'd started late in the morning and then lost time sitting by the road crying. She'd stopped for gas. Hunger had stopped her in Lincoln at Shoemaker's. That hadn't settled very well.

When the highway took her into Omaha, her grip on the steering wheel eased and she adjusted her shoulders, realizing how tight and stiff they'd become. She smiled a grim little smile as she navigated between multi-story buildings. The J.C. Penney building in Hastings had been the tallest thing she'd seen in two years. She felt a little intimidated by the traffic. She hadn't driven in a town bigger than Hastings since Connor had taught her to drive. All those buildings meant lots of people and she wondered about them. She knew about the art gallery, but she'd never been there. She wondered about nightclubs. Did people in Omaha listen to live music? Did they go out to dinner and dance to live orchestras? Maybe she could land there, stay close to Connor and Hope. *No, no.* She shook her head, continuing to flee eastward. *We would just keep hoping.*

Crossing the river into Iowa, she thought the Missouri looked a lot like the Cuyahoga in Cleveland, with its warehouses and the factories belching smoke along its banks. Then she left Council Bluffs, back into open country—and that enormous sky.

Bobbi didn't begin to relax until she saw Des Moines spread out before her two-and-a-half hours later. She hadn't slept much the previous night and she'd begun to doze at the wheel. She knew Des Moines. After all, she'd served her first months in the Army at Fort Des Moines. She looked for a vacancy sign, checked in, hauled her overnight bag into her room, nearly stumbling with weariness, and closed the door. She lay down for a few minutes, but the sounds of traffic and people rustling around outside lulled her to sleep. And sleeping so close to the base where she'd endured basic training took her back in her dreams.

"Wow!" Bobbi's friend Bonnie said as she straightened the seams on her stockings. "We'll finally get to meet some of the guys on this base."

The women had a night off, courtesy of the townsfolk of Des Moines and they couldn't wait. They fussed with their hair and competed for mirrors to apply makeup. When the bus arrived— the familiar cattle truck—they helped each other into the back and took their places on the benches. Bobbi watched the countryside spooling out behind the truck, awed by the open sky and how small the base looked in the middle of the fields. Jiggling and bouncing along, she noticed plot after plot of shattered stalks, standing broken in rows.

"What's that stuff?" she asked Bonnie.

"Corn stalks. They grow a lot of corn in Iowa."

"Looks dead."

"Harvested. That's the stalks. They'll turn the cows in soon."

"What for?"

"To graze the stalks and knock 'em down, pick up dropped corn, stir up the soil, leave their manure to fertilize next year's corn."

"Busy cows."

Bonnie grinned.

When they stepped off the truck in Des Moines, Bobbi blinked. "Where are all the buildings—skyscrapers, stores?"

GRAVY

"This is Des Moines, not New York or Chicago."

"But it's flat!"

"You're west of the Mississippi. It *is* flat. We don't have so many people we have to stack 'em up."

As they stepped into the dance hall, Bonnie stopped in the doorway. "Darn."

"What?"

"Look at that. Do you see any men? There must be hundreds of WAACs here, but no soldiers."

The rest of the women nudged Bonnie out of the way and stepped into the hall as another truckload of WAACs came in behind them.

"There are couples dancing."

"Yeah, but I don't see any men standing around. Just women, hundreds of women."

"We'll just have to dance with each other.

Once they'd visited the bar and found a table, though, one of the few soldiers arrived to ask Bobbi for a dance. They danced a quick jitterbug and a ballad before the guy, Burt, tried to lead Bobbi outside.

"I'm here to dance."

"The hell you say. C'mon let's get out of here." He gathered her around the waist and led her toward the door.

"I'm not going anywhere with you." Bobbi planted her feet. "I just got here."

"Why not, baby? I wanna get it on."

"Well get it on with somebody else."

"I want *you*. You women are all whores anyway."

Bobbi stared at him, her face flushing. Like she did back in her first nightclub, she came around with an open palm and slapped his face, leaving finger welts. She stared a minute more and began walking.

"You're not going anywhere!" He grabbed her arm.

She looked down at his hand for a moment and jerked away, striding back toward the table where her friends sat watching. In silence, the dance crowd parted.

Burt looked around at all the people now watching him, his face turning livid. Scowling, he took a step toward Bobbi, but another soldier stepped out to block him. "No, you don't. She's not interested."

Burt stared at the other man for a moment, turned on his heel, and strode out the door as the orchestra started with the first bars of the King Porter Stomp.

"That was . . ." Bonnie began.

". . . par for the course," Bobbi finished for her, eyes flashing. She tossed back a big gulp of her drink. *I just can't get away from it.*

The four didn't notice another soldier walking up to them until he leaned over the table, pulled a pair of khaki-colored panties from his pocket, and dropped it on the table.

"Burt's right," he whispered, looking at each of the women in turn with a conspiratorial wink. "My buddy gave these to me. Said he got 'em from a WAAC."

Bobbi frowned, grabbing the panties. "Got 'em from a WAAC, hell. He stole 'em off the clothesline last Saturday."

She stared at the soldier for a long moment. "Inadequate little wimps," she snarled, "always gotta say they did when they didn't." She continued to stare, eyes drilling into his. "Ruin women's reputations so they can feel like *big men.*" She stuffed the panties into her own jacket pocket. "Some men!"

The soldier stood, swallowed hard, and flushed—even his ears turned red. After glancing around the room, as if seeking an answer in the crowd around him, he cleared his throat a couple of times.

"Well?"

He looked at the table for a moment, then glanced at the four women. "I'm sorry," he stammered.

"You oughta be."

The other women waited in silence, studying their nail polish.

"You're right. I oughta be. I'm not like this."

"And yet here you are." Bonnie murmured.

"I guess I felt sorry for that guy. You just obliterated him." He looked at Bobbi.

"Sorry for *him!*" she snapped.

"Well . . . Look. I'm really sorry."

They stared in silence for a few moments.

"Sorry lookin'," Bobbi finally said.

"What?"

"You heard me."

"Um. Yeah. Sorry lookin'?"

GRAVY

Bobbi laughed. "Look, I'm sick of you guys gossiping."

"Um."

"You men are worse than a bunch of old women."

"We're . . ."

"But I appreciate a man who can admit when he's wrong." Bobbi held out her hand, "so let's start over." She looked him up and down. "I'm Bobbi Bowen."

He offered his hand. "Chuck Barrows."

"This is Shirley Shank, Dottie McCowan, and Bonnie Anderson."

Chuck pulled up a chair. It turned out that there were nearly a thousand WAACs at the dance and only about two hundred men, so the women sat and talked as they took turns dancing with Chuck and getting acquainted.

August 3-4, 1947 — Cleveland, Ohio

Hours later, when Bobbi opened her eyes to sun peering through a gap in the drapes, she smiled. Chuck had grown up on a farm like Bonnie and the two of them had hit it off. He and her friend had become nearly inseparable during the few moments when the Army didn't have anything else for them to do. Bobbi stretched, wondering what had happened to them during the past five years. When she reached for Connor, she remembered. *I'm not gonna cry. I'm just not.*

Bobbi pulled the spread over herself and listened to the sounds of people walking around and talking, rolling a cart past her room, opening and closing doors, and driving cars. She heard somebody shouting and the slamming and banging of a garbage truck loading up out back.

Maybe with buildings around her instead of those blank open skies that always seemed to watch her—and the wind pushing and pushing—maybe she could think. Bobbi had experienced isolation—even in crowded rooms. But somehow the indifferent crowd always seemed like a second skin. She'd never realized that until she'd spent her first few hours alone in a big house on a big prairie under huge implacable skies.

Bobbi hauled herself into the bathroom, trying not to think about Hope and if she missed her mommy. She wondered if Connor missed her and thought about calling. *Maybe I should turn the car around and go back—try to work things out.* She allowed herself to imagine Connor caressing her stiff neck and shoulders and kissing her lips, but she couldn't get past that. *That'll just make it worse.* She simply couldn't imagine making love with her husband. Even thinking about it left her queasy. She dismissed the thought.

She showered, yanked on some fresh clothes and climbed back in behind the wheel. She continued on U.S. 6 across Iowa, Illinois, Indiana, and two-thirds of Ohio, and arrived at the east edge of Cleveland around midnight. When she saw a vacancy, she checked in and fell, exhausted, into bed. She'd figure out what to do in the morning.

By 7:00 a.m., she'd returned to the car and started for Little Italy. During her years out west, she'd forgotten Cleveland's summer humidity. The open car windows left her hair a frizzy mass of damp curls. Her clothing stuck to her. She noticed cigarette butts and pieces of newspaper lying on the street, rough-looking men leaning in doorways. Six years before, she'd have never even seen those things, but after visiting her home city with Connor, they'd all become apparent.

She arrived at her parents' café during the breakfast rush. She greeted her dad in the kitchen, tied on an apron, and helped her mom wait tables. When they had a break, Ella stopped to stare at her.

"What're you doin' here?" She peered around her daughter. "Where's Connor?"

"In Nebraska. I'd hoped to stay with you."

"What for? Where's Connor?"

"I've left him, Mom,"

"Why? Looks like he's a good provider."

"He is, but . . ."

Ella frowned. "Are you crazy?" She looked around. "Where's Hope?"

"I left her with Connor's mom."

"What're you *doin'*?"

I'm afraid, Mom. I can't . . ."

"You knew you were marrying a shellshocked veteran. *Now* you're scared?"

"It's not like that."

"What's it like?"

"I'm afraid I'm turning into Grandma Shank. I think I'm going crazy."

"You probably are."

"*Mom!!*"

"Well, leaving that man who's doing such a good job of taking care of you—and all that security—never worrying about food or rent. That's what you said."

"I know, but . . ."

GRAVY

"Look Bobbi, you made your bed. Now lie in it. Don't expect us to take care of you."

"I wouldn't, but I've got to get started again."

"We can't support you. You'll have to pay rent and groceries."

"I just need a place to stay for a couple of weeks, until I can get a job and find an apartment."

"Still. We got nothin'." Ella stared at her. "How much did you bring with you?"

"How much what?"

"Money, Bobbi, money."

Stunned, Bobbi thought for a moment. "Maybe a couple hundred. Just what we had in the house."

"You can give me a hundred. That should take care of your share of expenses. And you can work here for your share of the rent."

"But I'll need deposits for an apartment and utilities. I won't have time to look."

"You'll figure it out. This isn't easy street like your farm with Connor taking care of everything."

"But . . ."

"Here," Ella smacked a key into her hand, "go get changed. I'll see you in an hour."

Bobbi realized her mother wouldn't budge. Ella started toward the kitchen. "Be sure you wear some comfortable shoes."

Inside her mother's apartment Bobbi closed the door. *Maybe that's what I'll be doing with the rest of my life.* She dragged her suitcase and overnight bag onto the couch. *Not even a Murphy bed. Well, it's just mom. Don't suppose she needs another bed.*

She slumped on the couch next to the bags, stretching her feet in front of her. *I need a good night's rest.* She shook her head. *I guess I'm not gonna get it.* She just couldn't get herself moving. She couldn't imagine why her mother was so mad at her. *She didn't even ask why I left—well, she sort of did. It sounded more like an accusation. Seems like she's jealous of the security Connor provides—provided.*

She glanced around the apartment, noticing the telephone. *Oh yeah, I was gonna call Mary.* She dragged herself off the couch and dialed the number. Ralph answered on the fifth ring.

"Oh, yeah," he said when she identified herself. "Mary said you'd called."

"Could I speak to her, please?"

"You could, but she's in the hospital. We've got another new baby, you know. She tried to tell you she was in labor last night, but you hung up."

"Guess I got in a hurry. That's your third, isn't it?"

"Yup. A little girl finally. Mary's tickled pink. In fact, all she can talk about is getting to the stores and buying something pink. I think this is gonna cost me."

"Oh, Mary's always been sensible."

"Yeah, listen, I gotta get to the hospital for visiting hours."

"Say hello for me. I'll try to get over there tomorrow."

"She said to find out how long you'll be in Cleveland. Said you didn't say much when you called."

Bobbi hesitated.

"Bobbi?"

"I'm still here. Probably for good. I'll probably be here for good."

"You okay?"

"More or less. You go take care of Mary. We'll talk later."

So much for an invitation to spend a couple of weeks at Mary's.
She checked her address book for Kate's number and dialed.
Kate answered on the first ring.

"Hi. Oh, I thought you were Ed. He's just getting back from
Chicago tonight. One of the salesmen died suddenly and he had
to take over that territory until they hired somebody. He's been
over there for two months, and I've barely seen him."

"That must have been lonesome."

"Yeah, he's supposed to call me when he gets to Cleveland so I
can have dinner on the table when he gets here."

"Then I'd better get off the phone."

"So what're you doin' in Cleveland?"

"We'll talk when you and Ed have got reacquainted."

That's that. Bobbi hung up the phone. *They're getting on with
their lives and I don't know what I'm doing. Startin' over, I guess.*

She opened her suitcase and dug out a plain black skirt and
white blouse. She hadn't worn a skirt in months. The shoes she'd
been wearing would have to do. After applying fresh makeup,
she sighed and headed for the café.

August 10, 1947 — Willow Grove

After a week and no word from Bobbi, Connor called Information
for her mom's number. He called and called. He knew his in-laws
were already at work by seven a.m. and that they worked late,

so he called late—apparently not late enough. They closed on Sundays, so he called Sunday without success.

By the second week, he couldn't sit still. Fortunately, he'd had plenty to do on the farm, but the nights were torture. Sometimes, with all the work done for the day, he would walk around the section. Sometimes the four-mile walk around that square of farmland helped him sleep. Often it didn't.

Finally, one warm, velvet night when the black sky opened to profound silence, after a long walk, he wrote Nora.

> Dear Sis,
>
> I'm here in our newly remodeled house after a trip around the section looking at stars. I hope you can see stars there, too. I know city lights block them. Are the lights back on, yet? I hope you and Daniel are okay making a life. It's been more than two years, so I hope Paris has been reconstructed.
>
> I've been walking around the section most nights. It's amazing what I see by starlight. Tonight, I went 'round the Meents section. The north bottom's a little muddy and I saw all kinds of animal tracks. There were a couple of deer again. I walked alone because Bobbi left me about ten days ago. Left Hope with Mom. She thinks she's damaged our little girl giving birth, and she says Hope's not safe with either one of us. You know about my problem, but she has these rages sometimes, Nora, and I don't know what causes them. She won't talk about it. I don't know what to do. I'm trying to stay alive here and hope she'll come back. I keep trying to call her, but I'm not getting through.
>
> Take care of yourself and Daniel,
>
> Connor

GRAVY

Writing to Nora didn't solve anything, but Connor felt a little better. Bobbi had never had as close a connection with him as Nora. They had grown up sharing all their silly little childhood adventures and he'd only known Bobbi a couple of years.

Besides, Bobbi had grown up differently. He'd hoped they would have years to grow together like he and his sister, but would he ever see her again?

August 11, 1947 — Cleveland

Bobbi couldn't wait to get back into Lake Erie. She'd had no water for swimming in Nebraska. The café was closed on Sundays, so she hurried to Euclid Beach the first Sunday. It might be her last opportunity before she got immersed in work.

She listened to the crowd on the beach, noticed the faint organic smell of lake water and Humphrey's Popcorn Balls being made in the popcorn stand, just like she'd made them when she was fifteen working in the park. It felt like a reset. She cut through the surf in a smooth crawl, then switched to a dolphin kick in deeper water. *God this feels good. Maybe I died and went to heaven.* She rolled and dove, water moving past her like a caress—like Jack swimming with her, their bodies twining together like otters. She smiled until it all came back, her first love murdered. She closed her eyes and banned that train of thought.

I've got to get a job. I'll think about that. She emptied her mind as best she could and started again. She looked forward to auditioning and she imagined swinging and singing some jazzy new songs. Even in the cool water, she could almost feel the hot spotlights and hear the clatter and clank of a dinner crowd. It would be so good to get back to singing for somebody besides the cows and the pigs. *And your husband.* She banned that thought, too.

240

She cleared her brain again, but Carl Short, her attempted rapist, intruded. *I WILL NOT think about that swine.* She laughed. *Now I know some pigs, I probably shouldn't insult them.* She remembered Tony Falgione escorting her around the LakeView, keeping the customers' hands off her. She'd just started out then, a naïve kid. He'd helped her stick with it so she could support her family. She remembered standing on the platform with him, waiting for the train that would take him to war. *Wonder what happened to Tony. Hope he survived. Maybe he could be my manager. He knows the music scene. He's level-headed.* With a gasp, she remembered their promise. She remembered the night sitting in his Chrysler DeSoto on top of that hill looking over the lights of Cleveland.

"How about," he'd said, "how about when this damned war's over," he'd twirled a lock of her hair around his finger, "and we both get back home," he'd tipped her head up and kissed her mouth, "how about we look each other up and," he leaned in for another kiss, "how 'bout, if we're both still alive and we haven't found anybody else," he cradled the back of her head in his hand and kissed her once more, tracing her lips with his tongue, "we look each other up and just see if we could be happy together."

Can't go there. Never loved Tony. Grateful for his protection. After Jack died it didn't matter.

She swam, round and round, as her mind swirled back through her life. *Seems like everything I touch goes to hell. There's something wrong with me, some kind of spell on me I can't escape.*

After a couple of hours swirling and twirling through her past, she waded onto the beach, grabber her towel, dried herself, and since she had money for the bath house, went in and changed. The whole afternoon stretched out ahead. *Guess I'll start looking for work.*

GRAVY

August 12, 1947

Bobbi left the café after the noon rush. She eaten nothing but a
slice of toast and her stomach growled as she stepped into
Danceland looking for Freddy Carlone. If she could get a gig,
even a one-nighter, she could get herself back in front of
Cleveland audiences. Her stomach growled again, reminding her
of Buffalo and nearly starving. As she crossed to the bandstand,
she realized she walked too fast. Short, choppy steps don't look
relaxed. She slowed down and squared her shoulders,
consciously taking longer, more leisurely, steps.

She approached the stage. "Hi Freddy."

"Bobbi?"

"Been a while."

"I haven't seen you in years. Just that night here with your
husband."

"I'm back now."

"Didn't work out?"

"Nope. So I'm lookin' for a job and I wondered if you could use a
female vocalist."

"Bobbi, I've already got a singer."

"Do you know of . . ."

"Hey, you wanna come in on the Saturday?"

"Sure."

"I can give my singer a night off and have you as a featured
guest performer. That'll get you back in front of an audience.
Saturday night. KFAU still broadcasts live. We'll promote you in
our radio ads and the marquee, too. That's about all I can do."

"That's a lot. Thanks. Do you know any other orchestras looking for a canary?"

"Not really, Bobbi. Seems like after the war, everybody wants to sing."

Bobbi hurried back to the café for a bite to eat before the dinner crowd.

She worked both lunch and dinner shifts on Saturday, then rushed over to Danceland, changed, and stepped on stage for the band's first set at ten p.m. Still there at four a.m., she changed back into street clothes after the last set. On the way out, she stopped to talk to Freddy. "Thanks for letting me do this, Freddy."

"People still like you, Bobbi. Hope this'll give you a start."

"Me too." Bobbi waved over her shoulder and took off.

The day after her performance at Danceland, Bobbi hustled over to KFAU to see if she could resurrect the radio show she'd almost had during the war. "I'm sure you can't do anything right now," she told the program director, "but I hope you'll consider me when you plan your winter programs."

"What else have you done besides the show at Danceland? I don't know your name."

Bobbi told him about singing and travelling with the bands before the war.

"But the gig with Carlone is the only thing recent?"

"I sang at a nightclub in Colorado Springs when I was off duty."

"But that was still what, two or three years ago?"

"Two."

"Bobbi, you sounded fine this weekend, but I'd like to see a lot more recent experience before I commit a half-hour block of airtime. Do you know the new music? Do you know enough to keep it fresh? That kind of thing."

"So come back when you've got another job?"

"I guess it's like that. Sorry."

"Me too."

As she approached other band leaders in other clubs, she referred often to her show with Carlone and all her experience before and during the war but couldn't even get an audition. They told her that her experience was outdated. They wanted to know where she'd been and why she hadn't been singing. The club in Colorado Springs made no difference. "You can't keep up with the music scene in Podunk County USA."

Day after day, as she looked for singing gigs between running her legs off at the restaurant, she became more aware that she couldn't pick up her career where she'd left off. And—she'd about run out of time. Her mom wanted her out in two weeks, and she couldn't rent an apartment without a job.

Dead beat after a second shift with her parents, she kicked off her shoes and dropped on her mom's lumpy couch, her left arm across her eyes. *Maybe I should go back to Nebraska.* She allowed herself to think about her little family; she was too damned exhausted to resist. Her daughter 's little body, kicking and squirming like she had that last morning, swam before her eyes. She remembered Connor stepping out of the house that morning, turning back, "I know last night was terrifying," he'd said, "but we'll work it out, Bobbi."

She noticed sounds on the street—people shouting and car doors slamming. She heard people moving around in the building, footsteps on the stairs, and her tense muscles relaxed. She didn't know if she could stand any more silent afternoons when the wind whistled through the screens and the heat pounded on the house. She didn't even have a name there. Hardly anybody called her Bobbi. She'd become Mrs. Conroy.

Nothing's changed. Hope's probably better off without me and Connor definitely is. He must not want me back very bad. It's been almost three weeks and he hasn't even called. She rubbed tired eyes. *It's you who left, Bobbi.*

Next day, as she hauled heavy plates around the restaurant, stacking them hand to shoulder, she kept trying to decide what to do. *I'll will have to start all over again—back to the bars and lounges. I wonder if I can stay sane in those places with men grabbing at me. Will that set me off?* She delivered a big order to a noisy table. *I'll just have to try. I don't know what else to do. I'll give myself another week to find something—anything—before I call Connor.*

The next afternoon, between shifts, she rushed to LakeView Jazz Club—all the way back to the beginning. She entered through the back door and found her way to Fred's office, stepping in as he hung up the phone.

"Bobbi. What're you don' here?"

"Lookin' for a job, Fred."

"Aw, come on. No kiddin' around. What're ya really up to?"

"I really am looking for a job, Fred." She gave him a steady look.

"After all these years travelling with the bands? What're ya tellin' me?"

"Long story, Fred, but I've been out of the business for a while and it looks like I'm starting over, so I thought 'what better place'."

"Well sure, you got a job, but—are you sure?"

"Yup."

GRAVY

"All right, Bobbi, then let's go talk to the band. You'll remember some of them." Fred hustled out of his office and across the floor, leaving Bobbi to keep up if she could.

He introduced band leader, George, none too happy about a new vocalist from out of nowhere. "You know, Bobbi, these guys still play the good stuff. None of this new Latin stuff."

"Oh, but you have to keep up with the times."

"Not for our crowd. When do you want to start?"

Bobbi agreed to sing on the weekend.

This is gonna be a dead end. No new music. But at least it's a job.

She returned to the café, worked her shift, and gave her notice like any worker off the street.

When she arrived at LakeView on Saturday, she noticed Tony hanging around in the shadows by the bar. Throughout the rehearsal, she kept eyeing him, wondering if he still worked there. Before she headed to her dressing room to change, she stepped over to say hello.

"What're you doing here, Tony?"

"The question is—what're *you* doing here? You outgrew this place ten years ago."

"So did you. You're not still working here?"

"It's a job."

"You got a family?"

"Nope, but I hear you do."

Bobbi studied her fingernails. "I do," she whispered.

"So, what *are* you doing here?"

246

"I have to get changed."

"It ain't like you to run out when it gets tough."

She kept walking. *If it were just tough for me.*

Skeptical at first, George began to loosen up as Bobbi maintained her professional attitude. She knew all the songs the band played and a lot more besides. One slow Tuesday night when the dance floor stayed stubbornly empty, she asked for a new tune. "You know *Begin the Beguine.* Why not play it?"

"Fred don't like that Latin stuff."

She grinned, eyes sparkling. "Let's just do it."

"Fred will have a fit."

"He'll get over it."

They played the song, but only a few couples move onto the dance floor.

"How 'bout you play *Brazil?* I've got a plan." After a short argument, the band started the tune. Bobbi stepped to the front of the stage. "Hey, how many of you know how to dance to this?"

A few people raised their hands.

She turned to George. "How much line can you feed me?"

He let the band keep up its own tempo and uncoiled some mike cord from behind the stage and pulled it out for her. "What're you doing?"

"Just keep playing for a bit." She pulled the cord and stepped off the stage. "Okay. "I'm going to show you. Tony, could you help me out here?" She stepped into his arms and they started into a Cuban Walk. "I knew you'd know how to do it," she whispered. Now, turn me sideways to the crowd." She raised her voice. "See, it's like this—slow-two, quick-quick. You hesitate a count on the first step."

Several couples stepped up and tried it. Bobbi abandoned Tony and walked around, trailing her mike cord, careful not to get tangled with the dancers. As she watched them, she glanced around to see both Fred and Tony, standing at the edge of the floor, arms folded across their chests. "See," she said, "it's easy. The hard part is the hip swing. You men keep your weight on your right foot and move forward with a slightly bent knee." She demonstrated with her left foot. "You women can do anything the men can—only you have to do it backwards." She got a bit of a titter. "Now, when you transfer your weight your hip swings."

Once she got them into the pattern, she stepped back on stage, coiling her mic cord. Soon the floor filled with people and she smiled at Fred. Fred said nothing, so they continued to slip in something new every evening. Bobbi began to enjoy her work again, although she left every night completely drained.

August 23, 1947 — Willow Grove

Trying to nail the last shingle on the barn before dark, Connor watched a strange car pulled into the yard.

"Well, I'll be damned," he muttered when his old flame, Pauline, stepped out of the driver's door. He watched her walk to the house and knock, then turn back to peer in the open garage door.

"Hi there," he called as she turned back toward her car.

She looked around, finally spotting him. "What're you doin' up there?"

"Fixin' some shingles. Be right down." He joined her in the driveway. "What're you doin' here?"

"Heard you could use a little company."

"What'll your husband say about that?"

"I didn't marry him, Connor."

"Mom sent me your engagement announcement."

"Well, I didn't marry him anyway."

"Thing is . . . *I'm* married."

"I heard. Heard she took off."

"She's back at her folks."

"When's she comin' back?"

"I don't know, Pauline. Soon I hope."

"I don't mean to be nosy, but I heard she left you and that baby and took off."

"Damn it! I don't know where people get this stuff."

"It's not true?"

"Oh, it's true all right. Just nobody's business."

"Connor, I just thought you could use a friend since Nora's not around."

"She's back in Paris."

"I know. I just had a call from her."

"*A call!*" He kicked a rock across the drive. "I s'pose she told you to come cheer me up."

"Something like that."

"Look Pauline, Bobbi's only been gone two weeks. My marriage is *not* over and I'm not looking for another romance."

"I wouldn't expect you to, but maybe someone to talk to? I'm a much better listener than I used to be."

"Pauline . . ."

"Listen, I drove all the way over here on a mission. Nora expects a report, so how 'bout you make a girl a cup of coffee and we just talk for a while—catch up a little bit."

"Pauline, I've got work to do."

"It's dark out there. What are you going to do this late?"

Connor stared at her, brain churning. "All right. Can't do any harm I suppose."

Connor fired up the stove and made some coffee. Then they sat in the kitchen reminiscing— about ghost lights and riding cows, all the neighbors that got sold out during the thirties. The boys that didn't come back and the ones who did.

"Connor, Nora said you went through some pretty rough stuff in the Army. Was it bad?"

"Yeah. I still have nightmares—daymares, too. I won't kid you. I scared my wife half to death. Cracked her sternum once when I thought I was back in New Guinea."

"That why she left?"

"Partly. Whole lot of other stuff, too."

"What I don't get is her leaving the baby—especially if she's scared of you."

Connor hesitated a long moment, elbows on knees, head hanging. "She's more scared of herself."

"Why?"

"Pauline, I don't know. I have thoughts, but I don't know, and she won't tell me," he looked up into her eyes. "Can we change the subject?"

"Sure." They were silent for a few minutes. "Remember all the weeds we chopped," Pauline began. "My gosh we cut a lot of cockleburs." She laughed. "Dad had to sharpen the corn knives every time we went out."

"We had plenty of cockleburs, but I remember the sunflowers. You know, Pop would see one of their little faces sticking up out of the corn and here we'd go on a search and rescue mission. Good training for all the chopping we did in the jungle."

After another short silence, Pauline asked if Connor still liked to dance.

"Oh yes! First time Bobbi and I danced together it was like we'd been dancing together all our lives."

"Waltzes and fox trots?"

"Those and we jitterbug—and I learned some new stuff in Panama."

"Maybe you can teach me."

"Yeah, when Bobbi comes back, we can all go out."

"Do you think she'll come back?"

"I don't know, but I've got to give it time."

"Do you have to wait at home by yourself?"

"Pauline, I'm not gonna lead you on. We made a great couple once, but I'm in love with Bobbi and I'm gonna do everything I can to get her back."

"Well, maybe you can take a break sometime and I can take you dancing."

"I'm going to Cleveland in a few days. See if I can persuade her to come home." Connor looked at the clock. "My gosh, look at the time! I've gotta get some sleep."

Pauline smiled, standing and putting on her coat. "Okay Connor, I get it. You're in love and you don't need any confusion."

He gave her a sheepish grin. "You understand?"

"I suppose I do. I'll tell Nora you're all right."

"Please."

August 15, 1947 — Cleveland

The following Monday, Bobbi and Ella awoke at about the same time. Ella sat and eyed her daughter as she made up the couch and put her bedding away. Ella cleared her throat.

"All right, out with it. What's got you so scared you have to leave your husband and baby? If Connor's beating up on you . . ."

"No, Mom, it's not that. He's been getting better."

"You're not afraid of *him?*"

"It's complicated."

"*Everything's* complicated. I thought you had that figured out by now."

"Well," Bobbi stopped folding sheets. "I *am* afraid when Hope gets to toddling around, she'll wake him up when he's napping."

"So, you make sure she's not in the room when he's napping."

"It's not just that."

"No, I don't suppose it is. But if you're saying you can't have her around her father, then she needs her mother. I *never* abandoned you."

"I know, Mom." She looked at the floor. "But I'm not any better than Connor."

"What's that supposed to mean?"

"I have these . . ." She searched for a word her mother would understand. "I have these . . ." She plopped on the couch and grabbed the pillow, hugging it to her chest. "I have these spells."

"Spells! What's a spell? I don't know spells."

"That's what Claire would call them. I just have these blow ups and I lash out." She paused. "I don't know what sets me off. I can be cookin' or cleanin' the house."

Ella waited.

"And I just blow up. I mean, I spanked Hope for spitting her peas."

"Oh, we all lose patience."

"No, Mom, not like this. She threw up and I spanked her for throwing up. Then I was spanking her for crying when Connor took her away from me."

Ella remained quiet for a long moment while Bobbi fished in her pocket for a handkerchief. "You're sure not like that all the time, are you?"

Bobbi blew her nose. "Okay. Here's what happened." She described the storm and her craziness. "I think Connor was gettin' through it when I blew up on him. We ended up clear under a big cedar tree. Hope was all by herself."

GRAVY

"Out in the storm?"

"No, in the house—in her crib."

"That's not so bad."

"But she'll be able to climb out of it before long."

"What happened to you, Bobbi?"

"I don't know." She wailed. She jumped up and paced the tiny living room. "I don't know. One minute I was all right and then suddenly," She stopped walking with the sound of the door latch echoing in her brain. She sat. "I heard the door latch click."

"What about it? So what?"

"Sh!" Bobbi raised her hand and looked past her mother— through her mother. "I heard the door latch and it sounded . . ." Tears started streaming and she began retching. She sat and swallowed hard. "It sounded like that—horrible—thing." She covered her mouth with both hands.

Ella let her settle for a moment. "What horrible thing?"

"That thing Dr. Powers used to stretch me out." She mumbled, clasping her hands in her lap.

"What do you mean stretch you out?"

She focused on her hands. "He said he could stretch my bony pelvis, and he put this thing inside me and forced it open—more and more every month to make me big enough."

"I can barely hear you, Bobbi. Big enough for what?"

"To give birth normally. He said I'm inadequate, narrow like a little girl."

Ella sat without a word. "Normally? What's normally?"

"Without the caesarian."

Ella glared at her daughter. "He raped you. You let him rape you."

Bobbi stared at her mother. "He never . . . It was just that thing . . ." She blinked. "It was an experiment. I found out it was an experiment."

"Experiment!! What experiment?! To see how often you would let him rape you?"

"He said he could expand my pelvis so I wouldn't have to have the caesarian."

"And you believed him?"

"I . . ."

"You must have liked it."

"Liked it?!" Bobbi exploded off the couch. "It hurt like hell! I bled every time. It felt like he was ripping me apart."

"But you kept going back."

"He's a specialist. He's supposed to know what he's doing. And I didn't want Connor to die."

"Connor? What're you talking about?"

Bobbi sat, fiddling with her handkerchief. "Powers's the only surgeon within 150 miles who's qualified to do a caesarian. He said if I didn't try the treatments first, he wouldn't do the surgery."

"So?"

"If I said I didn't want to go to Powers, Connor would have to know why."

"Tell him."

"I couldn't—can't—Connor would kill Powers, and then they'd kill him."

"Oh, that's nonsense. Don't exaggerate."

"I'm not!" Bobbi snapped. "He almost killed a guy in town the night we got the VJ Day announcement, because of the fireworks."

"That's different and you know it. That's not murder. He wouldn't attack a doctor."

"He did, Mom. When Powers said Hope didn't have much chance, he almost choked the doctor to death. He's been charged with attempted murder."

Ella got up and paced. "Do you think Connor will get off? You can't stay here."

"I think so. The doctor withdrew the charges and I think—I don't know. I hope so."

"What made the doctor . . ."

"I threatened him."

"With what?"

Bobbi faced her mother with a grim smile. "One of the nurses told me it's illegal to experiment on someone without telling her. I told him I'd tell."

Ella smiled. "That's my girl! See? It'll be all right. It's over. You need to go home now."

"I wish I could. It just sneaks up on me."

"Well Connor's gettin' over his stuff—or so you said."

"He is, Mom."

"Then you can too."

"But I can't . . ." Bobbi jumped up and started another pot of coffee.

"You can't stay here."

Bobbi measured the grounds into the basket. "I can't go back."

"Why the hell not?"

She turned and looked at her mother. "I can't be a wife to him."

"What does that mean, for cryin' out loud?"

"I can't stand to sleep with him—to have him make love with me."

"What happened to that gentle lover you told me about?"

"He hasn't changed," Bobbi hung her head, "I have."

"Well, just get over it!" Ella snapped. "Enough is enough. Quit feelin' sorry for yourself."

Bobbi stared at her mother without a word—about the silence and the wind whistling through the screens and how the sky bears down on you like an accusation. *Yes, I will have to stop feeling sorry for myself. If I'm ever going to sing with the Glen Miller band or have a radio show of my own, I've got to knuckle down and find a place to live.*

August 30, 1947 — Willow Grove

Mostly, Connor got through the days all right. He had plenty of work. He ate supper with his folks most nights and spent a little time with Hope before he went home. Nights, though, he couldn't help but panic. What would he do if Bobbi did get a job singing with a big-name band? What would he do if she never returned? How would he raise Hope all by himself? And then the worst question would squirm into his brain and eat away at his resolve like a cancer. What if she took Hope?

He played Wayne King records every night and sat in the kitchen with the dog at his feet, remembering Bobbi, hair a mass of curls pulled back in a headband, vaccinating a bunch of pigs. Or he would waltz to the music, imagining Bobbi in his arms. Sometimes, he got out the perfume bottle she'd left behind and sprayed a whiff into the air, inhaling deeply, remembering how Bobbi's fragrance had surrounded him when they danced together. Night after night, he sat with one hand absently scratching the dog and images of his absent wife running through his mind, as he tried to crowd out the questions.

Sometimes he fell asleep with his head on the table until the dog nudged him awake. Sometimes he awoke after the lamp burned out and the phonograph needle swished round and round at the end of the record. With swollen eyes and stiff neck, he would climb the stairs and crawl into an empty bed. Sometimes he would remember his Army friend, Ed, standing outside the barracks, smoking. Told him he shouldn't think so much. "It'll scare ya to death." He sure been right about that. What else had he said that night? Oh yeah. "Ain't yore life complicated enough already?" He'd got that right, too.

About a week after her first visit, Connor heard a car engine. He moved to the window in time to see Pauline, dressed in a crisp shirtwaist with bright pastels and a full skirt that swished in the breeze. Connor pulled on his shirt as he walked to the door.

"Hello. What brings you clear out here?"

"I came to rescue you."

He frowned, "Rescue me from what?"

"Yourself."

He leaned in the door frame, folding his arms across his chest. "What makes you think I need rescuing?"

"Nora said you'd be wallowing."

"Wallowing?!"

"Well, look at you. You're sitting alone in the kitchen listening to those maudlin Wayne King waltzes. You haven't even got enough light to read by."

"Don't feel like reading."

"No," she flashed, "just wallowing."

"I ain't wallowing!"

"Well, neighbor, whatever you're doin' it don't look like fun." She stepped back and folded her arms over her chest, giving him a critical look-over. "Here's the deal. There's dancing tonight at Club Ivanhoe in Hastings and I'm taking you."

"Pauline . . ."

"I know, I know. You're still married."

"I am, Pauline."

"I know. But you just can't sit around here and feel sorry for yourself."

"I'm not. I have work to do."

"It's Saturday and it's dark, Connor. You need to get out of here."

"But . . ."

"No buts. This is for your own good."

"Pauline, I appreciate what you're trying to do."

"Look. I'm not leaving until you get changed and go dancing with me."

"You're not listening. I love my wife. I'm not lookin' for someone else."

"Who says *I* am?"

"You . . ."

"Look Connor," she interrupted, "we've been friends since we were kids. Forget the romance. It didn't work out. Just take me dancing," She looked over his shoulder. "At least let me in so we can have a civilized conversation."

"Well . . ."

"Go turn off that awful record and get dressed."

He took a small step back.

"Just do it."

Back inside he sat at the table but jumped up again. "I'll make you some coffee."

"Sit down, Connor. It's too hot for coffee."

He sat again and scratched Freckles, refusing to look at Pauline.

"Look, if Nora were here, she'd be *draggin'* you out."

"She *is* my sister."

"Let's just say I'm fillin' in for her."

He rubbed the dog's silky ears and looked deep into the dog's brown eyes. Freckles whined. "You don't think it's a good idea to go out with someone else, do you?"

GRAVY

"We're not 'going out.' Friends. No strings."

"Tell that to the gossips. I don't want Bobbi hearing that I'm hanging around with another woman."

"She's in Cleveland. How's she going to hear anything?"

He eyed her while he buttoned his shirt. "Oh, all right. I don't suppose it'll do any harm."

"Of course, it won't."

He left the table and turned off the record player. "Just remember, I'm *very* married." He headed for the stairs. "Wait here. I'll get cleaned up a little."

He came down a few minutes later tucking a white shirt into a pair of tan slacks. She reached up to straighten his collar.

"Pauline," he warned.

"Okay. Sorry."

In the car, Pauline tried several times to start a conversation, but got only monosyllables in response. "What's that you're whispering?"

"Oh. It's nothing. I didn't know I was doing it."

"It's not that cadence Nora told me about—the names."

Connor colored. "Yeah."

"That's not allowed either."

"For Chrissakes!"

She's drove in silence for a few moments. "Sorry. Guess I expect too much."

GRAVY

When they got to the club, Connor noticed the lighting. "This isn't any brighter than my kitchen."

"It's a nightclub, Connor."

Once they had their drinks, Pauline tried to get Connor on the dance floor. Staring around the club he noticed several people from home giving him the eye. "This was a bad idea, Pauline, it'll be all over town I'm cheatin' on Bobbi."

"No, it won't. It's all over town that she left you. Nobody's judging."

"But when Bobbi comes home, if she hears—it'll be all over."

"Just relax. We're here now. C'mon, let's dance."

Obediently, Connor stood and led her onto the floor. After dancing a couple of numbers to the first live music he'd heard since Bobbi had left, he relaxed into the music. He couldn't help noticing how good it felt to hold a woman, to move to the rhythms of a pretty good band. He and Pauline had been partners before, so they danced comfortably together. He even had a little fun. When Pauline dropped him off at home, she walked him to the door.

"Pauline, I had a good time. Thanks. But I don't think we should do it again."

She stepped into his arms. Mechanically, he gave her a squeeze, then released her and turned to go inside.

"Connor." He looked back at her and she reached up to kiss him. He responded momentarily, then tore away and fled into the house.

"Jesus! That's the last thing I need." He stood watching her headlights swing around the willow tree and out the lane. *But God, it felt good. I wish it were Bobbi.*

He stepped into the living room and turned on the phonograph, pulling a Wayne King waltz out of its jacket and setting the needle. He closed his eyes and moved to the music. The face he saw as he danced was Bobbi's. *God, I wish she were here.*

September 6, 1947 — Cleveland

For a couple of weeks, Bobbi worked LakeView, struggling to adjust to the nighttime hours. It had been years since she'd tried to sleep during the day. She'd had to struggle to put a bounce in her step and energy in her voice. When she returned to her apartment just before dawn, she'd fall asleep immediately, but her husband and daughter stalked her restless dreams. She dreamed of Connor with another woman sometimes and woke crying. Sometimes it was Hope crying for her or standing by the window at Claire's house, watching for her. Those dreams woke her, and she would lie awake for hours telling herself she couldn't go back and risk hurting her family.

On a Saturday night in early August, she noticed a man seated right next to the stage leering at her. Something about his expression made her queasy. She struggled to ignore him and move naturally through her set, but she felt stiff. As she left the stage at the end of the set, he stood. She cast a forbidding glance in his direction. She didn't know how she'd react if he touched her so she fled in the direction of her dressing room. He reached for her, but she batted his hand away and ran, gagging.

By the time Fred caught up, she was rinsing out her mouth.

"Whatsa matter? You got the flu?"

"No. I'm just queasy. I'll be all right."

Fred watched her a moment. "Looks like more'n queasy. You look—what's that word—haggard."

263

"I'm all right."

"Look, I don't want you slappin' my customers."

"I know, Fred, I just had to get to the toilet."

"I see that. You need to go home?"

"Nah. I'll sing my last set."

"All right." Fred stepped out and closed the door.

When she walked back out for her last set, she saw Tony eyeing her from the edge of the dance floor.

For weeks, she struggled to stay upright during her sets and hidden out in her dressing room between them. She would sit in front of the mirror, her arms folded on her dressing table and her head resting there. By the end of the last set, she could barely put one foot in front of the other and she stumbled into the arms of a customer as she stepped off the stage. Cupping her breast, he tried to kiss her, but she turned her head and brought her knee up into his crotch, following up with a fist to the back of his head as he folded over.

Tony materialized beside her. "What're you doin'? You'll kill him." He grabbed the guy's elbow and helped him stand.

"Tony?" She gagged.

"Better get to your dressing room." He helped the guy outside.

Bobbi rushed backstage, swallowing bile. *There goes that job*

She heard Fred pounding on her dressing room. She rushed by him as he stepped in and heaved into the toilet.

"What's wrong with you?"

"I'm not feelin' so good." Bobbi grabbed a tissue from a box on her dressing table and wiped her mouth.

GRAVY

"Bobbi you can't . . ."

"I know, Fred."

"Look, we already had this talk—years ago."

"I know, Fred. I just don't know what gets into me."

"I'm sorry, Bobbi, I just can't do this again."

"Can't you give me another chance?"

"No, Bobbi. You hurt that guy."

"Well, he . . ."

"I know, Bobbi, but what were you thinking? Never mind. I don't think you oughta try to work in a place like this."

"Fred, Tony's still here."

"No, Bobbi. It was hard enough for him the first time, loving you with no future in it."

"I suppose not." She hung her head.

"I'm sorry, Bobbi. I don't know what's happened to you."

"It's a long story, Fred. You haven't got time."

"Well." Fred turned to go.

"Yeah."

When Bobbi left her dressing room, she found Tony waiting outside. "I'm takin' you home."

"It's all right, Tony. I have a car."

"I'll come get you in the morning and bring you back here to get it."

"Tony . . ."

"I'm takin' you home. Now come on." He touched her elbow.

She relaxed. "Oh, all right, Tony. It will be good to not have to drive."

She was grateful he didn't mention that her eyes look too swollen to see, but she'd looked in the mirror.

"Yeah, just to let your nerves settle."

She gave him directions and they arrived at her apartment in only a few minutes.

"I see you've stayed in the same neighborhood."

"Yes, it's convenient for now."

He handed her out of the car and walked her up to the door. "I can make it from here, Tony."

"That's okay. I need to know what door to knock on when I come tomorrow."

They took the elevator to the sixth floor. "Tony, I'm really exhausted."

"I don't expect you to invite me in. Just try to get some rest." He turned to go.

"Thanks, Tony." She turned and entered her apartment.

The next day, he arrived at two in the afternoon. She made him wait while she wiped her tears and splashed cold water on her face.

"You hungry?"

"Hadn't thought about it."

GRAVY

"Let's go get coffee before we get your car."

"Tony, I need to find another job—right away."

Tony took her to a quiet little place about a block from LakeView. "Listen Bobbi," he said once they were seated, "if that husband of yours was beating on you," He reached a hand under her chin, looking into her eyes, "I'll kill him, and you'll have your baby back."

"No!" Bobbi gasped.

"Look, I know a lot of women let their husbands beat them, 'cause they . . ."

"Tony, do you really think I'd be one of them?"

"Not the Bobbi I used to know."

"He's a shellshocked veteran, Tony, and he blows up sometimes. But it's not him."

"What then?"

"It's me, Tony. You saw me last night."

Tony took a gulp of coffee, studying her over the rim of his mug. "What *was* that? You were ferocious."

"That guy grabbed me and I just—I don't know—flipped."

"I know he was all over you. But I was right there. You didn't have to kill him."

"That's just it. I. can't. stop. myself."

"Why? What's goin' on with you?"

"I can't talk about it."

"If I knew what it was, maybe I could fix it."

"I can't!" Bobbi tore off a piece of her roll and stuffed it into her mouth as if to stopper it.

He started to speak, but she gave him a warning look.

"Well, all right, but what're ya gonna do?"

"Oh, Tony, I don't know! I always thought I'd get to sing with the Glen Miller band or the Dorseys or Duke Ellington."

Tony stared.

"You don't think I could do it."

"There's the moxie I remember, but you're not off to much of a start."

"I think I've got the voice."

"Yeah, but you're startin' over."

"I know. I gotta get hold of myself."

"I've been thinking, Bobbi, maybe I can get Fred to give you another try."

"I was hopin' you could escort me."

"That ain't gonna work. You're on your own, Sugar."

"But why?"

"Your husband's not the only shellshocked veteran."

"And there's more fights?"

"Yes, a lot more." He gave her an earnest look. "Do you think you could do it without me?"

"I'm not sure." Bobbi took a last sip of coffee and held up her cup for a refill. "I don't know what gets into me."

"Seems like you're scared of something." Tony fell silent for a long moment. "Bobbi, you look like you're strung out."

"I'm *not* doin' drugs!"

"No! I'm not sayin' that, but you look like you haven't slept in a year."

"More like, what's this, August 30? More like three-four weeks."

"That how long you've been back?"

"About that. I go to bed, and I'm pooped, but I wake up dreamin' about Connor or Hope and I lay there and stare at the ceiling."

"Hope. That your baby's name?"

Bobbi smiled. "Yeah. Doctor said there's something wrong with her. Said she'd be retarded." She stirred more sugar into her coffee and lit a cigarette. "He said not to expect her to learn very well."

"Aw. That's just crap!"

"That's what Connor and Henry say."

"Henry?"

"My father-in-law."

"Maybe the doctors here could help."

"Tony, she's safe with my in-laws."

Tony frowned. "She'd be safe with you."

Bobbi interrupted. "No, she wouldn't. That's what I'm trying to tell you. I haven't hurt her yet—except giving birth to her, but I've had a couple of blow-ups with her."

"You couldn't hurt your own child."

"I'm not so sure, Tony. Listen, I've got to go."

"What's your hurry?"

"I just have to get going. Figure out what I'm going to do."

"Maybe we can just talk it out."

"No! I need to go!"

"Gosh, Bobbi. It's all right. I'll take you to your car."

Bobbi stubbed out her cigarette and grabbed her purse, sliding out of the booth while Tony fumbled for a tip.

"You okay, Bobbi?"

"More or less. Let's just go."

"Okay, okay."

When they got to the deserted parking lot, Tony handed Bobbi out of the car and walked her around to the driver's side of her own car. "Well." He stepped closer and folded her in an embrace. "I'll talk to Fred." He tipped her chin up and kissed her.

For a moment, she responded, then shoved him away. He stared. "All right, Bobbi. Just remember, I'll always be here."

She opened her car door, crying. "I can't do this, Tony. I just can't."

"I know, Sugar. Just take care of yourself." He turned back to his car and left.

She started her car, still blinking back tears and drove aimlessly through the streets of Cleveland. Eventually, she found herself in the parking lot at Euclid Beach, staring out at Lake Erie, mesmerized by the waves lapping up on the beach.

GRAVY

September 6, 1947 — Willow Grove

Stopped for a snack around noon, Connor sat head in hands, slumped on a kitchen chair, a Wayne King Waltz playing on the phonograph. The waltz reminded him of dancing with Bobbi and how quickly she'd picked up new steps—even Nora couldn't follow as well as Bobbi.

She's gone a month and it already seems like a year. Even before she left, I missed her following me around, trying to learn everything. He shrugged. *With a new baby, I knew she couldn't do that anymore. I understand that. What I don't understand is what happened to our nights. I missed her in bed, even when she still slept there. I can't remember the last time we made love.* He shook his head, as though to rattle a thought loose. *What happened to the laughter in her eyes? Surely that was real.*

I wish I'd brought Hope home with me tonight. Maybe I wouldn't feel quite so lost if I could even watch her sleep. He groaned. *Bobbi's probably right. If something set me off, I could hurt her.* His mind ratcheted around that idea. *I could kill her.*

His dark thoughts dragged him back to New Guinea and all the good men he'd left there on that damned hillside. *Useless. Just useless. What did it get us stumbling up that hill, running and hiding behind blades of grass? For what? You get to the top, the fuckers order you back down—what's left of you. I never asked for that. None of us did. And it ain't over yet. My own wife don't trust me with my little girl and my mom ain't so sure. Who could blame them? I don't trust myself, either.*

He swept his arm across the table, smashing his plate and uneaten meal on the floor. He stood, strode into the living room, grabbed the record, scratching the needle across grooves, and flung it to the floor where he stomped it into pieces.

I don't know what happened. Everything was gettin' better and then Bobbi got pregnant. He frowned, staring at the broken record. He screamed, punching his fist into the wall. "I DON'T KNOW WHAT HAPPENED!"

271

GRAVY

He stomped back into the kitchen and swept pots and pans, a dish tub filled with dirty dishes, and miscellaneous kitchen utensils off the counters, splattering soapy water and dish shards. He grabbed his chair and demolished it against the wall, leaving ragged holes in the new sheetrock and exposing wiring that hadn't been connected to a power source yet.

He stormed out the back door, slamming it behind him. When it tore off the bottom hinge, he kicked it, tangling himself in the frame, which he ripped off its hinges, and threw into the spirea bushes. "BOBBI," he screamed at the sky, "BOBBI, WHAT HAPPENED?"

Glancing around, wild-dyed, he snatched up a piece of the door and bludgeoned the bushes to tatters. From there he strode through his hedge, breaking carefully pruned branches, and stormed to the weeping willow, thrashing it as if he were tearing through the jungle with a machete. *Why'd I do all this stuff, anyway? All this for Bobbi and where is she? What'm I here for? I'm no good for anything anymore. All I know how to do is kill."*

He remembered his service revolver, but he couldn't remember where he'd put it. He paused in his destruction and stood, thinking. Noticing the weight of the wood he held, he lifted it tentatively and then dropped it, still trying to remember where he'd put that gun. *Oh yeah, I gave it to Bobbi to put away. Didn't even want to know where it was those first few months. Don't know why I kept it.*

He stormed back toward the house. *Wonder where she might have stowed it.* He tried the top of the closet first, feeling around for the familiar shape. When he couldn't find it, he dumped everything off the shelf with one violent sweep of his arm.

He rummaged in the bottom of the closet without success, then pulled drawers out of the dresser and dumped them on the floor. He moaned when he pulled out the first of Bobbi's drawers, staring at a pair of nylons she'd missed. He pushed the drawer back into place. He glanced at her dressing table and gave his head a shake and moved on to the living room. *Maybe the bookcase.* He dragged handsful of books off the shelves. He pulled the cushions off the couch and the overstuffed chair. Nothing there. As he stepped into the kitchen and surveyed the possibilities, he noticed his hands shook. *So what? I'm gonna end this anyway. As soon as I find that gun.* He began dragging things out of the cupboards, dropping them in an angry heap on the floor.

He'd known, when he didn't find the gun hidden in the bedroom, that he wouldn't find it in the house, but he couldn't help himself. When he'd finished in the kitchen, he stepped over the shambles he's left and headed for the garage.

When he'd taken apart everything he could think to take apart, he sat on the front step, face buried in broad hands, and wept.

Henry's and Claire's Farmyard

Wind still for once, sky heavily overcast, Henry chopped sunflowers along the road ditch while Claire watered the chickens. Both hesitated when they heard Connor's voice. "I DON'T KNOW WHAT HAPPENED!" Claire set the bucket down and hurried over to Henry across the farmyard. "Do you think he's all right?"

"No."

"Should you go see about him?"

"Yes, but not yet. He's gotta get it out of his system."

Claire leveled an even gaze at him. "Do you think he'll hurt himself?"

"Didn't you say Bobbi gave you that damned gun he brought home?"

"Yes."

"Then nothing that won't heal." He turned back to the weeds. "Hope still nappin'?"

273

She flinched. "Oh! I forgot. I was just gonna water the chickens." Henry watched her bustle off, muttering. "I'm not used to a baby in the house anymore."

A couple of hours later, Henry wandered into the house, washed up, combed his hair, and put on a clean cap. I'm goin' over to Connor's."

"You take good care of him."

Henry made a quick glance around the yard when he stepped out of the car and walked up to his son, still sitting on the front step. "Looks like you've had a storm around here."

Connor gave him a red-eyed, sheepish look. "Wasn't a storm."

"Yeah. I thought not. How bad?"

"Broke things up pretty good."

"Well, that'll give you somethin' to do to keep your mind off your troubles."

"I don't think that's gonna help, Pop."

"Helped me a lot."

Connor stared at his father. "You? Whadaya mean?"

"You remember when we lost him woulda been your baby brother?"

"Yeah. All the time Bobbi was in labor, I kept seein' you carryin' Mom out to the buggy—limp and gray as an old dishrag. It's just a flash and then gone, just like the baby. I was so little then."

"Your mom's been feeling it too. And me. All that panic."

"But what I broke—that's nothin' with you."

"Hunh. When that doc tol' me your ma was gonna die."

"Die!"

"You an' Nora was at your Aunt Anna's by then. Wasn't nothin' I could do, just wait on her to die." Henry sat on the step next to Connor and looked out at the torn willow and the hole in the hedge. "Anyway, I felt so helpless and my wife in that hospital dyin'. I couldn't just set there like a damned vulture and watch. Henry glanced at his son, then scanned the torn screen and the pieces of the frame in the broken-up spirea. He took in the ripped-out hinge. "I come home and had me a regular fit."

"A fit!?"

"Oh, I throwed things and broke things and tore the place up real good."

"Nah."

Henry grinned. "What'd you say you learned in the Army? Demolition's easy?"

"But it's the buildin's tough."

"Let's go take a look."

"I don't know if I want you to see it."

Henry stood and slapped his son on the shoulder. "It'll be all right. A man can get to feelin' helpless and useless. Just makes you so mad you can't keep it in."

Connor stood and looked down at his dad, wondering how he always understood. "I was thinkin' about bringin' Hope over here to live with me, but maybe Bobbi's right. Maybe you and Mom ought to raise her. I can't take care of her." He nudged a dishpan with his toe.

"Of course, you can. Why can't a man can take care of a baby?"

It's not that. I'm afraid I'll hurt her."

Henry stepped over to look at the hole in the wall. "What happened with you two anyway?" He picked up pieces of the chair. "Bobbi says she's afraid she'll hurt her baby and now I'm hearing the same thing from you."

Connor began picking up pieces of plaster board. "We had a fit, both together." As the two poked around in the wreckage, Connor explained about the night of the storm. "What's weird, Pop," he concluded, "is that Bobbi blew up before me."

"What do you mean?"

"Well, I was tense as a cricket in a room full of shoes, but I had it under control. Then Bobbi . . then Bobbi started poundin' on my chest and screamin' and bitin' and kickin,' an' of course, that set me off."

The two had fished out three undamaged chairs and Henry sat, resting his elbows on the table. "Until somebody knows what happened to Bobbi, there's not much we can do."

"Pop, I can't figure it out."

"So what're you gonna do about you?"

"Work, Pop. I can stay out of trouble when I'm workin.' I'm just not sure what I'm workin' for."

"You got that little girl over there with her grandma, Connor. As to work," Henry gave him a wicked grin and looked pointedly around the kitchen. "That shouldn't be a problem. You'll have plenty to do to make this a place to raise a daughter."

Henry took another gander around the kitchen. "There's one thing, though. You can't leave Bobbi with her mother for long."

"She's not comin' back, Pop. She's just gone."

"We'll see. Give her some time." He looked around again. "It don't look like you'll be cookin' in here tonight. You better come on over and eat with Mom and me. Spend some time with that little girl. She's confused about where she belongs. She misses her mom." Henry walked out, levering the door into place on the way out.

September 7, 1947 — Cleveland

After Tony dropped her off, Bobbi spent most of the night at Euclid Beach, sitting in the car, staring at the lake, and allowing herself to think about Connor for the first time. She remembered Tony's kiss and it brought back images of Connor, sitting on a blanket surrounded by red rocks; the way he'd nibbled, barely touching her lips. For the first time in over a year, she felt desire and she let it overwhelm her. At least she knew the source of her sudden panics. It was not as simple as just getting over it like her mom thought. But maybe she could in time. Connor had learned to calm himself in thunderstorms—most of the time. Maybe she could learn too.

She stepped out of the car and walked the beach, thinking about the weeks she'd been in Cleveland, about the noise and energy, people walking and talking, whooping and hollering, clinking glasses and clanking machines. Out on the beach with only the sound of the waves, she thought about the silence on the prairie on still days, and the howling of the wind blowing against the house on others. She remembered clear, bald skies when it felt like someone peering in the windows where she had nowhere to hide.

She looked at the stars. There didn't seem as many of them as on the prairie. But they were the same stars. Connor had pointed out the Big Dipper and the North Star. She found them, wondering why the night sky looked so dim. City lights must drown out their brilliance.

Staring, she thought about starring with a top-name band. It felt wonderful singing with a band again, in front of a mic with people dancing and having a good time. She still dreamt of the

GRAVY

big bands—Tommy and Jimmy Dorsey, Glen Miller, maybe her own show.

She thought over her career, before Connor and before the Army. *I really had fun the night I won that contest, and all the times we visited other clubs. Tony was always gallant, escorting me around LakeView. Then all the tours and the cities.* Those years, only about three of them, all ran together in a brilliantly lighted blur of stage lights in her eyes and makeup lights on her face. *I was so scared the night Al Polizzi came in asking for me. At the house party, his bodyguards terrified me.* That night brought her back to Jack, though, and seeing that headline and his murder.

Then she remembered why she had quit. She'd liked the idea of serving her country, but she had her own reasons for enlisting— nearly starving in Buffalo, nearly getting raped by that sleezy club manager. He'd turned up in her nightmares, over and over, in the years since, but she always thought she'd come back to it. *Not always. I made up my mind, when I accepted Connor's proposal, that my singing career was over. But here I am.*

She climbed back in the car and sat, staring at the lake. She hadn't counted on Dr. Powers. *There's no place in the world I can get away from those men. I thought I would be safe on a farm in the middle of nowhere.*

She flipped on the car radio for a little noise. The first tune she heard, *Begin the Beguine,* reminded her of dancing with Connor—the warm, safe feel of him holding her, leading her, shielding her. And she decided, sitting in that parking lot looking out at the waves, that she would go home. She smiled. She couldn't wait to see her husband and her little girl.

Bobbi started the car, slid it into gear like Connor had taught her, and headed for her apartment. She'd throw her stuff in her bags and get on the road by dawn. *The rent's paid 'til the end of the month. If everything goes right, I'll call and give notice.*

What if it doesn't go right? She crowded that thought out of her head. *I'll worry about it when the time comes. Maybe I won't have to worry about it.* She slowed. *Connor hasn't even called.* She pulled up short in front of her apartment building, just staring down the street.

Well, you haven't called him. She stormed ahead. *I'll be in Nebraska in a couple of days. Then I'll know what to do.*

September 7, 1947 — Willow Grove

Next morning, Connor awoke to a pinpoint of light shining in his eye. Squinting, he looked around for the bright little beam. He yawned, stretched, and sat on the edge of the bed where that tiny bit of light still shone in his eyes. He lifted his hand to block the glare, then stood and located a reflection in the corner next to Bobbi's dressing table. He reached for what appeared to be a shard of broken glass and found a perfume atomizer, cut glass making rainbows as he lifted it. He brought it to his nose and inhaled his wife's favorite fragrance. It nearly brought him to tears. He decided to try calling again.

He scrambled into pants and hurried downstairs, buttoning his shirt. He hadn't tried calling in the morning. Maybe he'd get an answer. She *must* be staying with her parents. At least they'd know where to find her. He waited for the operator.

"Hi, Aunt Ollie."

"Hi, Connor, what can I do for you?"

"I want to make a long-distance call."

"Maybe somebody'll answer this time."

"I sure hope so." He gave her the number. The phone rang, and rang, and rang.

"Do you want me to let it ring some more?"

GRAVY

"No, Aunt Ollie. Thanks anyway."

"I'm sorry, Connor. Don't get discouraged now. I know you'll get her—or maybe she'll call you."

"I don't know, Aunt Ollie. Don't seem like she wants to talk to me."

"Aw Connor, she's confused. She'll get over it. Gotta go. Got another call." She unplugged and the line went dead.

When he put down the phone, he glanced around the kitchen, thinking where to start. He decided he probably ought to have a screen door in the heat, so he would start there—after breakfast.

He threw a few cobs and a splash of kerosene in the cook stove and lit a fire, thinking about Bobbi trying to figure out how many cobs to use to cook an egg. His mom had said something about how many cobs it takes to bake a cake and Bobbi was off—experimenting with numbers—how many cobs to make this and how many cobs to make that. While the fire settled down to heat the stovetop, he fished out the skillet and grabbed bacon out of the icebox. Noting that he'd need another block of ice, he grabbed a couple of eggs. He pulled out one of the three plates he hadn't broken and served himself, letting the fire die.

Before tackling the door, he re-shelved his books, put the cushions back on the chair and couch and tromped back upstairs to straighten out the bedroom. He had the front door lying on the porch, filling the ripped screw holes, when his dad arrived.

Connor looked up and smiled. "And you brought my Hope." He took her from his dad.

"Thanks, Pop. I called Bobbi this mornin'." He gave his daughter a squeeze.

"Any answer this time?"

"No. They must *live* at that restaurant." Hope squirmed and he set her on the blanket his father had brought. "So I'm fixin' the

280

door." He set back on his heels studying his daughter as she scooted herself around. "Y'know, Pop, I don't think she's retarded at all."

"Me neither."

"Bobbi's been makin' herself sick over it. I guess the doc told her if Hope didn't keep up with some milestones, she wouldn't develop right."

"Oh, that's horse apples. Kids don't do all the same things at the same time."

"Anyway, Bobbi just watched her like a hawk, looking for something wrong."

Henry studied the barn roof, noting some missing shingles. "Seems like them doctors got nothin' to do but scare people."

"Bobbi blames herself for everything."

"I know. That so-called specialist ought to be horsewhipped."

"I'd like to get my hands on him."

"You're already in enough trouble. You done there?"

"Yup," Connor ran a hand over the repaired screw holes.

Connor stood, picked up the baby with her blanket, and went into the kitchen.

Henry surveyed the damage. "That must have been some rampage."

Connor hung his head. "I was pretty upset."

Henry stared at his son. "I wanted to take another look and see what we need. I'll have to run home for some stuff—unless you have wood glue and clamps. He looked around again. "You'll need a little piece of that sheetrock they left behind." He poked at the hole. "You didn't throw it out?"

"No, Pop. It's stacked in the attic."

"Did they leave any of that joint compound?"

"I'll have to get some."

Henry took another look. "I don't know how to do this stuff, but I watched them some. I think we can figure it out. How about if you go to town and get the stuff. Get a blade too, like the kind they used?"

"Sounds good. I'll take Hope with me."

"Okay. And I'll go home and gather up the other stuff we'll need."

They met in the kitchen that afternoon. When Henry arrived, Connor had Hope sitting on the blanket, propped on pillows, reading to her.

"What's that you're reading?"

"Huckleberry Finn."

Henry chuckled. "I think that's a little beyond her understanding."

"Well, yeah, but if she's going to talk, she needs to hear words."

"Good point." Henry fished a bottle of wood glue and a knife from his pocket, picked up a chair leg and scraped off some old glue around dowels. "You didn't get to talk to anybody this mornin'?"

"No, Pop, still no answer."

"You tried callin' that restaurant?" Henry picked up another piece of the chair. "Here, hold this."

282

"Can't remember the name of the damn place, Pop."

Henry kept scraping old glue. "It's your in-laws' business, Connor."

"I know, Pop, but they ignored Bobbi so bad, I didn't care if we ever went back there." He gathered all the scraped pieces together.

"Okay, let's see if this thing fits together."

Connor held the two front legs in place while his dad tried all the other joints.

"They're still her parents." Henry pulled the joints apart. "Okay, now for some glue." He squeezed some into the joint and around the dowel and tapped it into place.

"I know. I know. I wish I'd paid attention. I just wish she'd left me some way to get in touch."

"How 'bout Information?" Henry glued and fit the next joint together.

"Aw, I tried that. Seems like there's hundreds of restaurants in Cleveland."

"Hmmm," Henry said, "We gotta hurry and get all these pieces together now."

They assembled all the joints and Henry showed Connor how to set the clamps with cushioning to prevent scarring the wood.

"Okay, tighten these down. The glue will squeeze out." While Connor tightened, Henry wiped excess glue.

"You know, Pop, I could drive right to that restaurant . . . to their apartment, too."

"It may come to that but give her time. Have you written her a letter?"

"No address, Pop. I wish she'd left her address book. I could call her friends."

Henry set the chair up on its four legs, checking the clamps.

"What if she gets a job with some big-name band? I'll never get her back."

Henry stood. "What if she does, Connor? Would you take that away from her?"

Connor glanced around, checking on Hope still playing with some kitchen utensils on the floor. "Pop, I've been worryin' about that since the day she left. You know, she wanted me to be her agent." He stood, retrieved his daughter, and brushed off the dust. "She may not be crawlin' but she gets around."

"She's just fine." Henry sat on one of the undamaged chairs. "What would you do? Would you try that?"

"I can't do it, Pop." He straightened his daughter's playsuit and set her back on the floor.

"Be a hell of a way to raise a baby."

"I can't force her to come back, though."

"You ready to let her go?"

"No!"

"You may have to."

Connor stood and paced while his dad watched. "But Pop." He stopped and sat beside his father. "In her note, she said she'd always love me." He stood and walked some more. "But she won't let me love her back." He picked Hope up and jiggled her on his hip. "She don't even know I've been callin' almost every day." He handed Hope to his father. "And what about *her*?"

"I don't know, Connor."

Connor walked. "I can't figure her out, Pop."

"I wouldn't give her more'n five or six weeks. Then you might have to drive over there. You gotta let her know you haven't forgotten her."

"That's right. She used to say that her parents never cared enough to keep in touch." He walked to the door and back. "I'll give her another three weeks. Then I'll go get her." He glanced out the window. "Can I borrow your car?"

From that moment on, Connor had a plan. He would repair everything he'd broken, replace the shingles on the barn, get his cattle worked and haul the steers off to the sale barn. He'd make a trip to Hastings to buy something nice for Bobbi—and get some new dishes. Then, on September 22, he would climb into his father's car at five in the morning and head to Cleveland to see his wife. He'd get there late at night, but he'd go find her first thing in the morning. Maybe she'd be ready to come home.

September 9, 1947 — Willow Grove

At the end of the day, carrying buckets to water a few the little trees he'd planted after the storm, Connor saw Pauline's Chevy coupe pulling into the driveway. "Damn!" He didn't suspect her motives, but he felt uneasy having her around as he prepared to go to Cleveland. He'd hinted that she should stay away, but she hadn't taken the hint. He picked up the buckets and walked to the car. "I have a bunch of trees to water, Pauline, then I'm going over to the folks to spend some time with my daughter."

"Give me a bucket and I'll help you."

He stared at her, watching the color creep into her cheeks.

"Pauline, I'm all right now. You don't need to keep checkin' on me every weekend."

Her color deepened and he heard a little tremor in her voice. "I don't want you to get depressed."

"I don't need a babysitter. I'm going to Cleveland soon to bring Bobbi home."

Pauline shifted her eyes to the ground, focusing on a pebble she nudged with her toe. "You finally got a call through?"

"I'm just gonna go get her."

She smiled. "What if . . ."

He looked out at his trees. "She may not come this time, but she'll damn well know I love her, and I want her back home." He turned to Pauline. "What're you crying for?"

"I'm not!"

"What's that tear streaking down your face?"

"Oh! I just wish someone loved me like that, you damn fool!"

Connor blinked, jerking as if to duck a punch. "Fool?" He picked up his buckets and turned away, starting for the tank, turning back after a few steps. "Sorry. Guess I've been absorbed in my own problems." He walked back to his old girlfriend. "You'll find somebody."

"I don't think there's any single men left around here."

"You won't find any hangin' around me." He stared at her for a moment, frowning. *If you'd waited instead of running off the minute I joined the Army without so much as a Dear John . . .*

"You're dismissing me!"

He continued staring. "I'm not."

"You are."

286

"I'm goin' to Cleveland in a couple of weeks."

"Can't we be friends?"

"We are—aren't we?"

"I guess so," Pauline sighed. "Yes. Of course, we are!"

"What were you thinkin'?"

"Never mind. Give me one of them buckets." She grabbed a bucket and headed for the tank. He followed and they watered the trees together in silence. When they'd finished, Pauline followed him into the house to wash up. "I know you're goin' to your folks to see Hope. Mind if I tag along. It'd be nice to see your folks, Connor. I don't think I've seen 'em since Nora left for Paris."

"Don't you have to be at work tomorrow?"

"I won't stay long."

"Guess it won't hurt anything."

"You walk over there, don't you?"

"Usually. It's only a mile."

"I can't believe she left you without a car."

"She was scared, Pauline. We both were."

"You haven't told me what about."

They climbed into her car and she turned to face him—waiting.

"And I'm not goin' to."

She smiled. "Fair enough."

They spend a couple of hours with Claire and Henry until Connor put Hope to bed.

"Gosh it's good to see you," Pauline told Henry and Claire. "It's been ages."

Claire gave her a motherly hug. "You've always been a good friend to my kids, Pauline. I know you've cheered Connor up. You know he's goin' to Cleveland in just a little while."

"Yes, I know. I hope it all works out for them."

When Pauline pulled into the driveway, Connor started to jump out of the car, but she asked him a question and then reminded him of something from their childhood and she kept him talking, losing track of time.

"Oh Connor," Pauline said at about ten thirty. "Could you make me a cup of coffee? I'm sleepy and I gotta drive home."

Connor's heart gave a lurch. It didn't feel right, but he led the way into the kitchen and made some coffee. Sometime after eleven, fortified with caffeine, Pauline jumped up to go. They stood on the step to say goodbye.

"I'm giving you a goodbye hug, Connor Conroy, and there's nothing you can do to stop me."

September 8-9, 1947 — U.S. Highway Six

Leaving Lake Erie, Bobbi hurried to her apartment where she scurried around throwing things, haphazard, into her bags. At seven that morning, she lugged suitcases down to the car. Two more trips and she jumped in the driver's seat and left the city, tapping her fingers on the steering wheel as she waited for traffic and red lights. Half an hour later, she skirted the edge of Lake Erie on U.S. Highway 6. She hoped she wouldn't get stopped, but fifty seemed like crawling, so she pushed it—maybe she could get away with sixty. She couldn't wait to get to Indiana where she wouldn't be breaking any laws.

By the time she reached Gary, she couldn't keep her eyes open. The excitement with which she'd started the day has dissipated and she had to stop, in mid-afternoon. She found a quiet motel and checked in, walked to a nearby diner remembering she hadn't eaten since she'd had the roll and coffee with Tony the previous afternoon. When she got to her room, she fell on the bed for just a minute before she washed up and changed. She awoke feeling energized. She saw sunlight leaking around the drapes. She shouldn't have stopped. She'd lost good driving time. Since she'd paid for the room, she decided to shower and change . . .

When someone knocked, she opened the door.

"Oh. I'm sorry I disturbed you."

"I need to get going anyway. I won't spend the night."

"You weren't checked in for another night."

"Another night? I just got here."

"You were here when I came to work this morning."

"No, that must have been someone else."

"I check the roster when I come to work. You checked in yesterday."

Bobbi stared. "What day is this?"

"It's Tuesday, Ma'am. September 9."

"What time is it?"

"Seven o'clock."

"Morning? Holy cow! I gotta go. You can come back in half an hour. I'll be out of here then." She hurried into the bathroom, stripping off her rumpled clothes on the way.

Showered and changed, she grabbed her overnight bag and ran out to the car, climbed in, and roared out of the parking lot. She settled in at sixty miles per hour, slowing as she passed through little towns—there must have been hundreds of them. She crossed into Iowa at ten thirty Central Time. *About five hundred miles to go. Not as many towns now. Maybe I'll be home by midnight.*

She tried not to think ahead, keeping her mind blank. No sense in getting all excited and finding out Connor wouldn't have her. No, she wouldn't think about what might happen in Willow Grove. She'd live on hope for a few more hours. When she crossed the Missouri River into Omaha, she stared at the buildings and sidewalks, and all the people walking around in the early evening. *Last chance, Bobbi. No more cities from now on.* Stomach growling, she stopped when she spotted a little café with a handy parking lot.

Once out of Omaha she felt like she'd driven onto another continent. *It's so quiet. Only the sound of the car. It's like I'm the only person left on the planet, blinded in that blaze of light, occasionally passing an artifact of some lost civilization—the white grain elevators coming up in my windshield then falling behind; an occasional farmyard with a man walking around carrying buckets of feed or water for his livestock.* As the sky darkened, she noticed the occasional farmhouse with a dim light, probably kerosene, visible through a window.

At about eleven thirty, she pulled into the yard. *Connor must have got another car.* As she circled the willow tree, her headlights lit up the front door. She saw someone on the step. "It's Connor," she whispered with an exhausted sigh. Then the two bodies separated realizing her worst fear—another woman. She stared a moment, tears streaming, as Connor walked toward the car, right arm shielding his eyes from her headlights.

When he touched the front fender, she managed to react, slamming the car into reverse and backing around behind the other car to escape out the lane.

Connor ran, reaching for the door when she stopped moving to shift. "Bobbi! Stop!"

At the end of the quarter-mile lane, she looked in the rearview mirror. Connor sprinted behind her about halfway up the lane. She couldn't believe he could move that fast. She slammed it into second and spun her wheels as she fishtailed onto the gravel, throwing dirt and rocks behind her. Before she dropped over the first hill, she looked again to see Connor standing in the lane, hands on his knees, panting.

I should have known somebody'd be after him as soon as word got out.

September 9, 1947 — Willow Grove

Connor noticed the headlights first. They'd started into the driveway before he could disengage.

"It's Bobbi," he whispered as he started down the sidewalk. He smiled and ran to greet his wife. "*She came home.* He'd already forgotten Pauline still standing on the step.

"Bobbi! Stop!" he yelled as she backed around and sped out the lane. He sprinted to catch up, laying a hand on the trunk before she accelerated. He kept running, bent over in a crouch as though he were ducking mortar rounds. He'd run about halfway out the lane, when Bobbi crested the first hill on the main road. He gave up then. He sprinted back to the house.

"She saw us. She'll think the worst."

Pauline sat at the wheel of her car. "I'm sorry, Connor."

291

"Move over. I've gotta catch her."

She scooted to the far side of the car. He gunned the engine. He sped around the driveway and down the lane. Pauline hung on, bracing herself on the dashboard. He hoped he could hold the car on loose gravel as he tore toward the three-mile corner. "I don't know where she went," he muttered as he neared the corner. "Shoulda caught her by now." He fishtailed around the turn and floored it until he got to the highway. "I've lost her." He stopped, peering up the road, looking for taillights. "She shouldna got away. I don't understand."

"She was way ahead of you, Connor."

"Not that far. I shoulda caught her."

He turned toward home. "You can drop me at Mom and Pop's. I'll borrow their car."

When they reached his parents' house, Connor slid to a stop, dust rolling up over the back of the car. He leapt out and stormed into the house, leaving Pauline to find her own way home. "Mom! Pop!" he yelled. "I need the car! Bobbi's here!" He ran up the stairs, two at a time. "Pop!" he yelled, "you awake? I need the car—now!"

He barely heard the baby crying as he focused on catching up to his wife.

Henry stepped out of the bedroom, closing the door behind him. "What's goin' on?"

"It's Bobbi, Pop. She came home."

Henry stared at his son, waiting for the rest of the story.

"She drove in the yard, and I knew the car by the headlights. Pauline was just leavin'."

Henry shook his head.

GRAVY

"I tried to catch her, Pop, but I don't know where she went."

"So, what're ya gonna do?"

"I wanna borrow your car and try and catch her. Make her understand." He stood facing his father in the dark.

Henry sighed. "Tomorrow's Wednesday. Today, I guess. You got any cash?" Connor turned out his pockets.

"I got nothin,' Pop. What if I have to drive all the way to Cleveland?"

"Let's go downstairs." Henry led his son down the narrow steps. He lit a lamp. "You better wait 'til you can get some cash."

"I can't, Pop, I don't want her thinkin' the worst."

Henry heaved another sigh. "Car's about empty." He got his wallet out of the top buffet drawer. "I got a few bucks, that'll maybe get ya to Omaha. You got a checkbook?"

"At the house."

"You'll hafta change clothes and pack some stuff for a few days anyway, just in case."

"Pop, I don't wanta fool around that long. I don't have the time!"

Henry eyed his son. "Take the time."

"But she's gonna think . . ."

"She already does."

Connor groaned.

"You're just gonna hafta convince her and don't start out looking guilty. You aren't, are you?"

"No, Pop. Pauline just got to talkin' about old times."

"Huh."

"She was leavin.' She insisted on givin' me a goodbye hug. That's when Bobbi drove up the lane. Caught us in her headlights."

"You better go get her 'fore she has too much time to get solid in her opinion. But be ready to stay a while."

Connor stared at his father, red-eyed. "Maybe she stopped in Hastings. She's probably tired."

"And mad as a wet hen."

"I gotta go, Pop."

"You drive careful son, ya hear me?"

By the time Connor had packed a few changes of clothes, turned the house upside down looking for some money, and located his checkbook and his wallet, the sky had begun to lighten. He strode out the front door, duffle bag over his shoulder, stowed the bag in the back seat and climbed into his dad's Chrysler New Yorker. He pulled out of the lane, driving at a sane pace, and turned north.

In Hastings, he drove around for hours, looking for the gray Plymouth—their Plymouth—at all the motels, By the time he remembered the parking lot behind the Lazy J, Bobbi had already left for Henry and Claire's.

September 10, 1947 — Willow Grove

After seeing Connor and Pauline, Bobbi drove to her in-laws', hoping to see her daughter, until she remembered the time. She turned around in their driveway and headed north to Hastings where she would spend the night. First, she had to get to Hastings, and she soon realized that she'd got herself lost again.

GRAVY

Driving country roads in the dark, she again had the sensation of being the last remaining human. She followed the tunnel of her headlights, around and around. When she found herself at the end of the lane, back at home—where she'd hoped to be home—she stopped and looked toward the house. When she saw not a flicker of light, she exploded. "He could have waited a month! It's only been a month!" Then she pressed the accelerator and stormed over the hill in a cloud of dust lit only by headlights and a three-quarter moon.

When she passed Henry and Claire's house the second time, she saw lights. *Damn! I must have woke them up. Maybe I should stop now.* She kept driving. *I'll apologize tomorrow. I can't deal with them now.*" The second time, she paid more attention. *I go three crossings this way.* At the three-mile corner, she stopped, peering through the windshield, trying to remember. Frustrated, she pounded on the steering wheel. *I couldn't have lived here anyway. I can't even find my way to town.*

She chose right and finally found U.S. 281. She sighed and drove straight north to Hastings, hoping she'd find a vacancy. When she reached Hastings, her vision blurred, she spotted a vacancy sign and pulled into the parking lot. Stumbling into the lobby, she rang the bell and waited, pacing, whispering to herself. "What'm I gonna do? What'm I gonna do? What'm I gonna do?"

When the clerk appeared, looking as disheveled as Bobbi felt, she checked in, took her little stack of towels and her key, and drove around to the parking lot in the back. There, she paced some more. *Okay, I'll go back to Cleveland. See if Tony has got Fred to budge. Otherwise, I'll find something somewhere else. I'll just have to control myself. I'll file for divorce.* She sat on the edge of the bed, face in her hands, sobbing. *A month. Only a month.*

When she'd cried herself out, she stood and began pacing again. *I'll file for divorce, then, when I get myself established, I'll come back and get Hope. I can't give them both up.* She tried to ignore the screaming voice inside. *What if you explode like you did with the peas, Bobbi? What if you hurt her? What if . . .?*

"Shut up!" she screamed. Someone pounded on the wall of the next room and she subsided, head hanging, and sat. Eventually, she levered off her shoes with her toes and swung her legs up onto the bed, pulling the side of the spread over her. She awoke when light came creeping around the curtains. She awoke groggy, feeling like she'd just butchered a whole flock of chickens, with that dead chicken smell in her mouth.

She stumbled into the bathroom and checked the mirror. A haggard old woman with puffy eyes stared back at her. "Ugh!" She turned away and retrieved her overnight bag, scrubbing her face with cold water to bring up some color. She soaked a washcloth in cold water and lay down for a few minutes with the compress across her eyes. She'd had to cover up exhaustion when she'd traveled with the bands. She knew how to do it.

With the swelling under control, she showered and dressed, stepping back into the bathroom for inspection. She added a little eye makeup and called it good. *Nobody'll ever know I spent the night crying my eyes out.* She gathered her belongings and left for her in-law's farm.

Claire came to the door, wiping her hands on her apron. "There you are. Connor's gone after you."

"What do you mean gone after me? I saw him at the house last night."

"He came up here in a panic. At first, we couldn't understand him, he was so shaken up."

"Whatever for?"

"Said you'd come to the house and Pauline was there." Claire said it as if it were the most normal thing in the world to come home and find your husband in another woman's arms.

Henry stepped up behind Claire. "Come on in the house. There's no sense standin' on the step. C'mon in and set down, so we can talk."

Bobbi complied. "Nothin' to talk about, Pop. Connor's got another woman. I left so he got on with it." Her dry throat choked her.

"That's the thing. He ain't got no other woman."

"No," said Claire, "he don't."

"It's okay. I saw him myself—last night."

"But that's just Pauline!"

"What Claire's tryin' to say. Pauline's an old neighbor. They played together when they was kids. She's been worried about him."

"We've all been worried about him."

"Well, she looked like she was more'n a little worried about him."

"Bobbi. If you hadna brought that damn pistol up here for Mom to hide, I don't know what he woulda done. He was lookin' for it after you left."

"He didn't think he had any reason to live anymore."

Bobbi's eyes narrowed. "It sure didn't take him long to find one."

"He ain't over it."

"Mom, he's probably just gettin' out of bed over there—with Pauline."

"He ain't over there at all." Henry said. "He come stormin' up here at midnight or so in Pauline's car and wanted to borrow our car to catch up with you."

"Well, he can't have us both."

"He don't *want* you both," Claire said, "Pauline's been comin' round trying to cheer him up."

"I remember now. Isn't she the one he was goin' with when he joined the Army?"

"Yeah. She went off and got engaged to somebody else."

Bobbi frowned. "She's married?"

"No. The marriage didn't come off."

"So now she wants Connor back." Out of the corner of her eye, she spotted movement next to the kerosene heater. Hope squirmed on a little roll-away bed in the corner near the stove, frowning and watching her mom. Bobbi caught her breath. "Hope!"

Henry gathered the baby into his arms. Hope watched her mother, while Bobbi struggled to keep her hands in her lap. "She's grown. Does she crawl yet?"

"No, but it's a little early for that," Henry said, "and you're not to worry about it. She's doin' just fine."

"Bobbi, Connor still loves you, and he wants you to come back more'n anything."

"You don't know how much I want to believe that, but what I saw did not look like wanting me back." Bobbi reached her arms out to Hope. "Hope, honey, would you come to mommy?"

Hope stared at her and Bobbi let her hands fall into her lap. She blinked back a tear.

"Give her a minute. She's not used to you now."

"That's just the point, isn't it? I screwed everything and everybody up. Hope won't develop right. She doesn't even know me." She looked at Claire. "Mom, I'm goin' back to Cleveland. I'll have to get some things settled and then I'll file for divorce so Connor can get back with Pauline. I don't have anything to offer him anyway."

"Bobbi! You can't do that! Connor doesn't *want* Pauline. He wants you!"

Bobbi looked at Hope and her daughter reached for her. Bobbi picked her up and walked with her, humming the little lullaby, "Chi baba chi baba chi wah wah . . ."

"I'll get things set up so I can take care of Hope, then I'll come back and get her. Connor's got Pauline now . . ."

"Connor's got no such thing! You want him to kill himself?"

Henry stood, raising his eyebrows at his wife. "Just listen to what Connor has to say. Would you do that?"

"I'm not goin' over there to *see* Connor after last night!"

"Bobbi! Didn't you hear us? He's out lookin' for you."

"He didn't come back?"

"No. He said he'd try to catch up with you before you got to Hastings. If not, he was going on to Cleveland and try to catch you somewhere in between."

"Why don't you just stay here. When he calls, we'll tell him to come back."

"I'm not sure."

"Just stay. Have you had any breakfast?"

"Well, no."

"Stay here and spend some time with Hope. Then you can thrash it out with Connor."

"I'll make you some breakfast." Claire jumped up as if it were settled.

"Oh, don't bother."

"It's no bother, Bobbi, I'll just fry you some eggs and bacon." Bobbi heard the rattle as Claire shook the ashes down from their breakfast.

"That *does* sound good."

Bobbi spent the day and the night, sleeping in Connor's old bedroom and remembering their first nights there—how embarrassed she'd been when the bed collapsed. And she allowed herself to hope. She knew what she had seen—her husband in another woman's arms. But the embrace had been so fleeting, just a flash in her headlights. Maybe, just maybe, Henry and Claire had told the truth that it had been a friendly hug. Maybe.

When Connor hadn't call by Thursday night, Bobbi couldn't take any more waiting. She decided to leave early, find her husband, and have it out. She walked out the door at five a.m., with a lunch of sandwiches and carrots, along with a thermos of coffee.

September 10-11, 1947 — U.S. Highway Six

In Hastings, Connor pulled into a Conoco station and filled up for the long haul. "Let me write a check for a hundred so I can take some cash with me.

"Can't do it."

"How about a fifty?"

"Look, it don't matter how much you write your check for. I ain't got any change as it is."

Connor wrote a check for the amount of his gas and jumped in the car heading east. At ten o'clock in the morning, he figured Bobbi had at least half a day on him unless she stopped somewhere. He would have to drive all the way to Cleveland. He arrived in Omaha, late-afternoon. He doubted he could cash a check after he crossed the Missouri River Bridge, so he again fussed with a station attendant for cash.

"Try that liquor store down there." The guy pointed to a neon sign down a couple of blocks.

Connor wrote another check for his gas and drove down the street. He only had two checks left. He tried to get a hundred but got a six-pack of Budweiser and a twenty, instead. He crawled back in the car. He considered driving on. The twenty might get him to Cleveland. He didn't have to eat, didn't need to sleep. His mind jerked back to the times on New Guinea when they had starved and run and fought without sleep, without water, until big, strong men simply collapsed in the heat. "Mendez, Wilson, Moore . . ." He sat staring out the windshield, seeing the rocky hillside where they died.

Snap out of it. You can do this. He figured he and Bobbi would have to spend at least one night in a motel and they'd have to eat on the return trip. And besides, he didn't know how long it would take in Cleveland. He drove down to Thirteenth and Farnam. By the time he found a bank and a parking place, the banks had closed. He would have to spend the night in the car and run in the minute the bank opened. He leaned back in the seat to wait.

Hours later, he opened his eyes in the glow of streetlights. He rummaged around in the glove compartment and found a can opener. "Thanks, Pop." He took a beer out of its cardboard cradle, levered it open and took a long, slow sip. "Mmmm." He coughed, "Warm beer."

By morning, he'd had a couple of little naps, finished the six pack, and had a full bladder to show for it. *No place to piss around here.* He considered driving down to the river, but it was almost time for the bank to open. He wanted to get going.

His cash withdrawal took longer than it should have. Since he was writing an out-of-town check, the teller called a manager and he had to wait, show ID, and wait some more. He didn't walk out the doors until nine-thirty.

* * * * *

A nine-fifteen, still watching for her in-law's Chrysler, Bobbi stopped at the light on Farnam and Fourteenth. She'd already driven for hours, settling on U.S. Highway 6 for the long haul to Cleveland. She glanced at the tall buildings of the financial district. *Hope I'll find him soon. Get this hashed out. Figure out what to do.* She studied the cars ahead. *Hope I'll recognize the Chrysler from behind.*

The light changed and she followed traffic down a block to Thirteenth. *What am I thinking? He left Wednesday morning. He'll be in Cleveland by now.* She glanced at the First National Bank, noticing a Chrysler parked out front. *That looks like Mom and Pop's car.* She shook her head. *Too bad it's not. I'd like to punch him in the nose right now.*

She again followed traffic across the Missouri River Bridge and back out into farm country. She noticed the open skies and horizons that stretched away for miles. In Des Moines, she filled up with gas and took a bathroom break.

* ** * *

With his cash in hand, Connor practically danced with frustration and discomfort. Once across the Missouri River Bridge, he looked for a patch of weeds, but he had to get through Council Bluffs first. *Damn! Get me outa here.* He finally screeched to a stop about a mile from the city limits, jumping out of the car, and plunging into the road ditch.

On the road again, he put himself into that place he'd found in New Guinea, where he numbed body and brain into complete focus on mission—not danger, not ability to perform, not mission's end, not the next step, only the task ahead. Boring duty, but he'd learned to endure boredom. Seventeen, eighteen, maybe twenty to twenty-five hours. He could stand almost anything for that long.

He looked straight ahead without noticing the fields and farms along the road. He barely saw the cities, only noticing route signs, streetlights, other traffic. What he did notice passed out of his mind as soon as it slipped behind him. About twenty miles east of Des Moines, the car took a sudden lurch to the left into oncoming traffic. Driving one-handed, Connor found himself staring at the grill of a Mack truck. "Crap," he yelled as he jerked his elbow from the window and wrestled the car to the shoulder, skimming within inches of the truck's high front fender and the driver's steps. Once he had the adrenalin surge under control, he climbed out and checked the tires. As he'd thought, the left front had shredded. He groaned. Still can't get rubber. Another holdup.

He sighed and got the jack and the spare out of the trunk. He changed the tire in about ten minutes, but he knew he had to get a new one before he went very far. All the other tires showed just as much wear as the one he'd removed. When he pulled into Grinnell, he stopped at a service station. When he pulled up to the service bay an attendant, the name on his pocket said Les, walked out wiping his hands on a grease rag. He leaned in the window.

"How can I help you?" He got the tire size and went inside, coming back in a few minutes shaking his head. "We can order it from Des Moines and have it here in about an hour."

"Or I can drive back." Connor checked his watch—twelve-thirty. He figured he'd lose about the same amount of time either way. "Order it."

He got something to eat and found a phone. His mom told him that Bobbi had spent the day Wednesday and left at about five that morning. She should catch up any time. *Maybe I should wait and watch for her.* He calculated driving time. *She must have passed through Omaha about the time I left. She may have already passed me.*

Numbed to the sameness of the road, the fields, and the little towns, Bobbi settled into the rhythm of the car engine and the wheels on the road. To keep herself alert, she sang. When her throat felt scratchy, she tried to stop before she made herself hoarse, but the empty hours created a vacuum where the melodies that poured through all her waking hours had to come out. She was singing *Begin the Beguine* when she passed Grinnell at one-fifteen. She glanced at the service station right beside the road but didn't really see it. She remembered the lunch Claire had made for her and nibbled as she drove.

* * * * *

With a usable spare in the trunk, Connor pulled back onto U.S. 6 and took his time, driving just under the speed limit and hoping he'd see the Plymouth grill in his rearview mirror. By the time he reached Davenport and the Illinois border, he hadn't spotted it. He resigned himself to driving all the way to Cleveland. He stepped hard on the accelerator, detached again from everything but the driving, driving without thought or emotion, conscious only of the road ahead. He barely slowed down to pass through the little towns along the way and that finally caught up to him just outside Joliet, when he saw flashing lights behind him. *Damn it! Damn it, Damn it, Damn it!* He pulled over to the shoulder. It only took a few minutes to get the ticket, but that was a few more minutes he'd fallen behind. Back on the road, he slowed down and numbed his growing frustration with more of the task at hand.

September 13, 1947 — Cleveland

Bobbi unlocked her apartment at about ten in the morning, bleary-eyed and cold. She dragged in only her overnight bag because she still hoped Connor would find her soon. Maybe he'd already got her address from her parents. Maybe she could just leave her things in the car and take them back home instead of hauling them in through the cold drizzle.

She looked around the bare room with its generic furnishings, remembering all the things she'd picked out when she moved into the house with Connor. She set the bag on the floor. *Maybe he decided I'm too much trouble and turned back.* She dropped her purse on the floor next to the overnight case and looked out the window for the Chrysler.

She flopped into a chair. *Nope. I won't think it.*

While she tried to decide whether to go to bed or to stay awake and wait for him, she dozed in the chair. She awakened a few minutes later, groggy, to the sound of someone pounding on the door. She jumped up, smiling and smoothing her rumpled clothes. *It's him!* She ran a hand through her hair and opened the door.

* * * * *

When Connor arrived in Cleveland, he remembered not a single detail of the trip, as though time had stopped in Omaha and resumed in Cleveland when he pulled up in front of Ella's apartment building. On that crowded city street, losing his wife for the second time nearly drove him to his knees. Thrust back two nights, with Bobbi returning to the farm and the taillights of the car going over that first hill, he almost felt the adrenalin rush pushing him out the lane on foot. He inhaled, coughing on the city air, and opened the apartment house door.

I'll just go up these stairs and knock on the door and I'll have a civilized conversation with my wife.

He trudged up the stairs, craning his neck to see the top of each landing, as if he expected to see Bobbi on one of them. When his knock got no answer, he stood, forehead against the door, waiting for his frustration to subside. He walked back down the stairs and stood beside the car wondering if they'd all moved away. He lit a cigarette and scanned the street, pacing. He

checked his watch. Nine-thirty. The restaurant was already
open. He dropped his cigarette, ground it out under his heel, and
leapt into the car. Five minutes later, he pulled up in the alley
behind the restaurant in a cold drizzle. When he stepped inside,
he took an immediate left and walked into the kitchen.

"Hey," said Paul, "get outta here!"

"Where's Bobbi?"

Paul glanced over his shoulder. "Oh, it's you."

"Where's Bobbi?"

"How should I know? I ain't seen her since she got that job at
LakeView."

"She's not staying with Ella?"

"Naw. She got her own place."

"Where is it?"

Paul turned a couple of eggs and checked on some hash browns.
"Around here somewhere."

"What do you mean somewhere? Where is she?"

"Look, you come tearin' in here yelling.' Whadaya want from
me?"

"My wife. I want my wife."

"Took ya long enough," Paul stepped over and stared into
Connor's eyes.

"Well, I'm here now. Where is she?"

Paul eyed him for a long moment, then turned back to the eggs.
"Ella has her address."

"God dammit! Where *is* she?"

Paul turned again staring, his mouth working. "She's out front waiting on customers, you asshole. Where'd you think she'd be?" He turned back to his grill. "Now get outa here and leave me alone!"

Connor stalked out into the dining room, scanning for Ella. When he spotted her waiting on a table, he made his way to her side. "Where's Bobbi?"

Ella kept writing in her order book. "And you'll have?"

Connor took her arm. "Where's Bobbi?"

Ella jerked free. "I'm working here. I don't know where Bobbi is. Now leave me alone." She turned back to the table. "I'm sorry about the interruption. Was there anything else?" When she'd taken everyone's order, she rushed back to the kitchen with Connor right on her heels. She turned in the order and he again demanded Bobbi's location.

"Paul said you have her address."

"Yeah. Get outta my way." Connor stepped aside as she grabbed the coffeepot and an extra glass of water and headed back out on the floor with Connor as close as a shadow. When she stopped suddenly, he almost ran over her. "Get outta here," she demanded in a fierce whisper.

"Not 'til you give me Bobbi's address."

"I don't know it."

He stood and glared, holding her gaze.

"Oh, all right! Go back by the kitchen and wait." She poured coffee and served the water. "I think it's in my coat pocket."

She followed him to the back room and retrieved a torn piece of paper. "Copy it and leave this right here." She pointed to an open spot on a small table and left.

He fumbled around the room until he found another order pad and a pencil. He scribbled the address and ran out to the car. Paul had said it was close by, he hoped he'd stumble on the street if he just drove around the area. Every moment he wasted was a moment she'd doubt what his parents had told her. He drove methodically, peering through the windshield wipers, going around block after block, looking for Random Road. At last he found the building and bounded up the stairs.

* * * * *

When Bobbi opened the door, she found Tony.

"Where you been? What happened to you? Are you all right?"

She sighed. "I'm fine. I just made a quick trip to Nebraska to see my daughter." *What do I tell him? I don't even know what's going to happen.*

"When'd you get back? I saw the car outside."

"Just now—an hour ago, I guess."

"You must be exhausted. I just wanted to let you know Fred's gonna give you another chance."

"Oh thanks, Tony. When does he want me to start?"

"He said to take a week and try to get your head on straight." He looked over her shoulder. Mind if I come in?" He wiped his wet shoes on the hall carpet.

"No, of course not. Tough night?"

"Yeah. I'm beat." He sat in the nearest chair.

"So that would be Saturday, wouldn't it?"

"Guess so. If that's too soon he'll probably give you more time."

They continued discussing Fred's terms. No hitting customers, of course. Chatting up the clientele between sets.

"All without you to keep 'em off me?"

"'Fraid so."

A knock interrupted them. Grinning, Bobbi jumped up to answer. The moment Connor stepped across the threshold Bobbi felt a charge—as if a thunderstorm had just blown into her apartment. She looked back at Tony.

"Bobbi, I just want to explain." Connor looked past Bobbi and spotted Tony getting up from where he and Bobbi had been sitting. "Who's that?"

"That's Tony, Connor."

Eyes narrowed Connor stared at the other man. "The bouncer you told me about."

"Yeah."

"What's he doin' here?" Connor frowned. "It don't matter. He don't need to be here."

"Connor . . ."

"I'm just leaving."

"You better."

"Stop it, Connor!"

He grabbed Tony and shoved him toward the door. Tony stood his ground.

"Bobbi, will you be all right?"

GRAVY

Bobbi looked from one to the other.

"God damn it!" Connor grappled with the bouncer, "Get outa here!"

Tony stepped out of Connor's grasp. "Bobbi, I'm not gonna let him hurt you."

Connor tried again to shove the other man out the door, but Tony stepped aside. "Get outta here! I need to talk to my wife— alone."

Tony backed up a step, watching Bobbi's face.

"Connor, just settle down."

Connor kept pushing and Bobbi watched his eyes turn red— something they always did when he went into battle mode. She tried to talk to him, but nothing penetrated his overcharged brain.

The men erupted into the hall, panting and snarling. Connor got Tony onto the floor in a chokehold when a door down the hall slammed open and a disheveled man stormed out looking like he'd just awakened with a whopping hangover.

"What's goin' on here?" He didn't wait for an answer, but slammed Connor to the floor from behind. "Don't know who started this but it's over." He kicked Connor in the ribs.

"Leave him alone!" Bobbi grabbed the man's arm. He shrugged her off and stood glowering while Connor lay gasping for air. Tony scrambled to his feet, coughing.

"Thanks," he croaked, offering a hand to the neighbor.

"Just get the hell outta here."

"C'mon Connor." Tony helped Connor to his feet, "let's get outta here."

GRAVY

"I need to talk to Bobbi."

Tony dropped Connor's arm. "Later."

The neighbor took a threatening step toward them both.

Connor glanced at the neighbor, then at Bobbi. "We have to talk."

Bobbi stared at him, noticing the snarl that distorted his mouth and the fire in his eyes.

"Come on, Connor. You need a nap."

"So do I," the neighbor grumbled. "Get the hell outta here."

"We're goin'." Tony turned to Connor, trying to steer him toward the stairs, but Connor shrugged him off.

"I can walk. Just get off me." He straightened with a grimace. He turned toward Bobbi.

"Just go." Bobbi shook her head. "You're scaring me."

Connor's shoulders sagged. He made eye contact. "I'll be back."

Bobbi slammed the door.

When she heard the two men's feet on the stairs, she fell onto the sofa, trembling. She hugged her knees, trying to calm herself. *He's not any better. He's worse. I was crazy to think this could work.*

* * * * *

Connor stormed to ground level with Tony right behind him. Ignoring the other man, he slammed into his car and sat staring at the Plymouth, noting Tony's bulk beside the door where he'd stopped to light a cigarette. "Damn it," he grumbled, "won't that guy ever leave?"

GRAVY

Connor pulled into traffic. He stopped at the first liquor store and bought a six-pack and a pint of Jim Beam to calm himself. He drove in the general direction of the lake. When he arrived at the parking lot at Euclid Beach, rain on the windshield distorted waves pounded onto sand. What he could see reminded him of go-back places abandoned during the thirties—empty acres of tall grass prairie blowing in the wind. He'd seen thousands of acres during his rambles around the West.

He considered stepping out of the car and walking into the waves until he couldn't walk anymore. Instead, he popped the cap off one of the bottles beside him on the seat. He leaned back with his arm over the back of the seat, chug-a-lugged the bottle and opened another. Gradually, he settled into a kind of calm, the kind of calm he'd found before battle when the men all knew what they had to do; when they knew they'd soon try to kill people they'd never met; when they knew those people would try to rip their guts out; when they knew they would most likely lose some buddies; and they knew there wasn't a damn thing they could do about it. He fidgeted with the label on the bottle, scraping at it with his fingernail, emptying his mind of everything but the bottle—and the next one. When an image of Bobbi slamming the door on him intruded, he checked his watch, deciding to return to her apartment in mid-afternoon. He hoped Tony wouldn't be there.

He opened another bottle, emptying his mind of everything but the wait and the bottle in his hand. By the end of the six-pack, his mind-emptying had stalled and a kaleidoscope of images he couldn't stop overwhelmed him. His brain ratcheted from Lone Tree Hill, standing over Hayes' lifeless body, to the hospital in Nebraska, glimpsing his wife's open belly through a swinging OR door, to the house he'd shared with Bobbi; to staring into the headlights of his very own car with a black sense of dread rising in his throat like bile.

He twisted off the cap of the whiskey bottle and took a slug. He *had* to calm down.

By mid-afternoon, he felt more agitated than ever. He might have decided to get sober before visiting Bobbi—but he didn't consider himself drunk. He might have checked into a hotel and got some sleep—but he'd managed for days without sleep in New Guinea, he didn't think he needed to rest. He would do those things later. He really wanted to settle things with Bobbi and take her home. He returned to her apartment where he leaned in the doorway and knocked, preparing himself to storm in if he saw Tony.

Bobbi answered and he pushed her aside, scanning the room for Tony. He saw fear in her eyes, but he ignored it. "Where is he?"

Bobbi hesitated, cringing. "He's not . . ." She drew a long breath. "He's on his way."

He grabbed her by the shoulders, breathing his alcohol-saturated breath in her face, his fingers dug in. "Bobbi, Pauline's just an old friend."

"Let me go. You're hurting me."

He let go and stepped back, weaving on his feet. "Bobbi, I want you to come home."

She stared at him, rubbing the bruises on her shoulders where his fingers had bruised her flesh. "I can't, Connor."

"Why not?"

She stepped back, stumbling into a chair. "Because." She hesitated and glanced around the apartment as if seeking an escape route. "Because." she studied something on the floor. "Because I'm going to." She looked into his eyes and down at his shoes. "I'm going to marry Tony."

Connor frowned. "But." He leaned against the wall. "But you came home."

"Yeah." She couldn't look him in the face. "I'll come back and pick up Hope as soon as I can get things settled."

313

Connor lunged for her, but she stepped out of reach. "You can't," he pleaded, slumping into a chair.

"It'll be better this way."

"No, it won't." Connor sat with his head in his hands.

"Connor, you've gotta leave now. I need to get ready to go back to work."

"Bobbi, I . . ."

"I'll file for divorce so you can get on with Pauline."

"Pauline's . . . I don't *want* Pauline!"

"Connor."

Connor looked up at her, anguish in his eyes.

"Connor. Don't hurt me please."

He stood and tried to embrace her, but she stepped away. "Bobbi." He dropped his empty arms to his sides. "I wouldn't hurt you."

"Just go, Connor, you're scaring me."

"I don't mean to."

"Go! Please!"

Connor gave her a long, searching look, then turned and left, stopping with his hand on the doorknob to look back over his shoulder for a moment as if to memorize her face.

GRAVY

September 13-14, 1947 — U.S. Highway Six

Dismissed, Connor stumbled down the stairs and outside the
apartment building. He stopped in the shelter of the doorway
and stared at the rain, coming in sheets by then. He reached into
his shirt pocket for a cigarette. He pulled a lighter out of his
pants pocket and fumbled to light up with shaking hands. With
both hands to steady the flame, he drew in a lungful of smoke. A
couple more drags failed to sooth him, and he dropped the
cigarette on the pavement and stomped it.

He walked to the car through the downpour, ignoring water
running down his face and under his collar. He climbed in,
gripped the steering wheel, laid his forehead on his hands, and
wept.

Once he'd composed himself, he drove back to the neighborhood
liquor store where he bought a quart of Jim Beam. The cashier
eyed him critically. "Mister, you look like hell."

"How much?"

"That'll be a buck fifty."

Connor peeled off a twenty.

"Looks like you already got a good start." the guy counted out
the change.

Connor stuffed money in his pocket and left, making no effort to
get out of the rain. He turned on the wipers and drove with no
particular destination, taking a gulp whenever he thought of it.
*I'm worthless. I can't do normal stuff anymore. I can't stop the
nightmares and the war. No wonder Bobbi wants someone like
Tony who doesn't have fits in thunderstorms, get into fights, and
scare her half to death.*

While he berated himself, he circled around Cleveland until he
settled down onto U.S. Highway 6, heading west toward Chicago
without really noticing. Somewhere between Sheffield Lake and

315

GRAVY

Lorain, he glanced at the fuel gauge and stopped at the next gas station. When he stepped out to pay for gas and use the men's room, he slipped in a puddle and fell half in and half out of the car, painfully wrenching his back. Levering himself with his elbows, he turned over and pushed himself onto his knees. He gingerly drew himself up and limped into the station house.

Back on the road, he drove into the gathering dusk, drinking steadily and peering bleary-eyed into the darkness. He cursed when another driver flashed his headlights to remind him. He switched on the lights then promptly forgot them, screaming at other drivers when they flashed their high beams.

Just outside Sandusky, he pulled into a gas station that had closed for the night and dropped off to sleep to the roar of rain bouncing off the car. He woke a few hours later, whispering the names. He grabbed the steering wheel to pull himself upright, squinting through the rain. Then he remembered Bobbi kicking him out, talking about divorce. He took a big slug of whiskey from the nearly-empty bottle and drove on, heading in the same direction as before—although it didn't really matter.

He drove through the night and into a gray dawn, barely noticing as the light gradually increased behind him. Traveling a deserted stretch of highway through heavy fog, he felt as if he'd driven into one of those places at the edge of the jungle where trees blocked the curtain of rain outside, and water dripped from leaf to leaf before it dropped to the forest floor. He saw only the glow of his headlights, reflecting off water droplets, and heard only the whisper of water lifted by his tires.

Half asleep, he noticed a painted turtle crossing the road ahead of him. "Must be lookin' for love," he muttered. He stopped and picked up the turtle, setting him on the floor of the passenger side.

"Here ya go ol' fella. Pr'aps we can talk 'bout this."

He crawled back into the driver's seat, drenched and shivering. "This ain't New Guinea, ol' boy." He eyed the turtle. "'s fuckin'

316

chilly out there." He pulled back onto the highway. "Now you just set back an' relax."

He had no idea how long he'd been driving when he pulled off the highway onto gravel at the three-mile corner. He plowed mud totally by instinct and years of practice. He pulled into his own driveway in the dark and stumbled into the house with the turtle tucked under his arm, automatically stripping out of his clothes on the porch and leaving them on the floor, along with the second, empty, whiskey bottle. He didn't remember where he'd got that, but he didn't stop to think about it.

Leaving the turtle to pace the porch, he dragged himself up the stairs and flopped onto his side of the empty bed. *Just like flopping into a hammock in the jungle. You're too god-damned tired to worry about what might kill you in the night.* He drifted off to sleep.

September 15, 1947 — Willow Grove

Connor awakened to another gray day, groaning as he opened his eyes. He closed them again and tried to remember why he needed to wake up. His head felt tight, like he'd got too much brain matter to fit in his skull—not that he felt very smart. In fact, so far, he hadn't had a coherent thought.

He tried to sit but moving tightened the strap around his forehead and his back screamed. He eased himself back down and lay thinking about what the hell he'd done to his back. After another few minutes, he elbowed himself onto his butt with another groan. Opening his eyes again, he squinted around the room, trying to remember where he'd landed. Recognizing his own bedroom, he looked for Bobbi, then remembered leaving Cleveland and the word "divorce." Elbows on knees, he lowered his aching head into his hands.

"Damn, I need a drink."

He stood, inching himself upright, taking inventory of the pain, and trying to remember what he'd done to his back. He struggled into some clothes and stumbled down the stairs, leaning heavily on the banister. The sound of shaking ashes down in the cook stove started a fire in his skull. He crept around the kitchen, dumping cobs in the stove and dousing them with kerosene, then dropping in a match. He lifted the coffeepot with care, filled it from the cold reservoir, and added grounds to the basket, all without making a sound louder than a snake slithering across the floor.

In bits he remembered the previous week, realizing he needed to return his parents' car. He burned some toast and ate it with a cup of coffee—mostly grounds, then headed out the door, tripping on the turtle and wrenching his sore back.

"What're *you* doing here?"

The animal retracted all appendages.

"Shy huh?" Connor picked it up and tucked it under his jacket.

He nudged the second, empty, bottle of Jim Beam with his toe, then picked it up and set it on top of the trash. Leaning over made his head feel like to would explode. He stepped out the front door, easing it shut holding onto the screen so it wouldn't slam. He looked at the turtle in his hand and decided he'd take it along to show Hope. He climbed in his dad's car and spotted the other Jim Beam bottle and a pile of Budweiser bottles in a heap on the passenger floor. He set the turtle on the seat and walked around to gather up the trash. Finding the cardboard holder for the bottles, he dumped the empties in and grabbed the whiskey bottle with the other hand, hauling it all to the trash wagon.

He returned to the car and sniffed. When he decided he couldn't smell booze, he cranked it over and drove to Henry and Claire's, pulling into the garage. He looked in the rear-view mirror and combed his hair down with his fingers, deciding he couldn't do much about his red, swollen eyes. He picked up the turtle, still retracted into its shell, and headed for the house, pulling the garage door down behind him. He found his dad reading *Capper's Weekly* and his mom in the kitchen baking a pie.

"Hi Mom." He walked through before she could get a look at him. "I parked your car in the garage."

Henry looked up. "How's Bobbi?"

"She didn't come, Pop." Connor hung his head. "Says she wants a divorce."

Henry remained silent for a moment. "That's not what she told us."

"She wants to come home," his mother said, wiping her hands on a dishtowel. "She couldn't wait. She wanted to catch up to you."

"Musta changed her mind." Connor stared at the floor. "Where's Hope?"

Claire pointed at the little girl. "She's scooted behind your dad's chair."

Connor grinned. "I brought something for you." He dragged the turtle out from under his jacket and set it on the floor where she could see it. He picked her up and set her on his lap, snuggling his cheek against hers. "That's a turtle. If you watch, his head and tail and legs will come out of those holes."

She looked at him and back at the turtle.

He looked at his father. "She wants to take Hope to Cleveland."

"Now that's all wrong," Claire said. "What happened?"

Connor told about getting to Cleveland and searching for Bobbi. "Then when I got to her apartment, there was some guy there."

"What guy?"

"His name is Tony. She says she's gonna marry him."

319

GRAVY

The turtle began to move across the linoleum and Hope squirmed on Connor's lap, watching. Connor set her on the floor and the turtle retracted. She poked the shell with one finger and backed away, then poked it again.

"It's okay." Connor picked her up. "You just watch, and he'll come out again."

Henry'd watched and listened. "What did you do when you found that Tony with Bobbi?"

Connor hung his head. "I tried to get him to leave so I could talk to Bobbi."

"Did he leave?"

"No. I tried to push him out the door."

"You didn't get in a fight?" Claire interrupted.

Connor looked at her, then back at Hope fidgeting on his lap." He handed Hope to his mother. "I gotta go home."

Claire stood, jiggling the baby on her hip.

"You'd probably better tell us the rest of it," Henry said. "D'you let your nerves get the best of you?"

"I couldn't help it, Pop! I been tryin' to get along here without her. You know how hard I've tried."

"I know you have, son, but the looks of you, you got yourself drunk. Was that before or after you left Cleveland."

"I had some beer to try and calm down."

"Oh, Connor!"

He looked at his mother, shoulders slumped. "I just wanted—my nerves were shot—I was just trying to calm down so I wouldn't—I didn't want to scare her."

GRAVY

Henry, leaned back and rubbed his jaw, "I think you scared her anyway."

"I guess it don't matter. She's just gonna divorce me, an' take Hope. I just can't." He sat, elbows on his knees and buried his face in his hands.

His parents reminded him that Bobbi had returned, and he should give her time. And keep working on himself. He resigned himself to working his ass off. Maybe that would keep him out of trouble. He spent the evening with his parents and his daughter then went home, put a Wayne King record on and tried writing a letter. By midnight, with a scattering of crumpled paper on the floor, he left the tablet and pens on the table, took the needle off the record where it had swirled for hours, and tramped up the stairs. By 2:25 he'd tried every possible position and couldn't find one that didn't hurt his back. He levered himself off the bed, struggled into his clothes, and clumped down the stairs. He read his last attempt, crumpling it into a ball and throwing it on the floor with the others. He gathered all the paper and dropped it on the live coals in the stove. It flared and died down while the grabbed a pile of cobs, inhaling the musty fragrance of dry corn and rich soil from the hog lots, and dropped them on top so he could brew coffee.

He sat down and wrote to his sister.

> Dear Sis,
>
> Well, I've royally screwed up. First there was Pauline. I wish you hadn't sicced her on me. She came to visit one evening and, when she was leaving, insisted on hugging me. That's exactly when Bobbi came home. Came in the driveway and saw the hug. Well, then, she turned around and went right back to Cleveland. I didn't even have a chance to explain.
>
> So, I followed her. When I got there, she had some other guy in her apartment. I panicked and made

321

a complete ass of myself. Got in a fight with him.
Scared Bobbi and she sent me packing. I don't
know what to do. She says she wants a divorce
and she's taking Hope. Says she's marrying the
guy. What'll I do?

Connor

When he sealed that letter, he stood and checked his fire,
clanking the lid onto the stove when he'd finished. He decided he
had no way to varnish his behavior. He tried again to write his
wife.

Dearest Bobbi,

I've been trying to write this for hours, but I don't
know what to say.

I guess the first thing I want to say to you is I'm
sorry. I was already mad when I got to your place.
What I really was—What I really was, was frantic.
I was so scared of losing you. Bobbi, I love you
more than anything and the thought of spending
the rest of my life like this, without you, puts me
into a panic.

I tried to call you every day at your mom's
apartment. Every day. Sometimes I tried first
thing when I got up in the morning. I tried in the
afternoon and late at night. So don't you think you
weren't missed. Don't think you *aren't* missed."

About Pauline. I know Mom and Pop told you
about Pauline, but I want you to hear it from me.

He got up and paced the little kitchen. *Just do it*. With a lot of
staring into space, he continued.

322

Pauline grew up on the next place. We were
neighbors. We all played together, her brothers
and sisters and Nora and me. We went to school
together. She just seemed the likeliest choice
because she was here. But I was never sure with
her. I am with you.

He noticed a gathering chill in the air, got up and shook down
the ashes, adding more cobs to keep the fire going.

Once I met you, Bobbi, there was no competition.
There still isn't. I want to hold you in my arms and
dance with you. You wrote in your note when you
left that you would always love me. That goes for
me, too, Bobbi. I will always love you.

He signed the letter, folded it, sealed it in an envelope, walked
out the quarter-mile lane into the rising sun, and put it in the
mailbox along with the letter to Nora and six pennies for stamps.
When he got back to the house, he climbed the stairs again,
crawled into the bed again, clutching Bobbi's pillow in a death
grip, and fell into a dreamless sleep.

When he awoke that afternoon, he resolved to work himself into
exhaustion and not to think about Bobbi. Maybe his letter would
help, but he doubted it.

September 17, 1947 — Cleveland

After Connor's visit, Bobbi returned to the LakeView, struggling
to keep her panic under control when customers got too close. To
begin with, at least, her withering stare kept the touchers at
bay. Tony did what he could to watch out for her, but the
customers who wanted to fight kept him busy.

The first Wednesday night, the only weeknight LakeView closed,
Tony dragged Bobbi off dancing. At Danceland, he found them a

table near the floor, and they ordered drinks. "So, Bobbi, you're still in Cleveland. I assume it didn't go well with Connor. He did come back, didn't he? Calmed down, I hope."

"Oh, I don't know, Tony. He came back all right, but not calm."

"He didn't hurt you?"

"No. Scared me. He was wild."

"Bobbi, that man is dangerous. He could really hurt you."

"I think he was getting better before I left him." She picked at her coaster. "But when he was here, he wasn't."

"He's out of control, Bobbi."

"Well, he was then."

"What did he do?"

"He'd been drinking."

"You *can't* go back, if he's drinking too."

"It's not like that, Tony. Normally, I drink more than he does."

"He doesn't have to drink all the time. Just once when he's mad about something."

The orchestra began their next set playing *In The Mood*.

"Let's just dance, Tony. I don't want to talk about it."

Bobbi found Tony's style adequate but uninspired. Although he gave her a strong lead, they suffered through a few missteps. She wondered vaguely what happened after he left on that train during the war. "I don't get to do this very often," Tony said after a stumble.

"Me neither."

GRAVY

They stayed on the floor for a slow number while Bobbi remembered dancing with Connor at the Peterson Club in Colorado Springs and how in step they were—even the first time.

"What ya thinkin'?"

"Oh nothing. Just remembering the club in Colorado Springs where I sang."

When they returned to their table, Tony had more questions. "What's it like out there next to the mountains?"

A flash of the mountains with Connor slipped through her mind. "Beautiful. You can go all the way up above tree line at night and see the lights of Denver spread out." She could almost feel Connor's arms around her as she gazed down at the city.

She jumped when Tony took her hand. "What're you thinkin'? You just drifted off."

"Sorry. I was just . . . Connor took me up there. I was just remembering." Bobbi decided to try another subject. "When you got on that train for Washington, where did the Army finally send you?"

"Oh, they really didn't send me anywhere. Made me a military policeman."

"An MP? I guess that makes sense. Where?"

"I ended up at Fort Benning. Spent a lot of time in Columbus—— Georgia that is. Just the same old thing."

"You're good at it."

"Maybe, but boring. Listen, tell me what it was like living on a farm? I just don't see you on a farm."

"I don't know, Tony. I *never* went hungry."

"Well, that's good."

"It's wonderful. I don't ever want to be hungry again—and it's not as boring as you'd think. Farmers are a whole lot smarter than you think."

"Must be quiet."

"You can't imagine—except when the wind blows. Then, you feel like it's sucking the breath right out of you. And sometimes the sky's so empty you feel like it's going to suck you up."

"Like Dorothy?"

Bobbi frowned. "Dorothy?"

"Wizard of Oz."

Bobbi chuckled. "Well, there are tornadoes. We had one that took down one of my father-in-law's grain bins."

"You're not thinking about going back to that God-forsaken place, are you?"

"I don't know, Tony. Connor's blow-ups aren't really his fault."

"But he has them. It only takes one."

"I know all that. But I'm really afraid of *myself*."

"Yourself? Why?"

"You saw what I did to that customer."

"What's that all about anyway?

"I can't talk about it."

"You've said that, but you have to. You should stay here in the city, and I'll take care of you.

GRAVY

September 20-21, 1947 — Willow Grove

Less than a week after he'd written to her, Connor got a letter from Nora. That evening before bed, he stoked up the cookstove, brewed coffee and read it.

Dear brother,

It sounds like you're in a mess. I don't know how you're holding up and whether you've heard anything from Bobbi, but I wouldn't give up yet. It'll take some time for her to get her divorce, so give her time to think. You said she came home once already, so she may not be all that committed to that other guy. Maybe she said that because you scared her, and she wanted you to leave. (You can be pretty scary, you know.)

While she's thinking you *must* get yourself under control. You told me about her blow-ups, and I agree with Bobbi that you can't both go crazy together. Not with a baby.

Since we don't know what's happened to her, you'll have to take the initiative—and I know that's harder than even I think—and I've seen some of the same craziness you have. But I also know you're getting better.

One evening before I left Nebraska, I remember you talking about the guy who lost his leg. You said he told you to come see him on the reservation. Maybe now would be a good time to do that. Maybe getting out on the desert and learning more about somebody else would get your mind off your own troubles for a while. Maybe it will help you come up with some new ideas about how to get your family together. Even if it doesn't help in that department, it might help clear your mind and give you some peace.

GRAVY

So that's my advice, Connor, for whatever it's worth. Remember you're my favorite brother and I believe in you.

Nora

Connor laid the letter on the table and took another sip of coffee. Jakes had still used crutches when they went from the ship to the hospital and lost touch. He wondered how his friend had adjusted to the new leg.

He remembered standing at the rail of the hospital ship and staring out at the ocean with Jakes and how peaceful it felt standing next to him, rolling with the waves. He smiled when he thought about his friend's obsession with peaches. It seemed like every time someone mentioned food, Jakes said, "Peaches would be better."

He had no address or phone number. When he looked at a map of Arizona and took in the size of the Navajo Reservation, he wondered how he'd ever find Jakes in the desert. "You'll find me," Jakes had said. Those were his last words when they'd left the ship. He guessed it might be time to go find him.

Next day when he joined his parents' for dinner, and a visit with his daughter, he'd made his decision.

"Pop, can you get along a while without me?"

"I think so. What you got in mind?"

"Think I'll go see Jakes."

"That's the guy from your squad?"

"First sergeant. Lost a leg. I want to see how he's getting along. Keep my mind off Bobbi."

"I wouldn't let her go too long."

"Nah, but I don't wanna go rushing back to Cleveland and make more of a mess. I've checked schedules. I can switch in Salina to the Atcheson, Topeka, and Santa Fe. That'll take me all the way to Winslow. I know how to walk. Did plenty of it in the 30s. I'll just ask people when I see them, where I can find Russell Jakes."

September 22, 1947 — Navajo Reservation, Arizona

He hopped off the train, ticket paid this time, shouldered his pack, and headed north on a skinny, potholed, blacktop road. He'd decided that he'd be safer on roads in case he got into trouble in the desert. Someone might come along. When the road forked, he saw a tiny sign for the Dilkon gas station and bore to the right. He watched and listened as a rainstorm climbed the sky. When it started pounding him, he felt right at home, back in New Guinea. Except it wasn't so humid.

Later, he walked up to a tiny station house with one ancient pump out front. It looked abandoned, but he heard shuffling inside. He dropped his pack outside and stepped through the open portal into the dim interior. The man behind the counter looked him over while Connor's eyes adjusted.

"You know you're on the Navajo Reservation?"

"Yup." Dripping, he looked around the room and back to the frowning station attendant. "I wonder if you could help me find Russell Jakes."

They guy's frown deepened. "Don't know no Russell Jakes. What you want him for?"

Connor hadn't expected a warm welcome, but he wondered how he could get through. He reached out a hand. "Name's Connor. I served with him in New Guinea. He told me to look him up. His name's Russell Jakes."

GRAVY

The man came around the counter, wiping his hands on a rag he pulled from his back pocket. When he shook hands, Connor could see himself getting sized up. He ventured another bit of information. "Last time I saw him, Jakes was still using crutches. I wanted to see how he's doing with the new leg."

"And you came out here into the desert lookin' for this guy? How'd you expect to find him?"

"I wondered about that when Jakes said to come, but he just said I'd find him. Guess he thought I'd figure it out."

The guy cocked his head. "You that sergeant can't stop talkin'?"

Connor chuckled. "I guess that's me."

"Jakes said you helped him out in that field hospital. Said the blood you gave that afternoon went into him when his leg started bleeding again."

"He never told me about that." Connor remained silent for a moment, thinking. "You know him then."

The guy nodded.

"Know where I can find him?"

After a moment's silence, the guy seemed to make a decision. "You can call me John. That'll be easier. If you don't mind waiting 'til I close up here—and riding in my rattletrap truck, I'll take you. I think he'll be glad to see you. He told us you'd be comin' sometime."

Dusk had settled when they crawled into John's truck, an old three-quarter ton with racks that flapped noisily.

"Looks like you've hauled some livestock in this rig."

"Yeah. Most of us raise sheep and goats."

"Meat animals?"

330

John gave him a sharp look. "What do you care?"

"Just makin' conversation." He glanced at the other man. "We raise pigs and cattle." He felt a guilty shock. *Somebody took it from the Pawnee.* He sighed. "Pop says sheep beller too much."

John grinned. "They don't say much long's they got plenty of feed and water."

"So that's the secret."

"Ain't no secret."

Silence fell and Connor thought he'd stay out of trouble if he kept his mouth shut.

"Jakes' been back 'bout two years now."

"Me too. Got to finish up the war bein' an MP."

"Jakes said you was pretty sick."

"Yeah. Better now. How's Jakes gettin' along? Did they fit him with a good leg?"

John peered across the darkening cab with narrowed eyes. "You'll have to see for yourself. Jakes'll tell you what he wants you to know."

They turned onto a rough sand and gravel trail, settling into a long silence. The truck rattled over deep ruts, making conversation difficult. After about an hour, John pulled into the mouth of a nearly hidden canyon.

"Jakes'll be somewhere in there with his sheep. He's got a shack about half a mile in, to your left. Follow the wall there. You should be able to find him."

"This was a long drive. Can I pay you for your time and gas?"

"Nah. Jakes' my friend." He stared at Connor for a moment. "You do him any harm, I'll find you, though."

Connor ducked his head. "Thanks for the ride. Maybe I'll see you again before I head home."

"Maybe." John shoved the truck into gear and took off, leaving Connor in a spatter of rainwater.

He started walking as his eyes adjusted to shadows. Mostly he felt his way along the canyon wall. When he got into the sheep herd, he talked to the animals, assuring them he meant no harm. He heard them breathing all around him, stepping aside and closing behind him. Jakes's two sheep dogs escorted him to a hogan. When they got close, one of the dogs barked.

"Hey, Jakes," Connor shouted, "It's me, Conroy."

Jakes immediately filled the low doorway, silhouetted in firelight. "Conroy. It's about time."

"John from the gas station at Dilkon gave me a ride to the mouth of the canyon."

"I told 'em to bring you up."

"How'd you know I was comin'?"

"Didn't know. Don't read minds, you know." He turned and hopped into the room so Connor could step inside. "If you came, I made sure you'd find me—like I said."

Connor glanced around at the comfortable shack. "Where's your leg? Didn't the Army take care of you?"

Jakes hopped to his place by the fire and sat.

Connor joined him. "Didn't the Army make you a leg?"

"Yeah, they did."

"Didn't they do it right? I'll make a lot of noise if they didn't"

Jakes held up his hand. "Take it easy, Conroy. They did what they could." He maneuvered his stump around where Connor could see it. "See, there's not much below the knee where I can strap it on."

"How do you get around?"

"It's easier to hop on flat surfaces. When I'm out with the sheep, I wear the damned thing. It's slow."

"You sure they can't do any better?"

"Settle down, Conroy. You have a bad habit of takin' too much responsibility."

"Sorry."

"'S all right. How're you doin? Still got the fevers?"

"Nah. Doc says my heart's actin' goofy an' I gotta watch my kidneys."

Jakes guffawed. "How do you watch a kidney?"

Connor laughed. It felt good. "They got tests I have to take every so often." He sobered. "How you gettin' along with loud noises?"

"Pretty quiet out here. I can curl up and wait out a storm if I have to. Think I'm gettin' better. You?"

"Me, too. Cracked my wife's sternum during one of those rip-roarin' storms, though."

"You got a wife?"

"And a little girl."

The men talked until late, catching up with their recoveries, or attempts to recover. Jakes talked about sheep and goats and courting a woman he'd known as a kid. "Don't know how she feels about a one-legged man," he said.

Connor talked about farming with his dad, meeting and marrying Bobbi in Colorado Springs. "She's left me, Jakes."

"When you hurt her?"

"No. That's the weird part." Connor talked about Bobbi's blow-ups and his bewilderment. "I thought I was the shellshocked lunatic," he concluded, "but sometimes she acts just like I do."

The men went to bed without solving either of their dilemmas.

September 29, 1947

After about a week, Jakes and Connor sat on a knoll in the canyon, watching the sheep. They shared a quick meal of dried goat, roasted corn, and ripe melons. As they finished up, Connor reminded Jakes of his obsession with peaches. Jakes took a long time to speak.

"You ever heard of Kit Carson?"

"Heard of him. S'posed to be one of our wild west heroes."

Jakes grunted. "Hero? Indian killer. Women, children, old people. Your year, 1864. Fall. Raided the canyons. Killed sheep, goats. Left them lay. Burned homes, crops. Forced people off the land. Many died."

Connor frowned, shaking his head.

"We'd taken care of our peach trees for hundreds of years."

"Peach trees! This is a desert."

"Huh. And yet we had fruit orchards in many of these canyons."

334

"God, I'm sorry Jakes. I can never make it up."

"Yeah. I know. You can't. Anyway, my people—we call ourselves Diné by the way. We survived. We came back and some of the trees had come up from the roots. The trees were in bad shape, but still growing. Twenty years and we had our orchards back."

"And you've been taking care of them all this time?"

"Yeah. All these canyons, wherever there's water." He eyed his visitor before continuing. "I've been working on a variety to extend the season. Here, they usually ripen between June and August, but I'm working on a later variety."

Connor laughed.

"What's funny?"

"I've always wanted to be a horticulturist and all this time I've been running around with one who's way ahead of me."

Jakes smiled. "I really like peaches—and the trees are my way of resisting."

"Resist away, my friend."

They finished their lunch in silence.

"Now," Jakes said, "we're gonna let the dogs watch the sheep and take a little walk."

Connor followed, watching his friend limp deeper into the canyon. Jakes stopped and began pulling brush away from the canyon wall. "Help me here."

As Connor pulled piles of weedy brush to one side, he saw a plywood door. Jakes wrestled it to the side and stepped in, gesturing Connor to follow. The cool interior housed a couple of crates deep under the wall. "We have to work these now."

"What's in them?"

GRAVY

"Breathe, man."

Connor took a deep breath. "Peaches!"

"They're the very last of the harvest."

Connor calculated. "So, you've extended your season almost a month."

"Not many this late, but I'll save some seeds and plant more." Jakes took a peach from one of the crates and handed it to Connor who bit into the tender flesh.

"This is great, Jakes. This is as sweet and juicy as anything I've ever tasted."

Jakes grinned. "We dry them and can them for winter and we sell the rest, along with the plums, apples, and—I'll show you."

"I had no idea."

"Most whites don't. We like it that way."

Jakes left the cave and pulled the plywood back in place. They covered it again. "Now we'll go see the trees."

They walked deeper into the canyon where a small artesian well dripped water into a trough that distributed it around the orchard. "They don't need much water down here out of the wind. Our little water source doesn't give much, but we've got good subsoil moisture from that constant drip. The mama trees' big root systems help out the new ones."

"You plant your melons in among the trees too?"

"Yeah. I put them in among the late bearing apples where they'll be harvested and out of the way when we pick apples."

As Jakes walked around the trees, pointing out the features of each, Connor realized his friend was enjoying the opportunity to show off. He remembered all the buckets of water he'd carried to

GRAVY

his own trees that first year and wondered if they would share a
little of the water they gathered through their leaves through
their roots—with a little fruit orchard. His friend's talk about
mama trees had him fascinated.

He noticed Jakes watching him. "I was just thinking about
planting an orchard at my place. My pioneer trees are about big
enough to break the wind. I don't have anything to block that hot
south wind, though. Maybe I could plant some fast-growing
poplars on the south.

Jakes chuckled. "Grows on you, don't it?"

Connor helped Jakes dry his last crate of peaches, learning all
he could. Then he hitched and tramped his way back to the
railroad. Rattling and shaking on the way back, he had a lot to
think about with much less desperation. If Jakes could breed
fruit trees without a degree, maybe he could too. He realized he
hadn't felt so relaxed in months.

October 6, 1947 — Willow Grove

When he returned from Arizona, Connor found an envelope
postmarked "Cleveland" in the mailbox. He ripped it open and
read it, standing at the end of the lane.

Dear Connor,

I got your letter. I guess I do understand about
Pauline, but I'm still afraid of us together. You
were <u>frightening</u> when you were here. I guess you
didn't hear me when I said I'm going to marry
Tony. I'll file for divorce soon.

Bobbi

337

GRAVY

Connor stuffed the letter in his pocket, striding back toward the house as if outrunning a prairie fire. He read it again before he threw it into the stove, watching it flare on the coals. He fit the iron lid back down with a clank and paced across the kitchen, fists balled, snarling about how he'd like to get his hands on that Tony.

He slammed outside to check on the cattle. So far none of them had found their way through the new fence he'd built that summer, but they always tested. He stopped in the garage and grabbed a fencing pliers from the peg board and put an handful of staples in his pocket. As usual, the walk, good grass, and well-conditioned cows settled his nerves.

Calves, trying to crawl under, had popped some staples off the fence. He hammered in new ones, still thinking about Bobbi.

She must not be in too much of a rip-roarin' hurry to marry that Tony if she hasn't filed for divorce yet. Nora might be right. Maybe I CAN change her mind.

At the end of the day, Connor had supper with his parents and spent a couple of hours playing with Hope, thoughts of Bobbi and Tony in the back of his mind. After he put his little girl to bed, he walked home in starlight so bright he could see his shadow. He lit a fire in the stove, put a record on the phonograph, and sat at the table with tablet and pen.

> Dearest Bobbi,
>
> I spend a few hours every day with Hope. I know you saw her a few weeks ago, but she's been learning since then. I brought home a turtle for her to see, and she follows it around on the floor. I know you been worried sick that she won't develop right after what that doctor said, but she's <u>fine</u>. I think her scooting around on her butt just means that she'll grow up to do things her own way—just like her mother.

He stood and checked his fire, adding a few cobs,
then turned the record over and set the needle on
the other side.

Bobbi, I'm sorry I scared you. I didn't mean to. I
expected to find you at Ella's apartment and then
I had to go to the restaurant, and I had to
practically wrestle them for your address—no
directions of course—so I wandered all over trying
to find your street—all that time worrying about
what you were thinking. So Tony was just one
surprise too many.

"Divorce," he muttered, jumping up to change the record again.
"How do I talk about that? Can I ignore it?" He decided to jump
right in.

I do remember you saying you want a divorce and
that you're marrying Tony. I just hope you'll
reconsider. We can have a really good life here,
Bobbi. I'm still getting better. Every moment I
spend with our little girl makes me better. For
her, everything's new and seeing her seeing new
things just makes *everything* seem fresh."

The phonograph needle whispered again, spinning at the end of
a song. Connor looked up at the clock. He'd been writing and
crumpling paper for more than three hours, one anguished word
at a time. He turned the record over and sat.

Bobbi, please don't divorce me until we've had a
chance to talk. I still don't know what's happened
to you that scared you so much (besides me, of
course), but surely, we can both conquer our
demons if we do it together.

He read the letter and decided it was the best he could do. He
signed it and walked it out to the mailbox. He still couldn't
imagine his life without Bobbi, but he'd reached a certain level of
calm. He'd learned to wait, and he could wait because he'd begun

to believe his mother and sister could be right. Maybe Bobbi made up the Tony marriage to get rid of him—because she was scared. What he must do is make sure there's nothing to fear.

October 10, 1947

Connor and Bobbi exchanged letters as Connor waited for the hammer to drop—divorce papers. The longer he waited, though, the more certain he became that he could change Bobbi's mind. He hadn't seen her for more than a month and he thought the time was fast approaching for him to make another visit to Cleveland. He worked on the combine with Henry, preparing for milo harvest, when his dad dropped a bomb.

In a steady wind, they tried to get the blades to work. "Hold on a minute, Connor, I think I see what's wrong. See that lever in there? Stick your hand in there and trip that lever. I can't quite reach it."

Connor tripped the lever.

"Good. I think that'll work." He walked around the combine to start it up. "What do you hear from Bobbi?"

"Pop, she still says she's gonna get a divorce. Maybe she'll change her mind. She just keeps saying she can't be a wife to me, whatever she means by that. I know something's happened to her, but I don't know what."

Henry hesitated. "I do." He picked up a worn blade and put it back down, then leaned against the lee side of the combine out of the wind.

Connor frowned. "You gonna tell me?"

Henry stared at his son. "I'm going to tell you something that you're going to hate. But you're going to stay calm and *not* do what you will want to do."

Connor stiffened, wiping his hands on a grease rag. "What'd I do? I'm writing letters so I don't scare her, but I want to go talk to her and hold her."

"I know, son." Henry took a careful look at the combine head. "Your mom told me something last night that just makes my skin crawl, something Bobbi's afraid to tell you because she's afraid for you."

"What? What can be so bad."

"It's that doctor. Dr. Powers."

Connor bristled. "Powers! I shoulda strangled him."

"Well, you almost did," Henry snapped. "So, forget it. Just shut up and listen."

Unaccustomed to his dad's tone, Connor subsided. Henry took another deep breath and sighed it out. "You know Doc O'Neill sent Bobbi to him because she needed an operation to have the baby."

"Yeah, and Powers told her she would likely die of an infection if he operated—scared her to death."

"She was a wreck."

"And she's still a wreck. She's not still scared of that, is she? It's over and she's fine. So is Hope."

"That's just it, Connor. It's not over for her."

Connor leaned against the side of the combine, "Whadaya mean?"

"Powers told her he could fix her so she wouldn't need to have surgery."

"That's nuts. You can't . . ." Connor's eyes narrowed. "What did he do to her?"

"He gave her some kind of treatments at each of her prenatal visits."

He frowned. "What kinda treatments?"

Henry hesitated as if still trying to decide whether he should go on. Staring into his son's eyes, he said, "I don't know all the fine points, but he put some kind of instrument inside her that opened up and he tried to spread her out."

Connor just stared back in silence, his mind churning. What did that mean? "He what?" He pushed away from the machine, still focused on his father's face as he began to comprehend. "I'll kill him." He strode off toward the house.

"Connor Conroy, you get right back here right now!"

Startled, Connor stopped.

"You're not going to kill anyone anymore." Henry lowered his voice. You'll stop, and you'll think, and you'll take care of Bobbi. Period."

Connor balanced on his toes, half-turned away from Henry, straining to keep going but knowing he had to stop. "Pop I can't let him get away with this."

"I know. But we've gotta be smart. Bobbi and Hope need you here, not locked up in jail."

"But . . ."

"Look, your mother and Bobbi wanted to keep this a secret. They were afraid that you'd fly off the handle and," he caught Connor's eyes and held them, "and do something stupid."

"You're tellin' me that bastard abused my wife, and I should get hold of my*self*?

Unrelenting, Henry continued to hold Connor's gaze. "Bobbi needs you to take care of *her*, damn it! She's all the way over there in Cleveland, trying to deal with this by herself . . . so stop the bullshit and listen to me."

Connor strode the few steps back to Henry, towering over him, eyes burning.

"Stop. Right. There." Henry poked his finger in his son's chest. "You're gonna *stop* this warrior stuff and you're gonna *think* about Bobbi and your little girl. And don't even *think* about goin' anywhere near that damn doctor. You got that?"

Connor deflated, sitting abruptly on the combine fender, scrubbing shaking hands through his hair. "I still want to kill him."

"I'd like to get my hands on him myself. But that's not what we're gonna do."

Connor had tears in his eyes. "What *am* I gonna do, Pop?"

Henry squatted on the ground with his back against the combine, gazing back toward the house. "You're gonna calm yourself down and forget about how much you'd like revenge and you're gonna think about what Bobbi needs."

"She needs Powers gone."

"Your mom's been thinking about this."

"What's she think I oughta do?"

"She says Bobbi's already humiliated."

"Powers's the one ought to be humiliated."

343

Henry held up his hand. "Says if you go off half-cocked, you're liable to shame her even more."

"She oughtn't be ashamed."

"Mom says she's still trying to think of it as a real medical experiment."

"*Experiment?*"

"Yeah. One of the nurses told her the doctor's been experimenting with his treatments."

"Nobody experiments on my wife!" Connor jumped up and started off again.

"Stop right there!" Henry yelled. "Haven't you heard a damn word I've said?"

"All right, all right." Connor turned back and resumed his place on the fender.

"Mom thinks she may need to think of it that way. She says you go stormin' off acting like you have to kill over it and Bobbi has to think she's ruined for you."

"*She's* ruined? That so-called doctor needs to be ruined."

"Maybe we can find a way, Connor, but what's important now is Bobbi. She's lived with this for almost two years already."

"I gotta go see her."

"I think it might be time, but you need to get hold of yourself first. Maybe right after harvest."

"I'll just show up. Go to that LakeView and wait for her . . ."

* * * * *

Across the farmyard, Claire stood peering through the window, wringing her hands and watching her husband and son, dark heads together by the side of the combine. She wished she'd never told Henry what the doctor did to Bobbi, and she hoped her revelation wouldn't end in disaster. Even though she swore him to secrecy, Henry insisted that Connor must know and that she wasn't giving her son enough credit. But she wasn't so sure. Connor wasn't the same man who'd helped her transplant the lilac bushes before he'd enlisted. Sometimes he frightened her— even just a few minutes before when she saw him across the yard, standing over her husband. It looked like a threat, and she feared for Henry. Connor had towered over his dad since he was about fourteen, but respect had kept him from challenging Henry. She could no longer count on that respect to balance whatever happened to him on those islands.

She let the curtain fall and scurried back to the kitchen when she saw the two men heading toward the house. *Maybe Henry's right. Maybe it will be all right.*

October 24-25, 1947 — On the Road

With the milo in the bin, Connor once again borrowed his parents' car and left for Cleveland. This time he knew where to go, and he had enough cash in his pocket to stay a few weeks. All through harvest, he'd noticed his dad watching him, but he'd kept his mind busy, planning his first meeting with Bobbi.

Before dawn, he headed east, squinting into the rising sun. He'd had a good night's sleep—at least as good as it got. Knowing what had happened to his wife gave him a place to start. He expected resistance, but he hoped Bobbi would learn to trust him again. Maybe in time she could learn to trust that the world's a good place to live. He could remember that kind of trust. It took him all over the west, believing in the kindness of strangers and the abundance of the wilderness. He'd had to struggle himself to regain that feeling after New Guinea. He still struggled.

GRAVY

On his father's advice, he forced himself to stop in some little town outside Gary, Indiana.

"You may not be able to sleep, but you can rest. Maybe read a book and clear your mind."

Connor had surprised himself when he dozed off reading and managed a few hours of sleep. He suspected that it helped knowing what he had to overcome instead of floundering in confusion.

He hadn't decided quite what he'd say when he saw her, and he hadn't decided where he'd go. He could go to the club, but she wouldn't let down her guard there. He imagined, after dealing with rowdy soldiers back in Colorado Springs, seeing Bobbi's blowups, and knowing what had happened in that doctor's office, that she had to struggle to control her panic when the drunks got too close. No, he decided, he'd go to her apartment.

But what would he say? *Bobbi, I know; or Bobbi, come home with me—I know; or Bobbi, Pop told me what happened; or I know what Powers did to you.* Nothing seemed right. *Maybe I should reassure her first. I could say, Bobbi, I know what Powers did to you and it doesn't matter.* Connor slapped his forehead with the heel of his hand. *Of course, it matters!*

He continued talking to himself until he pulled up in front of Bobbi's building at three in the afternoon. He'd moseyed that day, taking time for a leisurely breakfast and stopping again at noon in a little small-town café. He wanted to give Bobbi time for a good night's sleep after her night in the lounge. He had an opening line memorized and he muttered it to himself as he climbed the stairs.

"Just a minute," Bobbi shouted in answer to his knock—and then there she stood in the doorway and Connor forgot what he meant to say. They stared at each other for a long moment, then he stepped forward, bent her over his arm, and kissed her. She struggled at first, then relaxed and kissed him back. When he stood her on her feet, she stared in silence. "Wha'd you do that for?" she demanded finally.

"Shshshsh," Connor whispered, "I know."

"Know what?"

"I know what Powers did to you."

She gasped. "Is he alright? I told Claire not to . . ."

"It's all right, Bobbi, I'm not gonna kill him."

"You can't, Connor."

"I know. He's safe. Just come home with me. We'll work this out together."

"I can't, Connor."

"Can't why?"

"I'm trying to make a life here."

"Trying to deal with this all by yourself—singing in that sleazy bar."

"Those people gave me my start."

Connor could see he'd gotten off on the wrong foot. An image of Tony slammed through his mind, but he shut it off like a tourniquet on a bleeding limb. "I understand, Bobbi, but I'm talking about people who go there. You've got a whole family that loves you back in Nebraska. *I* love you."

Bobbi stared. "If you know, you know I can't be a wife to you."

"Can we go inside?" Connor asked, buying time. Inside with the door closed, he pressed his case. "I know it'll take time, just like it has for me."

GRAVY

"Even in time, Connor. I can't risk another pregnancy."

"I'll use a condom—when you're ready."

Bobbi began crying. "That's just it, I can't imagine ever being ready."

"Bobbi, what that doctor did to you, doesn't have to be forever—it *can't* be forever."

Bobbi stared at him hazel eyes narrowed. "I can't. Connor, I want you to go. Just go back to Nebraska—and marry Pauline—and be happy. I'm nothing but trouble."

"Oh, Bobbi." Connor took a step toward her, but she put her arm up to fend him off.

"Just go, please."

Connor turned as if to go, then turned back and caught Bobbi's eye. "I'll be back Bobbi. I'm not leaving without you."

"You have to."

"I'll be back." Connor started down the stairs. He heard Bobbi close the door behind him. He shrugged. *At least she didn't slam it.* "You don't leave anybody behind," he muttered to himself as he hurried out to the car.

He crawled behind the wheel and started the car. "Damn," he growled. "This is gonna take a while." He drove to the now-familiar liquor store.

"A quart of Jim Beam?"

"Nah, but I'm impressed you remember.

The clerk grinned. "I got a pretty good memory."

"I'll say. I just need a flower shop this time."

348

"You'll find one around the corner to your right and down . . . one . . . two . . . three . . . three-and-a-half blocks on your left. Are you sure you don't want some wine to go with them flowers?"

"Not this time."

At the flower shop, Connor ordered a dozen red roses and paid an enormous sum for them. "It's October," said the cashier. "We fly 'em in fresh from Mexico. That's not cheap."

"I suppose not. You got a card to put in with them?"

The clerk handed him a little rectangle.

"Bigger."

"That'll cost you for the card."

"Add it to the flowers."

"Pick out one from the rack behind you."

Connor grabbed a card with a single red rose on the front. "Bobbi," he wrote, "There's plenty of ugliness in the world. We've both seen our share. Try to focus on the beauty."

"You deliver?"

"Yep."

"Take these to apartment 6B, 1251 Random Road."

"Okay. That'll be ten bucks fifty-five, mister."

Connor handed him a twenty. "Is there a good hotel in the neighborhood?" He took his change.

"There's the Calibri over on 13th."

"Calibri! That's the name. Ralph and Mary Calibri. You don't know how much you've helped me out."

"Glad to be of service. I'll get these out right away."

"Thanks." Connor headed for the hotel. "Boy! That was easier than it oughta be."

Settled in his room, Connor immediately telephoned Mary. "Hello, Mary? This is Connor Conroy."

"Bobbi's husband?"

"Yeah."

"Bobbi isn't here, Connor. She's probably getting ready for work."

"I've just been to see her, Mary. I'm still trying to get her to come home with me, but she keeps saying she can't."

"I don't see her very much—because of her hours, workin' all night—but she always says she's getting a divorce, Connor."

"I know. She keeps telling me that, too. But it's been almost three months and I haven't got any papers yet."

"I don't think she's even seen a lawyer, Connor. Somehow something keeps coming up or she's too tired."

"I'm counting on that, Mary, but what about that Tony guy? Does she go out with him?"

"Well, he'd like her to." Mary paused. "And he could take care of her—he *has* been since she was a kid."

"Bobbi told me how he escorted her around the club like he was her boyfriend. Was he?"

"No, but he'd have liked to be."

"What'm I gonna do Mary? How do I get her to trust me?"

"She doesn't trust herself, Connor. You gotta make her believe in herself again. She usta be so," Mary hesitated, "scared of *nothin*'! I don't know what happened to her out there in the boonies. She says it isn't you, although you scared her pretty good last time you were here."

"Yeah, I know. I just found out myself what's scaring her and I can't tell you, but it was pretty bad. If only I'd known all along." He shook his head. *But I'd probably be on death row now if I had.*

"I don't think it's just that. She talks sometimes about the silence. Calls it empty silence."

"It sure is different from here."

"I'll bet you think it's noisy here."

"Deafening."

"See—and she says everybody out there expects her to be Mrs. Conroy—as though *she* doesn't matter."

"Not to me or my family!"

"Well, she had to make an enormous adjustment to start with."

"But she got along great at first. Mom said she made a better farm wife than girls who grew up on a farm."

"Farm wife," said Mary with a chuckle. "Who woulda guessed she could pull that off."

"Yeah, but I know she wants to sing with the Glen Miller orchestra."

"Doesn't everybody?"

"I think she's good enough."

"I think it's too late, Connor. When she signed up with Uncle Sam—it was just too much of an interruption. She can't get back in."

"That why she's back where she started?"

"Yup."

"I thought it was that Tony."

"Didn't know he was there."

"Hmmm."

"Look, Connor, I gotta go. The baby's cryin'. But here's the best I can tell you. You've gotta build her back up. Give her confidence back. Trouble is, that might just send her back to reaching for that gold ring—and for her that's the Glen Miller Band."

Connor hung up with a frown. *This feels like those first weeks, wonderin' if what's best for the girl's gonna make* me *happy.*

October 25, 1947

Connor decided he would take his next step at LakeView. Whatever else he knew, he knew that Bobbi needed to feel safe. He removed his shoes, plumped the pillows, grabbed his book, and lay down to read himself to sleep—probably a lost cause in the daylight. Shortening days allowed him some darkness, so he managed to doze. He arose at eight p.m., showered, shaved, and changed into slacks, button-down shirt, and a sports jacket. By nine, he stood with Tony in front of LakeView.

"Look Connor, I don't want any disturbances. They scare Bobbi. Why don't you go back to Nebraska and leave her alone?"

Connor looked at Tony a long moment. "Bobbi's my wife, Tony, and I'm not giving her up without a fight. She's worth it, you know." He reached out to shake Tony's hand. "There won't be any disturbance tonight. Not from me."

Tony took the hand and stared into Connor's eyes, frowning. "No, I believe there won't."

Connor stepped through the door and headed for a table next to the stage. He saw Bobbi start when she brushed by his table on her way out for her first set. He noticed the corners of her mouth twitch, but he couldn't decide if she suppressed a smile or a frown. Despite his focus, he enjoyed the music, although Bobbi seemed tired and a tiny bit out of sync. He doubted anyone else noticed.

When the band launched into one of the new songs with its smooth Latin rhythm, Connor couldn't help imagining Bobbi in his arms, dancing the steps she'd learned so quickly. Maybe soon, he told himself.

At the end of her set, he followed her backstage, glancing up to see Tony's eyes following him. He hoped the bouncer wouldn't interfere with what he had planned.

Bobbi didn't see him immediately when she stepped out. He noted the sag in her shoulders and how she threw them back as she prepared to step into the crowd.

"Bobbi." He offered his elbow. "How about I escort you around the club tonight?"

She jumped. "What're you doin' here? You gotta go home."

"We'll talk about that later. Right now, I'm gonna keep people's hands off you—if you'll let me."

Her smile barely moved her lips. "Maybe this once, since you're here."

"Good. That's settled."

She took his arm and they stepped into the crowd. She meandered among the tables, greeting customers, occasionally sitting to chat with a regular. Connor remained mostly in the background, standing aside to watch. Sometimes, Bobbi or the customer motioned for him to sit.

At one table, the customer—Bobbi introduced him as Chet—turned to Connor. "You're new around here. What brings you to Cleveland."

"Bobbi."

"That so? How do you know Bobbi?"

Connor glanced at his wife, then turned a steady gaze on Chet. "She's my wife."

Chet sputtered, looking at Bobbi. "Ya don't say. How long's this been goin' on?"

Bobbi looked at Connor. "About three and a half years."

"So, what're you doin' here?"

"I really like to hear Bobbi sing."

"I meant Bobbi."

"I gotta get ready for my next set." Bobbi jumped up and strode to her dressing room.

"What'd you do that for?" She glared at him in the dressing table mirror as he waited for her to touch up her makeup.

"What?"

"Why'd you tell him."

"We are. I'm proud to be married to you. Why would I hide it?"

"Connor, I'm getting a divorce."

354

"So what?" he challenged. "So, you can sing your heart out and be alone and learn to hate men?"

"I don't hate men."

"If you let what's happened change your whole life, you will."

"You don't know anything about it."

"Maybe not, but I know you're talented and smart—too smart to let one son-of-a-bitch ruin your life."

"I'm not . . . I . . . I . . ."

"I don't know how you get over it, Bobbi. I wish I did. But I know you can. I'm here to help you any way I can."

"You *have* to let me go. It's no good."

"Not gonna do that. He cocked his head. "I hear the band starting up." He offered his elbow.

She glanced in the mirror and shrugged.

He took her to the foot of the stage and returned to his table.

He escorted her around throughout the night, taking the role Tony had taken years earlier. They didn't talk much until the club closed at four.

"Let me take you home. You look bushed."

"Connor!"

"It's all right, I'll pick you up and bring you back tomorrow."

"You should be halfway home by then."

"I think you need to see a doctor about getting the wax out of your ears."

Bobbi stared, frowning.

"I'm not leaving until I'm convinced you've gotten Powers out of your system. Now let's get you home so you can rest."

"I've got the car, Connor."

"That's nice. I've got one here too."

"You have to take it back to Mom and Pop."

Connor took her elbow and steered her toward the exit. She forgot to resist.

"It's okay," he murmured in her ear. "Mom and Pop said to take as long as it takes." He opened the door to the parking lot. "They said you're worth the inconvenience."

Bobbi stopped walking. "They really said that?"

"Of course. Does that surprise you?"

She walked again to hide the dampness gathering in her eyes. "Uh huh."

"Let's take Mom and Pop's car." Connor hurried to catch up.

She stood, undecided, for a moment, then followed him to her in-laws' Chrysler. He handed her into the car and drove to her building.

"I can make it from here."

"I'll see you to your door."

"Connor." They looked at each other until Bobbi dropped her gaze. "All right." When she unlocked the door, she turned to Connor.

"Okay, Sweetheart, you get some sleep. I'll come get you about two."

He turned to go.

"Connor?"

He looked back.

"Thank you."

"Don't mention it." Back outside, he sat in his parents' car a few minutes, thinking. *I should have handled that better. We should be spending Sunday walking the beach and talking. What the hell am I gonna do all day?*

October 26-27, 1947 — Cleveland

Next morning, he slept late for him. At nine o'clock, after breakfast in the coffee shop, he stood at the front desk. "What is there to do around here on a Sunday?"

The desk clerk scratched his ear. "There's Euclid Beach." Connor shrugged. "How about the art museum?"

Connor remembered Bobbi talking about the museum and art school and how she hadn't got to go. Since he'd never visited a gallery, he asked for directions. Waiting for it to open, he walked Euclid Beach, listening to the all-too-familiar sound of waves crashing on the shore. Grateful for the calming sound, the fishy smell, and the rhythmic heaving of the lake, he stayed and ate at the Lake Lunch Cafeteria next to the pier.

During the afternoon, he wandered into the room housing Cleveland's collection of Gauguin works. At first, the lush color stunned him. As he gazed at the paintings, barely hearing the hushed voices of other visitors, he remembered the shattered islands he'd fought over in the Southwest Pacific and gazed at images of how they *could* have been. He envied the artist his time in the islands at peace. Staring at Gauguin's nude women, he winced, thinking of long it had been since he'd seen his wife that way.

The next afternoon, when Connor arrived at the apartment, Bobbi wasn't ready.

"Sit down for a minute, Connor, while I do something with my hair." She disappeared into the bedroom.

He sat next to the roses. "I see they got the flowers over here."

"Yes, thank you, but you've got to stop spending money and go home."

"I told you . . ."

"Yeah, I know. But you're wasting your money on stuff that'll just be gone in a day or two."

"You're worth it, Bobbi. We need more than bread, you know. Remember the Bread and Roses Strike."

"You know what happened to that. I read your card, Connor. The trouble with beauty is it doesn't last."

"That's nonsense." Connor jumped up and leaned in the bedroom doorway watching her. "I can close my eyes right now and see the yellow roses clogging the corner of Mom's front yard. You remember the smell?"

"I guess."

"Years from now I'll close my eyes and see you sitting there with your hair all gathered up in your hand."

She glanced at him in the mirror but didn't speak.

"Hey," he said, not wanting to overdo it, "you hungry? I'm starving!"

"I don't usually eat breakfast."

358

"Call it lunch then."

"Connor, we're just going to get my car. Remember?"

It passed through his mind to say *our* car, but he kept it to himself. "Lettin' me buy you food surely won't be dangerous."

"*Every*thing's dangerous." Bobbi looked him in the eye.

"Aw, that's not so." He extended his hands, palms up.

She looked at his empty hands. "Don't you and Pop have something to do with the cattle this time of year?"

"No Bobbi, but you're more important than the cows anyway." He decided to nudge a little more. "You're more important than any damn thing that needs doing on the farm."

She stared at him, then grabbed her coat and started for the door. When they got to the car, Connor drove to a diner he'd spotted earlier.

"Connor," she said when he pulled in.

"Bobbi." He turned to her and held her gaze. "I'm hungry."

She followed him inside. She said she wasn't hungry, but Connor noticed when the smell of hamburgers and French fries reached them at their booth near the counter, she ordered both and added a piece of cherry pie.

"Connor," she asked as they waited for their food, "how can you act like the world's such a great place?"

Connor's blue eyes focused on the far wall with an intensity that almost frightened her. "Well, I'm almost driven to my knees with despair when I think about what happened to all those good men that I led up that God-forsaken hill in New Guinea."

Bobbi nodded.

He looked back into her eyes. "I still say those names. Sometimes I say them when I'm frantic—in a storm or when something startles me."

The waitress brought their food and Connor picked up his knife and fork. "But now I say those names sometimes to remember how beautiful those men were."

He put a forkful of chicken-fried steak in his mouth.

"Weren't they . . ."

"Yeah. They were Indians and Mexicans mostly, and the Army used them like mules—used all of us like mules." He forked up another bite, gazing at the far wall for a moment before turning his attention to his food, eating a few more bites before he paused with mashed potatoes on his fork. "But they were men. Strong men. Proud men." He ate the potatoes. "They could work like mules, and they could stand up to anything." He dabbed a bit of his roll in the remaining gravy. "And they could laugh. They'd laugh until they rolled on the ground with tears running down their cheeks—right in the face of death."

Bobbi broke her silence. "But that's depressing. It's all the more reason . . ."

"But Bobbi, don't you see? They stood up to the worst—death and mutilation and *inhuman* slaughter—and they said, 'No you don't. We're men.'" He looked away. "Any they loved each other and took care of each other—*we* loved each other—until they took their last breath." He paused to regain control of himself. "And that, my dear, is beautiful."

Bobbi stared at him. "I'm trying to imagine how, in just a couple of years since you got off that island, you've managed to find beauty in all that horror."

"I can't answer that. It's just the way I feel." Connor waved the waitress over for the check. By the time they got to the car, he was exhausted, and he didn't want to pressure Bobbi, so he drove her back to the club. "Just remember Bobbi," he said when he opened her car door, "I'm not going anywhere."

He walked her to the other car, closed the door gently, and walked away. Then he went back to his hotel to read and rest. Staying alert to Bobbi's moods, doing his best to give her what she needed, and trying to control his own struggle left Connor drained. He spent the rest of the day lying on the bed with his book, between fits of pacing and peering out the window. He left the drapes open. Privacy be damned, he needed to see the sources of all that noise. He didn't know what threats might lurk out there—like standing in the house with a storm coming, wondering if it contained hail or a tornado and if he could get through it without becoming a quivering idiot.

About suppertime, he called home—just to make sure his folks didn't need him, or the car and to hear his father's quiet voice. Once he'd assured his son about the farm, Henry asked about Bobbi.

"I don't know, Pop. She still insists she can't be a wife to me."

"Well, she can't let that one man ruin her life."

"That's what I told her, Pop. But I'm afraid I may be here for a while."

They talked a little longer about the livestock and some repairs Henry had made to the equipment, then Connor hung up—a little calmer than when he'd called. At eight he got dressed, grabbed a bite at the diner, and headed for the nightclub to repeat the drill.

October 29–November 10, 1947

During the following week, he repeated the routine he'd established. He tried, on her nights off, to spend time with her,

GRAVY

but she refused, and he knew he couldn't insist. He couldn't help wondering what she did those days and nights.

He spent a lot of hours walking the beach. It reminded him of Panama and Australia, and the weeks aboard ships. It reminded him, too, of the prairie when the wind blew. He spent more time at the gallery, too, going directly to the Gauguin exhibit. He felt better when he could superimpose peaceful images over the shattered trees and torn people he'd experienced in similar places.

At last, on a Monday afternoon, Bobbi interrupted their lunch at the diner. "You know, Connor," she said, "I've been thinking a lot about what you said the other day—about your men?"

Connor glanced up from his hot beef sandwich. "And?"

"It's just not the same for me." She took a bite of her Reuben. I don't know how to explain this. You've seen and done things so much worse than me."

Connor caught her eye. He put his fork down. "It's not a competition, Sweetheart." He picked up his napkin and wiped his mouth. "It's not better or worse. Tell me about you, Bobbi."

She looked around. "Can we go somewhere else?"

Connor raised a hand. "Let me pay the bill and we'll go."

They walked to the car in silence and Connor drove toward the lake. "It doesn't seem like anybody's at Euclid Beach this time of year." He parked the car where they could watch the churning lake. "Tell me, Bobbi. How is it for you?"

"It's—When I was a kid, Mom and I went to the market and we saw this man, a bum."

"Yeah?"

"And he was all ragged and dirty, but he had the kindest eyes."

GRAVY

"Did he?"

"He didn't do *anything*. He looked at me and kind of smiled. I wanted to stop and talk to him." She looked out at the waves. "Mom took my hand and practically dragged me—I had to run." She looked back at Connor. "She spanked me and told me I should never go anywhere near anybody I saw on the streets. She said they're dangerous and they could hurt me." She frowned. "I suppose she was right." Her eyes filled with tears. "But I can still see those eyes and how sad they looked when Mom dragged me off."

"Not everybody . . ."

"I know, Connor, but my parents were out of work most of the time—and they bickered. They weren't like your Mom and Pop. They probably didn't mean it, but I felt like just another mouth to feed."

Connor remembered the way he saw his in-laws treat Bobbi, clenching his jaw in silence as she continued.

"And whenever Dad heard that someone got a job in the restaurant business, he'd go slamming around the apartment raving about one more chance for him being gone.

"When I got a chance to make some money singing—well, I snapped it up. It was great at first. We didn't have to worry about rent and groceries." She hurried on. "I was in the bandstand up above the crowd and nobody was drinking . . ."

"And then you had to sing in nightclubs and bars."

"Even that was fun sometimes. But somebody *did* try to grab me off the street, and Big Al Polizzi made me sing at his house party, and when my boyfriend, Jack, turned out to be his nephew—I really didn't mind. He was sweet and he protected me—and then I was out of a job and this nightclub manager tried to take advantage of me."

GRAVY

Connor just stared. "You didn't tell me. You poor kid!" He wanted to take her in his arms, but she looked like she might take flight and not come back, so he looked at the lake. "Bobbi, I'm sorry all that happened to you and I'm even more sorry you were too afraid of me to tell me about Dr. Powers. I'd still like to wring his neck."

"No Connor! You can't!"

"It's all right, Bobbi. You're more important than punishing him."

"You think I should forget it?"

"No! What he did *deserves* punishment, but it's more important now for me to help you get over it any way I can."

"That's what I'm telling you. I *can't* get over it."

"I believe in you, Bobbi, and I believe you can. But not all by yourself like this with people doing the very things that hurt you. You need the people who love you."

Bobbi peered out at the lake through a flood of tears. "I wish it were that easy."

"I didn't say it was easy." Connor risked taking her hand. He kissed the tips of her fingers. "Come lean on me for just a little while." He reached an arm around her shoulders. "You're practically rigid. Let it go for just a minute. Go ahead and cry."

And she did for first time in months, actually years right in the spot where she spent her last evening with Jack before they murdered him. They sat together with Bobbi's head on Connor's shoulder until she dozed off. Connor leaned his head against the window post and listened to her even breathing—in time with the pounding waves. He wondered for the first time if she'd missed the water back in Nebraska—and her friends. All his friends, his high school friends anyway, still lived close to home. And the singing. He remembered how she sang all the time. No

364

matter what chore engaged her hands, her throat always poured a stream of melody, like a river.

By the time she stirred, Connor's arm tingled with needles. "D'ja have a good sleep?"

Bobbi started, sitting upright. "I'm sorry. I just felt so safe for once."

"You are Bobbi."

"For the moment."

"For as long as I'm alive."

"I can't . . ."

"Listen," he interrupted. "I've been sitting here watching the waves and I wonder how much you missed the water in Nebraska."

"All the time, Connor. When I was a kid, I used to spend every summer afternoon at the beach—until I started singing at the nightclub. Even then, I'd slip down for an hour or two when I wasn't completely exhausted."

"I've been thinking." Connor twirled one of her short curls around his finger. "It wouldn't be the same, of course, but maybe you heard about the big dam they're building on the Republican River. It won't be Lake Erie, even when it fills, but we could go there sometimes. Take Hope so you can teach her to swim."

"Connor, you know it's not just the water."

"We could come back to visit your friends when the crops are in."

"Connor! I can't!"

"You gotta stop thinking about what you can't. That bastard, Bobbi, he's gonna *own* you."

"Damn it, Connor, I try *not* to think about him. It's when I'm *not* thinking about him that I blow up."

"Whadaya mean?"

She turned in his arms with her back against him. "There are things, Connor."

"Things?"

"Yeah, things that set me off. Remember the night in the storm when we both went crazy?"

"I think about it all the time."

"It was the latch on that shed. That kind of metallic click sounds like that damned thing he put inside me. The click sounds like locking it in place."

Connor stared.

"And the peas? They'd just brought me my lunch from the kitchen when Powers came in humming his little tune and started babbling about his *experiment*. I went berserk. There were peas on that plate and the smell . . ."

"Like the nail polish."

"Like that."

"What else?"

"Well, the obvious. I really hurt a guy one night. Almost lost my job."

"'Cause he got too close?'

"Couldn't keep his hands to himself."

"Must be torture moving around that club at night."

She looked at him. "It is. It's better with you there, but it is."

"Come home with me, Bobbi. We'll figure out the other things and I promise I won't touch you until you're ready."

"What if I'm never ready?"

"I won't let that doctor destroy our marriage. I believe you will be and that we'll laugh together again."

Bobbi smiled.

Connor pressed his advantage. "C'mon Bobbi, whadaya say? Come on home. You can beat on me for a while if you have to."

"But Hope."

"She can stay with Mom and Pop for as long as you think she needs to." Connor paused. Bobbi looked into his eyes, quiet and attentive, as though she listened for something.

"All right."

Connor held his breath, staring. "You mean it?" She nodded. "Well, all righty then," he said finally. "All right!"

Part Seven

November 16, 1947 — Cleveland

Connor wanted to hop in the car and head home immediately—before Bobbi could change her mind, but instead they spent a whirlwind week wrapping up her three-and-a-half months in Cleveland. The Sunday after she had sung her last set and said goodbye to her friends and her parents, they visited the gallery together. Looking at some Van Gogh works, Bobbi admitted that she'd always wanted to paint. "I accidentally got this voice, and there's not a moment when some melody doesn't pour through my mind but look at these poplars, and the sky. It's not my favorite, but Starry Night isn't here." She looked over her shoulder at Connor. "They'll be around forever."

He grinned. "I thought you said beauty doesn't last."

She shrugged and walked on.

"Wait a minute." Connor grabbed her hand. "I've been here before too—on those days when I couldn't see you." He led her to the Gauguin exhibit. "This is the country where we fought the war." He paused. "This is probably what it looked like before." He gazed again at the peaceful scenes. "When I saw it, the trees were shattered, so were the people. It does me good to see the places without the war etched on them."

"You know," he said as they left the gallery. "You might have been a great painter if you'd had the chance. Maybe we could get you some supplies."

"Oh, Connor, I wouldn't know where to start."

"Maybe they have art classes at Hastings College. It's not far."

368

"What about you?" Bobbi interrupted. "What about the GI Bill? You could go back to school."

"Dream on, fair lady. I aged out. They don't give education benefits to guys my age."

"After all you went through? What difference does age make? They didn't mind sending you into the worst of the fighting."

"Dunno. It's just not there for me. Anyway—what about it? You wanna go back to school? You could take a few classes to get you started."

"Oh, Connor, that time has passed. Just like the Glen Miller Orchestra. I'm just a washed-up old big band canary."

"You are not! You're only twenty-five. You've still got your voice. I just hope you'd rather be with people who love you. I've seen enough this week to know what a hard life it is—with men ogling you and reaching for you. You deserve better."

"Maybe I do. I'm not sure."

"I *am* sure. Damn sure. And once I get you home, we're all going to make damn sure you know it." He looked into her eyes. "Now where would you like to eat?"

November 19-December 22, 1947 — Willow Grove

Bobbi and Connor left Cleveland a couple of days later, arriving at Willow Grove after two long days of driving—since they both had to drive. They walked into a chilly house to find a few coals remaining of the fire Henry had started for them several hours earlier. They decided to go right to bed rather than starting another fire.

GRAVY

Next morning, while Connor took care of the livestock, Bobbi cooked the eggs and bacon Henry had left in the icebox along with a fresh block of ice. She'd just set the plates in the warmer when Connor slammed onto the porch cradling a bleeding hand.

"What happened?"

"Caught it on a barb—ripped off my glove. Connor got out the rubbing alcohol, but when he opened the bottle, Bobbi yelled and scrambled for the door, stomping outside and slamming it. Once he'd bandaged the cut, Connor joined his shivering wife on the porch.

"I can't believe I'm already going crazy. This was a bad idea."

"Bobbi, this is going to take a while. Be patient with yourself."

"I should go back."

"No, you shouldn't. You look like you're freezing. Can I hold you?"

She stared at him, thinking she should let him go. He stepped closer and wrapped his arms around her. She didn't object.

"Do you know what that was about? I think it helps to know."

She tried to remember what happened before she bolted. "I think it's the alcohol. Clinic smell."

"Maybe I should get iodine. What do you think?"

Bobbi snuggled into his chest. "I don't know. That was . . ."

"Rough, isn't it?"

"Yes. It's like somebody lit a fire in my stomach and everything's coming up."

Connor stood silent. She felt his breath in her hair.

"Is that why you were sick all the time when you were pregnant?"

She considered the idea, remembering all the times she got sick. "Maybe. It wasn't the alcohol. Not then."

"Let's go inside. Your teeth are chattering."

They stepped inside. "I'm just sorry you felt you had to bear that in silence."

She gave him a grim smile. "What makes you think I bore it in silence?"

"You *did* tell someone?"

"No. I drove out onto some deserted country road and screamed. Sometimes I cried. Sometimes I threw up. But I was never silent.

Connor stared. "It musta really hurt."

"Yeah. I need to get back at the dishes."

A few days later, the local dentist stopped in with his son, asking permission to hunt pheasants. "Sure," said Connor, "just stay out of the south pasture. I've got cows in there."

Eating breakfast with Bobbi, a series of shots and sent Connor cowering under the table. Bobbi crawled on the floor with him. "It's all right, Connor." She laid a hand on his forearm. "It's just hunters."

He gave her a sheepish grin as he crawled out and stood, giving her a hand up. "I forgot. We've always given people permission. I didn't even think about it."

Throughout the month, more aware of things that triggered their blowups, they helped each other through their episodes and consoled each other while they did. Bobbi began to believe

Connor might be right. Maybe with people who love her to help her she *could* get back to normal. Maybe they both could.

A week before Christmas, Nora arrived from Paris. Connor went pick her up at the depot under a blanket of gray clouds with sleet clicking on the windshield. As she stepped off the train, Connor grabbed her bags. "How long have you got this time, Sis?"

"I've got a month before I have to go back."

"That's great. We're having dances at the Legion Hall every Saturday now. Maybe we can all go dancing."

He pitched her bags in the trunk and jumped in the car. Driving out of town, he shot a glance at Nora. "What do you think about the situation in Palestine?"

"It's a disaster and we'll all pay for it for generations."

"That bad?"

"Worse. You remember all my letters complaining about the Allies' unwillingness to allow Jews to immigrate. There's this Jewish guy Weizmann who said back then that there were six million people in a world divided between places they cannot live and places they cannot enter. I'm ashamed of my country's unwillingness—with all its vast resources—to save those people's lives."

"So, they're all going to Palestine?"

"That's where they want to go. I guess they figure, if you're going to be hated anywhere you go, you might as well go back where you started."

"Sounds like there's a but in there."

"They have to sneak out of the British camps. Think about this." Her voice rose. "The war's been over for two-and-a-half years and they're still keeping these people who have suffered so much in camps with tents and Quonsets behind barbed wire."

Connor guided the car out of a skid.

"So now the Brits have turned it over to the United Nations."

"Maybe that will resolve it."

"Here's their solution. Make an independent Arab state and an independent Jewish state and let more Jews—many more Jews—go there."

"So where are all the Arabs now living in the Jewish state going to go?"

Nora snorted. "You've got it. Where indeed? There are hundreds of thousands of Jews who need a place to live, in addition to hundreds of thousands that Palestine has already absorbed. Where *will* they all go?"

After another long silence, Connor cleared his throat. "Do you ever think there are things that are just too big for you to understand, let alone solve?"

"Every day. I feel so damn helpless!"

"That's the realization I came to that last day in the jungle. That starving Jap soldier lying there dying had no more control over the war—or even whether we had one—than I did."

"Did that help?"

"Nope. But Jakes always told me I'm not responsible for the whole world. He said you gotta take care of your little, tiny bit and hope a lot of other people will take care of their bits. I guess that's all we can do."

"I just hope we all get better, collectively, at taking care of our bits."

"Me too, Sis, me too."

"We're almost home and I don't want to think about it . . . at least for a month."

"Okay, I really don't either."

Back at the farm, Nora dropped her bags, leaving them for Connor, and rushed to hug her sister-in-law. "You'll never believe how thrilled I am to find you here."

"I'm glad to see you too."

She pushed Bobbi away and looked into her eyes. "We all love you, Bobbi. Don't you ever forget that."

"It's hard for me to believe after the way I treated Connor."

"Mom wrote me about what that doctor did to you."

"God! Does everybody know?"

"You'll have to forgive her. She was hoping I could figure out how to help you."

"I guess it helps knowing I'm not in this alone. My mom told me to just stop feeling sorry for myself."

"That's awful!"

Bobbi looked away. "She's had to struggle all her life. I guess she thought if I didn't snap out of it, I'd lose everything. Maybe she was right."

Nora changed the subject. "It's almost Christmas and I've got a month before I have to go back."

They had supper at Henry's and Claire's, giving Nora a chance to get acquainted with her niece. After greeting terrified Jewish children entering Britain all alone at the beginning of the war, she could connect with kids pretty fast, and she soon had Hope reaching for her—until she saw the sadness in Bobbi's eyes. "I'm just a novelty, you know."

"You should have been her mama."

"Don't think like that." Nora pulled Hope onto her lap. "You're the one who hung on and hung on and hung on when she could have died waiting for that doctor. You're the one who'll be here when she learns to spell and when she goes out with boys."

"I've already abandoned her once. She still pushes me away."

"She may need some extra love," Nora gave her niece a squeeze and got pushed away. "She'll get over it. See, she pushes me away too. We just have to find other ways to make her feel secure."

"Bobbi." Connor stepped up behind her. "She pushes everyone away. I've told you that."

"This is just a crazy, stupid idea," said Nora, "but Mom wrote me about this, and I've been thinking. Maybe all the pressure when the doctor wouldn't do the operation felt like she was being smashed. Maybe hugs feel a little like that. It must have been frightening for her too."

Bobbi and Connor exchanged a glance. "I hadn't thought of that," Connor said. "Had you, Bobbi?"

She shook her head, looking into Hope's blue eyes. Her daughter grinned and clapped. "I think she's glad we're all here."

After supper they sat around the table chatting. "It's so nasty out tonight, Connor, why don't you and Bobbi spend the night here," Claire said as she followed Henry upstairs. "Your old room is all made up—yours too, Nora."

"Maybe we will."

While Connor and Nora caught up on old friends and family, Bobbi put Hope to bed.

GRAVY

After a few minutes, Connor gazed into the steady flame of the kerosene lamp. "Speaking of home places, how's Daniel doing with his?"

"Not so good, Connor. He's trying to decide what vines he can salvage to start over."

"You guys given any more thought to relocating here?"

Nora grinned. "Yeah. I'm going to look for land while I'm here. Daniel told me what to look for."

"That's great! After Christmas, Bobbi and I will help you look."

"I've already made a start."

"From Paris?"

"I wrote Grandma and Grandpa. Sent them our requirements so they could look for us."

"So, they found something?"

She squealed. "They offered their place at Guide Rock."

"Really?" Connor grinned. "They've been talking about retiring. Wanted to know if we wanted to farm it."

Nora chuckled. "They said the *kids* had all moved too far away. I want to take a look before I go back. If I remember right, it should be perfect."

"What do you need?"

"An east or southeast-facing fifteen-to-twenty-degree slope. Water, of course, but well drained. That will probably be the defining factor, considering our clay soils."

Connor stood and paced a few steps." I don't know if it'll be enough, but Grandpa's been composting just about everything he could get his hands on since he bought that quarter in . . ." he stopped to think, ". . . 1918, just after World War I. That's thirty years of cleaning the chicken house and the farrowing shed and scooping the barn and corral. He darn near wore out his manure spreader."

"I know. I'm counting on that. Besides all that, there are buildings and fences. I could use the chicken house and the barn." She smiled. "And the garden plot. I have missed growing things and the garden's been well composted too."

"You're gonna turn into a regular farm wife yet, but are you thinking about grazing cattle?"

"No. Just a milk cow, chickens, maybe a few pigs to eat. We'll have to build a wine tasting house—like a café, but that will come later."

Connor laughed. "You have to have wine first."

Just as Bobbi returned from putting Hope to bed, they made a date for the following day to visit Grandma and Grandpa, who would be home from their Christmas visit to Claire's little sister by then.

December 25, 1947

Less than a year old, Hope didn't understand Christmas, but she enjoyed ripping, crinkling, and throwing colorful paper around Henry's and Claire's living room. Everyone agreed to help her open the gifts.

Bobbi couldn't believe the stack of boxes with her name on them, but when Hope opened the first one (with a lot of help) she yelped. "A set of charcoals. What am I going to do with these?"

"You'll see."

GRAVY

Her next package, from Claire, contained watercolors, brushes, and a set of colored pencils.

"Connor, you've been talking too much. What can I do with these?"

"I promise, you'll see."

Amid opening and exclaiming over an array of gifts, Bobbi noticed the family seemed focused on her when she opened her last box. It was a large, relatively flat box from Nora. Inside she found tubes of oils, a palette, a couple of stretched canvases, an easel, and more brushes.

"I got them before I left Paris."

"Connor! I can't . . ."

"Remember what I said about focusing on what you can't do? Now here's your final gift." He handed her an envelope.

"Connor?"

"Just open it."

Inside she found the paperwork announcing her enrollment in night drawing and watercolor classes at Hastings College. She'd been kneeling on the floor, helping her daughter play with the paper. She leaned back on her heels.

"I don't know what to say."

"Sweetheart, just say you'll do it. The college only offers the two classes this semester, so you'll have to save the paints and charcoal for later, but you can get started right away. See the first class is right after the New Year. That's so you won't have time to back out."

"Believe me," Nora said, "you don't want Connor 'encouraging' you. That's how I ended up in the Foreign Service."

"I thought that's what you wanted."

"It was, but I'd have never done it if Connor hadn't goaded me into going back to school and taking the chance."

With tears in her eyes, Bobbi jumped up and hugged her husband. "Thank you, lover," she whispered in his ear. "I never could have dreamed I could have such a wonderful family," she said as she hugged each of her in-laws. She waved her enrollment form around. "And I won't back out.

January 28, 1948

Scrounging in the back of the closet for an old coat she thought she could make over for her daughter, Bobbi felt the cool, smooth fabric of her mother's emerald satin gown, the one she'd worn for her first audition. Distracted, she dragged it out and slipped out of her clothes, transforming herself into the big band singer. Heels, nylons, jewelry, even some silky underwear, it all fit. *Not bad after a pregnancy and messy abdominal surgery.*

She grabbed her hairbrush off the dresser and began crooning her theme song, *Blue Moon*, as she paced the side of the bedroom dragging an imaginary cord as if she were on a stage. As she sang, Connor stepped quietly into the room behind her and leaned in the door frame. "You really miss it, don't you?"

Turning with the hairbrush still in her hand, she nodded. "Sometimes it feels like I have a big hole in my chest, and I can't feel the rhythm of my own heart." She let the sentence drop, wondering if she'd hurt Connor yet again.

On the record player, Connor started her recording of his favorite, *Begin the Beguine*. Turning back to Bobbi, he held out his arms. She laid the brush at the foot of the bed and moved into them.

GRAVY

He whispered into her hair as he stepped forward into her retreating left foot. "You look sensational, Bobbi, just like the night I met you." Adapting a Cuban walk to the furniture in their living room, they moved together, hips swaying, slow step, quick, quick. In the middle of the room, where they had more space, they separated, hands joined, then came back together, moving into a turn before they stepped sideways, sidestep, quick, quick, into the big kitchen where they had more open space.

"What are you doing in the house this time of day?" she asked, as they passed the ice box on the way to the counter with its wash basin.

"Broke down again."

"I'll get changed."

"No, Bobbi, I don't think so."

Her recorded voice sang, "*and even the palms seem to be swaying.*"

"But the hay."

He guided her into another swinging turn. "It's okay, Bobbi. It's already late. The noon weather said clear tonight and sunny tomorrow. It will be just fine."

They separated again as he stepped forward on his left foot while she moved back on her right, slow, quick, quick. "I think we'll go to the Ivanhoe for dinner and maybe a little more dancing."

She brightened as her record crooned, "*a moment's divine, what rapture serene.*"

They came together then broke apart as he stepped back on his right while she moved forward, "That sounds wonderful. Hope can stay with Mom and Pop."

"Just what I was thinking."

He led her around the table and stepped back into the living room just as she crooned, *"Then we'll begin to know what heaven we're in, when they begin the beguine."*

As he took the needle off the record and turned the machine off, he said, with his back turned to her, "Bobbi, I'm afraid you gave up way too much when you married me. Are you sure you can stick it out here on the farm? We are so broke after everything that's happened, I can't offer you anything else."

"I think so. It's just the doctor and the surgery and the baby might die or be retarded. And then Pauline. I couldn't cope with it all. I *want* to be a good wife and mother."

He heard the desperation in her voice and recognized it all too well from the months of her pregnancy and the months before she ran back to the city.

"Bobbi, you *are* a good wife and mother. I'm just worried about that big hole in your chest."

"I love you and I want to be with you. It. is. just. so. quiet. here."

". . . and we don't get out much," he finished for her. "You know, Bobbi, I've just had an idea. There's no glamour or bright lights, but you could really help me, not just with that damned baler either."

"Yes?"

"It's going to get really busy around here now what with helping Nora and Daniel get that vineyard started and I'm supposed to be commander of the Legion Post. I have to get all the veterans in—and bring their wives into the auxiliary—if it's going to support itself."

Bobbi nodded.

"You're good at meeting people and making them comfortable."

"Yeah. So?"

"Would you be my membership chairman? You could sing at the dances, too. And nobody would try to grab you."

She took a moment to imagine how she would handle that. Then she gave him a wicked grin. "I would be your membership chair*woman*." She put the record back in its sleeve. "Do you think Mom could take care of Hope sometimes during the day. She'll be busy, too."

February 14, 1948

Bobbi leapt right into her chairwoman duties. As soon as she realized that Valentine's Day fell on a Saturday when all the farmers would be in town, she scheduled a dance. She telephoned every vet on Connor's list, especially inviting the wives and former WACs, reminding them that she had served too.

She set up a table at the entrance of the hall and asked everyone to fill out a 3x5 card with personal information.

"Hi, you're new, aren't you?" Bobbi handed a card to a hesitant woman who lagged a step behind her husband. "Or maybe I'm the one who's new." She smiled. "I'm not from around here. I'm Bobbi."

The other woman leaned close over the table. "Carol."

"I'm sorry, I could barely hear you. Was that Carol?"

She nodded.

"Carol, could I get you to fill out this card since your husband has already wandered off? If I can get your husband's name and your name, address and phone number, I can be sure you know about everything that's happening here."

Bobbi noticed that Carol looked pale and a little shaky. "Here. Take a seat beside me. Just fill this in, please."

Between talking with new arrivals and handing out cards, Bobbi glanced at Carol from time to time. She noticed her white-knuckled grip on the pencil and hesitation on the field for children's names.

Bobbi took a quick look at the top of the card. "John and Carol Horst. Didn't I see a birth announcement in the paper not too long ago?"

Getting no answer, she looked around to find Carol sitting with her head bowed, hands folded in her lap, silent tears flowing.

Bobbi jumped up, skidding her folding chair noisily away from the table. "Oh no. What's wrong?" She put her arm around the other woman. "What's wrong," she repeated. "Can I help?"

"My baby has cerebral palsy. He's . . . we can't take care of him."

"Oh Carol. I'm sorry."

"He's in Beatrice, at the Home. He took so long to get born—and then I had an operation."

Bobbi's eyes locked on Carol who seemed about ready to flee. For Bobbi, all the noise and rustle of arriving guests went silent as she felt heat surging up her neck and into her face. She was afraid to ask, but she had to, "Who was your doctor?"

Carol mumbled into her lap, "Dr. Powers in Hastings."

The day in the recovery room when she realized what Powers had done to her came back with a vengeance. She bit on a surge of anger and shame as she tried to keep from shouting. "I had Powers too."

Carol looked up then, eyes locking on Bobbi's. "Did your baby live?"

"Yes, she's fine. No thanks to Powers."

The women stared at each other for a moment. "Listen. This. is. not. your. fault." Bobbi whispered it and for the first time, she believed it.

She turned to one of the other wives, not even sure who it was. "Take over for me, please. I need to talk to Carol."

"Are you all right?"

"Yeah, yeah. I will be."

She ushered Carol into the silent kitchen and found a couple of chairs, setting them face to face. She settled Carol into one and she sat facing her, holding her hands. "Now. If you don't want to talk to me, you don't have to, but I think we've had the same horrible experience. Did Powers let you labor until you couldn't push anymore?"

Carol nodded. "I thought I was going to die."

"Me too."

Bobbi's face flamed and her eyes felt like they were on fire. She focused on her trembling hands. She didn't know if she could ask. She didn't want to ask, but she couldn't stop. "And did he give you treatments while you were pregnant?"

She heard a low moan and looked up to see Carol's eyes streaming with new tears. "It hurt. I thought I was going to rip apart. He left me there in the stirrups for half-an-hour every time with nothing to cover me. It felt like *years*. I felt . . . I felt . . . like . . . a whore," she whispered. "I thought, after that first treatment, about going to another doctor, but the nearest obstetrician is in Lincoln and that's four or five hours away, depending on the weather."

"Yes," Bobbi said, "we drove to the hospital in a snowstorm."

The two women sat silent, trembling hands joined, sobbing.

"Okay," Bobbi said, finally, gathering herself up. "Okay. And then he'd come back in and help you up and act like everything was normal and he was helping you so you wouldn't get a horrible infection and die."

"Yes. And then I would think, 'Well, he's a doctor and he knows best. I had to think that just to get through it."

"Me too, Carol, but he's not a doctor. He's a sadist and what he did to us . . ." She sat silent for a moment. "Oh my God. My mom was right. It was rape!"

For two years she'd tried to believe in her doctor, that he'd tried something new that might help the mothers who trusted him. She'd tried to believe that what he did was a mistake, not malicious. But for the first time she found herself unable to believe even that. The man who had claimed to be a doctor was a rapist.

February 17, 1948

"I've been thinking about that," said Connor a couple of days later when Bobbi told him about Carol.

"You've been thinking about Carol?"

"No. About Powers. About stopping him from hurting any other families."

"Connor, you can't."

"No, not by going after him." After a thoughtful pause, he continued. "I know it would be hard—really hard—but do you think you could tell Doc O'Neill what Powers did to you?"

Bobbi groaned. "What good would that do?"

"For one thing, we'd know for certain whether that's common practice—which I'm damned sure it's not." He took her hand. "And if it's not, he'll stop referring patients."

"But there's no one else any closer than Lincoln. I checked."

"I don't know what to do about that, but I think O'Neill can help figure it out."

"Connor, I don't know."

He gave her hand a squeeze. "Honey, if you can't, you can't, and I won't say another word about it."

The silence stretched for several minutes until at last Bobbi groaned. "All right. I do trust Doc O'Neill, and if it would keep other women from . . ." She couldn't quite say it yet. "And babies from dying or living whole damaged lifetimes." She shuddered. "I'll make an appointment."

"You're not going alone."

She looked into his eyes. "I don't know if I can talk about it in front of you."

He rubbed a hand across his forehead. "What if I told Doc what Pop told me, and you can just nod if I've got it right? Would that be any easier?"

She looked at the ceiling, taking a deep breath. "I don't know if anything will make it easier, but it has to be done before anybody else gets hurt." She took another breath, held it for a moment, and let it out. "Let's do it, as soon as possible, before I lose my nerve."

In minutes, Connor had made the call. He told the receptionist it was an emergency and had an appointment as soon as they could get to the office.

"Let's go," Bobbi said when he hung up. He grabbed his wallet and she grabbed Hope from the playpen. After dropping the baby with Claire with a promise of a later explanation, they headed for town.

Once inside O'Neill's office with the door closed, Bobbi started talking. She described the treatments, the endless labor, and her conversation with Carol. Connor explained what Powers had told him after surgery about the likely damage to his daughter. O'Neill asked a couple of questions, but mostly listened in silence. When they'd finished, he stood and paced the office, only a couple of steps each way. They watched until he resumed his seat.

"First," he said, "I want to thank you for your confidence. It couldn't have been easy to talk about this." He looked pointedly at Bobbi.

"No," she murmured.

"Second, you've confirmed my suspicions. Too many babies die and too many handicapped babies are coming out of that practice. I couldn't know about the so-called treatments or the long labors, though. Powers should have been doing the surgeries as soon as the mothers started labor."

He scratched his jaw. "In answer to your question, no, what Powers did to you and your friend Carol is not common practice. In fact, there is a body of malpractice law to address such things. I don't know how easy it is to make a case, but if you can afford a lawyer, I would encourage you to sue him. Maybe Carol and her husband would help."

He stood, took a few steps, and sat again. "Meanwhile, I'll have a coming to Jesus with Dr. Malcolm Powers. I'll remind him of malpractice law and ask him to think about the damage to his reputation if his doings got into the papers—not to mention the cost. That should encourage him to do things the right way until we can come up with an alternative."

He shook his head and inspected the ceiling. "I'll contact doctors in the surrounding counties and see if we can come up with some money for a clinic and I'll call the medical school in Omaha and see if they'll have some ob-gyn interns soon who might like to work in such a clinic. We've needed one for a while now."

He covered his face with his hands and propped his elbows on the desk. He looked up at Bobbi. "Young woman, I admire your courage, but I know it's not easy to get over this kind of thing. Please know that not all men, not all doctors, are like Powers and please, don't let him ruin your life or your marriage."

Connor stood and shook O'Neill's hand, and they left the office. Back in the car, he turned to Bobbi before he turned the ignition. "What do you think?"

"You know, for the first time in a long time, I feel like I can breathe."

"What you did in there, Bobbi, it's the bravest thing I ever saw."

Her eyes filled with tears. "What about all the guys in the Army?"

"That's physical bravery. It's different. You're my hero."

March 15, 1948

The whole family gathered at the freight station in Cowles when Nora's and Daniel's train arrived with a carload of balled and burlapped grape vines. While the railroad crew decoupled the car, Connor stepped forward to finally shake hands with his sister's husband.

"Welcome to Nebraska. I hope you'll be happy here."

Daniel shook his head and smiled. "Happier when I get my vines in the ground."

"We brought the truck, so we can start hauling right away."

Henry stepped up and shook hands. "We know your stock has been out of the ground for a long time, so we've been working on getting ready."

"I'm anxious to see the place. I told Nora what I need, but . . ."

"We don't grow grapes here," Connor finished for him. "So, let's get started. We'll help you load the first of your stock in the truck and we'll drive over to Grandpa's farm."

Daniel ducked his head. "Our vineyard in France was on Grandpa's farm, too. We'd been making wine since Louis the IV."

Without knowing how long that might be, Connor guessed it was a very long time.

While Henry talked to the railroad crew about when they could take their car, Connor and Daniel loaded the truck.

"We got that hillside graded and put in the terraces. We dug the wells—two of them. The windmills are ready to pump water down the terraces."

Claire herded Bobbi and Nora into the car. "We've redone Grandma's house."

"Same as our house," Bobbi added. "After Grandma and Grandpa moved to town, we knocked out the plaster and lath. We had Harm Obermeier wire it. REA will probably get to you soon, since you're so close to town. Pop watched the drywallers who did our place, so we did most of it ourselves this time."

Claire smiled. "Bobbi's turning out to be quite the construction worker."

"We got you some supplies and brought over some of the meat and vegetables we canned last fall—fruit, jams and jellies. You should have enough to get started. We figured we'd be feeding a crew of our men for at least a week or so."

Once in the truck, rattling over pinging gravel to Guide Rock, Henry talked about water. "The Geological Survey says the limestone formation underneath that second bench slopes toward the river, so you ought to have plenty of water to expand. Maybe you can water the next 50 acres with electrical pumps—although of course, the windmills are cheaper to run."

At the farm, they stepped out of the truck. Daniel spent a few moments scanning the hills. He walked to the cleared ground, picked up a handful of soil, and filtered it through his fingers. "Nice, loose, rich soils," he said almost to himself. "This will grow a lot of grapes. I wonder how different our wine will be," Daniel murmured.

"Doesn't that depend on the grapes?"

"Not entirely. The growing environment, particularly soils, plays a big part. For example, wine grown in the Bordeaux region is called Bordeaux and it has recognizable traits."

They hiked to the top of the gradual slope with Daniel sifting soil every few feet. At the top, they stepped off the top of the gentle ridge to the second windmill. Henry headed for the truck. "I guess we'd getter get started so we can find out what Guide Rock wine is like."

As they drove to the top of the slope, Henry suggested that Daniel should plant the first vine so they could imitate his technique.

Daniel began digging. "You handle these much like balled and burlapped trees. Set them about six feet apart. Do we have buckets?"

Connor grinned. "Plenty. The sheet rock sauce came in five-gallon buckets."

GRAVY

"Sheetrock sauce?"

"The joint compound we used on your walls. Nora told us how far apart the vines should be, so we perforated the pipe from the windmill every six feet here on top."

The three men gradually set up an assembly line with Connor digging, Henry setting the vines and Daniel following behind, back-filling and tamping the roots.

When they'd planted the last vine, Henry and Connor walked back to the truck while Daniel finished filling. Henry grinned at his son. "That boy's as fussy with his vines as you are with your trees."

Connor smiled at his dad. "I like him, Pop. He's a hard worker and look at how he handles those vines. He's got a patient, gentle hand on him. He'll be good for Nora."

"I reckon he will, and she'll be good for him, too. They've been through a lot together."

Henry stopped with his hand on the truck's door handle. He frowned. "You know, I've been thinking about you and your sister. You remember how you two took baby rabbits away from the dog?"

"Sure. I don't know how many survived."

"That's not the point. It was the kindness—although I don't think the dog saw it that way."

"Nora wrote me once about all the baby rabbits hiding in the woods in France and how she was helping Daniel save them."

"All the human rabbits the Nazis wanted to kill?"

"Right."

"That's what I've been thinking about you two. It takes a fierce kindness to risk your lives the way you two have."

GRAVY

"But Pop, I killed people."

"Nora told me about that starving Japanese soldier."

"I didn't save him."

"But you gave him comfort. I think a lot about how you took care of Bobbi, encouraged her, waited for her, even when you had your own struggles."

Connor shrugged. "That's what you would have done—or Mom."

"That makes me proud. What better testament to a parent than having raised kind children."

April 3, 1948

One rainy evening, Connor read while Bobbi finished crocheting a doily for Claire. Bobbi stood and took the book out of his hands. "Do you remember the weekend we went up to Kaley's in the Pines?"

"Sure."

"Doesn't the air feel like that tonight?" She hurried on." I know that was summer, but at that altitude . . ."

"Yeah, I guess it does. The wind's still for a change."

She straddled his lap and sat, looking steadily into his eyes.

Not sure what she wanted him to do, he put his hands on her waist as she leaned forward for a kiss, which he returned with enthusiasm. The kiss became deeper and deeper, yet she didn't pull away. Connor tried to be ready for her to take off, but she leaned back, holding his gaze, and began unbuttoning her blouse. He remained still, taking a deep, silent breath.

392

When she'd finished with the buttons, he risked helping her slide it off her shoulders and draped it over the arm of the chair. He considered unhooking her bra but feared that would spook her. He waited—continuing to look into her quiet eyes, satisfying himself that he saw no fear there. She reached for the hooks herself and again he slid the garment off her shoulders and laid it on top of the blouse—without breaking eye contact.

He placed his hands back on her waist, feeling the warmth of her smooth skin. After an interval of silent staring, she shivered, and Connor felt her skin tighten with goosebumps. "I didn't know if I'd ever be able to do this again."

He looked back into her eyes. "I did."

She moved his hands to her breasts and slowly leaned in for another kiss, as if each movement must be considered and decided. Connor, always ready to stop at any moment, knew that this time it would be rough for him to stop. Really rough.

She leaned back and released his hands so she could run her fingers over his chest and shoulders. He squeezed her nipples and took the right one in his mouth.

She groaned. "Take me upstairs." She stood and took his hand.

He lifted her into his arms. "This way's better."

Once in the bedroom, he set her down and hesitated, not sure whether she was ready.

She smiled at him. "Undress me."

"Yes'm." He unbuttoned her slacks and she stepped out of them as they slid down her long legs. When he'd removed her panties, he stood looking into her eyes, trying to determine if she were ready to go on. She stood exposed without any sign of revulsion or fear. She began unbuttoning his shirt and he allowed his hands to wander—until she broke away and turned toward the dresser.

GRAVY

Damn. I'm not sure how much more of this I can stand.

She turned back, unbuttoned and unzipped his pants and slid them off his hips, along with his underwear. "Hmmm." She glanced over his naked body. She handed him the condom she'd retrieved from the dresser. "You might want to cover that up."

He chuckled. "When'd you get that?"

"When Mom and I went shopping in Hastings last week."

"You've been planning this."

"Hoping, Connor. I don't know if I can do this, but I want to try. Okay?"

"Of course, but you're gonna have to take the lead so I don't rush you."

So, she did—and they did.

An hour later, they lay tangled in each other's arms. "How you doin'?" Connor asked.

"I'm doin' just fine. You?"

"Ecstatic. I don't know if this is normal, but at least we know now."

"That we can get there?" Bobbi finished for him, popping up and grinning at him.

Epilogue

When I was a child, I asked my mother about a journey we had taken together—a very dark, frightening, and noisy journey. She said there was no such journey. The closest we ever came was a car trip when I was little. But that wasn't the trip I remembered. In my memory, my mother held me close—too close. There were no windows and no light.

I know experts say one can't remember one's birth, but I know that my journey really did happen and that it was my attempt to pass through my mother's birth canal. My birth was particularly memorable, and those fearful days of darkness stayed with me until I was old enough to ask about them. For an infant with no language of sensation and very little experience, pressure may have transformed itself into noise, and even when I had the language to ask, I had no way to interpret the experience. Now I only remember asking and feeling that my mother's answer was evasive. I suppose, though, that Mom trusted the experts. She did that far beyond what was good for either of us. I'm sure she had no wish for me to remember the valley of the shadow we went through.

Through three days of hell, my mother held on to me. The placenta that tied us together did not separate as it might have during such a long labor and, together, we made it through the pain and pressure intact. She held me close. It was too close for comfort, but the doctor who predicted my short, hellish life and early demise simply did not know how tough the two of us were.

So, you see, every day of my life has been gravy.

The End

Author Bio

Just so you know a bit about me, I've been a truck driver, a farmer, an environmentalist, and a mother of sons all grown now. I'm a hugger of trees, lover of old folks, history, quirky science, and books. My mother's parents were restaurateurs and I like to try new recipes, although they don't always come out the way I expect.

I'm deeply concerned about human resiliency and how families and communities contribute to it–or not. Because I grew up in one, I'm particularly interested in extended families who have close relationships with the places where they live. This series seeks to bring together a family with the wisdom and support of several generations and a family with no ties.

As a farm kid, I got a hands-on introduction to one three-quarter-section piece of land–not by riding over it on a tractor, but by walking every hill and fencerow. It's provided me with a strong concern for the health of that land and the entire planet.

I must have my hands in the dirt, so every summer I disappear into my garden(s) where I grow fruits and vegetables as well as flowers. I live in town now, but my favorite parts of my double corner lot are the native grass and wildflower plots. They're nearly self-sustaining now.

My writing qualifications include a lot of living, some hard. I've worked most of my life as a writer, more than a decade for the Nebraska Game and Parks Commission and later for Martin Luther Home Society. My work has appeared in newspapers and magazines. I have also published two memoirs, a collection of essays describing my home on the plains, and two novels related to this one.

Other Works by This Author

The Reluctant Canary Sings: The only way to save her family was to sing, but her singing career never provided the safety or security she craved. Bobbi Bowen's story begins in Cleveland, 1937, the second dip of a double-dip depression. When she leaves the apartment she shares with her parents, she passes the Holy Rosary Soup Kitchen with its straggle of shuffling men and women in their bedraggled coats. At home she ducks her parents' fights—sometimes ducking a flying plate or saucer. The mob has a big presence in Cleveland, even post-prohibition, and there's a serial killer leaving dismembered bodies all over town. How will Bobbi navigate the hazards?

See Willy See: Caught in the run up to World War II, Connor considers enlisting, expecting he will go to Europe. Maybe he can protect his sister who's in Paris with the Foreign Service. But it's hard to think about leaving home and family, for another years-long exile. Filled with flashbacks of his travels living off the land and letters to keep him tethered to his family, Connor's story spans two of America's most disruptive decades (The economic Depression of the 1930s and World War II of the 1940s) in which Connor finds his most closely held expectations thwarted.

Threshold: A little boy stolen, a plainswoman married to the homliest man she ever saw, a Canadian homesteader who takes in his hired man and the whole, growing family, a husband in a hotel with a turtle in the bathtub, desperate to save a marriage—either one of them. This is a family like a prairie, woven of many strands.

Prairie Landscapes: The ramblings of one mind prowling the Great Plains, this book brings you face to face with the prairie and its creatures—a black cocker spaniel with a white necktie who befriended a runt pig—and an almost-immortal banty rooster. The landscapes stretch from eastern Nebraska's tall grass prairie to the grass-frozen sand sea called the Sandhills to the Pine Ridge in the northwest corner.

From Picas to Bytes: When Joseph Claggett Seacrest arrived in Lincoln, Nebraska, on April 1, 1887, the April Fool joke was on him—the newspaper job he'd come to take did not exist. This book chronicles 100 years and four generations of Seacrest journalism—from fights to establish and defend first amendment rights, to support their communities through donating money committees, to adoption of new technologies that kept the newspaper's doors open when most mid-sized dailies had died.

Reader's Guide

Connor and Bobbi come from very different lifestyles. Do you think they will be able to remain together in the long run? What will sustain them over the years? By the end of the novel, they've already faced some serious challenges. What do you think will challenge them in the future?

Why do you suppose Connor is able to woo his wife through her trauma? Does the support of his family make an appreciable difference?

What do you think motivated the author to write this book? What are the central themes of this novel? What issues or ideas does it explore? Do this couple's struggles have any relevance in today's world?

What do you find most surprising, intriguing, or difficult to understand? Why? What specific scenes or passages captured your attention? Were they interesting, profound, disturbing, sad? What made them memorable? What did they reveal about the characters?

What have you learned from reading this book? Did you gain any new perspectives?

If you would like to have the author participate in a club meeting either in person or by phone link or Zoom, you can contact Ms. Colburn at faithanncolburn@gmail.com.

Sample See Willy See

June 15, 1940 – Willow Grove, Nebraska

Connor couldn't stop worrying about Nora. If someone needed help, his sister would help. That could cost her life and it would be his fault. As he worked in hard sun chopping weeds from ditches and fencerows, machete flashing, shirt soaked with sweat, he thought about his sister over there in Paris with the Nazis poised on the French border. Wheat next to the tangled fence row where he worked made a dry, rustling noise in a breeze that barely stirred its stiff beards. A lone mosquito whined around his head. He looked down the hill toward the pond, dark and muddy with not a ripple on its surface. He'd give anything to get his sister into the silly little rowboat their dad had made for them when they were kids.

Only eighteen months apart and just the two of them, Connor and Nora had spent their childhood exploring the farm together. Their dad farmed a half-section, 320 acres. They had sun-scalded short-grass pastures to roam, picking yellow coneflowers, daisy fleabane, and round, pink balls of common milkweed. They chased butterflies—admirals, monarchs, black velvet tiger swallowtails. They climbed trees and looked into birds' nests, turned over clods and watched ants fleeing in all directions. That had changed with the dust storms and Connor's high school graduation, when he headed for California seeking a job. With over twelve million people in the United States unemployed, he'd managed to get a few jobs picking fruit. But when the crop harvest had run out, he'd managed to get on with the Civilian Conservation Corps. After his two years in the Corps, he'd become a hobo, riding the rails and living on the bounty of the national park system.

While he knocked around the country from park to park, living on what he could catch, trap, or pick, the Nazis had taken over

Germany and moved to take the rest of Europe. Rumors of Nazi death camps had spread throughout the country and his sister had decided to work right in the middle of it. Worse yet, Connor had goaded her into it. It drove him crazy that he remained safe at home while she worked at the edge of war. He whacked at a tough musk thistle releasing a sharp, acid odor from the severed stalk.

Still, he'd already lost his chance to go to college. He'd given up five years hopping trains, taking handouts, working the occasional odd job, and living on the land. Didn't he deserve a chance to build his future? Nora was doing what she wanted to do, anyway.

He took a savage swipe at a cocklebur. Whacking and slashing at firebush, sunflowers, burs, and hemp, he worked his way across the ridge of the hill, ignoring the dust he raised, inhaling its dry earth smell. The country still had to recover from the drought.

He could enlist, but there wasn't any point. America hadn't entered the war. No U.S. troops were headed for Europe. Maybe he could join the Canadian Army. That might get him close enough to save his sister—but he knew darned well she wouldn't leave until they closed the consulate.

GRAVY

GRAVY

www.ingramcontent.com/pod-product-compliance
Lightning Source LLC
Chambersburg PA
CBHW070743120726
47910CB00001B/151